BOLDFACED
LIES

Also by Charlene A. Porter

Cheryl's Clarinet
(with illustrator James A. Davis)

Tiger Woods, the Boy Who Loved Golf
(with illustrator James A. Davis)

BOLDFACED
LIES

A Novel

Inspired by True Stories
of the Real American West

Charlene A. Porter

Denver

BOLDFACED LIES
This is a work of fiction inspired by true stories of the real
American West.

By Charlene A. Porter

Published by:
Rose City Press
7496 E. 29th Avenue, Suite 172
Denver, Colorado 80238

www.charleneporter.com

ISNB, print edition, 1-934099-11-2

Cover design by Gillian Conte and Frank Foster
Interior design by Robert Howard

Manufactured in the United States of America
10 9 8 7 6 5 4 3 2 1

This book is dedicated to
Lucille Marie Russell Porter
my precious, beautiful, beloved mother.
Also, my angel.
I deeply and utterly love and miss you, Mom,
with all of my being.
Thank you-then, and always-for everything!
And to
John William "Bill" Porter
my strong, determined, beloved father.
Also, my hero.
I love and deeply appreciate you, Dad
with all of my being.
Thank you-then, and always-for everything!

Acknowledgments

The support, love, help, and encouragement, of all of the following, along with many others to numerous to be able to list them all, made Boldfaced Lies possible. Each and everyone has my sincerest, unending gratitude.

My parents John and Lucille Porter; My brother (deceased), Michael A. Porter.The Denver Public Library Western History Collection, The Pasadena (California) Central Library and branches, and all public and school libraries and librarians everywhere. The African American Leadership Institute (especially, Linda J. Williams, Norma Paige, John Marsh, and Nell Goodwin), Patricia Allen, Darlene Anderson, Marion Anderson, Henry Andrade, Elizabeth Ashley, Ray Bartlett, Reginald A. Bedney, Jeff Black, Omar and Jeweldine Blair, Clifton Blanchett, Joseph Boyd, Charlene "C.J."Bradford, Pamela Brown, Tony Brown, William Brown, Les Buffham, Lonnie Bunch, Lynette Burke, Norma Burnett, Tony Byrd, Guillermo and Laura Cabral, Rev. Dr. Johnie L. Carlisle (and the Congregation of First African Methodist Episcopal Church, Pasadena, CA), Carlos Camacho, Carla Claiborne, Gloria Clay, Bishop Cohen, (The) Colorado Black Firefighters, Leonard Collins, Gillian Conte, Keith and Marlene Cooper, LyDean Crews, Helen Criss, Mable Davis, James A. and Paula Davis, Denver Fire Station 3 and 29, Ofield Dukes, Gaile Dumas, Phyllis L. Duran, Steve and Julie Eisold, Renard D. Euell, Frank Foster, Four Seasons Ski Club, Cherie Francis, Sharon Francis, Cee Bee Franklin, Gregory Franks, Dennis Gallagher, Bridgett Gomez, Ellsworth Grant, Virlyn Grant, Lileth Habet, Henry Hammell, Gregory Hamlin, Bee Harris, Elisha and Mary Harris, Ronald Haskins, Allegra "Happy" Haynes, Lawrence and Clara Hill, James Hobbs, Holy Redeemer Church (Denver, CO), Robert Howard, Gloria Hine, John Hine, Murray Huff, Denise Jackson (Pasadena), Gary M. Jackson, Jayne Johnson,

Kenneth and Irene Johnson, Laurie Johnson, Rashida Kamal (Devi Noel), Clark Kepler, Amma Khalil (Iris Holliday), Jill King, Teresa King, Modupe Labode, Mirza Lavarrada, Charles Lewis, Mildred Lewis, Norm and Sienna Lewis, Rudy Lombard, George O. Love, Bob and Maureen Lucas, Jerry and Laura Malugeon, Araksya Manukeyn, Margaret Maupin, Randy Mazin, Linda Lou McCall, Carmelle McGhee, Anita McKissack, Terry McMillan, Barbara McPheeters, Joyce Meskis, Joelle Miller, Marifrances Miller, Russ Miller, Ruth Monroe, Ruth Moore, John Moreno, George and Marjorie Morrison, Pat Myers, Wanda Nave and Family, Charelszine Terry Nelson, Ray Newman, Michael Nixon, Norman Nixon, Tom Noel, Doris Owens, Rev. Garland Pierce, Clare Pitassi, Stephone Poole, Mario Powe, Emmett and Jimmy Powell, Stephen Quinn, Vickie Reece, Mark and Yvonne Rhaming, Connie Richardson, Fletcher Robinson, Roho (Don Davis), Keith Rogers, Angela Satterwhite, Denise Sawyer, Phom Sayavong, Gil Scott-Heron, Todd and Louise Skinner, Jan Shure-Hurwitz, Ronald Jemal Stephens, Paul Stewart, Lee Dora Smith, Patsy Jean Smith, George Sumpter, Leo Tavares, Eszylfie Taylor, JoAnn Thomas, Rosella Hightower Thomas, James A. Tolbert, Wallace Yvonne Tollett, Myrtle "Peggy" Underwood, Wayne and Wanda Vaughn, Hugh and Viv Wallace, Jonathan Washington, Ronald and Nina Washington, Roslyn Washington, Winter Weeks, Jessica Wendrick, James D. West, Maurice White, Eva Whitesell, Michael Whitesell, Bettye Wilkes, Larry and JoAnn Williams, Nancy "Bird" Williams, Sam Williams, Sherry Wilson, Linda Wright (Pasadena), Linda Glass Wright, Horace Wormley, Peggy Wortham, Katherine C. Wood. Also, every one of my wonderful, wonderful students, who taught me at least as much as I-hopefully-taught them. Above all, Thank you, Lord! I serve an awesome God.

Charlene A. Porter

James River Valley, Virginia

1862

Charlene A. Porter

*"Sweet Baby, hardly none a them white folks
white as they jest so sure they is."*

Aunt Pearl

Prologue

Euphrates O'Shea, the black one, fled the tattletale ruins of her twin brother's secret strawberry patch. Sticky, sweet, red berry juice stained her hands and mouth and the front of her flour sack dress. She was screaming like the bogeyman was 'bout to get her as she ran, zigzag, out of the stand of flowering dogwood trees.

Angus O'Shea, Junior, the white one, was on his sister's heels like one of Marse Henry's hounds chasin' a runaway.

"Damn you, Euphie," he shouted, "I'm gonna choke your skinny butt this time."

Euphrates knew her brother meant it too. It was the hottest blessed day of July and Angus hadn't slowed none.

She made it out into the grassy, blue sky, open, and headed down to the river bluff. Ever since Angus had helplessly watched their uncle drown two summers ago, he refused to go near water any deeper than his ankles. No way he was going to chance being within yards of the swiftly moving James River.

What did Papa call the river? A bed of broken bones and lost dreams.

Euphrates heard Angus yell at her again. He was gaining on her, darn him.

"You hear me, Euphie? I was gonna sell them strawberries. Would of got least fifty cents for 'em, too. Let's see how funny it is when I tell Mama on you."

Euphrates cut a look back at her brother but she didn't dare answer. They might have been born twins, but no stranger would of ever guessed it.

She had Mama's midnight-black eyes, high cheekbones, long legs, and the same deep cocoa skin. Her only trait from Papa was his flame red hair.

But looking at Angus was like looking back in time at what Papa must have looked like when he was a young boy growing up in Ireland. least ways peoples always said so. Same green eyes and wild, silky hair. Same pale skin and strong, broad shoulders.

Angus acted like Papa too. Kind one day, mean as a demon the very next. Now, his face was glowing, red as hot coals. Just like Papa's got when he took to lashing somebody.

Euphrates reconsidered her dash to the bluff.

Maybe it was better to go up to the big house and find Mama before Angus did. That is, if she wanted to save herself from one of Mama's "not-puttin'-up-with-anymore-foolish-ness" scoldings and punishments.

Seeing, with a glance, that Angus was gaining on her, Euphrates veered up the hill to the big house. To Marse Henry's.

She'd sneak in through the back, the kitchen door, then take the rear stairs up to the floor Mama was likely on. The third floor, the floor with the chillun's rooms.

The sun was still in its afternoon arch. Marse Henry wouldn't be back from Richmond till nightfall. Ma'am would be in her parlor, on the second floor, playing solitaire and drinking lemonade toddies least till dinner.

Euphrates wasn't usually allowed in the big house but whenever Marse was away, Mama let her come in and help with the chores. Then Mama'd have time to play with Baby Sister tonight 'stead of fixing dinner and going straight to Marse Henry's family.

She huffed and puffed the last few steps to the crest of the hill, then darted across the gravel path that divided Marse Henry's big white fancy house from the quarters, the rows of one-room shacks where everybody else lived.

She was out of breath and beads of sweat were running down her face. She took momentary refuge in the shade of a weeping willow and spied down the hill, wondering what had happened to her brother.

He had stopped too, at the bottom of the hill, and was bent over, with one hand on a knee, and the other hand to his chest, laughing.

He rose to his full height and waved Euphrates on. Thank goodness, she thought, sighing with relief, then just quickly realized she now had a new, even worse problem. If Angus let her escape he might go home, to their cabin, and find out she'd got into his cigar box, that he'd thought he'd hidden from her in Mama's quilt chest, and that had been brim full of silver coins and Federal dollars.

She knew Angus had been saving for that almighty *freedom* –whatever that was– day of his, but Clara and Lawrence needed the money more.

Marse Henry was going to sell them away from each other when he returned, so they had to run for it today. Theys needed to pays theys fare on the underground. If they got that far.

Euphrates waved gleefully back at her brother. He never could stay mad at her for long. Mama said theys was closer than most brothers and sisters 'cause theys had shared the womb. That theys had a bond couldn't *never* be broken.

That was probably true too, 'cause even now, at fourteen, theys was still each other's best friend. Least ways theys was til Angus found his empty cigar box.

Euphrates took a deep breath and cupped her hands to her mouth. "Nah, nah, nah, nah, nah, you-u ca-an't catch me," she called as loud as possible.

But as Angus walked away and Euphrates watched him, she suddenly understood something for the first time. How he got away with going into Richmond and passing himself off as Papa's younger brother. How he was able to pass for white.

Not only was Angus nearly as tall as Papa, but just now, as she studied Angus across the distance, she could've easily mistaken her own brother, for, for…one of Marse's own chillum. For a white boy.

The thought startled Euphrates, but it was silly, so she pushed it away.

She cupped her hands to her mouth again, this time to mimic the supposed sound of a ghost, and bellowed with all her might. "Ooooooooo. Oooooooooooooooooo."

That would get Angus's blood up. He hated when people teased him for being so light skinned.

Sure enough, he bolted around and lit up the hill after her. "I ain't kiddin', Euphrates. You messin' with my plans. 'Cause of you, I ain't got no strawberries to sell. And 'cause of no strawberries, no damn money."

Euphrates resumed her flight by skipping rapidly backwards along the gravel road, and away from the big house.

Bravely, she continued to taunt and egg her brother on. "Oooooooooooooooooo."

When, finally, he too made the crest of the hill, and flat land, Angus slowed to a walk to catch his breath. He was about to call to her again when he realized the danger ahead.

They had gone so far down the plantation's main road, toward the front gate, that when he turned around to look, the big house was barely visible.

As he turned back, to warn Euphrates not to go any further, she was already well past the archway of roses, standing out on the road to town.

Marse Henry didn't allow any of his property to even go as far as the plantation's stone boundary wall. Angus only got way with leaving 'cause Papa had convinced Marse to let Angus drive the wagon in to pick up the household's orders and supplies.

Anyone else who disobeyed found out jest how mean Marse Henry really was. Mama's sister, Patsy, had learned the hard way.

"Euphrates O'Shea," Angus shouted, "stop playin', and get yourself back here, now, else Mama's really gonna take a strap to you."

Euphrates wasn't studdin' her twin. She was gazing up and down the unfamiliar road, amazed that there was suddenly more to the world than she had ever imagined. Instead of her brother's voice, now all she could hear were the chirps and calls of birds and wildlife hiding in the unexplored forest in either direction.

"Hey!" she said, as if startled out of a dream. For the first time in her life she was taking in air what didn't belong to Marse Henry. Maybe, outside of Marse Henry's darn old wall, even she didn't belong to him.

Is this how Angus felt, she wondered, when he went to Richmond? What he meant by "free?"

Euphrates glanced back at Angus, then peered down each of the road's choice of directions. She took off running up the direction of road where the canopy of trees let through dappled sunlight.

She ran until she couldn't run anymore.

Amazingly, she was at yet another choice of diverging paths, again bounded on every side by thick forest. Were these trees truly taller? Greener? The air... sweeter?

A daring notion spoke almost aloud to her. Maybe, if she jest kept going, she could escape too. Like Clara and Lawrence.

She doused the spark of hope quicker than it had ignited.

She could never do that to Mama and Baby Sister. Or Angus. Papa had another family. His white family, so she wasn't so worried about him, but her mother, sister and brother needed her.

Yet, if this was as free as she was ever going to get, she jest had to see a little bit more of this strange new land, this heaven, before she hurried back home. And she did have to hurry. Somehow the morning had suddenly turned into late afternoon. If Mama had to look for her, it would mean a switch, for sure.

Euphrates ventured the path to the right. Along the way, she admired every bush, branch and bird.

Before long, she came upon a stretch of open land. A meadow. Its bounty of wildflowers was brazen with color. She had never seen such beauty.

A red-tail hawk dipped low enough for Euphrates to almost touch, then, just as quickly, it flew back out of sight. If only she could do the same.

She ran to the red flowers, to the blue flowers, to the yellow flowers, gathering bunches of them all, to take to Mama. The experience of choice made her giddy.

She wished she could take them all home, but now it was

even later, and her arms were full. She surveyed her surroundings for the path back.

The fading daylight made everything look the same. And the path? Had it disappeared right before her eyes?

A shiver of panic ran up Euphrates' back as she chanced measured paces first one way, then another. And another. There were only so many possibilities, weren't there? She stared up at the emerging stars for guidance.

From some mysterious place far away, booming cannon fire echoed.

Yanks?

Yanks. Her stomach knotted and her heart raced. Where, oh, where was Angus. He always rescued her. "Angus," she cried as tears welled in her eyes. "Help me."

But Angus couldn't answer her because he wasn't anywhere near. She was lost, and completely alone.

A faint breeze carried a hint of smoke. And something much worse. Much worse. Death.

From a torched plantation?

A sprinkle of ash and embers floated through the air, and a hot cinder burned one of her eyes. "Aghhhh!" she belted out, and blinked furiously with pain.

Her lungs began to hurt too. She was choking on the grayish haze settling all about her as the cannon fire continued to echo, again and again. Her bare feet absorbed the earth's trembling.

She tried to reason aloud with herself. "I's got to get to the river bluff. I's can make my way home from there."

Her stomach grumbled. How she wished she hadn't turned up her nose at the two-day-old square of cornbread and the soured cup of milk Mama had offered her for breakfast.

She pushed on, only to trip over a fallen tree limb. The branches of the limb raked her arms and legs as she sprawled.

The cuts and welps stung.

The light of the nearly full moon allowed her to see the trickles of blood from the deepest wound.

Standing up and brushing off, Euphrates reclaimed her determination to seek the river bluff. With steeled nerves, she began humming one of the lullaby's Mama always sang to Baby Sister.

After an hour, or so, Euphrates stumbled into a clearing, a brick structure stood in the center. Curious, she ran around to its front.

It had a wooden door which she didn't dare enter and seemed to be a washhouse, because anchored into the building's outer wall, at about the height of her father, were three long clotheslines, each extended out and held up at their opposite ends by wooden poles.

Each of the lines were laden with freshly laundered white sheets, all still damp to the touch and pungent with the aroma of lye soap.

Two, well-trod, paths, starting at the washhouse's doorway, formed a right angle and veered back into the forest.

Despite the swath of moonlight, more dense foliage shrouded the paths, making it impossible for Euphrates to see where either path ultimately led.

On nothing more than a gamble, she chose the narrower of the two paths. She was afraid, but not so much that a burst of playfulness couldn't break through.

She dashed back to the clotheslines and darted in and out, amongst the sheets, then sprinted up and down the rows created by the clotheslines, as if caught in a maze.

It had been a typical Virginia summer day, mercilessly hot and dreadfully muggy, and the cool sheets refreshed her arms and face. She stopped to hold one of the sheets to her cheeks.

The scent of the lye soap tickled her nostrils and caused

her to sneeze.

Upon opening her eyes Euphrates discovered the strawberry stains she'd imprinted on the sheets.

She'd forgotten that her hands and mouth were painted with the juice of her feast in Angus's garden.

"Uh oh!" A flood of guilt washed over her at seeing how she'd ruined someone's hard work.

Though no one was there to hear, she clasped her hands and pledged aloud, "I is so, so sorry. Someday, my word to God, I's find my way back here, and help you anyway I's can. I's hope I's hasn't gotten you in trouble."

For the first time ever, Euphrates would've almost rathered one of her mama's whippin's.

Pursuing her chosen path once more, she ran along it until she tired. She thought it curious for there not to be any big houses or cabins along the way, but soon enough all she was thinking about again was somehow reaching the river bluff.

The cannon fire had ceased.

An owl hooted from an overhead branch and fireflies darted about. Other than a chorus of crickets, all seemed peaceful despite the lingering stink of gunpowder.

She was so sleepy, and her mama must be worried sick 'bout now. She began to repeat Mama's favorite saying aloud, "Fear is not faith. Fear is not faith. *Fear is not faith.*"

The North Star twinkled overhead.

At last, she heard the faint sound of rushing water in the offing. She began singing Mama's favorite hymn.

Swing low, sweet chariot, comin' for to carry me home, swing low sweet chariot comin' for to carry me home. I looked over yonder and what did I see, comin' for to carry me home, a band of angels, comin' after me, comin' for to carry me home. Swing low sweet chariot, comin' for to carry me--

The unexpected sound of marching, a steady whomp, whomp, whomp, whomp startled her quiet. Whoever theys was, theys was coming toward her.

She had to hide. She dived into a thicket of wild roses, abundant with thorns, and crouched low.

From around the bend appeared a platoon of Yankee soldiers. A whole mess of them. Fifty, a hundred, maybe more. Every one with a musket settled on his shoulder.

She remembered the disappearing trick Angus used to play of stretching out face down in the tall grass so that no one could see him. She did as he might have, but her heart would not stop its awful pounding. All she could do was try desperately not to move or breathe.

"Lord Almighty," she prayed silently, "please, watch over me, else them northern devils gonna string me up just like Marse Henry say they did Big Sam and Moses. Amen."

As the soldiers paraded past, the thud of their boots caused the ground to rumble.

It seemed an eternity before all was quiet again, but something in her soul was telling her to stay put awhile longer.

As she lay there, her eyelids became unbearably heavy.

By the time she awoke, the sky was rouged with the very faintest blush of dawn.

She stood, brushed the twigs and dirt from her dress and hair, and tried to make-believe that all was well.

A breeze rustled, but quickly died. The sound of the river's rushing water was suddenly more distinct.

She hurried toward it.

In only minutes, she arrived at yet another clearing, this time, one with a windowless shack in its midst.

And, as investigation proved, twenty, or so feet beyond the shack was the river bluff.

Euphrates stood at the very edge of the bluff and peered

down just in time to witness the helplessness of an old buckboard being tossed and churned by the river's ferocious current. Any living thing would have suffered all the more.

The shack's banging door also unnerved her. Best she be on her way.

As she backed away from the ledge the gravely voice of a man stopped her heart cold.

"Over here, Missy."

Terrified, Euphrates turned in search of the person who had spoken.

"Uhhh!" she cried, at the sight of the monstrous ghostlike creature staring down into her face.

"Get inside," the creature demanded.

Suddenly, Euphrates realized that the thing wasn't a monster, or even a ghost. It was a man hiding his face and body under a sheet. A sheet with the same lye soap smell as the sheets outside the washhouse.

Jagged holes had been cut in the sheet large enough for Euphrates to see the man's eyes, nose, and mouth.

The man was aiming a musket at her. He grunted, then limped closer. His eyes were bloodshot.

"You ignorin' me, gal?" he said, and leaned even closer to her face. "I ain't gonna tell you again."

The man's stale, sour breath made Euphrates gag. She had to turn away.

"Oh yeah!" the man said, then jabbed the butt of the musket into Euphrates's stomach.

The jab caused her to fall to the ground, onto a sharp-edged rock that cut deep into her thigh. "Ohhhhhh!" she cried.

Before she could move, he put the musket to her head.

"Listen, gal. Either you do what I say, or I'll shoot you dead, right here. You choose."

Euphrates's thoughts were muddled, but she was aware enough to know that if she wanted to see Mama and Papa, and, Angus and Baby Sister, again, she had better do what the man wanted.

Ever so slowly, she rolled onto her knees, and, in spite of the pain shooting through her leg, managed to stand.

The man pressed a massive hand against her shoulder and forced her into the shack.

She stumbled but willed herself to remain upright.

He followed her inside and slammed the door closed. All was as black as Mama's cast-iron skillet.

She heard the man move toward her, then felt his calloused fingers on her face.

"You're a real pretty gal, you know that?"

Euphrates didn't know what to answer, but it didn't matter. The man grabbed the front of her dress and ripped it open.

She felt her face burn with shame and tried to cover herself with her arms.

"Uh huh! One of them uppity niggras. Well, I'll teach you," the man said, and knocked Euphrates's arms away.

He squeezed her small breasts until they hurt.

No man, or boy, had ever touched her, 'cept for Papa's hugs, but she could feel that this man's hands were sweaty and filthy.

His breathing went to shallow heaves as he roamed her young body. He reached for the sacred place between her legs.

She felt sick to her stomach, and not thinking, stepped back. He slapped her. Then gripped her throat.

"Uggghhh. Can't breathe," she pleaded.

When he finally opened his hand he let her fall.

He laughed as Euphrates gulped for air, but her relief was momentary. Without warning, he was down on all fours and on top of her with his mouth pressed against hers.

As he mashed the full weight of his man's body against her girl's body, she was crushed into the dirt floor.

She tried to struggle out from underneath him, but a sudden pain between her thighs made her want to die.

Something awful was trying to crawl its way out through her screams.

"Shut up, you little darkie, shut up," he spewed, as he thrust himself into her again and again. "Shut up."

*   *   *

Angus flattened himself against the outer wall of the shack.

He grimaced as he listened to a man's steady grunting tangled with Euphrates's scattered whimpers.

He gripped his spade tighter, flung the shack door open, and without hesitation, hurled himself inside.

He felt his way to the nearest corner, then waited for his eyes to adjust to the darkness.

A shaft of moonlight through the open door helped.

In the middle of the floor, a man wearing a sheet was hunched over Euphrates. The man was hurting her.

Angus held his spade high and crept closer to them.

The man stopped moving and grabbed for his musket, only Angus was faster and brought his spade down with as much might as his gangly fourteen-year-old body could let go.

The man hollered, dropped the musket, and bolted upright. "God damn it," he screamed, as he cradled his head.

Angus reached for Euphie, pulled her up, and shoved her behind him. He had to be ready to deliver another blow.

The man stood, then staggered toward the children.

Euphrates cringed but Angus did not flinch. Both of them saw the gleam of the man's Bowie knife as he pulled it from somewhere under the sheet.

As the man staggered closer and closer to them, he cursed and slashed at the air.

"Euphrates," Angus shouted, "get out of here. Now."

"No, Brother, I'm not leaving you," she cried back.

"Then stay behind me, against the wall."

For once, Euphrates didn't smart-mouth Angus.

He dodged the man's lunge, then swung the spade at him with determination. This time, though, Angus caught mere air.

The man took advantage of the opportunity, and pointed the knife at Angus's heart, backing the children into an opposite corner.

He towered over them.

What the man couldn't know was that Mama had raised them on the scripture of David and Goliath. Angus summoned all of his will and jabbed the handle of the spade into the man's stomach. Then, over and over, into the man's crotch.

"Aaggghhh," the man bellowed.

Angus jabbed him again, but this time the force of the hit knocked the spade from Angus's hands.

The man doubled over and fell to his knees, nearly landing on top of the spade.

All Angus could do was stare, helplessly, as the man bobbed forward and backward, hissing like a snake.

With no other choice, Angus finally made a grab for the spade, but the man leaned out and caught the handle, midair, yanking it out of Angus's grasp.

Pain, unlike anything Angus had ever felt, shot through his fingers and hands. His fingers felt broken, and the flesh of his palms was torn wide open.

The man got up and came at Angus again, but Angus could barely hold his throbbing hands chest high. He felt the knife slice down the whole left side of his face.

"Ahhhhggh!" Angus yelped as a searing agony raced from his temple to his chin. Blood dripped onto his shirt and hands.

He was stunned and dizzy, and felt like he'd been set on fire. In the confusion of it all, he heard the spade whap against the man's body.

Angus looked up just as the man wobbled, then fell.

Euphrates was standing over the man, trembling, and still holding the spade high above her shoulders, but somehow, the man clamored back to his feet.

This time, Euphie was either too exhausted, or too scared, to move, and only watched as the man bent to reclaim his knife.

Angus, though, wasn't about to allow the man to hurt his sister anymore. Instead, Angus ran in and pulled the spade out of Euphie's grip, then got between her and the man just as the man raked the knife through the air.

The blade of the knife nicked Angus's forearm, but Angus managed to keep hold of the spade and raised it as high as his injuries would permit.

"You shouldn't have hurt my sister," Angus said, and brandished the spade as if it were a sword.

The man guffawed, enjoying himself so much he threw his head back and tilted up on his heels, losing his balance.

He swirled his arms to try to stay standing.

Angus, now a gladiator, seized his chance. He batted the metal edge of the spade into the man's waist.

Blood seeped through the man's sheet.

A deathly quiet followed as the man looked down at the stain, pawed at it, and then silently crumpled to the ground.

For a long moment, the children held their breaths. Finally, Euphrates asked, "Is...is...he...dead?

"I don't know," Angus said, then added "but I sure hope so."

The twins waited, ready for anything.

Their fears were justified.

Before either one of them could react, the man rolled to his side and got to his feet, growling like a rabid dog.

Worse, he still had the knife. "I'm gonna kill you niggras once and for all," he said, and slashed the air.

Angus blocked the knife with the bed of the spade, and remained focused. "Euphrates, move."

Angus's body was racked with pain, and his senses were dulled beyond measure, yet there wasn't time to hesitate.

The man tried to turn and face Angus, but his feet tangled in the hem of his sheet.

At last, with one bash, then another, Angus obliterated the back of the man's head.

The man's blood spurted in all directions and especially onto Euphrates's and Angus's faces and clothes.

This time, though, the man fell with such a thud that the earth shook.

Euphie and Angus waited for him to stir, but at last, he had gone to his reward.

With measured caution, Angus finally spoke. "I, I think he really is dead now, Euphie. He can't hurt you anymore."

Euphrates answered with only a deep sigh. She felt a need to see the face of the man who had mauled and shamed her, and went over to his body.

She lifted the bloodied sheet to look. The shock of what she saw told in her voice. "Brother, it's…it's…I's mean…he's a white man. A Yankee soldier. What we gonna do?"

Angus stared at the spade, then threw it against a wall. "There's nothing *we* can do. I is got to get out of here, or, when theys find me, they is gonna string me up."

"No! Euphrates cried, and threw her arms around Angus's neck, clinging to him with her last bit of strength. "No, no, no, no!"

Angus loosened his sister's arms, and gently pushed her away. Then he knelt, unbuttoned and removed the soldier's shirt, and handed it to Euphrates for her to put on.

Next, he removed the man's pants, then stepped into them himself.

"Brother, what is you doin'? Have you's gone daft?"

"I got to get out of Virginia, Euphie," he answered. "With this half a Yank's uniform, I at least got a chance. And look at these boots. They's even better than Papa's."

Angus put the boots on, then they walked out of the shack into the fresh air. Both of the children breathed deep.

The pink and yellow light streaked across the horizon trumpeted the arrival of morning.

Euphrates could see that her brother had been badly injured. As a flap of skin hung open down the left side of his face. By the time such a bad cut healed, it would probably leave a great, ugly scar for the rest of Angus's life.

On their walk to the bluff's edge, an urgent concern pressed on Euphrates's heart. "Brother, the river's too dangerous," she said. "'Besides, you can't swim."

"I's don't have a choice, Euphie," Angus said calmly.

They reached the look-over and stared down at the James River's relentless current. Even with the dawn reflected on its surface, the water looked secretive and angry.

Euphrates turned toward her brother and studied his face. She didn't want to ever forget what he looked like. Tears, of love, and sorrow, welled in her eyes. She reached to touch her brother's face once more, but he held her hand back.

I'd better bury him first," Angus said, with a nod toward the cabin, then turned to go toward it.

Euphrates caught him by the arm. "No! I want to do it. And I's will hide the spade, too," she said.

Angus stared back at his sister, then, after a moment, kissed her on the cheek. "Tell Mama, I will always love her," he said. "And you. You be good. Help Mama takes care of Baby Sister."

Euphrates nodded, then cupped her hands over her face to keep him from seeing her cry. The smell of lye soap and the sight of the man's blood on her skin made her want to wretch.

She didn't want Angus to run away. She loved her brother and couldn't imagine life without him. Her eyes were still squeezed shut when she heard a splash.

She quickly dropped her hands and looked to see what had happened. Angus was nowhere to be seen, but he couldn't be gone. He just couldn't be.

He was, though. Maybe forever.

Euphrates resisted looking down at the river for as long as possible, then gave in. The water was dark and swift. A large dogwood branch floated along at the river's mercy, then, was suddenly swept under.

Again, she remembered what Papa called the river.

A bed of broken bones and lost dreams.

Euphrates's tears spilled and wouldn't stop.

"Angus," she called out across the river's vastness, "please! Please, come back!"

She waited on the bluff, for hours, every second her gaze searching the river for any sign of her brother.

*   *   *

For years afterward, Euphrates went to the bluff and prayed for Angus to reappear.

He never did.

Women K.K.K.
File Papers
For State Charter

Incorporation papers for the Women of the Ku Klux Klan have been filed in the office of the secretary of state. The incorporators and directors of the organization are Meta L. Gremmels, Dr. Ester B. Hunt and Laurena H. Senter, all of Denver.

Objects of the organization are given as the procuring and enforcement of just and equitable laws, upholding the constitution of the United States and the state of Colorado, teaching of respect for laws and law-enforcing authorities, furtherance of American principles, ideals and institutions, and relief work to alleviate suffering and distress.

Only white women of American birth over 18 years old are eligible for membership.

Denver Post, December 8, 1924

Denver, Colorado
1925

Charlene A. Porter

Chapter One

The *Rocky Mountain News* had forecast that Denver would begin 1925 buried under an old-fashioned plains blizzard.

The actuality was more of a gentle blanketing of snow. A cross between the light flurries that swirl back into the air on gusts of wind, and the heavy drifts that ice into mounds on utility and telephone wires, weighing the wires down so low that they sometimes snap and fall to the ground. The kind of snow that's back breaking to shovel and that makes streets nearly impossible to drive down, but that is great for rolling into jolly snowmen, or compressing into deadly snowballs.

The kind of snowfall that inspires old-timers to swap stories about the 1859 "Pikes Peak or Bust" gold rush, the days of the Wild West, and the years of the silver boom.

The times, when – seventy or eighty years back – , the territory that is now Denver was home to buffalo herds and populated by camps of Arapaho and Cheyenne Indians. When all there was to Denver were the makeshift trading posts and mining camps that sprung up between the confluence of Clear Creek and South Platte River.

"Yeah, and how about all them gosh-durn buildings in every direction. Banks, hospitals, schools, churches, libraries, hotels – even one built by some Colored fella name of Ford – and cinema palaces," one of the grizzled old men would say.

"Yep. And don't forget the e-leet dry goods stores and fancy amusement parks, roller coasters, Ferris wheels, and all. But that ain't the top of it. Now, houses and what not, springing up far out as can be," someone equally as time-worn would add.

"Truth to tell," yet another old-timer would pipe in. "But it's them country club bunch a sons and daughters what really got my dander up. They just plain showing off. I mean what's a body need with thirty rooms in one house? Why, they almost need their own brick factory to build one of them monstrosities. But then, there's them blasted au-to-mo-biles. Instance, last week, some crazy fool driving a long yellow De-Soto just about runned over me."

"Yep, know what you mean," the conversation would start all over again, "Denver jest ain't what it used to be."

There was one topic, however, even newcomers could join in on: the majesty and beauty of the Rocky Mountains.

Their thirty miles of snowcapped peaks stretched north to south, along the western boundary of Denver, as if created to be a daily reminder of God himself. The wagon trains that had tried to cross them to get west, used to take four, five, sometimes six weeks, or more…and a lot of them just couldn't make it across the steep passes or out of the deep canyons.

Now, in the two or three generations since the trail and mining days, small towns were nestled throughout the Rockies, while communities along the foothills, such as the little city of Golden, looked out over Denver and the other flatland settlements.

Indeed, it was to Golden's Table Top Mountain that young lovers drove to park and watch the swirl of red, purple, and yellow light ebb from the plains sky as Denver's street lamps came on.

All Margaret Browne knew of such excursions, however, was what she would overhear her stepson, Kyle, and his friends plotting whenever one of them could get the family automobile. But Margaret didn't like Kyle being twenty-five miles from home – especially with the bunch of hooligans he had taken up with lately – and always forbade his going. Lately, though, he disobeyed and went anyway.

It wasn't that she didn't trust Kyle, who after all, at seventeen, was really a young man…it was just that she tried to protect him from his father, who always accused Kyle of doing something wrong.

But then, Devin didn't trust anyone. He wouldn't even permit her, a grown woman of thirty-four, to learn to drive.

Today, though, was not a time for worrying. Both Kyle and Devin had gone off on their own, leaving Margaret alone in the house with her mother-in-law, Mother Browne, and their butler, Walter…which meant a rare chance for Margaret to leave the house without having to tell Devin where she was going.

But Margaret had to hurry. If Devin came home unexpectedly, he most likely would make her stay home.

And she certainly didn't want to ask Walter to lie for her, which she had already done several months ago, but which she had seen by the look on his face wasn't something he was comfortable with. She had to leave now, while Walter had gone to the drugstore for Mother Browne's new prescriptions. She didn't want to leave her mother-in-law alone, but she had little choice.

Margaret went to the hall closet for her coat and hat, and took her ice skates from their hook, and her sketch pad and pencils from their hiding place in a box marked Tree Ornaments.

Thankfully, she'd made sure to put the gloves Kyle had given her for Christmas in one of her coat pockets, and so she didn't have to go back upstairs for anything.

She walked out onto the front porch and she looked directly at the mountains. Their peaks were hidden by a bank of clouds that also covered the sun, and it had started snowing again. The day was gray and somber. The temperature, three or four degrees below zero.

She put on her gloves, walked down the porch steps to the sidewalk, then began the ten-block hike to the trolley stop on Seventeenth Avenue. She had remembered to line her boots with newspaper to insulate her feet against the cold, so her only real worry was trying not to slip on the seemingly invisible black ice that sheeted the flagstone sidewalks.

Most of the home owners on Grant Street, however, were conscientious and prided themselves on keeping the walks of their millionaire neighborhood well salted.

Margaret had walked only two blocks when a young woman with an infant in her arms passed by going in the opposite direction. The woman's gloveless hand were truning blue. Frostbitten.

Margaret took two more steps, then stopped, hesitated an instant, then pulled off her gloves and ran back toward the woman. "Here," she blurted as she came shoulder-to-shoulder with the woman, and held out her gloves. "Put these on. I'll hold the baby for you."

The woman looked at Margaret in disbelief, but handed the bundled infant over. The woman was shivering, but struggled to talk. "I, I, I don't know what to…"

"Please," Margaret said, as she pulled the baby's yellow blanket closer to its face, "there's no need to say anything. I already know." .

Ten minutes later, but still three blocks from her trolley-stop, it was Margaret's hands that had turned painfully blue. All she could do was push her hands deeper into her coat pockets and try to walk faster. She attempted to ignore her numb toes. After all, suffering an afternoon of winter weather was nothing compared to what she stood to gain for the rest of her life.

As Margaret waited for the trolley, she took her hands from her coat pockets and placed them, palms down, on her stomach. The baby growing in her womb was so helpless. She had to tell Devin, soon, that she was pregnant. But what if even that didn't stop him from beating her?

She tried to keep from feeling the pain in her bruised shoulder. She wasn't going to allow anything to keep her from searching for her daughter.

Devin didn't know that she'd had a child seventeen years ago, or he never would have married her. Somehow, she had to find the courage to tell him that too.

Clang. Clang. The trolley screeched to a stop and let Margaret on.

She chose a seat with as few people nearby as possible, and sat down with a deep sigh of relief. She filled the adjoining seat with her ice skates and sketch book and hoped no one would ask for the seat. Her hands and feet ached as they began to thaw. She realized that the morning was already gone.

Clang. Clang. The trolley bell turned Margaret's attention to the passing scenery.

Many of the storefronts along Seventeenth were still decorated for Christmas with candy canes painted on the shops' windows, and pine wreaths hung on their doors. She had the feelings that she wasn't so much passing through a commerce district, but rather through a lovely alpine village. "Peace on earth, good will to men," Margaret said softly, truly meaning it.

The seasonal tiding made her think of Gwen, who was Jewish but whohad been her best friend since childhood. now their lives were as opposite as ginger ale and champagne, especially now that Gwen had inherited her parents' fortune, yet she and Gwen still loved each other like they were the sisters each had longed for.

Margaret gazed out at The East Denver Ice Cream Parlor and Confectioner, where Gwen had kissed her first gentile boy.

And the Rexall Sundry and Drug Store, where Margaret had shoplifted a rouge. She had been so overcome with guilt that she had run straight home and spent an entire six hours on her knees reciting *Hail Marys* and *Our Fathers*.

Then came the nameless and wonderfully mysterious antique shop where they'd had the most fun. They had seldom purchased anything, but the owner hadn't seemed to mind. He had let them spend hours sorting through the overburdened clothes racks for items to try on, and they had found everything from antebellum hoop skirts, to Red Cross uniforms, to black silk kimonos.

Margaret never would forget when Gwen found that red hoochie-koochie dress with the fringe all around it, then put it on and sashayed around as if she were one of those women on Market Street.

"Penn-syl-vania," the trolley conductor sang out, and brought the car to a stop.

Two riders exited the car at the rear as new riders boarded at the front. The token box chimed with the deposit of each eight-cent fare.

One of the new riders, an attractive Negro woman who seemed somehow ageless, walked by the several empty seats at the front of the trolley, and made her way to a seat at the rear of the trolley.

Two other new riders, a boy and a girl, both about twelve years old, talked excitedly, and like Margaret, had ice skates. They stood in the aisle, near her, as they stomped slush from their galoshes and shook snow from their caps.

To avoid the assault of moisture, Margaret turned her face back toward the window.

Just as she looked out she saw a car skid across the icy street and crash into a telephone pole. The KOA radio broadcast that morning came to mind. The announcer had warned of downed power lines throughout the city. She tried to visualize what it all must look like.

South Denver and Englewood were mostly residential, but there were also orchards and sanatoriums. Those repairs would come last.

North, to the stockyards and factories of Globeville, and west to the mills and breweries of Golden, there would be a lot of people who needed safe roads to get to work, so crews were probably working in those areas already.

She had never been east, to the suburbs and airfields, so couldn't picture that part of the city. Maybe Devin would take the family on a drive out that way some weekend. Then again, the last time they'd been on a Sunday outing Devin had caused an accident, and had had to spend the night in jail for punching out the other driver.

If only he would allow her to learn to drive.

Margaret closed her eyes and hoped the gentle hum of the trolley's motion would quiet her thoughts. It didn't. Within seconds, her mind was aflame again with guilt and dread.

Why had she fooled herself all these years into believing the impossible?

Into believing that Devin would eventually fall in love with her...and no longer compare her to his deceased first wife.

Into believing that she, the daughter of a humble dry goods merchant, would eventually be welcomed into his family's social circle: Denver's Sacred 36.

Rather, she had to finally accept that she and Devin would always occupy separate worlds.

His, primarily polo fields and country clubs.

Hers, the working class neighborhood where she had grown up and worked in her father's store.

Devin hadn't even seemed to notice, or care, that she had retreated into a life of household duties and church bazaars. Her only saving grace was that she had begun to sketch nature scenes, and had found that she had a talent for it. She'd even secretly sold a few of her sketches to a local curio shop that reproduced the scenes on postal cards.

"Clark-son," the conductor announced. This time, however, Margaret was too lost in thought to notice those who came or went. Instead, she was replaying scenes of how Devin's drastically changed behavior over the past year. Before, he'd been merely inconsiderate, but during the past months he'd become brutish.

It was as if something about this newest scheme of his – some kind of membership campaign for a secret organization – had unleashed his vilest nature. He had become little more than cruel and violent.

There had to be more explanation to all of this than that her father had fallen behind on his monthly deposits into Devin's bank account – which is how the Brownes had managed for so many years to keep up appearances, and before Father Browne died, to pay off his betting debts. But what could it be?

Margaret's question led to thoughts of her father. She loved Angus deeply, but wished at least once a day that he hadn't insisted on her marrying Devin. Even after all these years, she could still hear her father's argument.

"Listen, lassie, this is a might good match. It's not everyone that can marry into a first class family like the Brownes. Trust me, there's a long line of other girls who wish they were in your very place."

Margaret wondered if this sacrificial social climbing existed among other races and cultures, or was it simply the white race's shortcoming? She found herself back at her worries about Devin, hoping that he hadn't mortgaged their house... which his grandfather had built during the Gold Rush.

She felt a flutter in her womb and glanced back out the window.

How ironic. After years of disappointment and heartache, and shedding her final tears for the child that she was apparently never going to have, she was at last pregnant. Three months.

Still, she couldn't shake the sense of mourning, only, for which child?

The one she'd raised?

The one soon to be born into a loveless marriage?

Or, the one who had been--.

No! She had to stop doing this to herself.

She saw a bony, filthy mutt scratching earnestly into a mound of hardened, dirty snow. An ache clenched her chest.

"Don't worry, you miserable thing," Margaret whispered, even though the dog couldn't possibly hear her, "spring isn't so far off."

Clang. Clang. The trolley continued east, down Seventeenth, past the boundary of Capitol Hill, toward her destination, City Park. If only she could make it that far before her breakfast wretched back up.

She closed her eyes for the briefest of moments' then was unsettled by what she saw when she reopened them.

Dr. Woods' office.

The sting of old hurts flooded her mind. No matter how earnestly she attempted to force the memory away, every detail of Dr. Woods' dingy back room was as clear to her as the day her father had taken her there.

The remembered smell of antiseptic so overwhelmed Margaret that she wondered if she was somehow about to be strapped to that same narrow bed.

Equally unbearable was her recollection of the nurse, a squat, heavyset blonde who wore wire-rimmed glasses and who spoke with an accent of some kind – Hungarian, or maybe, Polish and who had taken her wailing baby into the next room, never to be seen.

"Not good. Not good," was all the woman had said when Margaret had begged to hold her newborn baby. "She have new Mama now."

The same nurse had quieted Margaret by pressing a cloth full of chloroform to Margaret's face, but as she had drifted off to sleep, Margaret had clung to the memory of the word *she* as if it were a satchel full of gold nuggets.

It had been morning by the time Margaret awoke, and by then there was a new nurse, another woman she had never seen, who claimed to know nothing about any such baby. Her only role, the new nurse had declared, was to have Margaret dressed and ready to go home when her father drove up to the office's rear entrance to pick her up.

Margaret could still see her father's expressionless face when he had leaned across the seat of his Model-T to push open the car's passenger door. He had sped off as soon as she was inside the car, and had said nothing to her the entire ride home.

Like everything else her father had refused to acknowledge – his past, Margaret's mother, the baby's father – they didn't discuss the baby either. In fact, as soon as they had arrived home, and for all the months and years afterward, she and her father went on with life as if nothing out of the ordinary had ever happened. Not that Margaret didn't try, every once in awhile to bring up the subject. It was simply that her father ignored her questions, or left the room.

Exhausted by the memory, Margaret turned her attention to her fellow trolley riders.

A redheaded man of about twenty was sitting across the aisle. She decided that her father might have looked very much the same in his own young adulthood, forty-five or fifty years ago. But that was only a guess, because she didn't know her father's age, nor had she seen a photograph of him as a young man or boy. He probably hadn't allowed any to be taken. She wasn't absolutely sure that his real name was Angus O'Shea.

Again, Margaret wondered if the forbidden topic of his youth had anything to do with the scar that extended down his face.

She also thought of her mother, who had abandoned the family when Margaret was only six. But she hated thinking of her mother, who had never so much as written to explain. If it hadn't been for two old busybodies she'd overheard gossiping at a Holy Cross bake sale, she wouldn't have known that her mother had returned to Norway...or, that she was even from there. It had been the first time she felt happy that she looked most like her father. Before then, she cursed her unruly red hair. The stubborn streak she had inherited from him as well.

"Hum-boldt." Again, the trolley braked and its front and rear doors flung open. A swirl of snow flurries swept in on a gush of cold air and reminded Margaret of her destination. Her spirits lifted. She slipped a hand underneath her coat and tenderly caressed her stomach. She realized soon she would have to stop wearing a corset.

With her free hand she pulled a rosary from her coat pocket and entwined the long string of glass beads around her fingers. "Hail Mary, full of grace," she recited. "The Lord is with thee.

Blessed art thou among women; blessed is the fruit of thy womb, Jesus. Holy Mary, Mother of God, pray for us sinners, now and at the hour of our death. Amen. Hail Mary, full of grace. The Lord is with thee."

Once more, her thoughts drifted to the early morning because Devin had stumbled in, inebriated and stinking of bootleg whiskey and cheap cologne. He had threatened her with his fist at finding his supper cold.

She had to face the truth. Devin was becoming increasingly dangerous to her and the baby.

The trolley's gentle rocking came to a sudden stop and jolted her. She had to reach out to the seat ahead to brace herself. She looked at her hand and for a moment was alarmed.

Her wedding ring was missing. But then she remembered her visit to the pawn shop.

For the one hundred and twenty-five dollars she had received for her ring, she had settled the coal and grocery bills, and attempted to pay Walter his monthly wages, which he had refused to accept. Instead, she used that money to pay Mother Browne's doctor, and to have the leaky roof repaired.

She put her palm to the window and rubbed in circles until the heat of her hand defrosted the ice crystals. More shops came into view.

Clang. Clang. Happily, Weinstein's Bakery was ahead.

Happily, because during their high school years, it had been one of Gwen and Margaret's favorite places.

Mr. and Mrs. Weinstein were the nicest people Margaret had ever met, and their son Isaac – before he'd gone to the war and been lost at sea – so funny that he should have been in Vaudeville.

When Gwen's parents were out of town, and left her with extra money, the girls went to the Weinstein's bakery sometimes two or three times a week.

Still, no matter how often they went, Mrs. Weinstein always added one more cookie or cupcake to both their bags than either one of the girls had paid for.

Even if they discovered the bonus after arriving home, Margaret likewise always insisted that she and Gwen rush back to pay the extra nickel or dime.

As soon as Mrs. Weinstein saw the girls coming back in the door, she'd quickly send Mr. Weinstein to the basement storeroom for some suddenly needed item. And the outcome never differed.

The girls, out of breath from running, would hold out the money they owed, and Mrs. Weinstein would fold her arms, hunch her shoulders, and refuse to take it.

"So, I'm not so good with numbers," she would say, then add, "so, the world should end?"

At almost the same moment, Mr. Weinstein would reappear with his wife's filled request, and Mrs. Weinstein would shoo the girls on their way. Margaret smiled at the memory and eagerly awaited the cheery storefront coming into view.

But in its place there was only a small boarded up building with licks of black scarring its outer wall.

"What in God's name?" Margaret gasped. Where was the bakery? She squeezed her eyes closed and swallowed hard. She couldn't bear to look. Her thoughts became a screaming blur as the trolley continued past the burned structure.

It's, it's not possible, she thought. That nosey butcher, with his foolish blather, couldn't have been right. All he told were fibs. Besides, Devin had promised her that the Klan would leave the bakery alone.

"Gay-lord," the conductor called. The next stop was Margaret's, but she was barely able to breathe. For the baby's sake, she had to remain calm. She took deep breaths, then forced the air in her lungs back out.

A grizzled old man, wearing a tattered, dirty Chesterfield coat that must have once been of fine quality, was standing in the aisle, staring at her.

"Hey duchess, ya mind?" the man said.

His gravelly voice broke into her thoughts. "I'm sorry...what?" she asked, still hyperventilating.

"Ya mind if I sit?" he said, looking at her ice skates and sketch pad in the adjoining seat.

Margaret quickly looked and saw that all the other seats in the trolley were taken. "Oh, no, not at all," she said, thankful to be distracted. "We're practically at my stop anyway. In fact, "she added as she gathered her belongings, "why don't we just exchange places?"

She scooted out of her seat and stood, expecting the man to sit, but he remained standing. He was holding out a grubby palm in which rested a shiny silver dollar. "Thanks, duchess," he said, "that's right decent of ya. I'd like ya to have this...for ya troubles."

"Oh, no, I couldn't," Margaret said, admiring the coin. "It's awfully handsome though."

"Look Duchess, ya'd be doin' me a favor," the man said, then took her hand and emptied the coin into it.

"Thank you," Margaret said, for some reason joyfully relenting. Suddenly, she recognized the man. It was Silver Dollar Joe, one of Denver's last surviving '59ers, and once the most renowned tycoon west of the Mississippi.

He was now an impoverished old man and lived under the viaducts, but would appear in various places around the city giving away silver dollars.

Margaret watched him take her vacant seat, then turn his face toward the window.

She was glad that Gwen would be meeting her at the park so that she could tell her about all of this.

"E-liz-a-beth," the conductor called, and clanged the bell as he brought the trolley to the first stop along City Park.

Margaret took another deep breath. Now was no time to weaken. If the nightmare of her daughter being taken from her was ever going to become the dream come true of their being reunited, only she could make it so.

The trolley's rear door opened, and Margaret stepped into the crisp winter day. The sky was now cloudless and achingly blue. A few of the houses bordering the park had white smoke curling from their chimneys. The noon sun reflected blindingly bright off the snow. A perfect day.

Margaret took the closest path into the park and turned her thoughts to her child…who actually would now be a beautiful young woman of seventeen.

Chapter Two

Why Margaret thought she would be able to recognize her daughter she didn't know. She just knew that she would.

As she proceeded on the path to the City Park Lake she passed the sundial, and the two, side-by-side, bronzed cannons from the Civil War. A short distance more beyond a flank of pine, trees was the lake.

The iced-over surface of the lake held a kaleidoscope of hundreds of skaters, their chatter and laughter filling the air. Most of the ice skaters were school children still out on holiday, but the path surrounding the lake was just as busy with promenading adults. The benches that bordered the lake and path were mostly occupied by elderly observers.

Margaret found a vacant bench with a view of the boathouse and sat down to change into her skates.

After lacing up her skates, she took a few more minutes to pencil sketches: one of an overly rouged old woman; one of the boathouse admission sign; and one of a ring of child-sized angel figures impressed in the snow. Then she was ready, and set her drawing pad aside.

She cupped her hands to her mouth, blowing into them to warm them, then hurried out onto the ice.

Within seconds Margaret had smoothly blended into the counter clockwise flow of the other skaters and was gliding along effortlessly. She noted that despite the many skaters, and except for two or three slushy spots, the ice was holding up well. Just one *Danger* sign had been posted.

In the less crowded center of the lake, was a snow-suited child whose reluctant footwork and flailing arms reminded Margaret of her own beginner's efforts. Whether the child was a boy or a girl, Margaret could not tell. She just hoped that the teenage boys zigzagging wildly around a flock of teenage girls didn't scare the child.

They certainly didn't seem to bother the couple waltzing by arm-in-arm, at least not to any extent that Margaret could see. How wonderful it must feel to be in love, she thought.

She skated around the lake twice, looking into every face. But not one was her daughter's. She had to counsel herself to remain optimistic.

On the third time around she saw a young woman with waist-length brunette hair. A closer look though revealed that the girl was a honey-skinned Negro.

A half-hour later her hopes were raised again, only this time by a young woman whose hair was as red as her own. She sped up for a chance to look in the girl's face, but heard the girl make a grossly uncharitable comment to a boy who had accidentally collided with the girl's sister-like companion.

More dashed hopes. Margaret O'Shea Browne was confident that no child of hers could ever be so cruel.

She skated around the lake several more times, all the while paying attention to any newcomers to the ice or path.

But still, no luck. She had to fight hard not to feel discouraged.

Before she even realized it was three o'clock.

Margaret needed to get home, but Gwen, who had promised to meet her here an hour ago and to give her a ride home, was late as usual. She decided to wait for Gwen fifteen more minutes. If Gwen didn't arrive by then, she would just have to take the trolley again. She'd think of something to tell Devin.

She noticed that the condition of the ice was deteriorating. That, in some places, the water under the ice was even visible. Fortunately, this created no real problem as most of the other skaters had already gone.

Margaret was delighted to realize this. The day had been a failure in the most important way, but suddenly she had the rare chance to put aside her natural shyness and to practice her figure eights and pirouettes.

The few who had witnessed Margaret ice skating always spoke afterwards of her grace and skill. It was almost balletic, they usually said.

Nevertheless, by Margaret's own measure any talent that she demonstrated was futile, for the one person she had worked so hard to impress, her mother – who had taught her to skate when she was just a small child – had never returned to Colorado, and thus, had never witnessed Margaret's proficiency on the ice...nor any other part of Margaret's life, for that matter.

"Look, Mama, look," Margaret had said many times to an imaginary figure standing on the lakeshore, "look what I can do." But on the night of her sixteenth birthday, Margaret had finally accepted that her mother was never coming back, and decided that the endless practice was mere foolishness.

Ever since, she'd found it just short of painful to perform on the ice. Oddly, this opportunity to do so delighted her.

She had thought herself unnoticed, but the few skaters who hadn't yet gone home, gathered around to admire her display of artistry. Even a man strolling along the lake's path stopped to applaud and doffed his hat to her.

The audience joined in with cheers of "Beautiful." "Lovely." "Enchanting."

Her cheeks burned with embarrassment at such adulation. She decided to stop and jabbed the toe of a blade into the ice, bringing her twirl to an abrupt end.

In nearly the same instant, a small girl with a head of curly blonde hair broke through the gathering in a panic. She ran directly to Margaret and hid in the folds of Margaret's skirt. The spectators politely dispersed.

"Some mean old boys are chasing me," the little girl said, looking woefully up at Margaret. "They called me a kike and said they're going to rub snow in my face."

The child pointed into the park at a quartet of ruffians running in the direction of a large snowman. Beside the snowman stood an actual man who was lifting a small boy high enough for the boy to put the fedora he was holding on the snowman's head.

Margaret and the little blonde girl watched the little boy place the fedora on the snowman's head, then clap with glee. They continued to watch as the four older boys ran headlong into the snowman, busting it to smithereens.

"No!" both Margaret and the little girl cried. But their protests were useless. All that remained of the snowman was a ragged mound of snow at the man's feet. The four boys had already run laughing and shouting to the top of Museum Hill. They hadn't even paused to look back at their victims: a ruined snowman, a stunned father, and a brokenhearted little boy.

Margaret was speechless as she watched the father bend to pick up the trampled fedora. The little girl just wept and clutched Margaret tighter as they both listened to the little boy wail. Except the trouble wasn't over.

One of the older boys rushed back down the hill, tore the fedora out of the man's grasp, and scrambled back up the hill to his buddies.

Another one of the boys grabbed the hat and gave a victory yell. Then, all four boys scattered. Two of them disappeared into a stand of cottonwoods and another ran around to the side of the museum, but the one with the fedora bumped into a strolling couple as he ran past the front of the museum.

He shouted something undecipherable at the couple then also ran into the stand of trees.

Only it wasn't the prankish boy Margaret stared after. It was the couple he had run into. She watched, bewildered, as the couple sat on a bench overlooking the lake.

She might never have looked twice at the man, but his bright red scarf, which was the exact color of the one she had knitted and given to Devin for Christmas, had caught her eye.

She suddenly felt lightheaded and disoriented. She didn't even notice the woman, standing next to a chauffeured car, calling to the little girl.

"Miss Gertrude, come now," a stocky woman wearing a functional brown coat and a mannish hat, said in a thick Germanic accent, "the car is waiting."

The little girl obeyed and skated away from Margaret's protection without so much as a goodbye, but Margaret didn't say good-bye either. Her concentration was fixed on the couple sitting on the museum bench.

There wasn't any doubt about who the man was. It was her husband. Devin. Only, his companion was a, a...a *Colored* woman.

A Colored woman. Margaret didn't understand. Devin despised Colored people. She felt bewildered and numb, unable to look away from Devin and the woman.

She sensed someone skate around her as if she were a discarded object in the middle of a road, but she was frozen in place. A chill spiraled down her back as she watched Devin kiss the Colored woman. A deep passionate kiss.

When, finally, he drew back from the woman, Devin pulled his scarf from around his neck and draped it tenderly across the woman's head, tucking the ends of the scarf inside the woman's coat. Then he leaned in to kiss the woman again.

Margaret felt woozy. And lost. About to vomit. She had to put a hand on her stomach to keep from retching.

A *Colored* woman?

Margaret's eyes brimmed with tears.

She stumbled onto the ground, leaned on a tree, and bent over and heaved. By the time she recovered and looked back up at the top of the hill, Devin and the woman were nowhere in sight.

All she saw now was a trio of Colored boys about to launch themselves down the slope: two of them in inner tubes, and boy on a shiny red sled. The two in the inner tubes had hitched themselves together, with the legs of the boy in the rear hooked around the waist of the boy in front.

Next to them was the boy on the sled who yelled, "Ready. Set. Go."

The three boys shoved off, and bumped their way to the bottom of the hill.

The boy on the sled went faster, and farther, and almost reached the edge of the lake. "Man, that was fun!," he shouted. "Let's do that again."

Despite the dimming light of a winter late afternoon, the three boys eagerly ran back up the hill.

Margaret watched them go and she realized that other than the Colored boys, she was nearly alone in the park. She didn't know what had happened to Gwen, but for safety's sake, she didn't dare wait for her any longer. She scolded herself, then set out to skate back across the lake to the bench where she'd left her shoes and sketch pad.

Her mind was clouded with thoughts of Devin…and the Colored woman. She had to gather herself, or she was going to be crying all the way home, but at least, now she knew that her marriage really was hopeless.

She straightened her back, and started to step back onto the ice but the boy on the sled whooshed to a stop within inches of her.

"Sorry, lady," he said as he stood up from the sled and turned to go immediately back up the hill.

But Margaret didn't have a chance to answer. Instead, a snowball sailed past her shoulder and exploded against the boy's forehead.

"Awwwwww!" the boy yelped and fell to his knees.

Margaret rushed over to help him.

As she glanced around the otherwise serene landscape in search of the assailant, all she saw were the other two Colored boys, both of whom were almost back at the top of the hill. Apparently, they had no idea their friend had been badly injured.

As Margaret tried to hold the boy up until he was steady on his feet. She noticed someone rushing toward them.

"Yoo hoo," Gwen called with her customary gaiety, and of course, she had on yet another new fur coat. "Pet, watch out! Behind you!" Gwen said, pointing with alarm to somethingor someone behind Margaret.

Margaret looked over her shoulder. One of the boys who had taunted the little blonde girl and destroyed the snowman, was winding his arm as if readying for a major league pitch. Then he let out a savage yell and threw a snowball the size of a large orange at the other two Colored boys just as they reached the bottom of the hill again in their inner tubes. But, thank goodness, it missed.

The two Colored boys looked at each other with shock, then saw their injured friend leaning on Margaret's shoulder. "Man, let's get outta here," one of them said, "them pecker-woods are trying to kill us. Come on, we gotta get Billy."

The two friends rushed over for their buddy.

"Thanks, lady. We got him," one said as they took Billy out from under Margaret's arm, then arranged themselves, one each under Billy's shoulders and carried him away.

"But what about our rides?" Margaret heard one of the boys ask.

"What about 'em? They ain't worth dyin' over," came the reply.

Margaret watched them as they struggled to carry Billy across the park.

"Come on," Gwen said to Margaret, tugging at her arm, "there's nothing you can do."

But Gwen and Margaret were startled once more as the four white boys who had staged the ambush, seemed to come out of nowhere and make a run for the inner tubes.

The boy who had last claimed the fedora let the others scuffle among themselves for the inner tubes, while he made a running dive for the sled, landed perfectly on it, and held on as the sled shot out across the lake.

"Wow!" This is fun," Gwen and Margaret heard him say after the sled had skewed to a stop against a sign that read:

Beware!.
Thin ice.

His friends, who were scampering over the hill with the inner tubes, had him in real danger. Gwen and Margaret could hear the ice breaking under him as he stood to walk back to land.

Without even thinking, Margaret ran onto the ice and skated toward the boy as fast as possible, but the crackle of another fissure compelled her to edge the blades of her skates to a sharp stop.

If she went out any farther, she would be in just as much trouble as the boy.

"Hey," she called to the boy as she watched him crawl back for the sled, "you'd better stop right there."

The boy ignored Margaret.

"Hey!" she said, again, "are you crazy? That part of the ice is going to give way any minute."

"Back off, lady, and mind your own business," the boy answered. In one more reach, the fire red sled would be his for good.

There was only the barest hint of daylight remaining, but Margaret could still see the determined spite on the boy's face. She pleaded with him again. "Didn't you hear me? Do you want to drown?"

The boy didn't act concerned. He had gotten hold of the sled's pull rope and was trying to stand again, but his feet slipped out from under him. His well-worn street shoes were no match for the slippery ice. His backside hit the ice with a thump.

Then, once more, he tried. A harder thump.

Finally, he waited to catch his breath, then rolled onto his hands and knees, and began inching toward Margaret, though he still had the sled by its rope.

Margaret was holding her breath in disbelief. She heard another crack in the ice.

The boy panicked and retreated but one of his knees punched the weakened ice and his leg went into the frigid water.

The fissures surrounding him lengthened, then gave away. "Help! Somebody! Anybody! Help!" the boy begged as he struggled to escape. He was crying and gulping for breath, and his body was probably going into shock.

Time to save him was running out.

She heard him pleading again, this time through chattering teeth.

"La-la-lady, ya gotta help me. I...I, I can't swim. I'm freezing to death," he said, sobbing.

All that held him aloft were his arms extended outward atop the breaking ice. His strength and courage had clearly faded.

Margaret yanked off her coat, then stretched out on her side. Holding onto the coat by one sleeve, she threw it toward the boy and ordered, "Grab hold."

"I can't. I'm scared," he said.

"You can," Margaret scolded him. "Now do it."

"Are you crazy, lady? I said, I can't."

"Well, you'd sure better try," Margaret answered.

At first, he hesitated, but then he extended his hand toward Margaret's coat. He withdrew his reach a second later as another crack in the ice snaked toward him.

Ignoring the continuing whine and crackle of the ice, Margaret eased closer. "Try again," she demanded.

He did, and this time his fingertips grazed the end of the coat's sleeve.

"You're not trying hard enough," Margaret insisted. Now really try." All the while she was inching closer to him.

Again, he reached, and just barely grabbed hold.

Slowly, Margaret wriggled backward, stretching the coat sleeve into the likes of a taut rope. With great care the boy brought his other arm over and clutched hold of the sleeve with that hand too.

"Good. Now, whatever you do, don't let go," Margaret instructed.

She dug the toe end of her skate blades into the ice and did her best to anchor herself. Hand-over-hand, she pulled the coat and the boy toward her. Gradually, the boy's body emerged from the water, but her toehold began to slip. Holding her body as rigid as possible, Margaret pressed her toes down harder into the ice and continued to reel the boy in.

At last, like a hooked fish, the boy's entire body flopped out onto the ice. She could hear him sniveling.

She pulled him the rest of the way to her, grabbed the neck of his jacket and scooted them both backward to safety.

Once they were both on land and able to stand, Margaret quickly pulled off the boy's sopping wet jacket and put her own, less wet, coat around his shoulders.

With both of them shivering, she guided the boy toward Gwen's car. Even from a distance, Margaret could see the disapproval in Gwen's eyes.

Chagrined, but not heartless, Gwen handed her fur coat to Margaret, then put a cashmere blanket around the boy. As they all got into the car, Margaret looked up at the top of the hill.

No, it couldn't have possibly been Devin that she had seen. *Especially, not with some Colored woman.* She decided against mentioning anything to Gwen about it.

As they drove away, Margaret looked over the back seat at the boy. His mass of blonde curls lent him the appearance of a cherub, but his blue eyes had the gleam of the devil. He was staring out the window at the sled.

Within seconds, more bits of ice surrounding the sled broke away and the sled disappeared into the lake.

"Damn niggers," the boy muttered.

Chapter Three

The door chimes rang. Again.

Margaret was beginning to wonder if Devin had invited half of Denver to the meeting. She felt frazzled.

The constant doorbell ringing made her think of the ghoulish pranksters who trolled the streets every Halloween. Except, this was a night in late January. The only ghosts and goblins scaring about were the recruits Devin had invited into their home for another of his Ku Klux Klan meetings.

This had to be at least the fifth or sixth meeting within the past two weeks. Another meeting was scheduled for Sunday.

Had she not witnessed Devin's transformation – from hapless investor to zealous organizer – for herself, Margaret might not have believed her husband's change to be genuine or lasting. Yet, she had watched him closely the last months and could honestly say that she had never seen anyone so obsessed. His determination to sign up the most new Klan members in any western territory had revealed a level of ambition she had thought him incapable of.

And he had insisted that she join the women's group. The Kolorado KKK Ladies' Auxiliary. She had found the members narrow-minded and cold, and their meetings to be little more than long hours of hate propaganda, but since her involvement with them, Devin had stopped beating her.

If that's what it took to keep from getting her bones broken, then so be it.

The Auxiliary had almost as many members as there were men in the Klavern. And, she had to admit, the women's mission to close whore houses and illegal saloons did have a practical appeal. After all, if they didn't exist, Devin might be home more.

For now, though, welcoming Devin's recruits was her immediate concern. She invited the two latest arrivals in and extended her arms to accept their coats.

Like most of the other attendees, the two men threw their wet, heavy coats across Margaret's arms without so much as a "thank you."

Most of the coats smelled of mildew and stale cigar smoke.

As the two men stood in the foyer, they fell into a private, but audible commentary about the Browne's home.

"Blazin' buffalo balls, will ya look at that beaut!" said the man with thick rims of dirt underneath his ragged fingernails. He was ogling the magnificent chandelier overhead. "Now, I see why they call this stretch of Capitol Hill, Millionaires' Row."

What a crock, Margaret thought. Besides, most of the real money had moved a few miles south, to the Country Club Distric, or to the estates around Cheesman Park and the polo graounds.

The men continued their observations like gawkers at a circus sideshow.

"No kiddin'," the one with the sooty complexion said, then nudged his pal. "Take a gander at that, will ya..." He nodded toward the full suit of armor that stood sentinel at the base of the spiral stairway, then walked over to inspect it. He let out a long, low whistle. His eyes roved from the top to the bottom of the nearly man-sized shield bearing the Browne's family crest.

With childlike curiosity, he tested the point of the mannequin's spear. "Owww, damn it, " he cried and pulled his hand back. A trickle of blood ran from his fingertip.

His companion was still craning his neck, trying with all his might to see what was up the Browne's staircase.

"Come on, Frank," the bloodied man said as he inspected his flesh wound, "we got more important things to tend to." His statement was punctuated by wild cheers from the men who had arrived earlier.

Why, Margaret pondered, weren't all of these men home with their families on such a bitterly cold and snowy night?

If her guess was right, the whole lot of them – mill hands, factory workers, farmers, teamsters, policemen, ministers, laborers, mechanics, salesmen, bankers, doctors, lawyers, grocers, and barbers; you name it – were simply yearning for a little excitement. Something that would churn their day-to-day routines and put a spark in the winter bleakness.

From the snippets of conversations she'd overheard before the meeting, Margaret knew that many of the men had voted Republican in the recent national and local elections... for President Coolidge, Colorado Governor Morley, and Denver's mayor elect, Stapleton...not to mention just about the entire slate of new state senators and county judges.

"About damn time the Klan got some real muscle in these parts," one voter had boasted.

As Margaret laid the most recently collected hats and coats on the bench by the telephone table, the doorbell chimed again. This time it was a rosy cheeked boy.

Surprisingly, he at least removed his cap before stepping inside. "E-e-evening, Ma'am," he said to Margaret. "I-I-I'm late. M-m-mind if I g-g-go on in. I-I-I k-k-know the way."

"Please," she said, and took the boy's hurriedly discarded coat and galoshes. She couldn't help thinking that he wasn't even as old as her stepson, Kyle.

The boy went straight to the library but in his rush, left one of the doors ajar. At last, Margaret had a way to listen to Devin's sermon along with the others.

She set the boy's things down, then went to stand just outside the library doors. She was close enough to hear what was being said, but far enough toward the kitchen to have an alibi should anyone exit the library before she could disappear.

It occurred to her that there must be nearly fifty men packed into the library. After the meetings, they usually spent another hour inquiring about his maternal granddaddy's collection of Civil War memorabilia. Instead of a room full of books, the library's walls were devoted to an arsenal's worth of Confederate relics; mostly guns and swords.

In the northern corner of the room stood a flagpole bearing the Confederate states' flag, the Stars and Bars. Of the few books on the shelves, every volume glorified the southern cause.

Margaret tiptoed closer to the crevice between the doors and tried to peek in. Whatever Devin's proclamation, it was receiving lavish applause. It required several attempts for him to continue.

How amazing, Margaret thought. In private, Devin tells me the recruits are, "nothing but a bunch of northern yahoos and hick ne'er do wells." But to their faces, he greets everyone of them like they were a long lost brother.

"Shoot," he'd once admitted to Margaret, "if ten thousand fools all want to hand over 10 dollars of their hard earned pay envelopes, just so they can march through the city wearing sheets and mumbling nonsense, well hey, I say for them to step right up. I'm more than happy to oblige anybody. Besides, if so many others in the goodole U.S. are jumping on the KKK gravy train, then why should I be a sucker and pass it up?"

Margaret never found herself with an adequate answer.

She wondered, though, if any of the "citizens" he recruited had the foggiest notion of Devin's real intent. That he craved far more than just being Colorado's head membership salesman, the King Kleagle. The way he saw it, being able to pocket two dollars out of every Klectoken – the ten-dollar initiation fee – was nothing compared to the take the Exalted Cyclops of Klaverns was getting.

By bringing in so many new members, Devin was due for a promotion. And the better he made the state's Grand Dragon, Dr. Locke, look, the more reasonable his chances of being appointed head of his own Klavern. He just had to outmaneuver Locke's flunkie, MacDuff. It wasn't going to be easy, but Devin wasn't going to let some no 'count coal miner, from some back brush part of Ireland, come to Devin's own home town and walk away with all he'd worked for.

Margaret may not have known all the wheeling dealing that went among the Klan hierarchy, but it wasn't hard for her to see that Dr. Locke had complete control over what went on in Colorado. No wonder he was so egotistical and pompous. She hated thinking of what it meant if their lives became any more mixed up with his.

She heard the recruits fall silent again, then Devin continued.

"The Ku Klux Klan is a white man's organization," he said. "We teach, promote, and uphold the doctrine of white supremacy."

The applause began anew, but he must have signaled for them to hold on.

"The preservation of the white race, indeed, the very survival of Christian civilization, depends upon us. Unless the purity of white blood is maintained, you, me, our families, are all doomed. A real American has to be prepared to defend his birthright."

This time the men refused to be quieted. They stomped and yelled. The Chinese vase on the round mahogany table in the center of the foyer vibrated to the edge of the table. Margaret reached out for the vase just before it fell to the floor.

As she held the vase close, it reminded her of her life, which in so many ways was also toppling over.

She sat the vase under the table, then returned to her listening post. This was precisely the kind of audience Devin craved.

"The science of berry picking," he called it. Knowing which fruit was so ripe that when he reached out it practically fell into his palm. The bookcase ladder, which he had had built with extra wide steps, was where he did his berry picking.

He'd climb midway up the ladder, then speak to those looking up at him with all the eloquence and brimstone of a country preacher. By the end of his appeal, most every man in attendance was so full of ire and hate, they were ready to go out and burn crosses as soon as they could gather the wood and matches.

"Shhh," she heard the men prompt each other. She pictured Devin like she'd seen him rehearse in front of the bedroom mirror, mopping his brow with his handkerchief, then hooking his thumbs under his suspenders. She had to admit, he'd cultivated the sense of urgency to perfection.

"I'm speaking of that centuries old evil. Mixing white blood with that of Negroes," he said. "Why, did you know that now there are so many niggras with white blood flowing through their veins, you and I are in danger of looking up one day soon and not knowing who is who?"

The men sucked in their breaths in a collective gasp of disbelief and disgust. Devin let the image…of a light skinned, keen featured, straight haired Negro…sink into the men's minds a moment longer.

There was an uneasy quiet.

Margaret could sense the men shaking their heads in anger and suspiciously studying one another. Devin's puppetry had succeeded. One of the men let loose a blaze of profanity and hostile oaths. Others copied him.

What she didn't understand was why all the fuss. It wasn't as if niggras were wherever you looked in Denver.

True, there were the ones in household and courtesy employment, and the few who worked in the factories and as laborers, but for the most part they stayed on their own side of town.

Five Points. Or whatever it was called.

She had never even seen a Negro in Denver General Hospital. Not even during an outbreak of influenza.

And, just like in her father's dry goods store, Margaret knew the city's general policy was that Coloreds had to use the rear entrances, even when they were sent to pick up packages for their employers. The more exclusive shops arranged delivery of their goods to keep the matter from ever being of concern.

Of course, there were the complaints about the cinema and vaudeville houses admitting Negroes, but at least the Coloreds were restricted to the seats in the balconies. The "crows' nest," she believed their section was called.

The only real trouble Margaret had ever heard of Coloreds causing were the rare instances, usually on a scorching summer day, when two or three of their children would try to swim in the Washington Park lake with all of the other children. But they were always quickly shooed away. So, goodness, what problems between whites and Colored could there really be in Denver?

For just an instant, Margaret thought of her daughter's father. His skin had been more reddish and freckled than black or brown, and his hair, though coarse, had been almost blond. She had known the truth about him all along, that he was a Negro, but he'd never hidden that from her. His color hadn't mattered to her anyway.

For the sake of the future, if not the present, she forced the memory as far down into her soul as it could possibly go.

Somehow, her thoughts turned to Walter.

Walter's father had served the senior Brownes for years, long before Father Browne had been crippled in a polo accident. Indeed, the Brownes had almost considered Walter Senior a member of the family. They'd seen to it that Walter Junior and Devin grew up as playmates.

When Walter Senior died, there had been no question that his son would inherit his position.

Margaret had never met the senior man, but Walter Junior's skin was as dark as imported chocolate. It was obvious there couldn't possibly be any white blood in him. She did wonder, though, where he'd gotten his thick silky black hair.

She thought of the child in her womb, and her limbs flooded with fear. She crossed her arms over her stomach and hunched inward, but she was safe now. She had to keep reminding herself of that.

Unlike her first baby, this one was all white. He, or she, even had a father whose family tree could be traced back to

English royalty. She was worrying needlessly. Devin's resumed speech roused her from her morbid contemplation.

"I don't know about you," Devin railed, "but I ain't about to let the goddamned day come when some uppity niggra traipses his nappy-headed self up to me and tries to claim I'm his kin."

The recruits stomped and hooted their approval again.

"No sir," Devin went on, "not in this lifetime, nor in any one hence. Not if this Dixie-born-and-bred son, and I dare say any other red-blooded Klansman, has anything to say about it. I guarantee you!"

So this is what could turn a roomful of men into a pack of rabid dogs, Margaret suddenly understood. Hate piled so high and thick that it was all they could see or touch. All they could dream of or talk about.

Once again, she looked down at her stomach and smoothed her hands over its budding roundness. "Don't worry, little one. We're safe this time," Margaret said in a pained whisper.

She turned toward the mirror behind the telephone table and looked into it. She hoped to see her stronger self, the self which she had nearly forgotten about.

"And, somehow, I still have to find my daugh...."

A scream of torment came from upstairs. She knew that she should have been accustomed to Mother Browne's cries by now, but they were just as alarming today as when they'd begun several months ago.

Margaret always ran to her mother-in-law's side whenever the outbursts occurred, only nothing ever seemed to be truly wrong with her. Devin accused Margaret of being neglectful and impatient with his mother.

What Devin refused to understand was that Margaret loved Mother Browne. That despite Margaret's not knowing if her own mother was dead or alive, caring for her mother-in-law gave her a measure of relief, perhaps even a degree of hope.

"It's all right, Miss Margaret, I'll go," Walter said as he came into the foyer and headed up the stairs. He was carrying a silver tray on which sat a bowl of steaming tomato soup. "She wouldn't eat earlier," he said. "She's probably just hungry by now."

Walter seemed to understand Mother Browne better than anyone. As usual, Goldie, Kyle's dog – half retriever, half mutt – followed close behind Walter, happily wagging its tail as it trotted up the steps.

Margaret thought of the rowdy bunch in the library and for a fleeting moment felt an impractical sense of safety because of Walter's being in the house as well. She felt herself flush.

Thankfully, the door chimes rang again.

She fanned herself with both hands, then looked in the mirror to find any loose wisps of hair. She tucked the two or three loose strands back into place, then quickly went to answer the door.

The sight of a large burly man with a black patch over one of his eyes took Margaret aback. She was at a loss for words as he brushed past her and entered her home uninvited. With effort, she regained composure.

"Mr. MacDuff, this is such a…a surprise," Margaret said before MacDuff reached the library. "I, I don't believe my husband's expecting you."

She did not offer to take his jacket and cap, nor did he take them off. He simply ignored Margaret and went straight into the library without a word, firmly pulling the library doors closed behind himself.

Margaret winced and jigged backwards at the unexpected insult. She never had known the man to exhibit any manners, but treating her so rudely, in her own home, was inexcusable.

Putting him out of her thoughts, Margaret went back to the library doors and pressed her ear to one of them. Devin's speech was so aflame now that his voice transmitted even through the thick mahogany doors.

"Let me delight you with another fact, brothers," Devin said. "The mighty Klan is a Protestant organization. We shun all that is not the way our proud forefathers intended."

The applause seemed less generous this time, yet a few of the men did shout earnest approval. Devin continued.

"Brothers, we say to the world, truly and without apology, no Catholics and no Jews will be permitted to spread their filthy propaganda here. No siree."

This time, the applause was vigorous and Devin had to wait a long while before going on.

"And that's not all, loyal subjects."

"Tell, 'em boss," one of the subjects volunteered, only to be hushed by his brethren.

Devin took advantage of the moment and paused to regain their full attention. Nearly a full minute passed before he continued.

"You'll be equally pleased to know that this is purely an American organization. Only those who are one hundred percent Caucasian and native born are welcome. Which means...*No* spics, gooks, or spooks. *No* wops, kikes, or micks. In other words, if you weren't born here, then on my granddaddy's grave, you're not welcome here."

Hearing such blatant vitriol sent a chill down Margaret's back. She couldn't listen anymore.

What about her own father? His people were Irish. She did know at least that little bit about him. And not only that, her father and Devin had never had more than the odd word to say to each other. How did where her father's parents were born make her and Devin enemies?

For that matter, what about herself? She had the same blood as her father, and also like him, was Catholic. She put a hand to her throat, over the little gold cross suspended from a delicate gold chain that she'd worn since the day her mother put it on her.

It was all that she had left to remind her of her mother. Angus had burned everything else the morning after the evening her mother had hurridly packed and rushed out of both of their lives, forever.

She tucked the cross inside the bodice of her dress – out of sight of any it might antagonize – then felt for it under the fabric. She would have to remember to keep it hidden from now on.

Lost in the tangle of her concerns, Margaret had missed the last few minutes of Devin's speech, but she could hear that the men were nearly rabid now. This was probably the best time to make her entrance. After all, Devin had made it clear that her job, as mistress of the house, was to keep the room comfortable for his guests.

Eventually, she had received a rare compliment from him. He admired how she could slip into the library, straighten the chairs, clear away empty glasses, and stoke the fire, all with him barely knowing it. So, yes, this was the time to go in.

She neatened her hair, checked that her collar was flat, then squared her shoulders and opened one of the library doors.

She nearly gagged from the mingled odors of cigar fumes, body musk, and cheap whiskey. How dare these men, these strangers, turn her home into a saloon. Wasn't the purpose of prohibition to make liquor illegal?

Margaret decided, then and there, to finally accept the Klan women's invitation to join their chapter.

Upon surveying the library she became even more incensed.

The men were not only using Mother Browne's crystal candy dishes as ashtrays, there were also smoldering cigarette butts and cigar ends perched on the edges of various table tops, bookshelves, and the fireplace mantel.

Furthermore, an arm on a fragile, antique chair was broken; a puddle from a spilled drink was dripping into an opened end-table drawer, an ember was smoldering on the Persian rug, Father Browne's prized collection of five hand-carved smoking pipes – each with its own display stand - were all jumbled instead together in a pile at the end of the mantel, and the oil painting of Devin's granddaddy, the Colonel, was knocked cattywampus.

Worst of all, the Brownes' family Bible was on the floor and had footprints on it.

Devin was holding court near the flag stand, and apparently did not care about the damage to the library.

"Boys," Devin hailed as Margaret went about her duties, "the fiery cross is now ours to carry if America is ever going to be redeemed."

"Here, here," a man shouted.

Devin replied, "I say, America for Americans! Are you all with me?"

"Hell, yes," someone near Margaret bellowed.

Devin repeated, "America for Americans," and pounded a fist into the open palm of his other hand.

The men joined in, and began chanting, over and over, "America for Americans. America for Americans. America for…".

They were frightening Margaret. She wanted Devin to end the meeting before trouble started. She pushed her way past one man, then another, anxious to get to Devin.

MacDuff blocked her way, seemingly unwilling to budge. She tapped his shoulder, but he refused to look around.

Thankfully, the men's chanting was at last dying out. She could just lean around MacDuff and call to her husband from where she stood. She peeked around him, and just above a whisper, called, "Devin. Devin."

He looked partially in her direction.

She mouthed to him the words, "It's late, and the streets are getting icy. Isn't it time these men went home?"

The men were crowding around Devin and recaptured his attention. She was stranded in the crush of men trying to get to him when one loud voice from the back of the room drowned out all the other with, "Say, Pop, what's a woman doin' in here? Ain't this men's business?"

Margaret instantly recognized the voice of her stepson. Kyle. Somehow, she hadn't seen him come in. Perhaps he had entered the house through the kitchen and come into the library after her. If only she could locate him among the other faces.

As if reading his stepmother's mind, Kyle seemed to appear out of nowhere.

Margaret jumped when she felt his arm across the back of her shoulders.

All the chattering had stopped, and everyone, including Devin and Margaret, gave Kyle their attention.

"Hey, Pop. Maybe stepmom's a spy. Whadya' think?" Kyle, a foot taller than Margaret, stared down at her with a sneer.

Margaret braced herself and looked to Devin for help, but Kyle spoke first. "Just kidding, Stepmom. Don't get worked up."

"That's enough boy," Devin said, scowling at Kyle. The tension between father and son nearly crackled. Only an uneasy cough from a corner of the room caused Devin to relent. "My wife is quite right, gentlemen," he said, finally. "It is time that we adjourn."

The men grumbled but shoved their way out to the foyer, heading en masse to the stack of coats and hats.

Little of the camaraderie of just a few minutes ago was in evidence as everyone began to reach for his belongings.

Only Devin, Margaret, Kyle and MacDuff remained in the library.

Margaret was clearing a place on Devin's desk to put the Bible, but Devin and Kyle were locked in another of their stare downs.

MacDuff went over to them and laid a hand on each of their shoulders. "You've got a fine boy here, Browne," MacDuff said. "A real good soldier. I'd be mighty proud to have a son just like him."

"Listen, MacDuff," Devin said as he slapped MacDuff's hand away, "I don't know who you think you're bluffing, because it's no secret that this here boy of mine ain't nothing but a lazy, good-for-nothing runt. Furthermore, I'll thank you to stay out of it."

And with that, Devin reached for Kyle's ear and twisted it. He seemed to enjoy watching his son squirm with pain.

MacDuff's hand fell away from Kyle's shoulder as Kyle contorted his body in an effort to escape the pain.

It took Kyle's face and ear turning blood red for Devin to let go.

Even from across the room, Margaret could see pools of tears gathering in Kyle's eyes. Risking Devin's ire, she went to Kyle to comfort him.

"Your father's just full of himself, and bourbon, right now," she whispered in her stepson's uninjured ear. "You know as well as I do that by morning he won't even remember this. Just go up to your room for now."

Kyle gave his stepmother a woeful glance, but followed her instruction.

As he left the library, he did not see his father stumble backward and plop into a chair. But MacDuff did and walked to the front door shaking his head.

Margaret followed.

By now the others were gone, and it was just the two of them at the front door.

MacDuff opened the door and allowed a swirl of falling snow into the foyer. "Sure lookin' forward to summer," he said to Margaret, catching her completely off-guard.

She was about to reply when she felt a definite flutter in her stomach and looked down at her stomach to momentarily contemplate the miracle of the life growing inside her.

By the time she looked up again, MacDuff had already disappeared into the blustery darkness.

"Me, too," she said to herself, instead, as she joyfully realized that by summer's end she would be a mother. Again.

"Me, too."

Chapter Four

O h, yeah, and if you see J.D.'s skinny ass anywhere, tell that spook he'd better get on back here with my money. Tell him when he picks up Boots's numbers, to get me one of them catfish dinners."

"Sure thing, Miz Johnson," Rowena's errand boy, Billy, answered for the umpteenth time. Billy hated Thursdays. Most every Colored maid had Thursday afternoon off, and it seemed like at least half of them came into Rowena's then to get their hair "fried, pressed, and laid to the side."

Billy hurried out the door before Rowena added ten more things for him to do.

He needn't have worried. This once, out of all the years her shop had been open, she was closing early. Her clients had been reminded every week for more than a month. Mildred Hawkins had been one of the lucky few to get an appointment and was Rowena's last customer of the day.

"As I was sayin', Sister Hawkins," Rowena said as she caught the kinky hair at the base of the woman's scalp between the prongs of the hot iron, "I don't care if them dickty heifers never come in here again. Matter of fact, they can just stay they im-i-tation, o-fay, selves right up on Welton all they want. They just wantin' to be seen anyway.

Rowena worked the hot comb through Mildred Hawkins's nape – or kitchen, as Colored women called it – like she was trying to straighten out coiled fence wire.

"'Sides, just like Brother Garvey says, they money ain't any greener than anybody else's." The hot comb grazed the skin on Mildred Hawkins's neck.

"Good heavens," Mildred hollered, and jumped up. "Chile, forget them folks. You 'bout to burn me alive."

Rowena hated admitting when she'd made a mistake. She kept a stone face and looked at her customer like she didn't know what in the world was the woman's problem.

"Mildred, you gonna have to sit still now. I ain't got all day. Amy's train gonna be in at two forty-five."

Mildred Hawkins started to respond, but J.D. banged through the door.

"Hey, Brown Sugah," J.D. greeted Rowena, and blew her a kiss as he approached.

"Boy, don't you 'Brown Sugah' me. Where's my money? You more than an hour late." Rowena slammed the curling iron back down on the heating plate, and turned to J.D. with her hands on her hips.

"Calm down now, Sweetness. Everything's copasetic. I got most of your stash right here," J.D. said, patting his coat's breast pocket. "You know how old Miz Wilkes can get going. Man, that woman talks more than an RCA radio."

He took a wad of dollar bills from his inside pocket, then deposited it in the lidless cigar box on Rowena's counter. "Still gotta go by Boot's, though."

Rowena cast a sharp glance at J.D. She didn't like nobody

playing with her money. She'd picked too much cotton, and washed too many floors, to take one measly cent for granted.

The arthritis swelling her hands was another reason she needed to keep track of her accounts. She didn't know how much longer she was going to be able to do hair. Uh huh, wasn't nobody gonna play with her money. She had Amy's boarding school tuition to think about, and the mortgages on this duplex and the two apartment buildings.

"Look, J.D.," Rowena said, "you already late paying back the fifty from last week. I'd done told you, whatever you do, don't play with my money."

"Speaking of which," J.D. said, and slipped an arm around Rowena's waist, "when you gonna stop working so hard and let me take you to one of them picture shows?"

"Go on now, boy," Rowena said, and pushed J.D. away. "I ain't got time for your foolishness." She picked up the hot comb again and went back to straightening Mildred Hawkins's hair.

"Oh, right," J.D. said, as he looked at himself in the mirror and slicked back his do. "I forgot you done gone over to the other side. That Mr. Charlie, what be in the club every night, sure got your nose all open."

Rowena pretended not to see Mildred Hawkins's face light up with shock. Instead, Rowena just waved the hot iron in the direction of the front door.

"Now look, J.D., you crossin' the line. Besides, I ain't got time for no foolishness-yours, or nobody else's."

Her dealings with a white man wasn't nobody's business noway. She wasn't even sure how it had gotten started.

"And while you on the door tonight, don't be lettin' them friends of yours in either. I ain't in business for my health. I gotta make a profit."

J.D. had helped her improve the speakeasy's operations, but if he was thinkin' he was back in Harlem, he'd better think again. Denver wasn't no backwater, like Chicken Neck, Alabama, where'd they'd growed up, but it wasn't no Main street either. If she wanted to keep a decent clientele coming to the club, she had to be careful of who she let in. As if bootleggin' wasn't a hard enough business.

J.D. picked up the copy of Reader's Digest from Rowena's counter. He was about to make a comment on an article when Lulu came down the stairs.

She was a young, petit redbone from Louisiana. She worked part-time in the shop and fulltime in the club, and like the other girls Rowena hired, lived on the duplex's third floor. The second floor was Rowena and her daughter Amy's living quarters.

Lulu walked up to J.D. and stared up at him. Like many men, his knees got weak looking at a Colored woman with blue eyes. "How about you and me goin' to the movies. J.D.?" Lulu said. "I hear there's a swell Valentino flick at the Orpheum."

"Sure, baby," J.D. said, and looked over the top of the open magazine at Rowena, "why not?"

He tossed the magazine, sidled over to Lulu and chucked her playfully under the chin. "We can take in a matinee. Maybe, stop by Boot's afterwards for a little chow."

Lulu smiled broadly at J.D. as he transitioned to the door.

"I'll be back to pick you up," he said. "'Bout three."

The door slammed, and J.D. was gone. Other than the sizzle of the hot comb working through Mildred Hawkins's hair, the only sound in the shop came from Lulu humming as she gazed out the front window.

"Miz Johnson," Lulu said without turning around, "why those cops walkin' back and forth? They been strolling up and down this sidewalk half the morning."

"Girl, ain't you got nothin' better to do? What about them sheets that need foldin' and puttin' away?"

Lulu rolled her eyes at Rowena, and went back upstairs.

Rowena ignored Lulu's attitude. The girl was always pouting about something.

Rowena continued twisting strands of Mildred Hawkins's hair around the hot comb, and thought back. She had made her weekly payment, hadn't she? Mmm hmm, Monday, like always. She had even doubled it, like Devin told her to. So what did the cops want?

The shop door opened and shut. Rowena recognized her two uninvited visitors.

"Afternoon, officers," Rowena said, looking at Sergeant Smith and Lieutenant Kirby in the counter mirror. "You gentlemens have a seat, if you like. I'll be right with you."

Kirby, a Saint Nick look-alike, acknowledged Rowena's comment with a quick touch of his hat. He instructed his partner, Smith, to wait near the door.

Rowena knew a lot about Smith just by his sallow skin and bad teeth. He was probably a white trash Okie anxious for any chance to make himself feel superior to at least a Colored person. Only he really wasn't, and he knew it. He stroked his billy club like it was his manhood.

Mildred Hawkins didn't bother to look at her finished hair in the mirror. She jumped out of the chair and threw two crisp new dollar bills into Rowena's cigar box.

"D-d-don't worry about the change," she said, then grabbed her sweater from the wall hook. "Nice weather we're having," she said on her way past Lieutenant Kirby, but hurried out the door without waiting for his answer.

Rowena removed her apron and rinsed her hands under the washbasin faucet. After drying her hands on a towel, she turned toward Sergeant Smith. "You gentlemens care for coffee?"

"This isn't a social call, Miss Johnson," Lieutenant Kirby finally said. "We've got word there's a moonshine operation in this neighborhood, again. Now, you wouldn't know anything about that, would you?"

They both noticed something about the shop's cabinets had Sergeant Smith's attention. Lieutenant Kirby tried stepping in the Sergeant 's path, but Smith walked around him. Rowena and the Lieutenant stood looking at each other.

"Officer Kirby, sir, you're talkin' to a sharecropper's daughter," Rowena said, trying not to seem nervous. "I hears all kinda rumors, but my daddy taught me when I was knee high to a piglet, to let what people say blow in one ear, and out the other. He said life always more peaceful that way."

We're just asking, Miss Johnson. That's our job. Gotta ask, or we'd be remiss." He watched as the younger man studied a framed stock certificate for Marcus Garvey's Universal Negro Improvement Association's Black Star Shipping Line.

"Say, ain't that that troublemaker?" Smith said, jabbing his billy club up toward the certificate.

Rowena started to answer, but Smith had already found something else to interest him. The bottles of peroxide lined up on a nearby shelf. He reached for one of the bottles, but it tipped over and crashed to the floor.

"Oops," Smith said, feigning innocence.

Within minutes he had flung open the doors of all the cabinets, and emptied out or broke most of the bottles he'd found.

Lieutenant Kirby did nothing to stop him. The shop floor was awash with streams of liquid and globs of cream.

The only shelf that hadn't been touched was over the sink. Rowena held her breath as the lieutenant took down one of the ceramic jugs on the shelf.

He started to twist out the jug's cork, but Sergeant Kirby snatched the jug from the younger man's hands. "Look, Smith, quit dicking around. If you haven't found anything yet, there's probably nothing here. No use ruining the place."

"But, Lieutenant," Smith said, "I'll bet— "

"By the way, officers," Rowena said as she carefully stepped through the shards of broken glass on the floor over to the lieutenant, then rested a hand on his arm as she looked into his face, "I been meanin' to ask you gentlemens, when do tickets go on sale for the Policemen's Ball? There is a ball this year, ain't there? I always likes to support a good cause."

"Why, that's mighty generous of you, Miss Johnson," the Lieutenant said, and waved for Smith to move to the door.

"Yeah, yeah, okay," Smith said, and walked away.

Rowena took the jug from the sergeant and put it back on the shelf.

"Whew," Kirby sighed as he removed his cap then mopped his forehead with his uniform sleeve. "Now, where were we?" he asked Rowena.

"The Policemen's Ball," Rowena said.

"Ah, yes. I wish more of our commerce people were so civic minded. We'll be sure to send the tickets right over. How many did you say?"

"Ten. Twelve. I got lots a friends that I'm sure are interested too."

"Sure thing, Miss Johnson." Kirby said, then tipped his hat to Rowena and headed to the door. "Come on, Smith, let's move on. It's time for us to get back to the station."

The sergeant looked frustrated and confused, and seemed reluctant to go, but the lieutenant was insisting. Smith did an about face and followed on the heels of his superior.

The officers' exit from the shop coincided with someone bamming on the front door.

"Anyone here who can sign for these encyclopedias?" a man with a dolly full of boxes yelled through the screen door. "The people they're for, 'cross the street, ain't home."

"Sure," Rowena said, "come on in, just look where you step. Things are a trifle messy in here right now."

Lieutenantt Kirby held the door open while the delivery-man hoisted the dolly load of boxes over the door ledge and pulled it inside. Smith waited on the sidewalk.

"We'll get back to you real soon about those tickets," Officer Kirby said, then left.

Rowena turned her attention to the next matter. "You can set them boxes behind that curtain, Mr. Uh...?"

"MacDuff. Just, MacDuff. No fancy titles for me.

"If that's what you say. Don't make me no mind."

Rowena waited for MacDuff to move, but he just stared at her like he was waiting for something. Finally he said, "It's C.O.D., sister. I'll put 'em anywhere you want after I get my money."

MacDuff looked at Rowena and watched intently as she reached into the bodice of her dress.

"Here it is," Rowena said, and pulled out a roll of cash as big as her fist. "Hope we'll be able to do business again some-time." She handed it all to him.

"Don't see why we shouldn't," MacDuff said, taking the money, then counting it.

True to his word, MacDuff moved the boxes to the back room, but then left just as abruptly as he'd arrived.

The morning had been wearisome for Rowena. She went behind the curtain, into the dining room, which now served as a storage area, and switched on the overhead light. MacDuff had stacked the boxes in two columns of three boxes each.

In the top bureau drawer she found a pair of shears, took them out and opened the blades into a wide vee. She chose one of the top boxes, then pulled one of the blades along an edge of the box to cut an opening.

Too impatient to cut all the way around the box, she reached her hand into the slit she'd cut in the box and tore the top of the box back.

The box appeared to be filled with straw, but after quickly scooping the straw out with her hands, Rowena made her find.

A handsome new set of leather-bound books.

She lifted one of the books out and rubbed her hand across its smooth, dark brown leather cover. Then she cracked the book open and flipped through its pages. Having so many words about so many things in her very own hand intoxicated Rowena.

She laid her palm against one of the pages. The paper felt deliciously cool. Then she lifted the book to her face and smelled. She inhaled the book's scent as if it were fresh plowed earth. The page the book opened to had a picture of a girl riding a bicycle down a tree-lined road.

Rowena stared for a long while at the words under the picture. "I'm not scared a no stupid words," she said, finally. "I ain't no dummy."

A well of tears brimmed in her eyes, blurring her vision. One of the tears dropped onto the page and wrinkled one of the words under the picture.

She sounded out the first letter in the first word.

"B-b-b...," she said, paused, then tried again. "B-b-b...."

A light seemed to go on in her head. "Bicycles!" she declared with the delight of a child. "Bicycles were in-- ven-ted. Invented. Bicycles were invented in... in 18-16."

She looked at the rest of the paragraph, then slammed the book to the floor. "Oh, forget it," she cried. "I ain't got time for this foolishness." She had gotten this far without knowing how to read, hadn't she?

She reached into the box for another of the books, quickly opened it, then just as readily discarded it. In minutes. Most of the box's contents of a dozen books lay in a mangled heap on the floor.

Only two books remained in the box and unopened. She reached in for one of the books, then nearly tossed it onto the pile of others, but something about it felt the oddest bit different. She opened it.

"Hallelujah," she hollered. It was exactly what she had been looking for.

This book was carved out in the middle, and in the carved out space was a perfectly fitted silver flask.

Rowena took the flask out, twisted off its cap, and took a drink of its contents. She swallowed hard, then drank again. "Now, we're in business," she said, and set the flask and the book on the counter.

Rowena removed the last book from the box and found that it also had carved out pages and a flask. She set that book and its flask aside on the counter.

She grabbed the shears again and pushed the empty box off of the sealed one underneath.

There were four more boxes to open, but she had to hurry. She wanted Amy's visit home from school to be perfect.

Rowena smiled as she ripped the blade through the next box.

Chapter Five

A jarring hitch in the Zephyr's velocity caused Amy to awake with a start. She had tried hard not to doze off during the daylight portion of her train ride, but she'd spent most of the night tossing and turning in her seat. The train's sleeping berths were *For Whites Only.*

She had managed to make her teachers and classmates believe that she was white – what Colored people referred to as passing – but she could tell by the way the school's Negro maids looked at her that they knew better. Because most Negroes could detect someone who was passing. It was almost like they had the key to a secret code, which is why Amy avoided as much as possible, the Negro men who worked the railroad.

Many of the men stayed at her mother's rooming house during Denver trip changeovers, and out of respect for her mother, felt it was their duty to look after Amy. If any one of them ever caught Amy carrying on such a charade, he'd be quick as lightning to let her mother know.

Amy had learned this fact the hard way, four years ago during the ninth grade, when she'd come home for Christmas.

Since then, no matter whether she was traveling from Denver back to her boarding school in Chicago, or vice versa, the sixteen-hour train ride between the two cities always felt insufferably long to her.

She felt the train begin to decelerate, then saw the large Wynkoop Street steel archway that faced the front of Denver's Union Station with a brightly lighted "Welcome" sign. She favored the opposite side of the sign that read, "Mizpah," the Hebrew salutation meaning "May the Lord keep watch between you and me when we are away from each other."

As if responding to a theatrical cue, like in October when she'd played Desdemona in the annual seniors' play which this year had been "*Othello*", Amy's stomach cramped and her palms turned clammy. Only this time her bout of nerves had nothing to do with stage fright, and everything to do with having to face her mother.

She recalled the discussion with Elaine, the woman who had sat across from her in the dining room of the Chicago station while both of them had had breakfast and each waited for her particular departure time.

Elaine had spoken with a southern drawl so thick that Amy had had to strain to understand her. They had both ordered Danishes and coffee, and had fallen easily into conversation. Amy had wondered to herself if Elaine had used a whole bottle of peroxide to achieve bleached hair so blonde it was nearly white. Elaine's bobbed haircut, a version of the Gibson Girl style popular with cinema actresses, had given Elaine a deceptively sophisticated appearance.

The illusion Elaine had created had disappeared when out of the clear blue, she had confided that her daddy, a dirt poor tobacco farmer, whose great-granddaddy had once owned a big Virginia plantation and lots of slaves, probably had the sheriff and his gang of deputies on a state-wide hunt for her by now.

"But honey," she had said, "I'm on my way to Hollywood. All there was for me in Virginia was the same life as my mama, and her mama, and her mama before that. If I never drink or hear of mint julep again in life, it still won't be long enough."

Elaine had insisted that Amy share a secret too which, of course, Amy had known was coming because she had never met a white girl who had thought twice about divulging her most private matters. Even to a stranger.

Inevitably, the person who had been turned into an involuntary confidante was expected to tell some equally personal story.

Amy had considered shocking Elaine by revealing the reasons she had been expelled from school, which was something that would be obvious to everyone, sooner or later, anyway. Instead, for the sake of letting Elaine know that Negro parents were just as strict and concerned as any other parents, all Amy told was that her mother was going to have one holy fit when she found out, and especially when she found out it was too late to do anything about it.

Elaine had just stared Amy straight in the face, and shrugged. "Well, honey, I don't see where you really have a problem. A simple little lie 'll fix all that. It's not like your mama actually wants to know the truth. Least ways, my mama never did."

For a heartbeat, Elaine's advice had made sense. Just as quickly though, Amy remembered that the whole purpose of her diligently carried out plot had been exactly how things turned out. To get herself kicked out of school with no possibility of ever being able to go back.

It was in that same instant that Amy finally had a deeper realization. The consequences of what she'd done were going to last well beyond graduation day. They were going to affect the rest of her life.

The shock of such a reality had caused Amy to feel as if the blood in her limbs and face had turned icy cold. For once, she had been glad that her skin was so...beige. Otherwise, she would've had that blood-drained look so many of her classmates got when they felt embarrassed or scared.

The passenger car jerked again and snapped Amy out of her thoughts of the past, which was just as well, because what was done, was...

She looked out the window and saw detached boxcars abandoned on nearby stretches of crisscrossing tracks. The train's speed ebbed still more, then came to a stop, as it pulled alongside the concrete platform.

A dull ache throbbed at the back of Amy's head. She just didn't feel ready to cope with her mother. It was bad enough that the two of them were as different as burlap and silk, but the truth was that her mother mortified her.

Her mother talked like a plantation field hand and dressed with about as much class as a dime store mannequin. And that imported rosewater she always splashed on; it just blended with the smell of those putrid hair chemicals she was in up to her elbows every day, and created an even more nauseous scent.

All that was happening was her mother's fault anyway. In the end, perhaps it hadn't been the smartest thing to have done, but at least this way, she wasn't going to have to live down the shame of her mother showing up for her graduation.

She didn't even want to think about what if her plan had failed, or the extent she might have been forced to go to then. All Amy knew was that she was willing to consider anything if it kept her classmates and their families from learning the truth about her.

She'd been able to make them believe she was as well off and high bred as they were. That she was being raised by a wealthy great-aunt after being orphaned as a baby.

She had been determined to keep it that way.

But her fancy, shmancy boarding school and her stuck-up classmates were part of the past. If her mother taught her anything, it was that looking back was useless. For all their mismatches as mother and daughter, at least they agreed on that.

Everything else they talked about just ended up causing a lot of loud arguments and slammed doors.

Amy had sworn since she was a child that she wasn't ever going to say to her own children the kind of hurtful things her mother had said to her. She would only tell her children the good things about themselves.

She placed a hand on her imperceptibly rounded stomach. That time was going to come sooner than she ever imagined. She swallowed hard and gazed out the window again.

Another passenger train, a stainless steel Zephyr, like the one she was on, sped by only feet away on a parallel outgoing track. Observing the opposing motion made her feel so queasy and disoriented that she had to close her eyes and take deep breaths.

Could morning sickness happen in the afternoon?

What appeared to be a young boy and a young girl, accompanied by a young woman, who was perhaps the children's nanny occupied the seats ahead of Amy. The boy and girl began to pound their small fists against their section of window, yelling, "Mama. Papa. Mama. Papa," nearly in unison.

Amy's moment of respite was gone. She opened her eyes and looked out as the train screeched to a halt. The station was crowded with people and baggage carts.

A smartly dressed man and woman were smiling and waving furiously to the boy and girl.

The woman's voice was muffled by the coach's thick window glass, but Amy could still make out her words. "They're home, they're home. My babies are finally home."

Other people on the platform began to crowd close to the train. Amy couldn't help but notice the eager looks on many of their faces.

Amy's fellow passengers were standing in the aisle, gathering their belongings. In no time, they were pressing to exit. Only Amy remained seated.

Ever so casually, she glanced out the window again. There was no sign of her mother. She didn't know whether to feel relieved, or hurt. There, unavoidably, in the forefront of her mind, was her heart's most troubling question. Why did it all have to turn out like this, anyway? All she had ever wanted was to attend Mitchell Elementary like all of the other children in the neighborhood, but no-o-o, that wasn't good enough for Rowena Johnson's daughter.

Then, last year, as she was packing to return to school after summer vacation, her mother made a surprise announcement.

"Sweet baby," her mother had said in her familiar, I done made up my mind on this so you might as well not even waste your breath, tone of voice, "I been waitin' and prayin' fo' your graduation day since before you started school. Ain't one person in this family ever got them a high school diploma before. So, come June, I jes' wants to see for myself when my precious daughter changes all that."

That was the first time Amy had ever experienced pure panic. After a week of self-torment, she'd come up with a sure-fire way out. Only, who would have known that by March, she would feel so differently?

She felt someone gently tapping on her shoulder. "Miss. Miss. Is everything all right? This is Denver. The last stop."

Amy looked up into the face of the most handsome Colored boy she had ever seen.

He was wearing a porter's crisp white jacket and cap, and though he was tall, he couldn't have been any older than she. His raven dark eyes were intent, but kind. A deep cleft in his chin gave his face a chiseled appearance.

Automatically, she checked off the major objections her mother would voice against him: Too dark, too nappy headed, and going by the Pullman porter's uniform, more than likely, poor.

"Uh...yes," she answered, "everything's perfectly fine, thank you." Although her heart was pounding, she desperately wanted to maintain the poise that had been drilled into her at school. "You could hand me my hat box, though, if you wouldn't mind."

She pointed upward, to the overhead rack.

"Not at all," the young man said, then grabbed a large round Saks Fifth Avenue box by its gold cord. He offered Amy his free hand. "Is there anything else I can assist you with?" he asked.

"No, I'm sure not, but thank you anyway," Amy said, and refused his hand. She couldn't help but notice that his shoulders were too broad and muscular for his jacket. She had to avert her eyes from him as she rose from her seat.

She strode ahead of him, to the door.

After inhaling and exhaling a deep breath, she turned and entered the passageway, then descended the train's steps to the station platform. To her surprise, her mother was standing there waiting for her. Her mother was amazingly well dressed, as if she'd been tutored for the occasion. She had on a tasteful gray woolen suit and a fashionable fox stole. Even her shoes were matching gray pumps.

"Sweet Baby," Rowena said, flinging her arms wide.

"Mama," Amy responded weakly to her mother's exuberant greeting and embrace.

Right away Amy could tell that her mother's concentration wasn't wholly on her, that the porter had caught her mother's disapproving attention.

With her usual command of things, Rowena quickly looped arms with Amy and handed a five-dollar bill to a porter standing in front of them, an elderly stoop-shouldered man who was given a description of Amy's luggage and told where to find Rowena's car.

Before Amy had a chance to speak again, her mother was pulling her in the direction of the station stairway. "We'd better hurry home, child," Rowena said. "I done cooked you all your favorites. Hot water cornbread, candied yams, fresh picked collard greens, and, smothered pork chops. And, of course, banana crème pie."

"That's nice, Mama," Amy said, forgetting about the young man and her hat box, "but I'm not really hungry right now. Maybe I'll be a little later. Right now, I was sort of hoping that when we got home we could just sit and talk."

"Sweet Baby, you know I ain't got time for sittin'. My club's open tonight. You and me'll have more 'n enough time for chitchat later on."

Amy hid her disappointment behind a half smile. She'd been right not to get her hopes up. She followed her mother's backward glance and saw that the young porter was busy helping other passengers. Her mother wasted no time regaining her attention.

With her hand gripped firmly under Amy's elbow, Rowena steered them through the crowd.

Amy could almost hear her mother thinking…Ain't any no 'counts with big ideas goin' to latch onto this child.

In less than a quarter hour Amy's luggage had been loaded into the trunk of the Packard, and she and her mother were on their way home.

As they drove away from Union Station, under the huge bronze Welcome Arch, Amy felt hard pressed to believe that the sign's greeting included her. She cast a sidelong look at her mother and wondered if things between them would ever improve. So far it didn't seem like it.

Rowena slammed on the Packard's brakes. She'd come within a foot of an elderly Mexican couple crossing at Wazee. Instinctively, she'd reached across the seat to prevent Amy from flying into the dashboard and window.

"Damn foreigners," Rowena protested and pummeled the steering wheel.

Before the couple had gotten as far as the curb, Rowena's foot was back on the gas pedal. She continued driving up Seventeenth Street, planning to turn left on Lawrence.

The streets were unusually congested with traffic, and for some reason, a horde of people that seemed to have come out of nowhere, was running up the sidewalks in the same direction as Rowena and Amy were driving.

Two white men, crossing together from the west side of the street to the east side, darted between the cars and ran in front of the Packard without looking. Again, Rowena had to brake suddenly. She started to honk at the men, but instead, muttered a string of curses. She seemed oblivious to Amy's distress.

The situation was rapidly becoming unmanageable. Other drivers were literally abandoning their vehicles in the middle of the street to join the crowd. Rowena's own auto had become completely hemmed in.

Amy scooted up to the edge of the Packard's front seat, and strained for a better view of whatever was going on. "Mama, what is it? Something awful must have happened."

"Sweet Baby, this ain't no main stop, like St. Louie, or New York. This is Denver. Probably ain't nothin' more 'n a couple of prairie hicks beatin' up a drunk Indian."

Amy glared at her mother with disgust. Nothing had changed. Well, maybe the times, but certainly not her mother.

Rowena looked at her daughter with a sly smile, but Amy turned away. Rowena offered a second guess. "Well, I did hear them talkin' in the shop today 'bout how President Coolidge was goin' to be visitin' here a day or two. Maybe that's what's causin' all the commotion."

"Why don't we go see for ourselves," Amy suggested, anxious to get out of the car. The steady stream of people was quickly turning into a surging river. As they brushed past, the Packard was thumped and jostled. Their mingled voices were escalating into an incomprehensible din. "I suppose if the rest of the city is in on it we might as well be too," Amy yelled, trying hard to mask a need to remain calm.

Rowena shrugged, and yelled back. "That ain't a bad idea. Just be careful gettin' out. These white folks 'd jest' as soon trample us to death." Amy started to respond to her mother's comment, but was distracted by swelling numbers of hurrying pedestrians.

"Now!" Rowena shouted and pushed open the door.

Amy hesitated, but her mother gave her a reassuring glance. After finally managing to escape the car, then working their way around to the front of it, Rowena took hold of Amy's elbow once again, and led her daughter forward.

"Mama," Amy shouted, "doesn't all of this excitement kind of remind you of when you closed the shop for the day and took me to Lincoln Hills? It was for that big Fourth of July picnic. We had so much fun. Remember?"

Rowena attempted to answer, but the sound of her voice was drowned out. She tried again, only louder. "Ain't no way I could forget. But it was the Juneteenth picnic; most all of Five Points was there," she said, practically yelling into her daughter's ear. "You was just six years old, and cute as can be in that yellow jumper I sewed for you, least that's what everyone of them judges for the "Little Miss" contest decided. Guess that's why my precious won first place, huh?"

For once, Amy and Rowena looked at each other, and both smiled. Rowena tenderly pushed a strand of Amy's hair away from her face.

"I'll bet if those judges saw my Sweet Baby all growed up, she'd win whatever contest they got for all grow'd up girls. All them other missys just have to go on home. Speakin' a which, I think we jes' oughta make plans to go on up to that picnic again this year. Might be kinda fun. What d' you say, Sweet Baby?"

Her mother's voice sounded oddly sincere to Amy, yet Amy didn't answer. She's heard it all before. Instead, she ran ahead of her mother, like she used to when she was a little girl and they would spend Sunday afternoons walking through City Park. Like then, her curiosity was getting the best of her.

She reached the wall of onlookers and nudged her way closer to the front, but a phalanx of men attired in business suits and homburgs still blocked most of her view. She had to stand on her tiptoes and peer over their shoulders to see anything.

All that was visible from her vantage were the tops of rows and rows of pointed white hoods passing by.

She looked back for her mother but could see that Rowena was stranded behind the outer layer of onlookers and had a curious, almost pained look on her face.

Amy started to call her, but a man who was standing behind Amy, pushing to get through, leaned into her and accidentally shoved her forward to the front of the wall of viewers.

The shock of what Amy saw was nearly too much to comprehend. An army of Ku Klux Klansmen, dressed in their

white robes and pointed hoods was tromping by. Whomp.
Whomp. Whomp.

All that could be seen of the men's faces were their eyes and
mouths through cutouts in the hoods' masks. The thought that
any one of these Klansmen could be a milkman, or a teacher,
or a judge – but that his identity and membership in the Klan
could be kept a secret – sent a chill down Amy's spine.

In the last few years, there had been numerous newspaper
stories about the Klan's inciting race riots in other cities, and
reports from around the country about Negro men who had
been abducted from their homes or off public streets by local
Klansmen, then coated with boiling tar and rolled in feathers,
or even lynched. Amy just hadn't wanted to believe any of it.

During her visit home for Christmas, Amy had overheard
a conversation in her mother's beauty shop about the cross
burnings that were happening on Ruby Hill in South Denver,
and the ones taking place west of Denver on Table Mountain,
but she hadn't wanted to believe that either.

After all, like her mother had said, this was 1925, and this
was Denver. Denver, Colorado. The place where less than a
hundred years ago great Indian tribes camped at the base of
the beautiful Rocky Mountains, and massive buffalo herds
roamed the open plains for as far as the eyes could see.

Where, now, tourists came to visit the famous Museum of
Natural History to see the dinosaur skeletons, or came to
take souvenir coins home from the U.S. Mint...the home
of Buffalo Bill and the unsinkable Molly Brown, and where
some of America's largest gold or silver or cattle fortunes had
been made, and lost. And made again.

Denver. Frontier territory, land of the free, home of the
brave. Not some part of the backward south.

Amy looked up the street to determine how much of the
parade had passed by. The men's brigades extended up

Seventeenth Street as far as the eye could see. The rows of men marching in front of her were just the tail end of the company.

Following behind the men was a large squadron of girls and women. They too wore robes and hoods, but their faces were uncovered. They smiled and waved as if they were in a beauty pageant. All their onlookers gleefully smiled and waved right back. All, except for Amy. She was still trying to make sense of this.

Next came troops of boys and young men. Like their mothers and sisters, they were outfitted in robes and hoods and also revealed their faces. The first section consisted of the grade school boys, and the next section of junior high school boys. Despite their youth, they were as regimented as well trained soldiers.

Bordering both sides of these sections was a drum and fife corps playing the anthem, *Dixie*. The corps members wore three cornered hats and vests and breeches reminiscent of those worn by their colonial brethren, and evoked stirring thoughts of the American Revolution. Their drums and lutes were festooned with red, white, and blue ribbons that fluttered like Old Glory. The parade-goers lining the sidewalks cheered and saluted the Klan's display of patriotism.

The man next to Amy began to whistle to the drummers' and pipers' music, then to march in place and to sing to it.

"I wish I was in the land ob cotton, old times dar am not forgotten, look away, look away, look away Dixieland," his voice rang out.

One of the man's flailing elbows almost jabbed Amy in her face. She managed to duck just in time. The next thing she knew a goodly number of those standing along the parade route were singing too.

"In Dixieland where I was born early on one frosty morning, look away, look away, look away Dixieland. Den I wish I was in Dixie, hooray, hooray, in Dixie and I'll take my stand to lib and die in Dixie."

The sound of the music trailed off as the boys' unit and the drum and fife corps moved on, but many in the crowd, especially the man next to Amy, sang on.

"Away, away, away down south in Dixie, away, away, away down south in Dixie. Away, away, away down south in Dixie."

Behind the children, the women, and the musicians, came an even more earnest group, an infantry of young men. Amy had never seen anything like it. Their faces appeared cold and stone-like and the perfectly executed...one, two, one, two...of their steps resounded like thunder.

Amy looked into their faces. For the most part, they looked so clean-cut and all-American, as if they should have been playing a game of baseball at a church picnic, or working the soda fountain at a Dolly Madison creamery.

None of them could have been older than eighteen or nineteen. If she'd gone to school in Denver, to East High or Manual, some of them might have been her classmates. She felt compelled to search for just one who was out of sync.

She looked down at the young men's feet, but rows and rows went by in absolute precision.

Finally, there was one marcher, about midway into a row who seemed distracted and who was decidedly out of step with those surrounding him.

Amy quickly looked up to see his face. At almost the same instant the boy looked directly over at her. His blue eyes were shockingly familiar. Amy could see that he was just as stunned. His face had gone pale.

He marched on, then the ground beneath her became unstable. The whomp, whomp, whomp of the marchers' boots thudded mercilessly in her ears and she had to gasp for air.

"Kyle!" she was at last able to cry in disbelief. She felt lost and uncertain. Frightened. Thankfully, she felt a comforting touch on her shoulder. Rowena had pushed through the crowd and was at her side.

"Humph," Rowena said at seeing the marchers up close. "I thought I left all this in Alabama. Let's get back to the car."

Amy hoped her mother hadn't seen the look on her face. She wasn't ready to do any explaining.

They hurried back to the Packard and were grateful to find that some of the cars around them had already left, leaving them a way to drive out of the quagmire of those still parked.

Rowena put the key in the ignition and started to turn it, but a violent shake to the car caused her hand to be flung off of the key.

Rowena and Amy looked up simultaneously. There at the front of the Packard was a rosy cheeked boy wearing a backward applejack cap and a tattered sweater. He couldn't have been more than ten or eleven years old. He had his palms pressed onto the hood of the automobile and his mouth screwed into a wicked grin.

"Beat it, kid," Rowena shouted and jammed the heel of her hand against the car's horn.

The unexpected blare of the car's horn caused the boy to jump backward in alarm, but he quickly regrouped and came forward again; he used all of the might in his juvenile body to rock the car back and forth.

"Niggers!" he shouted.

BLEEP, Rowena fought back with the car horn.

"Niggers!"

BLEEP. BLEEP. BLEEP.

"Niggers! Niggers! Niggers!"

BLEEP.

The rosy cheeked boy kept on rocking the car, and Rowena Johnson kept on blaring her horn.

Amy, hunkered low in her seat, was clutching her stomach. "Not Kyle," she said, weeping. "Oh no, Lord, not Kyle."

Chapter Six

A my opened the door of her bedroom, uncertain of what to expect. Every time she had ever returned home, her mother had changed the room somehow. Last summer it had been the new canopy bed.

This past Christmas, flowered wallpaper.

"What in the world?" Amy said as she stepped into her room. This time it was a whole new color scheme.

Gone were the matching pink-flowered curtains and bedspread she'd finally learned to live with.

In their place was a frilly yellow and white ensemble. And a new rug.

Oh well, she wasn't going to have to live here forever.

At least, Mr. Scruggs was still in his place, snuggled against the new pillows in the window seat. He was missing one of his black button eyes, and some of his stuffing was peaking out a torn seam on his side, but Amy loved her old teddy bear. Not throwing him away was the one promise her mother had ever kept.

The promises to find Amy's birth certificate, and the promise to tell Amy about her father, were always conveniently postponed. Something just wasn't right about it all.

Someday, soon, though, she was going to insist that her mother tell her the truth. "Isn't that so, Mr. Scruggs?" Amy said to her old chum, as she grabbed him up and hugged him to her. His soft, nubby fabric was as comforting as ever and still had the faint scent of lilac talcum powder that her mother had sprinkled into his stuffing when she'd sewn him.

Amy sat on the window seat and looked around the room as if she were a tourist orienting herself to a change of hotels.

The new décor was pretty.

Perhaps this whole situation wasn't going to be as difficult as she had feared. She just wished that her mother didn't work so much. Wished that the two of them had more time together.

But what difference did it make what she wished? She knew all too well that wishes were entirely useless.

Amy decided to unpack and set Mr. Scruggs on the bureau. Her mother's odd-jobs man had already brought the luggage upstairs to her room.

All of the pieces were neatly arranged, from smaller to larger, near her closet. As she reached for the largest suitcase-she discovered the stack of gift wrapped packages arranged on the settee.

She selected the small oblong box from the top of the stack and shook it.

From the sound it made, her guess was that the box held a necklace. An expensive one knowing her mother. Probably the pearls she had been promised for graduation.

But Amy didn't want, or need, a string of fresh water pearls, or anything else that could be bought. All she wanted and needed, was her mother's undivided attention. Something she'd never really had.

Without even taking off the box's ribbon and wrapping, Amy threw the box against a wall and crumpled to her knees. "Oh, help me, somebody. Please, help me," she cried, and curled into a ball. This wasn't a homecoming. It was the beginning of a prison sentence. She stretched out onto the pretty new carpet and lay there as if unable to get up.

With her ear pressed to the floor, Amy could hear strains of jukebox music and laughter coming from her mother's speakeasy, two stories down, in the basement.

She sat up and covered her ears with her hands, but that accomplished little. She looked around the room, desperate for a solution.

The radio console that she'd considered just a hideous piece of junk, practically called to her. "Oh, thank goodness," Amy said with a flourish worthy of an audience.

Amy sprang to her feet and went to turn on the radio.

She turned the adjacent knob in search of a station. At first all she got were loud *skitch, skitch* sounds that hurt her ears, and several barely audible transmissions.

Just as she was about to give up, she found KOA.

The announcer was a man with an easygoing voice.

"Up next, for your nightly entertainment, Denver, we have that sensational local orchestra, Professor George Morrison and his Melody Hounds, featuring the lovely Miss Hattie McDaniel. Listen now, as she sings her much requested, 'Got the Sam Henry Blues'."

Amy turned the radio's volume dial as far right as possible. The orchestra's overture, bluesy and plaintive, filled her room. She began to sway in time to the music's rhythm.

Miss McDaniel, the Negro Sophie Tucker, as the public called her, belted out her song.

I'm just a wandering child, just a wandering child, wandering 'round this big ole world alone, with no place to call my home.

Amy danced over to her vanity table and observed herself in the mirror. As she rolled her hips, the newspaper clipping, glued to the top corner of her full length mirror, drew her attention.

It was a photograph of beauty pageant contestants posed in their swim suits.

The girl in the center wore a wide diagonal sash, and held a trophy engraved, *Miss America, 1924.*

Amy pretended she was the girl in the center of the photo and strutted up and down the length of her room, across her imaginary stage. The music continued to accompany her.

My mother begged, Sam Henry don't you go. Sam Henry don't you go, but I turned my back, and went my way, and now all I've got to call my own is the low down Sam Henry blues.

She returned to the mirror and studied the photograph again, putting one hand on her hip, and the other hand to her hair, she worked to get the contestants' pose just right.

She glanced from the view of herself in the mirror, to the photograph, back to the view of herself, then back to the photograph. With two or three minor adjustments she eventually perfected the alluring stance.

For a moment, Amy felt an unfamiliar sense of self-satisfaction, but then, she noticed an undeniable difference between herself, and all the girls in the photograph. Especially, the girl with the trophy.

Every one of the girls in the picture had white skin, while her skin was a certain shade of brown.

She tore the Miss America picture down and ripped it into confetti, dancing as she threw the confetti about her and Hattie McDaniel sang...*This time, when I get back home...oh, I said, this time, when I get back home – to my mama's shack - no more will I roam.*

As the song ended, Amy stretched out her arms and sprawled back onto the floor. Her breathing was quick and ragged.

After a minute of recovery, she raised up to a sitting position with arms held high. "Ladies and gentlemen," she hailed her invisible audience, "the *real* Miss America."

Beads of perspiration were trickling from her hair onto her face. "Whew," she said, "the temperature in this room must be a hundred degrees."

She stood and went to the radio again, this time to turn it off, then crossed the room to the window seat.

With one knee perched on the seat's cushion, she unlatched the window and flung it open, leaning her head and body out into the night.

As she bathed her face and arms in the cool, late March air, she gave thanks that it was spring.

A corner street lamp extended its amber glow only a few feet. Except for the dim cast of starlight, it was dark in front of the duplex. All she could make out were the patches of snow still on the ground.

Someone walked into the light of the street lamp and stopped. The someone seemed to be a man, and he was carrying what looked like a case of some kind.

He seemed lost and unsure of which way to go.

As Amy's eyes adjusted to the night lighting, she recognized that the man was the porter who had helped her on the train. He was holding her hat box.

She watched him as he walked from the street corner to the duplex, but waited until he turned onto the sidewalk to the porch before she spoke. "Hello," she called to him. "Nice evening."

He looked up, obviously surprised. He had on his own clothes this time. A long raccoon coat, and one of those funny looking porkpie hats. He snatched the hat from his head. "Yes, he replied, "very nice."

"Can I help you?" Amy said.

He held up the hat box. "You forgot this. Your address was on the tag, so I thought I would just…"

"I'll be right down," Amy said, ducking out of the window before he could finish his sentence.

She tore open the rest of the gift wrapped boxes and tossed their contents of new skirts, blouses, and dresses into a pile.

Confused by such a selection, she finally reached for a red pleated skirt and a simple white blouse, and changed into them.

Next, she spritzed her wrists and throat with lilac water, then quickly brushed her hair.

She checked the results in the mirror and gave herself a nod of approval. Something was missing though. She went to the box she had thrown against the wall and ripped its wrapping off. Sure enough, the box contained a choker of beautiful pearls. She hastily put it on.

As she was about to run down the stairs, Amy looked down and saw that she was barefoot. The first floor's linoleum covering would be cold but she was in too much of a hurry to go back to her room and rifle through her luggage for a pair of shoes. She vaulted down the steps two by two.

There was a light switch at the bottom of the stairs, but Amy ignored it. No need to light up the hallway like a Christmas tree. Besides, other than her school dorm, this was the only house she had ever lived in. The first floor of the house was dark, but she knew every corner by heart.

Only she had forgotten about the mysterious stack of boxes she had seen that afternoon in the middle of what used to be the dining room. She stubbed a toe, royally, against the corner of one of the boxes.

"Owww!" she yelped. "What in the heck?"

She hopped back to the light switch and flicked it on. There was a narrow path between the stacks of boxes but she'd missed it entirely. She flicked the light back off and this time used her outstretched hands to guide her safely to the curtain that divided the room from the front hallway.

Once at the front door she turned on the porch light.

She hastily counted to ten then opened the door as if she'd been expecting a guest all along.

"Come in," she said, graciously. It was impossible for her not to notice the young man's look of bewilderment as he stepped aside, into the semi-darkness. "We live upstairs," she quickly explained. "The first floor is my mother's beauty shop."

"Smart!" he said, and handed her the hat box.

She set the box on the chair that was next to the small table with the telephone. "This was really nice of you. Thank you," she said.

"It was kind of on my way home. No big thing," he said.

She could tell that he was trying to think of something more to say, but her mind was just as blank. That he was so darn handsome wasn't helping her any.

"Oh my, I'm sorry," she said finally, and gestured to take his coat and hat. "I've completely forgotten my manners. You must be cold. May I offer you a cup of hot chocolate? It's the least I can do."

"Thank you," he answered and happily took off his coat and hat. That would be real nice."

Amy hung his apparel on the beauty shop's coat stand, then extended her hand to him. "Maybe we ought to at least introduce ourselves," she said. "I'm Amy. Amy Johnson."

"My pleasure," he said, shaking her hand a little too enthusiastically.

Amy found his slightly unsophisticated charm refreshing and attractive, and let him go on shaking her hand until he realized what he was doing. She had to stifle a giggle when she saw his embarrassed reaction to his own behavior.

Another awkward silence left them just staring at each other before he realized that Amy was still waiting to hear his name.

"Oh, right," he said apologetically, "us, Anthony…Hudson."

At precisely the same moment they both gave into tension- relieving laughter. That made Amy even more hopeful for the chance to get to know him. "The kitchen's in back," she said. "Follow me."

She tried not to worry about what Anthony must've been thinking as they walked between the boxes to the kitchen, or about the loud jazz music that could be heard coming from the basement.

She offered no explanation, and gentlemanly, he asked for none.

In the kitchen, she offered him a seat at the table. As she stood at the stove warming the milk for the hot chocolate, they talked like old friends.

They had a lot in common. Mainly, they were both boarding school brats. Only, the school Anthony had attended was a military academy, and he'd graduated last year, two years ahead of his class. He was just working on the railroad until he started Howard University in the fall.

Amy liked everything about him. She especially liked that he didn't ask her about what was going on in the basement.

What class, she thought as she set Anthony's cup of hot chocolate in front of him.

Before Amy could sit down, he stood up and moved to pull her chair out for her, then waited for her to sit. Her mother might not approve of Anthony's dark complexion, or, of his job, But Amy didn't care. All she knew was that he treated her with respect and that she enjoyed talking with him. They went on conversing for almost an hour.

When she reached over to take his cup to refill it, he stopped her, touching her hand lightly and thoughtfully, like he had on the train.

"I really should be going," he said. Only, instead of letting go of her hand, he held it tighter.

He was a year younger than Amy, but his grasp felt like that of a man's. The heat from his palm seemed to spread through her whole body.

The table parted them, but he stood and moved his chair next to hers, still not letting go of her hand.

She had a terrible realization. Under the circumstances she probably shouldn't even be sitting here with him.

"You smell wonderful," he said into her ear.

Amy closed her eyes and waited. She felt Anthony's lips touch hers, but a sudden cacophony of breaking glass caused her to jolt back. Anthony jolted back too and nearly tipped over in his chair.

The two of them looked up to find Amy's mother standing in the doorway to the basement stairs. A tray of shattered drinking glasses lay at her feet.

"Not in my house," she exclaimed.

The splintering glass had caused a cut on one of Rowena's legs, and blood dripped onto her shoe, but the look in her eyes warned Anthony and Amy they had a far greater concern.

Rowena's face visibly hardened as she stepped closer to them. "Keep your hands off of my daughter," Rowena said, her eyes narrowing to slits. "And get out of my house."

Anthony stood and tried to extend an apology. "I, I'm very sorry, Mrs...."

Rowena moved in front of Amy and shoved Anthony in the chest, hard, causing him to stumble backward.

"Right now, damn it."

Chapter Seven

Margaret set the vase of freshly cut April daffodils on Mother Browne's nightstand, hoping for at least a smile from her mother-in-law. "I know you might not believe it, but I grew them myself," Margaret said.

Mother Browne didn't answer or even smile. But then, for the last eight years she rarely had. A stroke had left the entire right side of her body paralyzed, and the whole of her face slack. Most days she simply stared into space, as if suspended somewhere between life and death.

The estate's gardens had taken on a similar countenance. With his mother bedridden, Devin had fired the groundskeeper and diverted the maintenance funds to his own use. In the years since, as his gambling debts had mounted, even the mansion's interior fell into disrepair.

Margaret had protested his selling off their home's fixtures and furniture, but as he always reminded her, it was his family's home, and he was his parents' only heir. And his father was already dead. Why wait when he could have it all now.

Most of it anyway. In the meantime, he didn't want to hear Margaret's mouth about it.

Fortunately, he hadn't objected when she had rescued a patch of the land to plant and tend her own garden. After all, whether he admitted it or not, it was a good portion of her harvest that kept them all fed. Whatever produce was left over, she bartered for dairy and bakery goods.

The flowers were something new she was trying. The Waterford vase she'd put them in was the only piece of Mother Browne's crystal collection she'd managed to hide from Devin.

Margaret crossed Mother Browne's room to open the drapes.

As she flung back the maroon velvet panels, a flood of morning light quickly lifted her spirits. She unlatched the French doors and pushed them open, stepping out onto the balcony.

The air was clear and crisp. She stretched her arms and gazed into the distance with wonder.

"Ahhhh," she sighed to herself, as much for Mother Browne's sake as for her own. Mother Browne, "Just look at those beautiful snow-capped peaks. Have you ever seen anything so stunning?"

As if she expected a response, Margaret stood aside to give her mother-in-law a clear view from the bed.

"Why..." Margaret continued, "I think it's even possible to see all the way to Golden today. What do you think?"

Mother Browne turned her face against the pillow and remained mute. Still, for her mother-in-law to move at all was progress. But then it had seemed to Margaret that Mother Browne had at least begun to try to communicate these last few months, even if just to express her displeasure about something.

For some reason, Margaret was convinced that her mother-in-law was trying to tell her something. Something important.

So far Margaret hadn't been able to interpret her mother-in-law's moans and grunts, nevertheless she was going to keep trying. Perhaps there was something in the room that Mother Browne wanted closer to her, or that she wanted to hold.

Unfortunately, there were so many knickknacks, books, and photographs in the room thatMargaret had no idea of what to single out. She would just have to continue to wait patiently until Mother Browne could make it clear to her. For now, though, it didn't matter. Mother Browne was asleep again.

Margaret stepped back inside the room, but left the French doors open. It was the perfect opportunity to get her dusting done. She pulled an old piece of flannel from her pocket and went about the room.

She handled every object with respect, aware that each one represented a significant time or place in her mother-in-law's once glamorous and passionately lived life.

She was especially careful as she picked up the silver framed photograph of her deceased father-in-law, as it was the last one taken before his crippling polo accident.

As Margaret wiped the frame's glass she thought once again of how fate had so cruelly altered her husband's life… and ultimately her own life as well. A truth it had taken her years to piece together.

All the versions of the Brownes' family history she'd been told had been riddled with lies.

As always, before setting the picture back down, she recounted the truth to herself to keep it straight in her own mind, and to tell Kyle, whenever it was the right time.

In the year following his father's misfortune, Devin had gone from being a spoiled little rich boy, to a child grieving his father's suicide. Apparently, however, the greater tragedy had been the loss of the family fortune due to Father Browne's swindling business partners.

It had only been due to the foresight of Father Browne's own father that the family estate was owned and maintained by a trust fund.

"The truth is merely a matter of perception, my dear," Mother Browne had instructed Margaret shortly after Devin had brought her home as his bride.

"So true, Mother Browne, so true," Margaret said, mostly to herself, as she placed the photograph back in its place on the bureau top, then continued to stare at it. It was amazing, she noticed, how much Devin had come to resemble his father.

Margaret allowed herself a wistful thought. What if, under other circumstances, her husband might have been a different kind of man? A hard worker, like her father. Not some con artist willing to do whatever it took to get money.

Still what was done, was done, including, soon, her marriage.

She moved to the bookshelves, making quick work of them, then arrived at the painting over the fireplace; a large oil portrait of Mother Browne when she was a debutante.

She stood back to admire it for a moment.

For the thousandth time, Margaret wondered if there really was a wall safe behind the painting, and if there was, if it really held the gold nuggets Devin swore it did. Lately, he'd been threatening to break into the safe, but Margaret hoped he had at least some shred of decency left. Stealing from his own mother had to be too far even for him to go.

She dragged a chair close to the fireplace and stood on it to reach the painting. Just as she swept a cobweb from the painting, she heard Mother Browne moan.

She turned to look at her mother-in-law and even from across the room could see that the woman was trying, desperately, to say something.

Margaret hastily got down from the chair and rushed to Mother Browne's bedside. Sitting on the bed, Margaret clasped the woman's hands between her own.

For the first time ever, the two women looked directly into each other's eyes. Margaret didn't need an interpreter for what she saw. Mother Browne's eyes were full of fear. What Margaret had to strain to understand was the meaning of her mother-in-law's moans. Margaret felt certain that she was asking for something, only what?

Margaret looked around the room for clues.

Was it something from a shelf?

In a drawer?

A favorite piece of jewelry…or one of the figurines brought back from mother's travels? Perhaps the bronze statuette of the Eiffel Tower on her bureau, or the ivory bust of an African child on her desk.

Margaret let go of her mother-in-law's hands and walked around the room, gently touching one thing then another.

As Margaret neared a corner table that held only a large open Bible, one of Mother Browne's hands began to tremble.

"Is this what you want," Margaret asked. "The Bible?"

Tears began to run down Mother Browne's cheeks.

Relieved, Margaret lifted the heavy leather covered book and brought it to her mother-in-law's bedside. She held it so that Mother Browne could look directly at its pages, which were time yellowed and musty.

It was printed in English and German, with the English text in the left-hand column, and the German text in the right-hand column. Between the "Old Testament" and the "New Testament" were pages that folded out to reveal a family tree. All the names were German.

Mother Browne reached toward the Bible. To help her, Margaret held the book closer, and set Mother Browne's hand on top of the pages.

Mother Browne pushed at one of the pages as if trying to turn it.

"All right," Margaret said, and began turning the pages, leafing back through the "Old Testament". She had not the least idea of what they were looking for.

Then, there it was, between the Psalms. A daguerreotype pushed into the fold.

Margaret had never seen Mother Browne look so happy, even the atrophied muscles in her face appeared to regain their elasticity.

Margaret removed the decades-old photograph and held it up for Mother Browne to see.

Mother Browne began to weep. "Mama, Mama," she moaned.

The people in the photograph seemed to be a family. There was a smiling little girl, about five years old, with dark, waist-length hair held back with a ribbon, and she was wearing a long gingham dress with a peek-a-boo crinoline. The little girl was leaning into the lap of a stoic looking Indian woman whose hair was also dark, but straighter and even longer, and parted into two braids.

The woman's buckskin dress and moccasins might have been ceremonial. Her posture in the high-backed chair was positively regal.

Behind the girl and the woman stood a tall, pale, white man, with a head of abundant, light colored curly hair. He was dressed in a tweed jacket and lederhosen, and had a hand resting on the woman's shoulder.

His gaze, straight at the camera, bespoke the pride of possession.

On the back of the photograph were two lines of writing in brown ink too faded to read.

Margaret put the photograph into Mother Browne's palm, and held her hand under Mother Browne's so that the woman didn't have to use her strength to hold the picture close enough to see. Mother Browne was decidedly smiling.

The bedroom door was closed, but Margaret could still hear the muted chimes of the grandfather clock at the bottom of the stairs. The church social committee would be arriving soon, but right now this was more important.

Margaret leaned over and kissed the old woman on her forehead. "I know, I know," Margaret said as she gently smoothed a strand of Mother Browne's hair back into place. It was impossible not to notice how her mother-in-law's widow's peak and high cheek bones matched those of the woman's in the photograph, or how Mother Browne had the same upturned nose and piercing stare as the man in the photograph.

Then, Margaret realized something even more incredible.

The little girl in the photograph was Mother Browne. The telltale proof was the mole at the corner of Mother Browne's mouth, which was in exactly the same place as a mole on the little girl.

A strong knock at the bedroom door caught Margaret by surprise. She quickly put the photograph back between the pages of the Bible, then carefully closed the book. "Come in," she finally called.

Walter entered the room with a luncheon tray. "I took the liberty of bringing this up a little early since you mentioned that you have a committee meeting this afternoon. I hope I wasn't out of place."

"Not at all, Walter," Margaret said, praying that he couldn't see the blush she felt rising in her face. "That was most thoughtful of you. Thank you."

Margaret watched Walter closely as he arranged Mother Browne's plate of food and her eating utensils on a small table. She sucked her breath in at what she noticed. Walter had a widow's peak identical to that of Mother Browne's *and* the woman's in the picture. He also had the same strong jaw line of the man, and the straight, dark hair of the woman.

Margaret's mind raced to try to understand.

She was probably just letting her imagination run away from her, she quickly decided. Walter was a Negro. How could there possibly be any resemblance between him and Mother Browne? And the people in the photograph, whoever they were?

As Walter finished setting the table, Margaret opened the Bible just enough to sneak a second look at the picture.

Yes, the likeness between Walter and Mother Browne and the people in the photograph was clearly evident. But what did it all mean?

She looked at Walter, again, and then back at the photograph. A yet more starling awareness came to her. *Walter and Devin had remarkably similar profiles.*

Granted, Walter was an inch or two taller than Devin, and also, Walter had dark brown skin, especially compared to Devin's ruddy complexion. Still there was no mistaking their familial likeness.

"It's just not possible," Margaret said, forcing the thought away. She slammed the Bible shut, set it on the floor and shoved it under the bed skirt with her foot.

"Pardon, Mrs. Browne. What did you say?" Walter asked Margaret as he moved the vase of daffodils to the luncheon table.

"Nothing, Walter. Nothing at all. I was just…just thinking aloud."

"Of course. I do it all the time myself," Walter replied with a polite smile. "Here, let me help you fix mother's pillows."

Walter plumped the pillows in back of Mother Browne's head, then added several more that were sitting on a nearby chair.

Margaret just stared at Walter as if it was the first time she'd ever seen him. He seemed not to notice. He simply picked up the plate with the soup bowl on it and handed it to her.

Unavoidably, the tips of their fingers touched as the plate went from one's hand to the other's, causing a shock in Margaret's body. She felt her nipples stiffen against her corset.

The plate and the bowl of warm soup wobbled between their grasps and the bowl of warm soup nearly slid off onto Mother Browne's bed. "Oh, no!,." Margaret cried just in time for Walter to pull the plate safely away.

Margaret felt flushed but hoped desperately that neither Walter nor her mother-in-law noticed.

Apparently he didn't, and Mother Browne had her eyes closed.

"I'll excuse myself now, Mrs. Browne," Walter said, "unless, of course, there's anything else I can help you with. I need to prepare the refreshments for your ladies' meeting."

"That's perfectly fine, Walter. Thank you, very much, for bringing up my mother-in-law's lunch," Margaret said while busying herself with some inconsequential rearrangement of the items on Mother Browne's nightstand.

"Not at all, Mrs. Browne. It's my pleasure," Walter said as he bowed slightly, then took a step back toward the door.

For the briefest moment, Margaret allowed herself to look at Walter as he left the room. Fearful that her mother-in-law might be sensing her discomfort, Margaret quickly lifted a spoonful of the soup to the woman's lips and coaxed her to swallow.

After only three or four spoonfuls of the soup Mother Browne turned her face away again. Margaret set the bowl on the table, took the damp washcloth that Walter had provided and cleaned Mother Browne's face and hands.

Margaret felt she was beginning to understand her mother-in-law. "Would you like me to read to you for a little while," Margaret asked her.

Amazingly, Mother Browne nodded yes. It seemed too that her face had assumed a certain softness.

Margaret removed one of the extra pillows from behind Mother Browne's head, and straightened the bed covers, then retrieved the Bible. She settled into a nearby chair and turned to the pages where she had found the daguerreotype. She selected Psalm Thirty-seven.

"Fret not thyself because of evildoers, neither be envious against the workers of iniquity. For they shall soon be cut down like the grass, and wither as the green herb.

"Trust in the Lord and do good; so shalt thou dwell in the land, and verily thou shalt be fed. Delight thyself also in the Lord; and he shall give thee the desires of thine heart."

Margaret looked up and saw that Mother Browne had already fallen asleep, but she decided to read on, quietly, for herself.

"Delight thyself also in the Lord; and he shall give thee the desires of thine heart. Commit thy way unto the Lord; trust also in him; and he shall bring it to pass."

Margaret let the Bible rest against the roundness of her expectant tummy, and closed her own eyes for a moment.

She thought again of the prayer that she recited every morning and every night, the prayer that one day she would find the child she had given birth to seventeen years ago.

She opened her eyes and propped the Bible back up to read a bit more.

"And he shall bring forth thy righteousness as the light, and thy judgment as the noonday. Rest in the Lord, and wait patiently for him; fret not thyself because of him who prospereth in his way, because of the man who bringeth wicked devices to pass."

Mother Browne was sleeping soundly. Margaret closed the Bible and set it aside, then stood and kissed Mother Browne on the temple. After gathering the luncheon plates onto the tray, she left the room.

As Margaret stepped into the hallway, she gently closed Mother Browne's door behind her. The grandfather clock chimed again. It was eleven-thirty; she had to hurry. The committee members were due any minute.

She headed for the stairway but stopped just short of taking the first step down. Some vague instinct was urging her to go back down the hallway to Kyle's bedroom. Like any good mother, Margaret obeyed the instinct.

For a long moment she stood outside of her stepson's bedroom door wondering what to do. Now that he was a young man, she tried hard to respect his privacy, expect she was becoming worried about him. Besides, the door was ajar, and it was going to be hours before he returned home. It couldn't hurt just to peek in and make sure that everything was all right.

Still holding the luncheon tray Margaret pressed a hip against the door, only something prevented the door from moving. Undaunted, she pressed against the door harder, this time also using her shoulder. Whatever it was was behind the door was heavy, and certainly needed to be put back in its place, she scolded silently.

Finally, she was able to push the door open just far enough to get into the room. To her great dismay, the room was a horrific mess. The bed sheets and blankets were halfway on the floor, dirty clothes were strewn everywhere, and not one book was standing upright on its shelf.

But what was behind the door?

She turned to look.

There were three wooden crates, each stacked one on top of the other.

The side of each crate had a picture of a skull on it, and two words printed in boldfaced black letters above the skull:

Warning.

Dynamite.

Margaret gasped and dropped the tray. The china dishes the tray had held broke into numerous shards.

Margaret staggered backward but bumped into a box filled with empty pop bottles. A box next to that one was brimming with oil rags. What in the world was Kyle up to?

She opened the window to air out the room and started to clean.

First, she righted all the books, then put the cars from Kyle's train set back on their track.

Next, she gathered his dirty clothes into a pile for washing. As she had always done, she checked his pants pockets for forgotten belongings.

In one pair of pants she found a cap pistol. In the pocket of another pair, a BB-gun.

From his shirt pockets she gathered two self-rolled cigarettes, a bowie knife, and three silver bullets.

It was as if she were in the room of a complete stranger.

Margaret looked at Kyle's closed closet door, but heard the sound of Walter's voice, and a few seconds later the voices of a group of women. Oh dear, the church social committee had arrived. Still, Margaret's instinct was bidding her to open Kyle's closet door.

Hesitantly, she pulled the closet door open and reached in to pull the light chain. She felt as if she had fallen into a nightmare.

A panel of drawings – of Negroes hanging from ropes slung over tree branches – was painted on the closet's back wall.

Filthy words were scrawled underneath.

Behind the few clothes properly on their hangers, hung a long white robe with a KKK emblem sewn on the right-hand chest area.

Margaret wondered if the world had actually caved in on her. She had to hold one hand over her mouth to keep from vomiting, and one hand on her stomach to reassure herself that the baby was safe from all this vileness. She wept tears of disbelief and fear.

She grabbed an empty duffel bag from the closet floor, tore the Klan robe from its hanger, and stuffed it into the bag. Stepping back out of the closet, she gathered all of Kyle's dirty clothes and pushed them into the bag too.

The bag was barely big enough for all it needed to hold. She heaved the bag onto the bed, and made a mental note to return for it later.

Lastly, she bent to pick up the tray and the broken china.

As she stood to leave, yet another instinct bid her to look on the back of the bedroom door.

She pushed the door back, away from the stack of boxes, and gagged at the sickening sight of what she saw.

Kyle's childhood teddy bear was hanging from a rope tied to a nail lodged in the door. Its eyes were gouged out and an arm was torn from its seam. Stuffing hung out of its insides and its fur was singed.

Margaret's first wave of emotion was fear, but it was quickly drowned by a deep sense of sorrow. The stepson she had raised so lovingly had been turned-by his own father, by her husband-from a dear boy, into a repulsive hatemonger.

That night, Margaret waited – and waited – for Devin to come home. It was nearly sunup when he finally staggered in, drunk, reeking of dime store perfume and stale tobacco.

Margaret lifted her head from the dining room table, where she had fallen asleep waiting, and looked at her husband pleadingly. "Devin, all of those sick Klan ideas you've been forcing on Kyle are polluting his heart, and his mind. And worse, he's becoming hateful and mean. Destructive."

Devin slurred something back at her and wavered to and fro until he rested against the wall. "Don't you tell me how to raise my son," he finally managed to say. "Kyle is my blood. Not some immigrant trash...like you, and your father."

Margaret ignored the insult. She had heard it so often that it no longer hurt. "But what you're teaching him is vile. Have you seen what's in his room? It's frightening."

Devin grabbed Margaret by the arm. "You becoming a nigger lover?" he spewed, and twisted her arm until she faced him.

"Please, Devin, that's painful," she begged.

"Painful? Ha! I'll show you pain if you ever mouth off to me like that again, or ever criticize my son again."

Devin drew her close enough to spray spittle in her face. "Do you hear me?"

"Yes, Devin, I hear you."

Tears of pain spilled down her cheeks.

He yanked her arm again.

"You don't like it, you can just go the hell back to your two-bit father. I don't need his damn money anymore, anyway. That was my hard-up mother's idea, the crazy old bag."

Devin pushed Margaret away, slamming her into the dining room wall.

Sparks exploded in her head as she slid to the floor, and her arm hung limp at her side. There was a loud ringing in her ears but she could still hear her husband cursing to himself as he stumbled up the stairs.

"She remained on the floor, and rocked back and forth, hugging her stomach and weeping. "It's all right, baby. We'll be gone from here, soon. I promise."

Chapter Eight

With his socks stuffed in his shoes, his shoes tucked under his arm, and his jacket tossed over his arm, Devin tiptoed across Rowena's Oriental rug, to her bedroom door, glanced back at her still asleep under the covers, and opened the door as quietly as possible.

He'd already heard a rooster crow from somewhere out in one of the neighboring yards, but if he hurried, he'd be home before Margaret was any the wiser. Like so many other mornings, he would just sneak into the house through the French doors in the library, and claim he'd slept, all night, on the library sofa.

As he exited into Rowena's hallway, and softly closed the bedroom door behind himself, Devin felt a stab of guilt and regret. Deep down he knew that Rowena deserved better than this, but their fates were sealed. If it was possible for him to feel love, what he felt for Rowena was the closest he'd ever gotten. She was the only person who had ever understood him, and how she explained things made sense to him. But that was all beside the point. He'd be ruined if it ever got out that she was anymore than his mistress.

It was no real secret that the men in his family had had Colored mistresses at least as far back as his great-great grand-daddy, but if he was going to achieve his rightful position in the Klan, sooner or later he'd have to give up Rowena.

Right now, though, it was too early in the day for Devin to be weighed down with such matters. He crept down the hall. Past Rowena's daughter's room. Past the boarders' rooms. Down the stairs through the kitchen. Out to the screened-in back porch.

He needed to sit to put on his socks and shoes, but instead of having a chair, the porch was cluttered with stacks of wooden crates. He took one of the crates and sat on it.

As he finished tying his second shoe, Devin heard the rooster crow again. He looked up to see the blush of the April dawn give way to a wash of brilliant sunlight. He had to get going. He stood, buttoned up and tucked in his shirt, put on his jacket, then pushed open the screen door, and hurried down the porch's rickety wooden steps, up the backyard walkway to the alley gate.

He was halfway down the walkway when the wood-framed screen door clapped closed. The double bang clob-bered his head with pain, making it impossible for him to take another step. "Agghh!" he cried, and winced at the throbbing in his skull. "Frigging rot gut."

As far as Devin was concerned, all this prohibition non-sense had gone far enough. Here it was, 1925, and after seven years, the Feds were still telling everybody what they could and couldn't make, what they could and couldn't sell – or buy – and what they could or couldn't drink.

Thanks to the two-timing politicians, and those meddling teetotaler dames, a decent bottle of booze was getting damn hard to come by. From what he heard, now even the Catho-lics' communion wine was just watered down grape juice.

Lately, Rowena's bootleg whiskey was getting just as bad. The batch last night had tasted like a drugstore cold remedy, or something out of the backwoods. Whatever ingredients her suppliers were using to make the stuff wasn't helping his stomach or brain none too much either.

As he waited for the pain in his head to subside, he gave thought to his whereabouts. He was smack in the middle of Five Points. The neighborhood his father used to call Spook Town and Jigville.

When he slipped into the neighborhood late at night, the surroundings looked like any other working class environs. And in the speakeasies hidden here and there, most of the patrons were white, so he still felt at home. It was just in these early morning hours, when he was leaving Rowena's, that it was hard to ignore.

Across the fence, in the next yard, a pretty young taffy – colored woman was hanging sparkling white, wet, bed sheets on a clothesline. Devin admired the steady way she went about her work. He nodded hello to her, but she kept her gaze averted, gathered her wicker basket, and fled into her house.

A formation of cackling geese drew Devin's attention skyward. The pain behind his eyes and at the back of his skull, throbbed anew. He shielded his eyes against the bright morning sun and watched for a moment as the birds flew north, homeward, for the spring.

"Lucky good-for-nothing bastards," he groused and continued on the two or three steps to the gate. When he reached it, he knew that the gate was latchless, so just gave it an easy push.

It swung wide open and let out to a rutted dirt lane.

That was one of the qualities Devin liked about Five Points, its relationship to the unadorned and genuine. It might have been only three square miles on the northeast side of Denver, but for all the Negroes' troubles, their community maintained an air of hospitality he couldn't remember experiencing on his own side of town. He'd have traded the paved alleys, any day, for what he sensed existed in Five Points.

As he walked up to the end of the alley, to where he'd parked his Olds, Devin made the observation that nearly every backyard he passed had a portion of the yard staked for a garden. It made him think of the melon patch he'd had when he was a boy.

He saw an old man seeding one of the gardens and felt tempted to stop and help, but then he berated himself for the impulse and hurried past.

He switched thoughts to how pleased he was with himself for having been so clever to park in the alley this time. He had solved two problems. The need to make a quick getaway in case the cops raided Rowena's speakeasy, and more importantly, the need to keep his secret life a secret.

He'd paid an old drunk two bits to keep an eye on the Oldsmobile, and to wipe the dew off of it come daybreak. It was better service than he got from the college boys who worked summers at the country club.

The aroma of coffee and bacon wafting from a nearby kitchen caught Devin off guard. Damn he was hungry. Margaret would just have to fix him breakfast when he got home. And she'd better do it with a smile.

"Wait a horse's ass minute!" Devin said aloud as he stopped in his tracks. Again, he shielded his eyes against the sun, only this time to make certain they weren't playing tricks on him.

Sure enough, he was a stone's throw from the end of the alley, but there was no Oldsmobile, just two shiny black Model Ts parked bumper-to-bumper.

He walked up to the front car and kicked its back tire. "Shit, I know this is where I left it." Devin said, and scratched his head.

The driver's side door of the Model T that he'd kicked swung open, and a short, heavyset man stepped out. He was wearing a tan-colored cashmere overcoat and a large-brimmed dark brown hat that shaded his eyes.

The man threw a set of keys into Devin's chest, but Devin's reflexive effort to slap at the keys to grab them failed. The keys landed in the dirt.

"It's around the corner," the man said in a gravelly voice, "parked in the front."

Devin's heart froze at the thought. Not because of anything to do with his marriage, but because his Grand Dragon, Dr. Locke, took it personal when any Klansman violated Klan laws, especially if that man was an officer. Any violation branded him a traitor.

Traitors died.

Consorting with a Colored woman was just about the worst violation possible.

"If it'd been up to me, all this talk would 'a been over," the man said to Devin evenly. "But the boss says he owes you a favor. If you don't have the two grand you owe him by Saturday night, next time the cops'll find your wheels. Only they'll be reeling it up from the bottom of Sloan's Lake, with you in it.

"Capisce?"

"Sure," Devin said, glancing just over his shoulder. Out of the corner of his eyes he could see that a gun was poked through an open window of the Model T. Devin added nonchalantly.

Hoping to conceal his nervousness he added, "It was always my intention. I just got caught up in uh, in uh,... in business. You know how it is."

The man gave Devin an expressionless face. "Boss don't go in for excuses. Just wants his cash."

With that, the man walked back to his Model T, got in, and sped away.

The second Model T, with the gun still pointing out the window, followed closely behind.

Mud and debris flew from under the tires of the cars and splattered onto Devin's face and jacket.

Devin stooped to pick up his ring of keys. Every one of the keys had been bent or broken off.

* * *

Margaret rang the kitchen bell again. Walter still didn't answer, which wasn't like him. She leaned over the upstairs banister and called to him. "Walter?"

As Margaret waited for a reply, she heard the back door open and close, then the sound of footsteps and the scurrying of Goldie's paws across the kitchen's linoleum floor. Goldie was Kyle's dog, but she followed Walter everywhere. Margaret felt relieved. Walter hadn't answered the bell because the dog and he were outside.

Margaret called to Walter once more. "Walter, can you come here please?"

Goldie rushed in first with her coat of silky golden hair flying and her paws clacking across the foyer tile. The retriever darted up the stairs and nuzzled against Margaret's calves , begging to be petted.

"You old spoiled thing." Margaret said as she reached down to pat the retriever's head, "Where's Walter, huh?"

Margaret didn't realize that Walter was looking up at her. His arms were full of firewood. It was spring, but the house somehow always held a chill. "Yes, Mrs. Browne, is everything all right?"

Walter's voice startled Margaret, but its soothing timbre caused her to blush. She stopped playing with Goldie and took a small step back. She didn't want Walter to see her like this and to possibly misunderstand. She spoke without looking over the banister at him.

"My husband just called. He said to pack a picnic lunch for the family. He's taking us to the mountains for the afternoon."

Walter was quiet. Margaret thought she could sense his puzzlement. As she waited for Walter to respond, she watched Goldie trot back down the steps to him.

Walter seemed to hesitate as he spoke. "Are you quite sure he said, 'to the mountains'? The weather's still a little cool for sitting outdoors, isn't it?"

"We'll just wrap up good," Margaret said. "Fresh air is exactly what Mother Browne needs. Now please, Walter, hurry. Devin wants us ready to go as soon as he gets home."

Margaret couldn't help herself. She stole a glance down at Walter but just as quickly wished she hadn't. His expression betrayed his disapproval. It was a look he boldly displayed more and more often. Maybe Devin was right. Maybe the Coloreds were forgetting their place.

Margaret decided to overlook the matter for the time being and rushed back into Mother Browne's room. She was going to have to search her mother-in-law's closets, and perhaps even the trunks in the attic, for an adequate coat and hat for the woman to put on. It had been years since the family had been on an outing together.

* * *

Kyle glanced in the Oldsmobile's rearview mirror to see his grandmother who was sitting in the back seat. She was staring blankly out the window.

"Hey, Gram," Kyle said loudly in deference to Mother Browne's diminished hearing, "hold tight, we're taking a curve."

Kyle yanked the auto's steering wheel to the left and leaned into the driver's side door as if he was swerving around one of the loops of the City Park Speedway. "Urrrrrrrrrrrrrrrrrr," he screeched, imitating the sound of tire rubber burning against road.

He stole another glance in the mirror. His grandmother was still gazing out the window, seemingly oblivious to his daring.

"That's okay, Gram," Kyle said as he relaxed back against his seat, "you're still my favorite girl."

Kyle looked forward again but slowed his maneuvering of the steering wheel to cruising speed. His father was outside the Olds motioning to him to roll down the window.

He did.

Devin reached in through the window opening and slapped Kyle in the back of the head. "Out of my damn seat, boy."

Tears welled in Kyle's eyes but he quickly blinked them back. He was determined to prove that he was a man now and could take whatever his father dished out. He slid across the seat to the passenger side of the Olds, then lifted himself backwards over the front seat into the back seat. He took special care not to jostle his grandmother.

As Devin took over the driver's seat Kyle suddenly felt like a child again. Mother Browne was still peering out the window as if nothing had happened.

Kyle thought about his grandmother as he watched her and wondered what the heck she was looking at. Sometimes he didn't know if he loved her, hated her, or just plain missed her. Since her stroke there'd been no one, except maybe his stepmother, sometimes, to take up for him and to stop his father from always hitting him.

His father began to bam the car's horn. After a minute he changed to pressing on it for long intervals causing it to blare almost continuously. Kyle hated this ritual between his father and stepmother.

Finally his stepmother rushed out of the house and joined them in the Olds. As his father turned the key in the auto's ignition Kyle couldn't help but think about how odd it felt for the whole family to be going somewhere together. Still, for all the years in between this and their last outing, little had changed.

As always, they rode in silence.

They were only a few minutes from the house when they turned west onto Colfax Avenue and headed toward the mountains. In half an hour more they were in the foothills with Red Rocks Park just ahead. The park's prehistoric formations of sandstone slabs jutted out of the earth at dramatic angles, and never failed to amaze him.

Devin drove through the entrance of the park and followed a winding road up to a bluff.

In another few minutes they were parked at a picnic site. The blustery weather had apparently discouraged any other tourists. All of the picnic tables were empty and the fire pits cold. Not even a deer roaming the forest was insight.

Devin led the exit from the Olds and everyone except Mother Browne helped unload something from the trunk.

"Anybody want to help me get a fire started for hot dogs?" Margaret asked as she spread out a red and white check tablecloth on the picnic table.

"Boy, you do it," Devin said to Kyle. "I'm going to take photographs."

"Oh, Devin," Margaret said with a sigh, "we just got here. Can't the picture taking wait?"

"You starting in already?" Devin said, glaring at his wife. "I thought if I did something nice, you'd at least go the day without griping for once."

"Devin, you know that's not what I'm doing. It's just that I thought…"

"Thought? Thought what?" Devin said with a smirk. "You see, that's the problem right there. Who asked you to think? When I want your thoughts I'll let you know. Right now I'm going to do what I said, and I don't want to hear any guff."

Devin turned his back to Margaret and looked for Kyle.

Kyle was helping his grandmother walk to the picnic table but glanced up just enough to see the familiar look of veiled resignation. Devin walked away from them, toward the forest, but Kyle didn't follow.

Devin stopped, turned on his heels, and glared at Kyle. "Didn't you hear me, boy? I said you're coming with me."

"Yeah, I heard you," Kyle said as he placed his grandmother's shawl on her shoulders.

"Don't get smart, boy. I never mouthed off to my old man a day in my life and you're not going to do it with me. Now let's get a move on. I need to find an interesting backdrop for the family photograph, and I want to get the picture out of the way while the light's still good. You see what you can find over in that direction, by those pine trees, and I'll check over along the bluff."

Devin walked to a distant grouping of boulders that were sitting on the edge of the bluff. Kyle obeyed and headed toward the grove of tall evergreens.

Once among the trees, Kyle found a slightly worn path that led into the forest. He couldn't resist the urge to explore, and decided to look for the photo setting on his way back.

He followed the path and smiled at hearing the crunch of the trees' fallen needles under his shoes. Before he realized it, he'd gone so far on the path that the picnic tables had disappeared from view, but he went on anyway.

After awhile, the path broke into two directions. Kyle allowed his instinct to guide him to the right. After a short distance, the path forked once more, and again he went right. He sensed that he might simply be going in a big circle. If his guess was correct, he would end up somewhere near where his father had gone, but it was probably time to be getting back.

Kyle turned to go but heard a strange sound nearby, the sound of quick, sharp jabs, like maybe metal hitting rock. He moved toward the sound until it seemed to be just on the other side of a large berry bush, but something in his gut told him to stay hidden.

He crouched low behind the bush and used his hands to part a slight opening between its branches. Kyle could just barely see his father, across the way, on the bluff. The sound was the repeated scrape of a shovel against one of the boulders near the edge of the bluff as his father dug dirt from beneath the boulder.

Kyle let go the berry bush branches and stood. He was motionless but stared into the gray sky trying to figure out what his father was doing. Nothing realistic came to mind.

When he returned to the picnic site he was out of breath from running, but his timing was perfect. His father was approaching from the direction of the bluff, and calling to everyone.

"Let's all go down to the bluff," Devin said as he neared the picnic table. "I found a great place for us to take a family picture, and if we go now the lighting 'll be perfect."

Margaret looked with dismay at all the food she'd arranged on the table and the places she had set. There was even a canning jar emptied of its pickles and refilled with wildflowers for a centerpiece. Her eyes met Kyle's but he quickly looked in the direction of his father.

Devin was waiting for them. He called to his family again. "Come on, you all, let's get going. The light's changing every minute. It'll be too dark before we know it."

Curse words spilled into Kyle's thoughts but for the sake of his grandmother and stepmother he kept them to himself. Instead, he helped his grandmother up from the table and circled his arm around her waist to help her. The three of them walked down to where his father waited.

As they neared the bluff and the boulders where Kyle had seen his father digging out the dirt, Kyle felt his stomach knot.

Devin arranged each member of his family into place in front of the boulder, then hurried back to the tripod where the camera sat aimed at them. He checked the composition of the picture in the camera's viewfinder.

Margaret was on the right. To her left was Kyle, and on Kyle's left, Mother Browne. A backdrop of trees and the boulder framed Margaret and Kyle, while a swath of sky and an edge of the boulder shone behind Mother Browne.

After a last adjustment to the camera's lens, Devin ran back and stood to the right of Margaret.

He activated the camera's shutter by means of a button in the palm of his hand that was at the end of a long cord attached to the camera.

The loud click of the camera and the bright flash of its light bulb startled Mother Browne and caused her to lean back suddenly against the boulder.

The boulder moved.

At first, there was just an uneasy creaking sound, but then it amplified to an ungodly cracking noise as the boulder tore from the earth and rolled backward, disappearing over the ledge of the bluff.

As fast as his instincts would allow, Kyle lunged for his grandmother and grabbed her arm before she could continue her fall backward. She cried out feebly as he yanked her toward himself and closed his arms around her frail body.

I'm so sorry, Gram," Kyle said. "I didn't mean to hurt you, but everything's all right now."

Margaret rushed to her mother-in-law and stepson and flung her arms around both of them. For the first time in years Kyle didn't pull away from her.

The three of them just stood there, frozen into place as they listened to the earsplitting sound of the boulder crashing against the rocks below. Devin was still standing apart from them. A cloud of rust-colored smoke and debris bellowed up from the mountainside and dusted them all with a reddish residue.

Margaret tried to shield Mother Browne's eyes and mouth, while Kyle held Mother Browne steady. Despite everything, she seemed unaware that they'd all barely escaped with their lives.

"Come on, Gram, let's go back to the car," Kyle said.

As he and Mother Browne walked toward the Oldsmobile he could plainly hear the heated exchange between his father and stepmother.

"How in heaven's name could you allow such a thing to happen, Devin?"

"Hell, she's old. What do you care?"

"But Devin, she's your own mother."

"So what? I'm sick of waiting for her to die. That money my father left is rightfully mine and I intend to have it, one way, or another. I need it."

Kyle paused to let his grandmother rest and used the moment to look back. His stepmother was reaching for his father's shoulders, but his father pushed his stepmother away and slapped her to the ground.

His stepmother lay there, in a heap, and sobbing into the dirt and holding her stomach, crying, "My baby, my baby."

* * *

As the Brownes drove back into Denver, the sky was darkened by storm clouds and a driving rain. West to east, Colfax was littered with stalled out cars and accidents. An old pickup, heading south on Federal Boulevard, hit a pocket of water at a stop sign and nearly sideswiped the Olds.

Eventually, they pulled into their driveway in one piece. Devin got out of the car without a word to anyone. Just as he reached the front door, Walter came out to meet the family with an umbrella, but Devin brushed past Walter nearly knocking him to the ground. Walter quickly recovered and ran to the car to hold the open umbrella over Mother Browne and Kyle as Kyle helped her out of the car.

Walter leaned into the Oldsmobile's open door and spoke to Margaret. "Wait here, Mrs. Browne. I'll be back for you as soon as we get Mother Browne inside."

Margaret nodded but kept her face forward so that it stayed hidden in the darkness.

Walter reached out to take Mother Browne's free arm but Kyle pushed him away. "Keep your hands off my grandmother, nigger," Kyle said, then rushed Mother Browne into the house without the shield of the umbrella.

For a long moment, Walter stood speechless.

Margaret got out of the car and stood beside him. She went to touch his sleeve but drew her hand back just as he turned to look at her. The light escaping from the house shone onto the side of her face. Even in the night and the pouring rain, Walter could see that Margaret's cheek was black and blue.

Their eyes locked in an eternity of words unspoken. Ever so gently, he touched Margaret's shoulder, but a booming thunderbolt rumbled the night and sent them both running into the house.

Chapter Nine

Margaret paced back and forth in front of the parlor window. It seemed to her the postman had been late every day this week. He was late today, as well. For what must have been the hundredth time she moved the curtain panel back for a peek outside.

Still, no postman.

She let the curtain panel go and resumed pacing.

Despite Devin's tormenting her, the first five months of her pregnancy had gone well. Only recently had her hands and feet swelled, and only now was she beginning to walk with a slight waddle.

But Margaret wouldn't have traded places with anyone.

She wanted, and loved, the baby growing inside of her with all her heart. Something she'd been too afraid to do when she was a pregnant, unmarried, seventeen-year-old with a deeply prejudiced father.

Like always, the memory still caused her to feel heartsick. And, sometimes, like now, it also triggered a shortness of breath. For the baby's sake, she forced herself to calm down by caressing her stomach.

"This is May, precious," she said, talking to her unborn child. "Come September, you'll be in my arms, and we can leave this place. I still don't know where we're going, but wherever it is, I promise that it will be peaceful and safe. That's all that will matter. Everything else will come, in time. Somehow."

The thought of having to survive, all on her own, half exhilarated Margaret and half frightened her. She tried to resist the fear, but at times it subjected her to bouts of depression and wishful thinking. Over and over, she would ask herself why she hadn't been able to make Devin care for her, or at least, their baby. Maybe then she would have had a reason to consider staying in the marriage.

But there was no use in trying to fool herself. Despite all of her efforts, Devin hadn't so much as helped her to pick names for the baby.

She had finally given up asking for his input, and had chosen two names on her own. *Iris*, if she had a girl, after her favorite motion picture star. *Jake*, if she had a boy, because her father had once said that's what he would have named a son.

The grandfather clock in the foyer chimed again. It was noon. By requesting the letter she hoped for to be sent to her home she had taken the foolish chance that Devin's daily habit – of being away from the house until dinner – would go unchanged.

Yesterday, though he'd surprised her and come home for lunch. She had offered countless Hail Marys praying that he didn't do the same today.

She was praying even harder that going to the Mother Cabrini Orphanage hadn't been just another dead end in the search for her daughter. *Time…was running out*. But she couldn't go anywhere until she knew, for certain, that her oldest child was all right.

The Mother Superior had promised to find out what she could, but had also warned Margaret not to have unrealistic hopes.

Margaret's deepest concern though, was that she'd already done everything she could think of to find her daughter. If the orphanage couldn't help her, she couldn't imagine what to try next. Not that that was going to stop her.

Nothing, outside of death, would, or could, stop her. Not ever. Not until she found her daughter. However long it took, or however far she had to go, one day she was going to find her.

Again, Margaret stopped pacing and chanced another look out the window. This time the postman was opening the gate. It was all she could do not to run to the front door to greet him. Instead, she forced herself to watch through the curtains until he walked up the porch steps.

As the postman stood in front of the mailbox he was partially out of Margaret's view, but she could still see him as he searched through his leather bag. From the bag he removed a small package wrapped in plain brown paper, a handful of business-sized envelopes, and two magazines, Harper's and Vanity Fair.

In quick order, she heard the mailbox open and close, and then heard the postman's heavy footsteps as he left the porch.

To give him enough time to leave so that he wouldn't see her when she went to the mailbox, Margaret counted, slowly, from one to ten.

Just as she mouthed the number seven, the parlor's quiet was broken by the ringing of the telephone in the foyer.

She stopped counting and held her breath. She could feel her heart thumping wildly as the phone continued to ring.

At last, she heard Walter answer it.

She listened to Walter talk. Whoever had called, they weren't asking for her. She felt a sense of relief. All she wanted to do was get the mail.

She rushed to the front door and outside to the mailbox.

Her hands trembled as she pulled open the mailbox. From it she took the package, the stack of envelopes, and the magazines.

She put the package and the magazines back but sorted anxiously through the envelopes.

Tears of pain and frustration welled in Margaret's eyes. She had been wrong to hope. Not one of the letters was addressed to Mrs. Margaret Browne.

With her heart heavy from disappointment, she kept hold of the envelopes and took the package and the magazines back out of the mailbox, and turned to go inside.

She hadn't heard Walter come to the door and collided with him as she stepped forward.

The package, the envelopes, and the magazines all fell to the ground. What she saw as she looked down at the scattered mail made her believe that her tear-blurred vision was merely playing tricks on her.

There, on the porch floor, poking from under the cover of Vanity Fair, was a palm-sized white envelope, addressed to Margaret in perfect penmanship.

As Walter bent to retrieve the fallen mail Margaret practically pushed him out of the way. "No," she shouted, "let me."

She kneeled down and slipped the small white envelope into her pocket, then gathered the other items, stood, and handed them to Walter. "Please put these on Mr. Browne's desk," she said, avoiding Walter's eyes.

"Yes, ma'am," he replied with the stiff formality he'd lately adopted, then carefully accepted the mail from her hand.

Neither one of them wanted to suffer the possibility of even just their fingertips touching.

"That call was from the Denver police. The local precinct,"

Walter said, seemingly more to break the tension than to give her the news. "Mr. Kyle has been arrested for vandalism. The officer wouldn't go into any more detail than that since Mr. Browne wasn't available. I told him that I was sure Kyle's stepmother would be on her way to the station as soon as possible to take care of the matter. Shall I call a taxi for you?"

Margaret felt perplexed and worried. "Yes," she replied, forgetting to avoid Walter's eyes. "Please."

*   *   *

Margaret stood on the sidewalk in front of the police station and studied the two-story building's entrance as if beyond its doors waited some unimaginable terror. She had never been in a police station and feared that her well-intentioned effort, to secure Kyle's release from custody, might result in doing her stepson more harm than good.

"Hey, Lady," a man's voice in back of Margaret barked, "how much longer ya plan on blocking the bloomin' door? Nobody's got all day."

Margaret stiffened and looked around. A ruddy-faced Denver police officer, with a Colored woman he had firmly grasped by the arm, was leaning in close to Margaret's ear. She felt her face go flush. "Uh, uh, I was just, uh…"

The officer didn't wait to hear Margaret's responce. He just pushed his way past her. "Come on, Lulu," he said to the Colored woman, in what struck Margaret as an oddly familiar tone of voice.

Margaret noted the woman's dress; a red satin flapper sheath, fringed from top to bottom so that it shimmied when she walked. It was similar to one that Gwen brought from Paris. The Colored woman's hair was even styled like Gwen's, cut in a bob and marcelled.

But never had Margaret seen a woman with such a haughty attitude. Not even among the country club members.

No matter how rudely the policeman jerked the woman, or how much she struggled against his hold, the woman managed to keep her head high, and her back and shoulders squared.

As the police officer pushed the station door open and took the woman inside, Margaret got a peek into the station lobby.

She saw another police officer, this one sitting behind a desk that was atop a platform, and a line of ordinary citizens that extended back from the desk.

Just as the station door was about to close in Margaret's face, she pushed the door back open and hurried inside. Immediately, Margaret knew that she had entered a foreign world.

A fist of fear clutched at her chest.

The woman in the red dress was studying Margaret as if trying to remember their knowing each other some long ago time or some far away place.

Embarrassed that such a woman, a Colored woman, would dare to meet eyes with her, Margaret blushed with indignation.

The nerve of the woman, Margaret thought, as she turned on her heels and headed to the police desk. Anyway, she needed to get this matter with Kyle behind her. She headed toward the line of people.

"Psst. Psst," a boy's voice beckoned. "Mrs. B., over here." Margaret stopped in her path.

She looked about but saw no one she knew. Perhaps she was just tired and imagining things. After all, the day had been anything but easy.

Again, she headed toward the desk. The line was the shortest it had been since she'd entered the station. She wasn't going to waste anymore time getting in it.

"Hey, Mrs. B.," the same voice called, "we're over here."

This time, to her amazement, Margaret saw her stepson Kyle, and his friend, Spud.

They were sitting next to each other in chairs obscured by their location in a dark corner. Like the Colored woman, they were handcuffed to the chairs. It was Spud who had called to her. Of course, in his usual disrespectful manner.

A rare flash of anger jolted Margaret's composure.

Hadn't she forbidden Kyle to pal around with Spud? He was an ill-mannered urchin who, apparently, never had to report home. And the way he spoke, and dressed, it was obvious that his background left a great deal to be desired.

Obviously, her warning about Spud had been right. If only Kyle had heeded her fears.

As soon as she and Kyle stepped foot outside of the station the first thing she was going to do was to make Kyle swear that he would stay away from Spud, and all the rest of that unsavory bunch of boys.

Once more, Margaret looked over at the Colored woman. She admired the woman's grace and especially the way she held her head erect and kept her back so straight.

Margaret drew in a breath so deep that her chest lifted. She, herself, was a far cry from being a Colored woman but there was nothing that said she couldn't raise her chin and square her shoulders too. Besides, it was simply good posture.

Oddly, Margaret's improved carriage made her feel a sense of kinship with the Colored woman, and, unexpectedly, a modicum of confidence. In fact, Margaret felt able to meet the police captain head on now, and just wanted to get to his desk. She needed to get Kyle out of this awful place, and to take him home, where he belonged.

She turned back toward the desk. The line of people was gone, but now the police officer at the desk was reading a newspaper.

As Margaret stood silently at the front of the desk, she stared at the front page of the Rocky Mountain News until she gathered the pluck to speak. "Umm, pardon me, officer. I'm here to see about my stepson," she said.

"Yeah, yeah," the captain said without putting down his paper. "Name?" he said, and turned a few of the paper's pages.

"Name?" Margaret implored.

"The kid's name, lady. What's the kid's name?" the officer said, and turned several more pages, still without the courtesy of looking into her face.

"Oh, ah, ah...," Margaret quickly looked at Kyle, then once more over at the Negro woman.

The officer crunched his newspaper closed and stared at Margaret, impatiently waiting for her to answer.

"Kyle. Kyle Browne," she said, finally.

The captain's expression quickly softened, and his face turned a bright red.

"Browne, you say? Not Devin Browne's boy?"

"Yes, that's right. Someone called our home, saying he was here. My husband wasn't in, so I came. I hope that's all right."

"Why, of course it is, Mrs.," the officer said, then leaned forward. "Your boy's probably had a very fine upbringing," he whispered, "but, between you and me, you might not want him hangin' around with the likes of that friend of his."

He nodded slightly in the direction of Spud. "That there's trouble looking for trouble, if you know what I mean?"

"I do indeed, officer," Margaret said, "however, I thank you for the advice. I'm sure my husband will be grateful as well. May I take Kyle home now?"

"Why sure, Mrs., and you can have your husband come back later and see to the small matter of paying for the broken synagogue window, and for the Mexican's peanut cart that was turned over. Witnesses, you know. Your husband is a, uh, a, a lodge brother of mine, which guarantees him to be a trustworthy bloke. I'll send a sergeant right over to uncuff your boy. What about his friend?"

"Well, he is just a boy, officer," Margaret said, glancing over at Spud. "I'm sure Mr. Browne will want to pay his fine too."

The officer nodded in agreement and signaled a nearby sergeant to go and release Kyle...and Spud.

"Humph," someone behind Margaret said, "isn't that just dandy."

Margaret turned to see who it was.

She was stunned to be looking into the face of her husband's mistress. His Colored mistress.

Margaret felt her own face prickle with the heat of anger and embarrassment.

She tried to step by Rowena, but Rowena extended a leg and blocked Margaret's way. Margaret remained calm. Rather than allow herself to be frustrated, she merely attempted to pass by on Rowena's opposite side. This time, though, Rowena stepped fully into Margaret's path and collided with Margaret's pregnant belly.

Margaret stepped back in alarm, instinctively putting her hands to her stomach as a shield. She looked to the officer for help, but new arrivals to his desk blocked Rowena and Margaret from his line of sight. Margaret was left to fend for herself. She felt frightened.

She also felt someone, besides Rowena, looking at her.

Margaret let her eyes dart to the arrested Colored woman, but the sergeant unlocking the woman's handcuffs stepped in between the woman and Margaret, and obstructed their view of each other.

Margaret decided to walk away from Rowena, but Rowena stayed right with her.

"Not so fast, queenie," Rowena said and grabbed Margaret's shoulder.

More exasperated than anything else, Margaret stopped, mid-step, and squarely faced Rowena.

"Take your hand off of me," Margaret said as quietly as possible, then jerked loose of Rowena's grasp as Spud and Kyle approached.

Ignoring Rowena, Margaret spoke to Kyle. "We can leave now. Your father will be down tomorrow to pay the damages. And Spud, I'm sorry, but I'll have to ask you not to come to our house anymore. You boys apparently aren't a good influence on each other, and it would be better if you went your separate ways."

"What?" Kyle protested and stomped his boot into the ground.

"Kyle!" Margaret pleaded, hoping her stepson would notice the Colored woman listening to their every word. "Please don't argue with me, especially not here. We can talk about this later, when we get home. Now, let's go."

Kyle and Spud hurried ahead of Margaret, and brushed past Rowena, causing Rowena to stumble backward slightly.

Margaret realized that now was her opportunity to escape and hurried past Rowena, only Rowena unencumbered by pregnancy, was faster than Margaret, and met up with her again just outside the police station's front door.

Margaret guarded her stomach again. She had to watch helplessly as Spud and Kyle ran across the street and disappeared out of her sight.

Rowena watched too, but laughed. She seemed to be enjoying herself at Margaret's expense.

The Colored woman the policeman had brought in was now standing behind Rowena yet seemed to want no part of Rowena's efforts.

Margaret waited for Rowena to regain her composure then looked Rowena in the eyes.

After a lull of only a second or so, Margaret reached out and slapped Rowena.

The passersby on the sidewalk came to a dead halt and looked on the two women in amazement. Rowena just looked stunned and held her hand to her cheek.

Margaret was equally stunned. Her arms and hands felt numb and her legs were wobbly. It took a squad car screeching to a stop at the curb to snap her back to full awareness.

Margaret realized that she had let her chance to get away. She hurried down the street without even a glance back at Rowena.

＊　＊　＊

It was blocks before Margaret dared to stop to rest.

She felt dizzy and needed to steady herself. She leaned against the wall of a building, then realized that she needed to sit.

She took a deep breath and looked around to get her bearings.

The building was the Orpheum Theater palace. If she went inside she could sit for as long as she needed and get something cool to drink. Thankfully, admission was only ten cents.

She bought a ticket for the matinee screening of Charlie Chaplin's, The Gold Rush, but once in the lobby decided to go to the powder room instead of going in to watch the film. The vanity area of the powder room offered plush sofas.

As she sank into the sofa in the far corner, Margaret remembered the envelope stuffed in her pocket. Had it really been just this morning that she'd put it there?

With a trembling hand she retrieved the envelope and studied it a long moment before opening it.

Finally, it was now, or never. She decided on now, and ripped the letter open.

The letter's message, *Dear Mrs. Browne, I regret to inform you*, might as well have been a dagger lunged into her heart.

She cried out in pain and crumpled the letter in her hand. Her tears continued until her sobs reduced to dry heaves.

After nearly an hour of crying, she had only enough strength to smooth the letter back out, and to read it once more. It still began with, *Dear Mrs. Browne, I regret...*" This time, though, she shredded the letter into confetti, then brushed the bits of paper from her lap.

She felt sick. She had to get air.

She ran out of the powder room, then out of the theater.

She had walked a mile toward home before realizing that she had forgotten her handbag on the powder room sofa. Only it was raining. And late. There would be trouble if she wasn't home before Devin. She had to go on.

The distance couldn't possibly be much farther.

By the time she turned onto her street, Margaret's feet ached and she was nauseated and shivering. It took all the strength she could muster to walk up the driveway to the house. She was within ten steps of the door when she collapsed onto the puddle-riddled gravel.

*　　*　　*

Walter had gone upstairs to check on Mother Browne and to use her room as a lookout.

Margaret should have been back by now, and from Mother Browne's room he could watch for Margaret's return. Before he went back downstairs, he looked out the window again.

Margaret was lying still and crumpled in the driveway.

Walter rushed out of Mother Browne's room, down the stairway, and out the mansion's front door.

As soon as Walter reached Margaret he kneeled and lifted her into his arms, holding her tightly against his chest.

His racing heart told him to run back into the house, but he'd been a medic in the war and knew that her condition was too fragile for him to do anything but walk slowly and gently.

The splatter of down-pouring rain mingled with Walter's tears.

As soon as he brought Margaret inside the house, Walter laid her on the parlor sofa, then went for a cold cloth to put on her forehead. She was moaning and tossing, but her eyes were closed as if she were asleep.

When Walter returned with the cloth, Margaret's eyes were open but they seemed to be looking at something, or someone, far away. Her moans had turned into a plea for help.

"My baby," she cried, "my baby. Please, don't let them take my baby." She clutched at Walter's arms and struggled to get up.

"Shhhh," Walter soothed, "no one is going to take your baby. Your baby's fine. Just try to get some rest."

After awhile Margaret quieted and closed her eyes again.

All that Walter could do was to put a blanket over her and wait. It would be improper for him to sit alone in the room with her, but he was afraid to leave her unwatched.

He chose a chair against the farthest wall and settled into it, hoping that Margaret's husband would get home soon.

An hour later, Walter awoke to Margaret's screams. She was inconsolable and nearly hysterical.

He needed to get her to the hospital, but how? Devin had the car, but worse, because Walter was Colored, he would be stopped at the hospital entrance. Negroes weren't allowed admittance to the city hospital.

Yet, sending her alone in a taxi was also out of the question. And, what if something was wrong with Margaret's baby?

Perhaps that was what she had been trying to tell him.

He had to go for help, now. There wasn't enough time to wait for Devin.

Walter went to the phone book and searched for the listing of Margaret's best friend. Was it unlisted?

Instead of calling, he decided, he'd have to go get Gwen.

Forunately, he'd chauffeured the two women many times, and could find Gwen's estate easily. He would run there.

He had run as fast as his legs would carry him once before. The night Klansmen had tried to run him down. That time it was to save his life.

This time, he would be running to save the woman he loved.

Chapter Ten

Angus O'Shea, Margaret's father, was a constant worry to her. Although he'd never remarried after his wife, Ingrid, had deserted him – leaving behind their children, seven-year-old Margaret, and ten-year-old Frank – Angus had done a good job of raising them until Frank had been stabbed to death in a street brawl when he was fifteen.

From then on, Angus O'Shea might as well have crawled into the grave.

Nevertheless, Margaret knew that her father had made every effort to give her a good Catholic upbringing and to assure that she had what he considered life's essentials.

Above all, he'd wanted Margaret to have respect, and for that reason alone, he had arranged a marriage for her into one of Colorado society's blue blood families, albeit a poor one now. He'd even gone so far as to guarantee his son-in-law a substantial yearly stipend.

But her father's once strapping frame was weakening from age, and his powerful handshake was now just a memory.

It had become Margaret's turn to do for him. For the last two weeks, she'd worked with him afternoons in his dry goods store. It also gave her the longed for chance to try to talk with him about his past.

All of her life, he'd been so secretive about where he'd grown up and the people he'd come from, that it created a craving in her for the answers. He even refused to tell her his age.

Of course, any questions about her mother were treated with an icy dismissal. "Now leave it be, lass," he'd say, "no good can come of it."

It had taken Margaret years of prayer to forgive her father for the years he'd virtually neglected her after her brother's death, but now she utterly revered her father. She thought his slight Irish brogue was charming, and she considered it an honor to have inherited his flaming red hair.

She was especially proud that Angus was one of Denver's most successful and respected businessmen. He was likewise known for his philanthropy. Their church parish, an annex to the city orphanage, and a wing of the veterans' home, stood as testament to his generosity.

He was a particularly easy touch for any old-timer claiming to have served in war. He practically cried into his ale at the mention of the war between the states, or, as it now was called, the Civil War.

Even that old black woman who'd been peering into the store's windows – every day, for weeks now – had received the benefit of Angus's soft heart by his forbidding Margaret to shoo the woman away.

If, in another day or so, the woman still wasn't gone, Margaret was going to have to take matters into her own hands. They simply couldn't afford to have Coloreds loitering outside the store.

Today, though, there were too many customers to worry about extraneous nuisances. Margaret set the basket with her father's lunch behind the counter, tied on an apron, and pitched in to help him and Will, his clerk.

"Why, Mrs. Myers, it's so lovely to see you."

"No, sir, we don't seem to have that size, but I'll be happy to see if we can get it for you."

"Why, thank you. My father opened O'Shea's Dry Goods over thirty years ago. He'll be pleased to know of your compliment. We hope you will come again."

Before Margaret knew it, she had rung up a number of sales and nearly two hours had passed.

"Papa. Why don't you rest a bit, and eat. Will and I can handle things on our own for awhile."

"Not a bad idea, lass," Angus said. "I'll just tend to the gent what come in to pick up the firearms he ordered, then set myself down for a bit. I'll just be in the back getting his merchandise."

Margaret's stomach knotted. She had ecognized MacDuff's tangled mame of blonde hair the moment he'd come into the store, but she'd hoped that he had decided against making any purchases. For an instant, she even wondered if MacDuff was following her. Why had he chosen this store to buy his guns from?

She avoided making eye contact with him, but she knew that he had already seen her. He was standing at the gun counter and rapped the glass so hard that it rattled loudly and caused Margaret to jump with alarm.

"Can I get a little help here?" MacDuff shouted.

A man and a teenage boy examining fishing rods were two feet away from MacDuff. The man grabbed the rod in the boy's hands, stuck both of their rods back in the wooden barrel filled with other rods, and moved the boy along.

"What is it we can do for you, Mr. MacDuff?" Margaret said, looking around nervously.

"Why, Mrs. Browne, I'd no idea you were affiliated with this fine emporium."

"It's my father's store. He went in the back to get your... your..."

"Rifles, Mrs. Browne. Rifles. Can't be too prepared you know."

"I don't know what you're talking about, Mr. MacDuff. At any rate, is there something from this case you want to see?"

MacDuff started to point to something on display, but Angus emerged from the storeroom carrying two long, shallow boxes.

Angus set the boxes on the countertop and opened one.

In it were four new hunting rifles.

Margaret looked at her father, but he was looking at MacDuff who was already examining firearms.

With a grunt of satisfaction, MacDuff lifted one of the rifles from the box, then pressed the butt against the socket of his right shoulder.

Holding the underside of the barrel with his left hand, MacDuff hooked his right forefinger into the trigger, squinted his left eye closed, then fixed his right eye on the sight scope. He pointed the rifle around the store like a hunter in a forest aiming at live game.

First, he settled on two shoppers with their backs to him. Then on a wall shelf with a display of toy soldiers.

Two children, a boy and a girl, each richly dressed but poorly mannered, were orchestrating a duel between two of the soldiers.

An elderly woman, several counters over from the children, looked up from her shopping to see MacDuff pointing the rifle in the children's direction. "Noooooo!" the woman screamed as she dropped a bolt of fabric onto the floor.

With the ferocity of a mother lion the woman lunged toward the children and grabbed each child by the scruff of the collar. The children kicked and bawled as she directed them out of the store.

Exasperated, Margaret stepped into MacDuff's field of view, wrapped her hand around the rifle's barrel, and pulled the rifle downward.

"Mr. MacDuff, you're scaring our customers away, and I don't blame them. You've managed to alarm me as well." Margaret laid both of her hands protectively on her bulging stomach. "Please. Take your merchandise, and go."

MacDuff cocked open the barrel of the rifle, peered intently down the empty shaft, then clicked the barrel closed. "No harm meant, Mrs. Browne. After all, we're on the same side."

Margaret answered him with an icy glare.

MacDuff seemed oblivious, but he did put the rifle back in its box, and the lid back on the box. He slammed his hand down on the top of the box, and then held his hand out to Angus to shake. "If you ask me, old man, it's times like these we white men have to stick together."

Angus weakly clasped MacDuff's open palm. "True, Mr. MacDuff. Most true."

As soon as the handshake ended, MacDuff took possession of his boxes of rifles. He seemed not at all bothered by the weight of the boxes, and walked directly to the door.

With his hand poised to open the door, MacDuff turned back to Angus and Margaret with a last comment.

"By the way, Mrs. Browne, your pap and mine look so much alike, they could be brothers. Now, ain't that a funny thought. If it were so, that'd make you and me cousins, wouldn't it?"

Margaret chose to ignore MacDuff's comment. Before the door closed behind him her attention was back on her father. He looked tired and drained to her. She hoped he would agree to close early tonight.

The store was suddenly empty of customers, but somehow that same Colored woman who kept lurking outside had managed to come inside.

Right then and there, Margaret decided that no matter what her father said, something had to be done about the woman. "Papa, I insist that we…"

Angus interrupted his daughter as if she hadn't spoken. "Oh, lass, I almost forgot. I promised to let Mr. Hwang know the moment I'd finished making the birthday surprise he asked me to make for his Mrs..

Angus reached under the counter and brought up an ornately crafted wooden birdcage. "Oh, Papa, it's so beautiful."

"Would you mind taking it over to him?" Angus asked.

"Of course not," Margaret answered, and hugged him.

Angus put the cage into a Del Monte Peaches box and handed the box to her.

She headed straight to the door with it. "I won't be long."

A few steps shy of the door, Margaret remembered her resolve. She returned to the counter, where Angus had begun logging the day's transactions into a thick ledger.

It took Angus a moment to acknowledge his daughter, but when he did, he closed the book and gave her his full attention.

She leaned close to his ear and whispered, "What about…?" she said, nodding toward the old Colored woman. "Shouldn't we call someone to come get her? The police, or the asylum?"

"She's an old woman, Margaret. What, who, can she hurt?"

"You're probably right, Papa. But she's so odd."

"There's no law against that, lass. Now, stop worrying, and get."

The short trek to Hwang's Laundry was one Margaret had traveled often. So often, and for so long, that the Hwangs, who were first generation Chinese immigrants, treated her like a second daughter. It was an honor she gladly accepted.

Ming, the Hwangs' daughter, and Margaret had become best friends over the years. After a time, they considered themselves to be more like blood sisters, than foreigners, to each other.

Probably not more than a handful of non-Chinese had ever been invited into the Hwangs' living quarters, but the Hwangs had made Margaret feel more at home in their back-of-the store apartment than she'd ever felt in her father's home. Or even now, in her own home.

She waited patiently at the laundry's counter until Mr. Hwang's customer left with her husband's package of freshly washed and pressed white shirts.

As was customary, Margaret bowed to Mr. Hwang. "My father hopes this is to your satisfaction, Mr. Hwang," she said, bowing slightly, then handed him the Del Monte box.

Mr. Hwang returned the bow then accepted the box. "Your honorable father is a great artist, American daughter. His creation will delight my dear wife endlessly."

Mr. Hwang bowed again. "Please thank him for me. Thank you, also, for bringing it to me. Ming will be most sorry that she missed you. She is at the market. Will you care to wait for her?"

"Yes, I would love to wait for Ming, honorable Chinese father. It's been months since I've seen her."

"She misses you as well, my child. Please. Go inside and make yourself comfortable. It's no good for soon-to-be mama to stand all day."

Margaret smiled at Mr. Hwang's acknowledgement of her pregnancy, and bowed once more. After an exchange of several more bows between them, she walked down the narrow corridor leading to the Hwangs's living quarters.

As Margaret went behind the beautiful red silk folding screens that divided the storefront from the apartment, she had the same thoughts, as always. How wonderful it must be to know other parts of the world.

To walk down ancient streets and to smell exotic scents. To taste new foods, and to hear unfamiliar words. To experience worlds upon worlds beyond the only one she'd known since birth. If only she'd had more courage when she was younger, she might have traveled, at least, out of Colorado.

The Hwangs' sitting room furnishings were secondhand, but the walls were decorated with original watercolors of cranes and mountainscapes. The desk set up with Ming's ancient typewriter, where nightly she completed her correspondence school assignments, sat against a wall.

Pushed against another wall was a card table where Ming had spent countless hours teaching Margaret the Chinese game of mahjongg, and where Margaret and Ming had filled out crossword puzzles as a way of helping Ming to learn English.

It was a genealogy chart, which nearly covered a third wall, that most intrigued Margaret about the room.

On the chart, Mr. Hwang had painstakingly accounted for more than two hundred and fifty years of Hwang ancestors.

Margaret couldn't read Chinese characters but she knew that each set of brush strokes named an actual person. The record of so many generations never failed to capture her imagination. What she wouldn't give for Angus to tell her about her own relatives.

She closed her eyes and tried to visualize at least one of her grandmothers, but her efforts were futile.

*   *   *

Angus knew it would be awhile before Margaret returned from the Hwangs, so he told Will to go on home. He could finish the closing duties of straightening and restocking on his own. He just hoped the old Negro woman would leave without him having to tell her to.

She was camped in the chair outside the changing room, slumped to one side of the chair, as if she were sleeping.

Half an hour later, when the clock struck six, she was still there. Angus walked over to her. "Auntie, you have to move along. We're closed."

The old woman didn't answer.

"Listen, old woman," he said, leaning in closer to her, didn't you hear me? It's time for you to go home. We're..."

The old woman put a frail hand on Angus's forearm and squeezed it, causing him to choke back the rest of his statement.

The strength of her grip surprised him. "Brother, it's me. Euphrates!"

Angus looked at the woman like she was crazy. Margaret had been right and he'd been wrong to let the old woman take advantage of his kindness. He yanked his hand from her hold.

"All right, old woman. I don't know what it is you want, but you won't find it here. Happily for you, I'm a peaceable man. You have one more chance to leave before I call the authorities."

The old woman stared up into Angus's face. Tears brimmed from her eyes. She seemed unable to catch her breath.

"Brother," she said, again. "I've prayed and prayed for this day. For just one more glimpse of you before I pass on. Are you so truly lost that you cannot embrace your own sister?"

Angus's patience had been exhausted. How dare this decrepit mammy assault him with such a ridiculous claim? He should have allowed Margaret to have her carted off in a straightjacket.

He forced the woman up with an unsympathetic yank at her arm.

"You're going to regret this mischief, Auntie."

"No, Brother. On our dear mother and pap's graves, I swear, it is you who will regret this moment."

The woman unloosened her arm from his grasp, then placed her hand over the silver locket pinned on the bodice of her dress.

She unpinned the locket and held it out to Angus.

Angus stepped back from the woman, but he was trapped by the display counter behind him.

Undaunted, the woman stepped toward Angus and forced the locket into his hand. "Open it," she insisted, then waited patiently until he did.

Angus began trembling as he worked the clasp that held the two sides of the locket together. He seemed in danger of letting the locket fall from his hold, but eventually he succeeded in opening it.

On one side of the locket was a tintype of a white man whose angular features were an exact likeness of the old woman's...that is, except for her very dark brown skin.

On the opposite side was a tintype of a very dark-skinned Colored woman whose coarse hair, broad nose, and thick lips were a duplicate of Angus's own.

"God rest their souls," the old woman said and crossed herself. "You do recognize our folks, don't you, Angus? And surely, you remember this locket Pap gave Mama? She never took it off, not even when she worked in the fields. I just couldn't stand to bury it with her, though. It was all I had left of them."

The proof of his relationship to the old woman was too much for Angus to bear. He stole a look in the changing room mirror and saw a likeness he'd hidden from for more than sixty years. First one tear rolled onto his cheek, then another. Within seconds it was a torrent of tears.

"What do you want from me, Euphrates?" Angus asked.

With her fingertips, Euphrates tenderly traced the long scar that ran across her twin brother's right cheek.

"Only to love you, dear brother. For whatever time I have left. And to thank you, for saving my life, that awful night so many, many years ago."

Angus was as distraught as an injured child. "But, but, I'm a...I mean, I live as a white man now," he said quietly. "For my daughter's sake, it must remain so."

"I didn't come to hurt you, Angus. Or your daughter. After all, she's my niece. Nevertheless, it has taken most of my life to find you. God willing, I have enough time left for you to find yourself."

* * *

Margaret rushed into the darkened store, frantic because she had lost track of time. Devin would be furious that she had been away from home the entire day, but she had to say good-bye to her father.

Instead of his being in his upstairs apartment, Margaret found Angus still in the store. He was sitting alone in the chair by the changing room, staring into the mirror. He looked to her like a man who had just received his death sentence.

"Papa," she said to him, and gently touched his sleeve.

Angus did not look at her. He seemed lost in his image in the mirror. Go home, lass. It's late," Angus said to his daughter. "You've no business being here now."

Chapter Eleven

J ust shut your trap, kid, and give me a minute," MacDuff said as he turned away from Kyle and pulled a crumpled, hand-drawn map from his overalls' bib pocket.

Maybe he'd gotten the landmark wrong and missed the turn-off, or, gone too many blocks. He doubted it though.

He couldn't read no fifty-cent words, or cipher numbers worth a darn, but his hound-dog sense of direction and memory kept him employed as one of the top delivery truck drivers at the Gates brothers' tire factory.

Now, here it was, the first week of July, exactly six years later, and counting. He knew his way around every square block of Denver. That is, with the exception of Five Points, which had never been a part of his route, anyway.

He'd only agreed to the occasional side jobs to this part of town as a personal favor to Dr. Locke. And, he had found that beauty shop okay that time.

MacDuff flipped the map from front to back, once, twice, then a third time. The paper the map was drawn on was jagged on one side, and long with red lines. The kind of paper that was in business ledgers.

The numbers on the map matched the numbers on the gate post he and Kyle were standing in front of, but this operation looked too big time to be a jig's. Since when did niggers own warehouses and trucking companies?

He spit out a stream of well-chewed tobacco, successfully aiming it at the group of dahlias along the fence.

MacDuff cocked his head toward the fancy-shmancy shingle over the gate. "You able to make out any of the scribble scrabble on the sign?"

"What?" Kyle asked, absently, as he stared across the street at the pretty brown girl seated at a desk visible in the window of an insurance company.

The girl was waving back at him.

MacDuff spit – the spew of his tobacco and saliva splattered onto the toe of Kyle's boot - and slapped Kyle in the back of the head.

"Hey!" Kyle said, rubbing his head, and looking MacDuff up and down.

MacDuff was taking a swig from his flask. He capped it and threw it back onto the seat of the truck through the open driver's side window. "Stop screwin' around. We're here on business. You damn near bad as your ole man."

"My ole man and I ain't... ."

"Forget it, kid," MacDuff interrupted. "Just tell me what it says up on that sign. I can't make out all them loop-de-loops."

"Well," Kyle said, "the top line says, 'D.L. Hudson and Son. The second line, 'Hauling, Storage, and Refurbished Goods.

Bottom line... ."

MacDuff delivered another smack to the back of Kyle's head. "Look! Bottom, top. Top, bottom. Do I care? Just read the friggin' thing."

"Okay. All right," Kyle said, holding up his arms against any further of MacDuff's assaults. "It says, 'Fair rates; hard work; quality merchandise.'"

For a long moment, MacDuff was quiet.

"Humph!" he said, finally. "Niggers somehow get more than two nickels to rub together and suddenly they imaginin' they high and mighty."

He spit again.

This time, Kyle managed to do a double step backward before the juice hit ground.

A second later, a larger truck than their own rumbled up behind them.

They both jumped at least a foot closer to the gate.

The truck, an old pick-up, was weighed down with a full bed of used lumber.

The truck's driver, a muscled Colored youth no older than Kyle, sounded the truck's horn.

Kyle and MacDuff just watched as an older Colored man pulled the gate open, and the truck drove into the vast storage yard beyond the gate.

As the man controlling the gate started to close it, MacDuff jammed the gate open with his foot. "Hurry up, boy," he said to Kyle, indicating for him to go. "I ain't got all day."

The man at the gate remained expressionless, but waited until Kyle and MacDuff were inside the yard to close the gate.

Kyle and MacDuff walked a few feet into the fenced acreage and looked around.

Among the snake-like aisles of old appliances, discarded automobile parts, and the crates filled with who knew what, were Colored men sorting the items into various barrels.

The Colored men looked at Kyle and MacDuff momentarily, but didn't stop working.

A three-story wooden building sat at the back of the property. MacDuff noticed the blinds close in one of the building's upper windows. He headed toward the building and signaled Kyle to follow.

They passed the truck, which had just driven in.

"Hey, boy," MacDuff called to the driver, "this Hudson's place?"

The gate-opener looked across at the truck driver. "Anthony. I think that ofay's talkin' to you."

Anthony's arm and chest muscles bulged as he lifted a stack of lumber onto his shoulder. He barely looked at MacDuff. "If that cracker wants to do business with my dad, he's sure off to a wrong start," he said loud enough for MacDuff to easily overhear.

All of Anthony's co-workers laughed, but still didn't slow their efforts.

MacDuff clenched his fists, and waited for the answer to his question.

He didn't get one.

Kyle watched MacDuff's face turn red.

MacDuff studied each of the Colored men's faces. One by one, he burned them into his memory. He especially wanted to remember Anthony. The smart aleck.

"This might be a junkyard," Anthony said to the others as he watched Kyle and MacDuff go into the building, "but nothing my dad owns depends on one measly dime from a white man. For sure, not one country enough to be using a match stick for a toothpick. And what about that blonde ass bumpkin' with him?

Now, there's a hoot."

* * *

"Wait for me down here," MacDuff said to Kyle, as they climbed the stairs and reached the building's second floor.

Kyle scanned the bales of rags dominating the floor's open space, and decided to sit down on the step he was standing on.

MacDuff continued to the third floor.

There, he found a sea of desks staffed by Colored men and women. Some of the people were typing, and some were talking on phones and filling out forms.

A group of three or four was meeting around a large wall map of the city. MacDuff noted the little flags pinned in various locations on the map.

An attractive, dark-skinned woman walked toward MacDuff.

"Good afternoon, Mr. MacDuff. I'm Miss Forbes, Mr. Hudson's secretary. He asked me to show you to his office."

MacDuff was speechless as the secretary led him down a wide aisle between the desks.

For the most part, the men and women continued working, but one of the younger women had stopped typing and was watching MacDuff as he approached. As he passed by her, he smiled and removed his hat.

She blushed and looked down at her keyboard.

"This way, Mr. MacDuff," Miss Forbes reminded.

The back of MacDuff's ears burned with embarrassment.

In a few more steps, Miss Forbes and MacDuff reached a door with a clouded pane of glass in its upper half.

"Uh, Miss Forbes," MacDuff said to her before she could open the door. "I've a..., lost my glasses. Out of curiosity, would you mind telling me what it says on the door?"

Miss Forbes read the gold imprint on the door's window. "Hudson and Son Moving and Storage. Hudson and Son Real

Estate and Property Management. And, Hudson and Son Domestic Employment Agency."

"Hmm. Thank you," MacDuff said.

Miss Forbes opened the door and waited as MacDuff walked into Dwight Hudson's office. She left the two men alone, but left the door slightly ajar.

"MacDuff," Dwight said, and put down the contract he was reading. "Come in, come in." Dwight rose from his chair and went to greet MacDuff with an extended hand.

MacDuff ignored Dwight's hand, and instead surveyed the office furnishings.

Leather sofa, mahogany desk, crystal lamp, two oil paintings, and a wall of shelves full of leather-bound books.

Okay, MacDuff said to himself.

He'd figured he could get five hundred for the job Hudson had hired him to do, but seeing all this, wasn't no way he was going to let him off for less than a grand.

Dwight closed the door.

"Something the matter, MacDuff?" Dwight asked as he offered MacDuff a Cuban cigar from a silver humidor with the initials DCH engraved on the lid.

"Seems crazy all this has to go," MacDuff said.

MacDuff selected one of the cigars, then held it under his nostrils and inhaled. "Ahhh!"

Dwight lit his guest's cigar, then his own.

"Depends on how you look at things," Dwight said as he blew a puff of the pungent smoke into the air.

Dwight reached in the silver box again, took a fistful of the habanos, and stuffed them in the bib pocket of MacDuff's overalls. Then he dumped the remaining cigars in the wastebasket and threw in the humidor after them.

MacDuff eyed the box. He could've bought a dozen rifles for what that box was probably worth.

"Personally," said Dwight as he climbed a rolling ladder positioned along the floor to ceiling bookshelves, I find sentimentality useless, and boring. A man gets stuck in the past that way."

Dwight scanned the upper rows of the shelves, then pulled down two books. "On to bigger and better is the way I see it. Except for these."

He held a gilt-edged volume of The Collected Works of William Shakespeare, and a tattered, string bound copy of Uncle Tom's Cabin.

"This one," he said as he descended the stairs and wriggled the Shakespeare in his hand, "was my mother's gift to me for graduating high school. 'Son,' she said, 'you read this, cover to cover, and you'll be prepared for anything white folks try to throw at you."

"Man, was I disappointed. It was one thing, never getting Christmas, or birthday presents, but all I'd ever wanted, since I was old enough to know, was my pop's pocket watch. He'd promised it to me the day he died. Only, Mama hocked it to buy this. I've almost incinerated it more times than I can count, yet for some reason, I just can't do it."

Dwight set the Shakespeare volume on his desk blotter.

MacDuff made no comment.

Then Dwight untied the string around the Uncle Tom's book and removed two shot glasses and a small sterling silver flask from its customized pages.

"God rest my mother's sweet soul, MacDuff. Turned out, she was one hundred percent right. As usual. In fact, it was the best advice anyone ever gave me."

Dwight poured whiskey from the flask into the glasses. "Join me for a little thirst quencher?"

MacDuff accepted the offer.

Dwight took another puff on his cigar, and then raised his glass into the air.

"You're a smart man, MacDuff. If you've got a daughter, you're probably the type who doesn't want her marrying my son," Dwight said, and took a healthy swig of his drink, "but any man that gets my money damn sure better be willing to drink my liquor."

Dwight Hudson and MacDuff clinked glasses.

"Saluda," said Dwight, and waited for MacDuff to drink.

"Whatever you say, Hudson," answered MacDuff, and quickly downed the imported, and very illegal, whiskey.

Instead of drinking any more of the whiskey, Dwight poured the contents of his glass into a potted plant. Then, he reached for an envelope tucked inside the middle pages of the Shakespeare book and opened the envelope.

From it he took a map that was drawn on a long sheet of paper that was jagged on one side and had red lines. He handed the paper and envelope to MacDuff.

"This is the down payment…and, a better map. More specific. I don't want any mistakes. Study it, then get rid of it."

MacDuff tucked the envelope in his bib pocket. "I've been at this a long time, Hudson. I don't make mistakes. Ever." MacDuff held out his glass for a refill.

Dwight obliged, pouring the flask's contents into MacDuff's glass until the last of the amber liquid had been emptied. "You're my kind of man, MacDuff. Who knows. Maybe, somewhere, way back, we're even kin." He watched for MacDuff's reaction to this supposition.

MacDuff didn't take the bait. He just tilted his glass toward his mouth and let its residue drip down his throat.

Dwight walked to the window and opened it. "Come here, MacDuff. I want you to see something."

MacDuff moved to the window, yet remained arm's length from Dwight.

"That's my boy," Dwight said, nodding toward Anthony, who was just unloading the last of the lumber, "the whole reason for everything I've built and struggled for. My pride. My joy. Nothing I wouldn't do for him."

Dwight patted MacDuff's bib pocket. "To be specific, this here is so he won't ever have to be just another nigger under the white man's foot. I'm willing to pay whatever it costs to insure that. Get my point."

MacDuff hooked his thumb under his overalls bib, and spit with a dead aim into the wastebasket.

"Like I told you, at our first meeting, Hudson...my work is guaranteed."

Charlene A. Porter

Chapter Twelve

The Palace Hotel's red-velveted and chandeliered lobby, where conversations were usually held to the lowest possible decibels, bustled with the comings and goings of summer travelers.

Just as quickly as a bell hop deposited suitcases to one suite, he was summoned to another for bags waiting to be carried down.

Much of the clientele was made up of seasonal regulars whose entourages included maids and butlers. From political dignitaries to visiting royalty; from old money to new money; if there was to be a visit to Denver, accommodations at the Palace were a must.

The local Ku Klux Klan considered the Palace their headquarters and made regular use of the hotel's meeting and banquet rooms. Tonight, however, the Klan had the Palace's domestic staff up in arms.

Mr. LaFonte, the hotel's manager, rushed to the main ballroom and pulled the Denver KKK's Grand Nighthawk, its sergeant-at-arms, aside.

"Monsieur MacDuff, pleez. This beautiful establishment ez one of the finest in the world. I insist that you people not stand on the furniture. We can send out the broken end table for repair, however, I fear the King Louis divan is a complete loss."

MacDuff lifted the pixiesh man by his lapels, and pinned him against one of the lobby's onyx pillars.

"Listen, bub, by my count, the Klavern has stuffed your pockets with enough dough to pay for fifty of them Louis whatever you call 'ems. Seems to me, you ought a be showin' us a little more hoss-pitality."

Mr. LaFonte's face turned blue as the heavily starched collar of his white shirt dug into his throat.

MacDuff shoved him another foot higher and watched him squirm for air. "After all, you wouldn't wanna offend Mayor Stapleton, now would ja?"

"Ugh, ugh," Mr. LaFonte croaked. "I think this has all been, ugh, a mis-, ugh, under-, ugh standing."

"That's exactly how I see it, LaFonte," MacDuff said. "I knew we could see eye-to-eye." He released his hold on Mr. LaFonte's jacket and let him crumple to the floor. He snickered at Mr. LaFonte's efforts to untangle himself, and then abruptly turned his attention to Kyle and Spud.

"Boys, this shindig's about to get underway for real. Better get on upstairs to your stations."

Spud and Kyle looked at each other like they'd just won brand new Red Flyer Schwinn bicycles. This was the moment they'd been preparing for ever since last month, when MacDuff had deputized them into the Klavern's security detail for special events.

Inductions such as tonight's Klanvocation were second in importance only to cross burning rallies.

Experienced Klexters weeded out spies who tried to enter a ceremony, usually with lethal results for the trespassers, but

Spud's and Kyle's duties were equally important, especially their assignment tonight: to safeguard the Klavern's higher ups.

"Man," Spud said, "I didn't think this night was ever gonna come."

"Tell me about it," Kyle shot back. "And wait'll my old man sees me. Bet he won't be so fast to plunk me upside my head now."

"He might not, but I will," Spud said playfully, and boxed Kyle's ear.

"Boy!" Kyle said, holding a hand to the pain, "Cut it out. I'm tired of your crap too."

As usual, Spud ignored Kyle. Instead of a reply, he issued a challenge. "Last one to the top of the stairs is a nigger lover," he said, and took off running up the plushly carpeted stairway.

"Ain't gonna be me," Kyle said, and followed immediately on Spud's heels.

There were eight flights to go up, but youth was on their side. By the third landing they were neck and neck, but on the stretch of floor between the sixth and seventh landings they nearly mowed down a doddering old man and his young nurse. Kyle took a moment to apologize to them, and to make sure neither one of them was hurt, but that gave Spud the winning edge.

By the time Kyle reached the eighth floor landing, Spud was already there, sprawled in a chair, trying to catch his breath. "Better, huh, watch, huh, out, man, huh," Spud panted. "Word's gonna, huh, get out, huh, you a nigger, huh, lover."

"Shut up, Spud. Some things ain't funny. Like I've said, I've had enough of your stupid jerkin' off."

Spud cut Kyle a sideways glance and burst into laughter.

Kyle just waved him off and went to round up the other boys that had been brought in to help him and Spud.

They had been sneaked into the hotel through the kitchen's back door, and had kept out of sight by putting on waiters' uniforms and riding up to the eighth floor in the service elevator.

Each one had been paid with a pop bottle full of cheap bootleg whiskey, so Kyle hoped they weren't all drunk and passed out in the vacant room he'd found to hide them in.

By the time Spud joined Kyle on the ballroom's balcony, which Kyle had selected as the best vantage point from which to see MacDuff's signals to them, Kyle had already assigned the other boys to various posts. Some would monitor exit doors and the hallways. Some would stay behind and in front of the stage that had been built in the ballroom earlier that afternoon. All the rest would mingle among the crowd of recruits on the ballroom floor and keep their ears and eyes open for any hints of trouble.

Over the course of the next hour, more than four hundred Klan enlistees entered the ballroom. As they milled around, waiting for the swearing-in to get underway, Kyle studied them. For some reason, they brought to his mind the stockyard animals herded into pens, just before slaughter.

After awhile, the air inside the ballroom was tense with anticipation, but the stage remained dark. Only the red, white, and blue bunting that decorated the stage scaffolding, and the barely visible chairs across the center of the stage, a throne-like one, flanked by six others – three to the left, and three to the right – taken from around the hotel, gave any indication of an impending event.

The recruits had begun to gripe, but then, suddenly, a hush came over the ballroom.

Two robed and hooded Klansmen, each holding a burning torch, had stepped onto the stage, and now stood sentry at the front corners of the stage. A minute later, six more Klarogos walked up the stairs to the stage. They proceeded to line the back of the stage.

The presence of the eight torch bearers created an ominous stir, but the start of a low drum roll caused the hair on the back of Kyle's neck to stand.

As the volume of the drum roll increased ever so slightly, Colorado's three Grand Titans, each of whom ruled over his own Province, came onto the stage and stood in front of the chairs to the left of the throne.

Next, the local Kludd came up. He was not a chaplain by virtue of any religious ordination, yet he was as esteemed as any other Klan officer. He stood in front of the chair to the far right of the throne.

After that, the drumming became louder.

MacDuff, Denver's newly appointed Klaliff, came on stage and stood in front of the chair that was two chairs to the right of the throne. To all but the innermost circle, that MacDuff was now a vice-president was a complete surprise. For Spud and Kyle keeping the secret had been a test of their loyalty to MacDuff.

The next increase in the volume of the drumming was expected, but not the addition of the flutes. The crowd murmured approval.

Devin, the newly appointed Exalted Cyclops, was on his way up to the stage stairway.

In comparison to the response MacDuff received, there was almost no surprise that Devin was the Klavern's new chief officer. After all, he had recruited nearly half of the chapter's current membership, as well as a goodly number of tonight's inductees. Devin stood in front of the remaining chair, the one just to the right of the throne.

Then, the drumming stopped.

The flutists continued playing, but only softly as a contingency of helpers removed the undecorated stairway, and put in its place one festooned with red, white, and blue banners.

A brass band entered the ballroom to the tune of "Dixie," and caught every man in the audience completely off guard. This time they outright cheered. As Colorado's Grand Dragon, Dr. John Galen Locke, entered the ballroom and made his way onto the stage, it might have seemed to some that it was the second coming.

He went directly to the throne and sat. The recruits hip-hip-hoorayed their illustrious realm leader as they might President Coolidge.

After the audience's prolonged ovation, those to the left and to the right of Dr. Locke, sat too. Finally, with Dr. Locke's ever so slight nod to Devin, the induction ceremony was under way.

Spud and Kyle were mesmerized. They watched intently as Devin, with a nod imitative of Dr. Locke's, then signaled MacDuff.

MacDuff responded by standing, stepping forward, and rigidly holding out his arms chest high, then clasping his arms over his heart.

At this, two flag bearers entered the ballroom in lock-step. One man carried the Confederate Stars and Bars, the other man, Old Glory. They brought both flags onto the stage and posted them in the stands at the left and right front corners of the stage, saluted Dr. Locke and his cabinet, then about-faced, and left the stage.

MacDuff, who was still standing, turned to Dr. Locke, and fell on bended knee.

"Your excellency, the sacred altar of the Klan is prepared. The fiery cross illumes the Klavern."

Dr. Locke was silent, but Devin spoke. "Brother, why the fiery cross?"

"Brother," MacDuff answered, turning toward Devin, "it is the emblem of that sincere unselfish devotedness of all

Klansmen to the sacred purpose and principles we have espoused."

MacDuff bowed his head to Dr. Locke, then returned to his chair.

Next, Devin stood and walked close to the edge of the stage. "My terrors and Klansmen," he said to the audience, "what means the fiery cross?"

All four hundred plus recruits recited from memory. "We serve and sacrifice for right," their voices rang out.

Devin pulled a Kloran from a hidden pocket in his robe and opened it to pages book marked with a red ribbon. He didn't so much read from the book as hold it as a sort of bible.

"Klansmen, all," he said, "to avoid any misunderstanding, and as evidence that The Knights of the Ku Klux Klan do not seek to impose unjustly the requirements of this order upon anyone, we require as an absolute necessity your affirmative answer to each of the following questions with an empathic 'Yes!'."

He made eye contact with random members of the audience, and then continued. "Is the motive prompting your ambition to be a Klansman serious and unselfish?"

"Yes!" the men answered vigorously.

"Are you a native-born, white, Gentile, American citizen?"

"Yes!" they replied.

"Are you absolutely opposed to and free of any allegiance of any nature to any cause, government, people, sect, or ruler that is foreign to the United States of America?"

"Yes!"

"Do you believe in the tenets of the Christian religion?"

"Yes!"

"Do you esteem the United States of America and its

institutions above any other government, civil, political, or ecclesiastical, in the whole world?"

"Yes!"

"Will you, without mental reservation, take a solemn oath to defend, preserve, and enforce the same?"

"Yes!"

"Do you believe in clannishness and will you faithfully practice the same towards Klansmen?"

"Yes!"

"Do you believe in and will you faithfully strive for the eternal maintenance of white supremacy?"

"Yes!"

"Will you faithfully obey our constitution and laws, and conform willingly to all our usages, requirements, and regulations?"

"Yes!"

"Excellent!" Devin said. "Just one more thing. Who will answer this last question for one and for all?"

"I will," Kyle yelled from the balcony.

Every head turned his way.

Devin was obviously displeased at being upstaged by his own son. "Very well, young man. Then tell me, what if one of your party should prove himself a traitor?"

Kyle answered without hesitation. "He would be immediately banished in disgrace from the invisible empire without fear, or favor. Conscience would torment him, remorse would repeatedly revile him, and direful things would befall him."

Devin locked eyes with his son, and asked, "Every one of your brothers in oath knows and is certain of this?"

Kyle scanned the audience for averted eyes and shifting feet. Mentally, he catalogued a tall, redhead boy, and two senior men.

"Yes. All this they now know and are certain of. They have heard, and will assuredly take heed."

"So be it," Devin hailed. "A Klansman always speaketh the truth. A lying scoundrel may wrap his disgraceful frame within the sacred folds of a Klansman's robe and deceive the very elect, nevertheless, only a true Klansman possesses the Klansman's heart and soul."

Devin returned to his seat as MacDuff accepted a scroll from Dr. Locke.

MacDuff then walked to the edge of the stage and unfurled the scroll, and read from it to the more than four hundred newly sworn in Klansmen.

"Sirs, we congratulate you on your manly decision to forsake the world of selfishness and fraternal alienation and instead, to emigrate to the delectable bounds of the invisible empire and become loyal citizens of the same.

"The prime purpose of this great order is to develop character; to practice clannishness; to protect the home and the chastity of womanhood; and to exemplify a pure patriotism toward our glorious home land.

"You must unflinchingly conform to our requirements, regulations, and usages in every detail and prove yourselves worthy to have and to hold the honors we bestow. Don't deceive yourselves. You cannot deceive us. Moreover, we will not be mocked.

"Above all, understand that mortal man cannot assume a more binding oath; character and courage alone will enable you to keep it.

"Always remember as well...to keep this oath means happiness and life. To violate it means disgrace, dishonor... and, death. May honor, happiness, and life, be yours, evermore, our beloved brothers of the robe."

The men in the audience whooped with joy.

"Man," Spud said to Kyle, "this is one hell of a night."

"Hell, is right," Kyle said under his breath.

*   *   *

An hour later, half of the men in the ballroom audience were stranded in the slow moving lines in front of two sales tables.

One table held Klan robes. The other table, a variety of hoods.

Two veteran Klansmen operated the cash registers. They were ringing up purchases as fast as they could collect the money.

Some of the men waiting in the lines were becoming impatient. Several began to push and shove. A Klexter had to be called over to help dampen flared tempers.

The men who had already bought their new costumes were guided toward another section of the ballroom where two more tables had been set up with Klan paraphernalia to buy. One table offered a choice of sashes and emblems; the other, a selection of various sized Confederate flags and recent issues of the locally published *Kingdom Kall* newspaper.

Also available on the tables were recruitment pamphlets for the inductees to take to their friends and family members.

Dr. Locke had finally signed off on Devin's campaign to hold a cross burning on the nearby city of Golden's Table Mountain. Only Devin wanted the event to be more than just a rally. He intended for it to be an end-of-summer spectacle. Something the members would talk about through the entire winter and be anxious to top the following summer.

To achieve such results, he needed the caravan that would drive the twenty-five miles from Denver to Golden to be made up of hundreds and hundreds of Klan families. Better yet, thousands and thousands.

If tonight was any indication, Devin's plan was well on its way to succeeding.

MacDuff had his own ideas. He wasn't about to let Devin Browne, or anyone else, claim any of the glory he'd been working so long, and hard, to realize.

The hubbub among the new inductees suggested only that the Klan rank and file were ready to go wherever and whenever called.

It was more a matter of who called them first.

A swell of soprano voices in the adjoining banquet room suddenly caught the attention of the men in the ballroom. The men hushed. Many of them had wives, daughters and mothers and sisters among the women next door, the Klanswomen of Kolorado.

A bespectacled banker type who was trying on his robe and hood, snatched off his hood and held it to his heart, like he would a hat in a show of respect. He spoke just above a whisper to the rugged cowboy-looking gent standing next to him. "My wife, Sarah, and our two girls, Elizabeth and Ellen, practiced that song around the piano for a whole week. They never let on that the women's auxiliary could sound that good."

The women's singing was indeed clear and strong. Many of the transactions in the ballroom ceased as more and more men listened.

Mine eyes have seen the glory of the coming of the Lord; He is trampling out the vintage where the grapes of wrath are stored; He hath loosed the fateful lightening of His terrible swift sword, His truth is marching on.

The women's voices grew louder.

Glory! Glory! Hallelujah! Glory! Glory! Hallelujah! Glory! glory! Hallelujah! His truth is marching on.

Now, all of the men paid rapt attention.

I have seen Him in the watch fires of a hundred circling camps; They have built Him an altar in the evening dews and damps; I can read His righteous sentence by the dim and flaring lamps, His day is marching on.

Again, the volume of the women's voices escalated.

Glory! glory! Hallelujah! Glory! glory! Hallelujah! Glory! glory! Hallelujah! His truth is marching on.

"Whad' ya say?" Dr. Locke bellowed.

The women's final chorus of the "Battle Hymn of the Republic" nearly drowned out Devin's attempt to reply.

He has sounded forth the trumpet that shall never call retreat.

"I said…we need to finalize the plans for the cross burning on Table Mountain."

He is sifting out the hearts of men before His judgment seat.

"Sounds like a good idea," Dr. Locke yelled back. "I'll talk it over with MacDuff."

Devin cursed underneath his breath, while the women's voices lifted to a crescendo.

Oh, be swift, my soul, to answer Him, be jubilant, my feet. Our God is marching on. Glory! glory! Hallelujah! Glory! glory! Hallelujah! Glory! glory! Hallelujah!

The women finished their anthem as if the last words – sung slowly and deliberately – were the most important words they would ever utter.

His truth is marching on.

Their refrain seemed to hang in the air.

Devin's attention, though, was still on Dr. Locke and MacDuff as he watched MacDuff whisper into Dr. Locke's ear.

On the ballroom floor the banker and the cowboy were engaged in a heated exchange.

"Dab blain women got no business in men's affairs. What are you, a pantywaist?" the cowboy said.

The banker raised his fists and egged the cowboy on. "Don't you dare insult my women folk. They could probably think circles around you. Blindfolded," the banker retorted.

The cowboy threw a punch square at the banker's nose.

The banker's glasses flew off his face and landed under the boots of another man.

Someone else spun the cowboy around and delivered a mean set of knuckles to his jaw.

Within a few seconds, a whole ring of men were in fisticuffs with each other.

Dr. Locke signaled the Klexters to get in there and break it up. He motioned for Devin to go too.

Devin hesitated, but saw MacDuff jump off the stage onto the ballroom floor ahead of him, and followed suit. He quickly found himself in the midst of a boxing free-for-all.

The banker knocked Devin unconscious with a wild right hook.

He still hadn't come around by the time the hotel doctor arrived. "It doesn't look good," the doctor warned. "Someone better hurry next door and get his wife."

*　　*　　*

Margaret knelt beside her husband, and using her shawl, gently brushed the dried blood from Devin's face. As two Klexters were about to lift Devin on a stretcher, she noticed Devin trying to say something.

"Wait," she told the men, and leaned over Devin so that her ear was close to his mouth.

His words were barely audible to her.

"'Mountain?'" Margaret asked, and looked at Devin in hopes of some clue as to what he was trying to tell her.

The hotel doctor grasped her shoulders and drew her back.

"I'm sorry, Mrs. Browne. We must get your husband to the hospital right away. I'll have someone drive you there."

As the stretcher was lifted and Devin carried away, he continued mumbling over and over, "Mountain. Mountain. Moun...."

Suddenly, Margaret thought she understood. For the past two months, planning the rally and cross burning on Golden's Table Mountain had been Devin's singular obsession.

It was his best chance to completely win Dr. Locke's favor. If MacDuff took over, Devin would lose out on everything.

"I'm not going to the hospital," Margaret announced. "I have to meet with Dr. Locke."

"Pardon me?" the doctor said and snapped his black bag shut.

"My husband needs me to... Oh, never mind. I'll just get there, to the hospital, as soon as possible. Thank you, for your help."

"Of course, you do understand, Mrs. Browne, that your husband has a severe concussion? There may be problems, complications that we cannot detect here."

"I was a volunteer nurse, during the war. I do indeed realize that my husband's injury is serious. I'm just doing what he asked of me. Now, please hurry and get him to the hospital. I'll be along as soon as possible."

"Mrs. Browne, may I say that you are a remarkable woman. I'll be sure your husband receives the best of care."

"I have every confidence that you will, doctor."

Devin and Margaret's eyes met a last time as he was carried out of the ballroom.

She sighed heavily. "And I'll do my best, as well."

*   *   *

Watching all this made Kyle want to puke. If Margaret had seen him up in the balcony, she had not let on.

Spud, meanwhile, had edged away from Kyle and was studying MacDuff's every move.

Chapter Thirteen

Saturdays were usually O'Shea's Dry Goods' peak business day. This early July afternoon, however, most of the streets of Denver were deserted, and thus many city businesses, too. A county-wide tornado alert was in effect for the entire day. Reports were that funnels had been sighted as close in as Littleton.

Also, a blustery morning rainstorm had caused extensive damage to trees and property, while the second half of the day had brought intermittent bullet-strength hailstones. Anyone with any sense had stayed safe and sound at home if possible.

Under the circumstances, Angus O'Shea planned to close early. He just hoped that Margaret wasn't on her way. He'd tried to call his daughter to tell her not to come to the store, but the raging weather had downed numerous utility and telephone lines. The radio announcers had repeatedly cautioned everyone to try to stay wherever they were, but Margaret always had been too much like him. Obstinate. She never believed warnings of danger were meant for her.

At just a little before four o'clock, she dashed into the store windblown and nearly drenched. "Hi, Papa. I brought you supper," she called to Angus as she removed her slicker.

Angus wanted to scold his daughter. Why, he wondered, hadn't his no good son-in-law forbidden her to go out in all this, especially since she was so far along in her pregnancy.

Damn him.

Before Angus could reply to Margaret, a young Colored woman, with a small Colored boy in tow, and a Colored infant in her arms, came into the store as well.

Unlike Margaret, who was already behind the counter, the woman halted just inside the door and looked about nervously.

Angus walked toward the woman but he stopped midway and waited for her to explain herself. Even on a day with so few sales he didn't want Negroes to get wrongheaded ideas about his policies. Like at any other department store in town, they were supposed to go around to the back. He had tolerated the old woman who came in from time to time, but that was because he had chosen to ignore her in the high hope she would eventually just go away. He crossed himself and thanked his lucky shamrocks he hadn't seen her lately.

The young woman pulled the little boy holding her hand closer to her side. "My son has a fever," she said to Angus. "I was hoping we could come in here until it cleared a little outside. We just missed the trolley. I don't think another one is due for half hour, or so."

Angus had both of his arms extended with his palms facing out and up in the universal gesture for "stop," but just as he started to send the woman on her way, Margaret stepped in front of her father and interrupted him.

"Of course, you're welcome to come in," Margaret said, and reached for the little boy's free hand. "Sit and rest yourselves. There's no hurry."

Margaret sat the little boy on one of the two chairs next to the dressing rooms, and kneeled down to unbutton his jacket. The little boy sneezed.

"God bless you," Margaret said to him.

"Thank you," he replied quickly.

The woman, and the baby she was holding, settled nervously into the chair, and Margaret and Angus went back to the counter.

"Papa," Margaret said, just above a whisper, "I think we ought to do something to help them. That woman doesn't have an umbrella, poor thing, and the little boy's fever worries me. I touched his forehead and he's burning up. He needs to get home as soon as possible."

"Lass, you'd help the entire wide world if it was up to you. I think she'll be just fine on her own."

"But, Papa, what if I was her? And had your grandchild with me?" Margaret asked, and put her father's hand to her pregnant belly. "Wouldn't you want someone to aid us?"

Angus sighed deeply. "All right, lass. We'll walk with them to the trolley, but that's as far as we go. Just know it's against my better judgment."

"Thank you, Papa," Margaret said, and stood on her tiptoes to kiss her father on his ruddy cheek.

* * *

Clang! Clang! The Downing Street Trolley screeched to a stop, and its doors whooshed open.

The Colored woman turned to Margaret, took her infant daughter from Margaret's arms into one of her own, and lifted her son by his arm onto the trolley's step, then climbed up after him, leaving Margaret and Angus standing on the sidewalk.

"Wait!" Margaret called to both the woman and the trolley driver as the driver reached for the lever to close the trolley door.

"Papa," Margaret said, and looked up at her father pleadingly. "We can't let them ride alone. What if something happens? The little boy really is very sick."

The trolley driver pitched in his two cents. "You folks coming, or not? I got a schedule to keep."

Angus said nothing, but his look of resignation told Margaret that she'd won him over. They followed the woman onto the trolley and Angus dropped the coins for all of their fares into the glass box.

As the woman tried to guide her son down the trolley aisle he wanted to stop and watch the coins trickle down the chute. "Ooo," he said at the musical sound the coins made on their journey to the bottom of the box.

Margaret and Angus waited patiently for his fascination to subside, but his mother cut short his observation and led him past all the empty seats in the front of the trolley to a seat nearer the back of the car.

Margaret and Angus chose the seats directly across the aisle from the boy and his mother.

The trolley had only one other rider, an innocent-faced young man who reminded Margaret of her step-son, Kyle. She couldn't help wondering if this young man had also been infected by the Klan's hate campaign. It sickened her all over again to think of how involved her own husband was in such evil.

Margaret offered a silent prayer of protection for the young man, then turned to look out her window.

The storm had subsided, for the most part, but the sky was still gray with clouds. Margaret wished that it wasn't so overcast so that she could see every detail of the neighborhoods the trolley was passing through, for, in all her thirty years, this was the first time she had ever been north of Seventeenth Street, or east of City Park.

Angus just sat rigidly, and mum, and stared straight ahead.

The little boy put his head in his mother's lap and went to sleep, while his mother cooed at the now awake baby.

"I never asked you their names," Margaret said, looking past her father and across the aisle at the woman.

"Oh. They're named after my mother's parents," the woman said and caressed her son's coarse hair, "But I always thought the names were too old-fashioned. I shortened his to Gus, from Angus, and the baby's to Lia, from Delia."

Margaret couldn't help but notice that Angus's face seemed to drain of blood at hearing the woman's reply. And…that he and the little boy had the same first name.

"How adorable," Margaret said. "I wish I could do the same." She looked at Angus but he refused her gaze. "I mean," she continued, "name my baby after one of his, or her, grand-parents."

Angus seemed to choke.

Margaret grasped her father's arm and peered into his face. "Papa, what's wrong?"

It seemed a long while before Angus finally answered.

"Nothing, lass. At least, nothing you need vex yourself about. It's just best that we return home as soon as possible."

"Of course, Papa. It can't be much farther now."

The Colored woman had no choice but to overhear Margaret and Angus's conversation, and offered a solution. "Please, don't worry about us. We'll be fine. We just have to go to Thirtieth Avenue. You know, in Five Points. We get off at Welton and only have to walk a couple of blocks. If you get off now, the trolley ahead of this one should just be turning around, and you can catch it to go back. You've been more than kind to see us this far."

"Don't be silly," Margaret said. "It wouldn't be right if we didn't take you to your door. Besides, I'll feel better knowing we did the right thing for Gus. Papa and I will be able to get back okay."

Clang! Clang! The trolley came to a stop and a young man, who had been on when they boarded, disembarked.

The rest of the way, Margaret, Angus, the woman, the boy, and the baby, all rode in silence.

Margaret tried to recall what she'd heard about Five Points. She knew that Walter went there on his days off, but their conversations dealt strictly with his duties as the family butler. Otherwise, all she knew of Five Points was something she'd heard at a debutante tea.

"My dear, Five Points is like a quaint little village," a large woman who had had on a ridiculous-looking hat with great long feathers sticking out of it, had said to her. "And, I'll tell you how I know. One of the times I needed my girl to work on her day off, I had to drive to her house to tell her because she didn't have a telephone. Well, I tell you, I never, in all my life, experienced more uppityness. It was a Sunday, and them niggras were promenading up and down Welton dressed like they'd just stepped out of Neusteters. Or, Gano Downs. I mean, really!"

Margaret laughed, not at the memory of the comment, but at the memory of the woman's ridiculous hat.

*   *   *

How odd, Margaret thought, as she, her father, and the Colored woman with her little son and infant daughter, stepped from the trolley. Five points looked just like any other neighborhood cared about by its residents.

As they walked, they passed a barber shop, a florist, a hotel, a clothing store, an insurance agency, a Rexall drugstore, a soda fountain and a grocery.

Odder still, Margaret realized, was that her father walked like he knew where he was going.

He had never mentioned anything about Five Points.

A man they passed seemed as though he were about to speak to Angus, but Angus remained stone-faced, and the man went by without a word. Margaret thought she could sense the man staring at them as they walked on.

A similar experience happened a block later, when a woman exiting a beauty shop acted for a moment as if she recognized Angus, but the woman quickly apologized for her error, and walked ahead.

Their journey along the next block was uneventful, and at the corner, the woman had them turn onto a street lined with modest, but well-kept, brick homes.

Although dusk was turning into evening, Margaret could see that someone in one of the houses was peeking at them from behind a lace curtain.

Apparently it was a great a curiosity for an elderly white man, a white woman, and a Colored woman with her children, to be seen together, she wondered.

About midway in the block, the Colored woman led them up the walkway of a pleasant little house with a porch bordered by bushes of red roses in full bloom. "This is my mother-in-law's house," the woman explained. "My husband and I are living with her while he works on the railroad. Sometimes, he has to be gone for a week, or more, but he makes twice what he could in a factory. Especially with tips and all."

When they reached the front door, the woman handed Margaret the baby, then searched her pocketbook for her keys. A handsome brown-skinned man opened the door before she could find them and pulled the woman into his embrace.

"Sugarpie," the woman hollered. "You're home!"

* * *

The woman, whose name Margaret finally learned was Betty Jo, invited Margaret and Angus in and introduced them to her husband, Arnold, and her mother-in-law, Mrs. Johnson, who was a war widow.

Angus seemed anxious to leave, but Margaret felt exactly the opposite.

Almost at once, Margaret realized what she had been missing her entire life. What these people had. Family and a real home; people who really loved and mattered to each other, and a place to live infused with that love.

These people, she realized, didn't call themselves family just because they had the same last name, or, because they went in and out of the same doors every day. And their house was far more than just a place to eat and sleep. No, these people were an honest-to-goodness family because they truly cared about each other, and their home was where they were nurtured and shared that love, a place where they'd be deeply missed if something prevented them from being there.

Even with the walls painted pale yellow, the living room was too small for the overstuffed sofa and chairs, which looked like they might have had a first existence in a posh estate, but it was tidy and decorated with taste. The aroma of pot roast and fresh baked biscuits wafted in from the kitchen.

"I hope you're staying for dinner," Mrs. Johnson said. "I knew I cooked extra for some reason. Please just excuse me a minute while I go see how everything is doing."

Gus pulled loose from Margaret's hand and followed his grandmother through the adjoining dining room, and into the kitchen. Margaret wished, with all of her being, that she could follow after them.

Arnold offered Angus and Margaret seats while Betty Jo went upstairs to put Lia down.

At first, Angus and Arnold engaged in little more than small talk, but in no time they were swapping stories about cities they'd both been to.

Arnold, on his routes as a dining car waiter.

Angus during his days as a teamster.

Margaret, meanwhile, made herself at home and studied the collections of framed photographs.

Those atop the fireplace mantel.

Those atop the player piano.

Those on the wall above the dining room sideboard, which featured a large, gilt-framed, sepia photograph of a strikingly good looking Negro man in an army uniform.

Betty Jo came back downstairs and walked over to Margaret, who was in the dining room staring at the picture of the soldier.

"My father-in-law," Betty Jo said, indicating the man in the picture. "He was a captain in the army's 815th, all Negro, division. He died on the battlefield, in France. My husband still has every one of the hundreds of Parisian newspapers and magazines his father sent him, stored up in the attic. I keep telling him they're more fire hazard now than anything, only he still won't throw them out. He swears he's going to use them one day to teach himself French."

Margaret noticed a hint of sorrow on Betty Jo's face and quickly tried to change the subject. "Your mother-in-law never remarried?"

"Nope," Betty Jo answered. "But I think having her sister here really helped. They bought this house together with both their savings. Aunt Euphie's health has been declining lately. When she comes downstairs for dinner you'll see that she's really the strong one."

"Were they born in Denver?" Margaret asked.

Betty Jo shook her head no. "Virginia. They worked their way west as cooks for a traveling vaudeville troupe. Got to Denver, and decided to stay."

"Betty Jo, child," said someone coming down the stairs, "now what tales are you telling about me and Baby Sister?"

Margaret had never heard such a loving voice. She quickly turned to see who it belonged to and immediately recognized the old Colored woman that had been loitering in her father's store.

Then, she saw her father's face go ashen and rushed to where he was sitting. "Papa? Are you all right?"

"We have to leave, lass. Now. And don't argue with me."

"But Mrs. Johnson is expecting us to stay for dinner."

"I said, not to ague with me. We have to leave, Now!"

Arnold looked perplexed. "Betty Jo, call Mama from the kitchen. I think Mr. O'Shea might be ill."

"No, he's not ailing any," Aunt Euphie declared as she worked her way slowly to the bottom of the steps. "Are you, Brother?"

Margaret couldn't understand why the air in the house had suddenly seemed thick and hazy.

What was this woman talking about? And how did she have the audacity to call a white man, especially one she didn't know, brother?

Angus didn't reply. Nor move.

Margaret didn't understand. Maybe Devin's friends were right. Maybe the niggras were getting beside themselves. Then, again, perhaps this poor old woman was just dotty.

Margaret turned to Betty Jo and Mrs. Johnson in hope of receiving a rational explanation. Little Gus was standing between them.

Not wanting Gus to hear her question, Margaret whispered to the two women, "Is she touched?"

Betty Jo and Mrs. Johnson, both, just as perplexed, could only shake their heads. Betty Jo seemed to want to speak, then just hunched her shoulders, instead.

What was going on here?

Angus was still sitting in the same chair with his elbows gored into his knees and his head buried between his hands.

The sunlight blocked by the stairway banister laid an image of dark and light stripes across his back.

Aunt Euphie went to him and put her hand on his shoulder. "It's all right, Brother. We're your family."

Angus began to sob.

Still not looking up, Angus reached for his sister's hand. Decades of loss, loneliness, and grief poured out through his flood of tears.

He didn't yet realize that his new found family was anxious to embrace him.

Finally, he stood and wrapped his long lost sister in his arms. His tears started all over again, except that *this time* they were sobs of relief...and even joy.

He held Euphrates back by her shoulders and for a long moment, peered into her face, then held her close again, then held her again at arm's length to take her all in.

Tears were flowing down both their faces now, and he began to laugh. A great, free, healing laugh.

Euphrates managed to tell him, "And this," her arms extended - to Margaret's amazement - to Betty Jo's mother-in-law, Mrs. Johnson, "is our Baby Sister, Lee Dora. Dora, come give our brother, my twin brother and your big brother, a hug."

Lee Dora crossed the chasm of the last seventy-plus years in less than a second, and ran to be included in her brother and sister's embrace and reunion. "If only Mama, and Papa, could see us now."

Margaret thought she might faint. She backed away from her father, and stumbled. Betty Jo and Arnold both moved quickly to steady her, then gently guided her to a seat on the sofa.

"Have you known all this time?" Mrs. Johnson asked.

"Yes. Except I also knew that Angus was passing for white. If he'd learned about us being here, it would have destroyed his life."

Euphrates took the several steps over to Margaret and put her hand on Margaret's shoulder.

"More important, I knew that his daughter had been raised to believe that she was white. Why should I have caused her world to fall apart? All I wanted was to see Angus one last time before I die."

Margaret leaped to her feet, and shouted at Euphrates. "What are you saying? You're just crazy. A crazy, old, Colored woman."

Margaret went to her father and tugged on his arm. "Come on, Papa. We have to go. We have to get out of here."

Instead of budging, Angus placed his hands firmly on Margaret's shoulders, then gazed into her face for what seemed forever. Finally, he pulled her close but began to weep again.

Margaret wanted nothing to do with this madness. She just wanted to go home. She pushed herself away from her father and hurried to the door. "For the last time, Papa, it's time for us to go home. This is all such insanity."

"No, lass, what was insanity, was spending all these past years pretending I was something I wasn't. I'm not white. I'm Colored. Up till now, my life has been nothing but lies. *Bold-faced lies*. I even believed them myself."

"Papa! Stop it!" Margaret pleaded and held her hands to her ears. "I don't want to hear any of this foolishness. Please, let's just get out of this house. Everything will be fine again as soon as we get some fresh air."

"No, daughter, it's not fresh air that we need. It's truth that you and I need, however bitter. Try to calm down so that we can all make sense of this...together."

"Make sense? Of what? Are you trying to tell me that I'm Colored? You, all of you, tear my life apart, and you want me to just calm down. Maybe you're all crazy."

With that, Margaret ran to the front door, flung it open, and ran out into the night.

She didn't know where she was running to, but she knew it had to be somewhere away from her crazy father, and those... Colored people.

*   *   *

A single street light, at the corner around which they'd turned earlier, gave Margaret the only hint of which direction to take. She could hear her father calling to her from the porch of the house, but nothing could ever make her go back there.

She prayed to be sent in the right direction, and pressed forward.

By the time she reached Downing Street, a trolley car was coming. She ran to the stop.

She was grateful that she hadn't had to wait, but she had no money with her. The driver, in no humor for tall tales, insisted that she disembark immediately.

She might as well have been lost in a foreign country. She started walking.

A Colored man approached from the opposite direction.

Her heart pounded and her heart constricted. As she and the man neared each other, she could hear him whistling.

He continued past her, and he and his music faded into the night. He hadn't even tipped his hat to her. How dare he show a white woman such disrespect? Could it be that he somehow knew too...that she was now a, a – she couldn't bring herself to say it - a Colored woman?

She put her hands out in front of her face and examined them. Nothing about them seemed to have changed. She still looked white, so wasn't she?

Light from the inside of a storefront illumed the patch of sidewalk she was about to cross. She peered into the storefront window.

Seven or eight Colored men and women were stationed at individual easels arranged in a large circle. Each person was sketching, or painting, their version of the model in the center of the circle; a twentyish Colored man in a tweed jacket sitting in a chair reading a book.

The model, the young man, raised his head slightly and smiled at Margaret, but by the time someone else looked to see who was there, Margaret had moved on.

Farther up and across the street, a stream of merrymakers were exiting their cars and going into a building with an awning that extended from the door to the street. The words, Café Society, were scrolled across the front of the awning.

From a closer vantage Margaret could see that many of the people entering the place were white. Also, some of the couples were Colored men with white women, and, white men with Colored women. The Negroes with other Negroes seemed to be the equals of the whites. It was all very strange.

What kind of nightmare, or dream, was she having? Maybe she was crazy too.

She considered, for a flicker of a moment, going inside, but decided instead to watch from across the street. From the deeply shadowed doorway of a closed business office.

Every time the door to the club opened, she could hear laughter, and music. Jazz. Hot piano jazz.

She felt disoriented, and terribly afraid. Only, of whom? Of what? No one had harmed her. She'd barely been noticed.

It occurred to her that the home she'd just been in was no different than the homes of white people. And except that the people in that house were Negroes, they acted the same as anyone else.

The only difference had been the array of their skin colors. Sable, tan, coffee, olive, bronze, even alabaster. One of them even had blue eyes.

She decided to go back to the storefront. She was an artist too. What was there to be afraid of if she went in and asked for their help?

Looking in the window she saw that the people were packing up, and some were already on their way out.

Thankfully, there was a church on the far corner. She could go and sit inside of it until she could figure out what to do.

She crossed the street, went up the church steps, and was relieved to find the front doors unlocked.

She entered the vestibule and immediately felt a sense of relief. The sanctuary doors were unlocked as well.

She approached the altar and knelt. Her tears dropped onto the altar railing.

"Dear, Lord...

Who am I?

What am I?"

Chapter Fourteen

A my turned off her nightstand lamp, stepped out of her nightgown, and climbed into bed. The cool, percale sheets gave her naked body welcome relief from the sultry, late July evening.

She had closed her bedroom door for privacy's sake, but the inch of space, between the bottom of the door and the threshold, permitted a shaft of hallway light into her room.

Shadows flickered every time one of the girls who worked in her mother's basement speakeasy, and an all too eager john, walked by her room – on the second floor of the duplex – on their way to, or from, one of the third floor rooms.

Many nights, the foot traffic kept her awake well past midnight. She beat a fist into her pillow and hoped this wasn't going to be another one of those nights.

The speakeasy was a private, *secret*, club for wealthy white men. Amy wasn't allowed to enter the club – ever – but from what she could tell, the men seemed to have an insatiable desire for Colored women. Her mother made sure the men had their choice of every hue of woman in the Negro race. From porcelin white, to coffee, to ebony.

Every one of the girls was beautiful, and every one of them busy every night that the club was open.

For Amy, the worst part of laying awake was that the same discomforting thought always returned; that operating the speakeasy, and selling bootleg liquor, was how her mother had been able to pay Amy's boarding school tuition, not to mention, how she afforded giving Amy so many expensive clothes, and how Amy had been able to spend last summer, with her classmates, in Europe.

Oh, God, why did it all have to be like this? The memory of a childhood rhyme taunted her.

If you're black, get back. If you're brown, stick around. If you're white, you're all right.

Her mother was trying so hard to give her a white girl's life–and why was such a life theirs anyway?–when all Amy wanted was to be herself. Whatever that was.

She didn't even know anymore. Black; white. White; black. Black *and* white. What difference did it make anyway?

Who made up all this foolishness? And why?

Amy turned to the wall and squeezed her eyes shut. To no avail.

She kicked her covers to the foot of the bed and sat up.

At first, she leaned against her headboard, but then she scooted into the middle of the bed, pulled her legs up to her chest and folded her arms across her knees. Resting her head on her arms, she breathed deeply, then let go a torrent of tears.

"It'll be different for you, precious, I promise," Amy said to the child in her womb.

Her declaration gave her an idea. She dried her tears and looked over at her teddy bear, Mr. Scruggs. Instead of giving the baby up for adoption, she would marry the baby's father. Now she just had to find a way to tell him that she had changed her mind. That they could run away and elope like he had pleaded with her to do during her Christmas vacation.

He didn't know that she was pregnant, but she would tell him soon enough. Their situation was still impossible, but there had to be some state in this whole big country that would allow them to live there in peace.

Amy reached toward her lamp, but stopped. The full moon shined bright enough into the room that she could do what she needed to without turning on a light.

She went to her closet and selected a skirt, a blouse, and her lowest heeled shoe. Within minutes, she was fully dressed.

Next, she went to her bedroom door and listened for the sound of footsteps in the hallway, or on the stairs.

For the moment, at least, she heard nothing.

She started to open the door, then thought of another way out: the outside stairway on the side of the house that her mother had had installed for the third floor boarders.

The window next to her bed let out onto the stairway's second floor landing.

She climbed out of her window onto the stairway landing, then tiptoed down the wooden steps to ground level. Of all the antics she'd pulled at the boarding school, this was the first time she'd ever gone anywhere alone in the middle of the night. She would have to be careful that no one saw her. They might get the wrong idea.

She decided to go out the back gate and walk through the alleys until she was a few blocks away. But what Amy found in the backyard startled her. It had been turned into a parking lot for luxury automobiles. Buicks, Stutzes, and Oldsmobiles were squeezed in alongside Lincolns, Cadillacs, and Packards.

She worked her way through the maze, but reached the gate just as a Bentley came down the alley with its lights off and parked alongside the fence. Its occupants, two men wearing top hats and tuxedos, and a woman in an evening gown, exited the Bentley, opened the gate, and proceeded up the backyard walkway to the outside basement door.

Amy had to duck down between the cars in the yard and wait until the trio went inside. She heard one of the men give the secret knock: Rap, rap, rap, a long pause, and rap, rap.

Strains of the player piano and a tangle of talk and laughter could be heard when her mother opened the basement door to let the newly arrived clientele in.

When the door closed, the night was quiet again, except for the hoot of a nearby owl.

A shooting star sailed across the darkness.

Amy glanced upward just in time to see it disappear from view, but the sky was aglitter with millions of more stars.

"Uhhh!" she gasped, at the beauty of it all.

Except for the street lamp on the corner, the block was dark. She walked in the direction of the light.

As she neared the lamp, a young man, – white, she immediately noted, – stepped from the dark and stood directly under the beam of light.

At first, her heart raced with fright, but then she recognized his smile. She started to run to him, and then halted before her next foot left the ground.

"Kyle!" What are you doing here? This is too dangerous." She meant to sound angry, except the lilt and tremble in her voice betrayed her. "Besides, believe it or not, I was on my way to see you."

Kyle had moved closer to Amy and was reaching for her

hand to pull her into his arms.

She struggled futilely against his strength, then relented. His breath reeked of cheap whiskey.

"Well," he slurred, "now you don't have to go anywhere. Furrr-ther...more, my beautiful brown sugar, I wasn't about to let you just walk out of my life. Haven't you figured out, yet, that I love you. To hell with my daddy, and the whole damn lot of his goons. It ain't like some of 'em don't have their own cup of brown sugah on the side."

Amy hated Kyle's calling her "brown sugah" and strained to be released from his hold for his ignoring her longstanding request to stop doing so.

He simply held her all the tighter, then kissed her long and hard.

Once more she attempted to resist Kyle's embrace, and passion, only, he overpowered her, again, pulling her out of the light of the street lamp and into the deep shadows of a nearby tree. "I need you, Amy," he said, and kissed her forehead, her cheeks, her nose, her chin, her lips. "I need you, and don't want to be without you. I could care less about the color of our skins being different. Are we the same height? The same weight? Born on the same day, or in the same month?"

She nodded no.

"What in hell difference can the same skin color mean? It's stupid! I'd love you if you were polka dot, and I was plaid."

"Sure, that's what you say, here, in the dark shadows of night. But what happens when your friends turn against you, or your father kicks you out of his house. You'll care then."

"Shhhhh," he said, as he stroked her hair, "let's not worry about any of that right now. Right now, let's just be here, with each other." He loved the texture of her hair, especially underneath where it wasn't so straightened. Where he could feel its strength and that it had a mind of its own. "Look," he said, holding and gazing at their clasped hands, in the dark, we can't even really tell what color either of us is. I could even be Negro, and you, white." This time he kissed her full on the mouth, only, with a tenderness that words could not convey.

Still, Amy struggled to get free of Kyle, and finally, he relented, dropping his arms to his side.

She stepped back and straightened her clothes.

"But, Kyle, you know what'll happen if they catch us." She had discarded her resolve to tell him that she was carrying his baby. "First, our parents would kill us, then, they'd still be so full of hate, they'd probably also kill each other."

Kyle ignored her comment, and instead bent to kiss her neck, then her shoulders. Before moving to her breasts he laid his hand on her stomach to anchor himself.

His hand could not lay flat. Her stomach was full and rounded.

Amy stiffened and tried to push his hand away, but it was immovable.

He searched her face for an answer. "Why…, why didn't you tell me?"

His arm slackened and his hand fell away from her before she could answer.

"What difference would it have made?" Amy asked, tears swelling in her eyes for the third time this evening.

She waited for Kyle to pull her close again, but he didn't. Instead, he just looked at her, as if she were a stranger that he wanted to slap.

A police car turned onto the far end of the street and drove slowly past her mother's house. The headlights of the police car nearly revealed Kyle and Amy under the tree.

Neither of them seemed to breathe until the vehicle was well down the next block.

After a long moment of staring at each other, Kyle stepped away from Amy, deeper into the shadows. Amy's tears wet her face as she waited in vain for him to hold her again.

At last, he reached for her hand, but it was too late. Amy jerked away from him before he could get a good hold of her.

"Stay away from me, Kyle. Don't ever come near me again."

Ignoring her, he made a second try and successfully locked her into an embrace.

"Amy, you've got me all wrong. It was just the shock of finding out this way. You caught me off guard, that's all. I mean, us, having a baby? It's just not something I ever thought about. Did you?"

Shame burned her face. She'd not only thought about it. She'd plotted it.

"I don't care what you meant, Kyle Browne, or ever thought about. Just let go of me."

She pounded her fists against his chest until he relented, and this time, she backed away from him.

He let her go.

When she reached the curb, she turned and ran across the street.

"Amy! Please! Come back," Kyle called after her. "We'll figure it out. I love you. Nothing else really matters."

"You're a liar, Kyle Browne," Amy yelled over her shoulder at him, "nothing but a boldfaced liar."

His actions had said as much. She was black, and he was white. He didn't have the courage to stand up to anyone who thought that was reason enough to keep them apart.

She stopped running, and started walking, where she didn't know. Not home, was all she knew. She'd ruined her life, all for the sake of finding a way to keep her mother from attending her graduation and embarrassing her. All so her classmates wouldn't learn that Amy was Negro, not white, as she had led them to believe. She could barely see through her tears.

Wasn't there anywhere in the world that a person's skin color didn't matter?

She stopped and searched the heavens in hope of an answer, but a wide swath of clouds had masked the stars. Clearly, the answer was no. No, there wasn't one corner of this world where a person's skin color did not matter.

* * *

Amy had no idea where she was, all she knew was that she was exhausted and desperately needed to rest.

She pressed a hand against her stomach. "Don't worry, baby. I won't let anything bad happen to you."

She trudged on until she came to a school building. The moonlight illuminated the name inscribed over the doorway. Manual High. The school she would have attended if her mother hadn't insisted she go to a boarding school.

She sat on the school's front entrance steps.

"Ooo, ooo," an owl hooted from somewhere in the dark.

The homes across the street from the school were modest, made of brick, and well kept. One of the houses stood out from the others. Its yard was bordered with neatly trimmed hedges, rather than a fence, or nothing, and the upstairs windows had wrought iron balconies.

The drapes in the front room window of the house were open and Amy could see that a party was going on.

It occurred to her that no one would see her if she approached the house and looked closer. She went almost as close as the porch.

What a time the party-goers seemed to be having. Everyone was laughing and smiling. The men were all handsome and wearing suits, and the women all beautiful and dressed in the latest flapper fashion. If she weren't seeing this with her own eyes, she would have never believed that Negroes lived this well.

The most elegant of the women was a blonde only a shade darker than herself. For a moment, Amy imagined herself in the woman's place.

The woman turned and looked out the window before Amy could move from sight. Seconds later, the front door of the house opened, and a young man stepped out onto the porch.

Amy turned to escape, only she didn't see that she had stepped into a flower bed. She tripped and fell face forward into an arrangement of petunias.

Her face blushed hot with embarrassment as she spit the dirt out of her mouth, then rose up on her knees and sat back on her heels.

A man's open palm reached down to help her up. "I think I'd better get you home," said a voice she was startled to recognize.

She looked up, hardly believing her eyes. "Anthony!"

She was humiliated beyond words. Why did he have to be so darn handsome?

He waited for Amy to take his hand, then cupped his other hand under her elbow and helped her stand.

"I'll be all right," she said. "Really."

"I believe you," Anthony said, hesitating before he removed a petal from her hair, "but at least come sit on the porch with me before I drive you home. I could get you some milk, or punch."

Amy could feel her cheeks burning. Before she knew it, he was settling her onto the porch swing.

"I'll be right back. I just have to go get the car keys from my dad."

Actually, Amy was grateful that he'd left her there alone. At least for a brief time, this house was hers. This life was hers. Anthony was hers.

The front door opened again, only this time it wasn't Anthony who appeared. It was the woman Amy had seen in the front room. The two of them, she and the woman, could have been mistaken for mother and daughter.

The woman took a sip of whatever was in the glass she was holding and threw the rest of it out toward the flowers. Most of the drink went into the petunias, but some of it wet the end of the swing, and the side of Amy's face.

"Dear," the woman said, looking down on Amy, "I don't know who your folks are, nor am I interested in finding out. I simply want you to understand that whatever you have in mind regarding my son, won't work. I repeat, will *not*, work. This party is to announce our son's acceptance into Howard University…somewhere he'll be out of the clutches of girls like you. Am I making myself quite clear?"

Amy stared at the woman a long moment, trying to figure out how to respond. First impressions were hard to undo.

"Ma'am, I don't know what you're talking about. And, believe me, your son is the last thing on my mind right now. In fact, we hardly…"

The front door swung open again, and Anthony hurried out, to his mother's side. "Okay, Mom. That's enough. Dad's looking all over for you."

*   *   *

Anthony drove up in front of Amy's house, parked, and turned off the ignition.

Amy was thinking about what he had just said. She wasn't sure she believed him. "You're trying to tell me that your mother is a sharecropper's daughter? That she picked cotton when she was growing up?"

"Hey, don't let the fake back east accent, and the fancy party fool you. Can't nobody cook a pot of collard greens like my mom. Grows them herself, too, in a garden in our backyard."

Amy looked at Anthony incredulously, unable to picture the glamorous woman she'd just met, on her hands and knees, digging in the dirt.

Anthony seized the moment, and put his arms across the back of Amy's shoulders, drawing her close.

She felt his longing as strongly as she felt her own. He leaned in to kiss her, but she offered her cheek instead of her lips. "I can't. I just can't," she said.

He tried again, but she froze. She cared too much about Anthony to lead him on. "I'm pregnant," she blurted. She felt like she might faint. She wished he'd take his arm from around her shoulders. "Didn't you hear me? I'm pregnant."

"Of course, I heard you," he said. "Anything else I should know?"

Amy didn't appreciate his humor. "Very funny," she said, afraid to look at him.

He removed his arm from around her, but turned her face toward his. "I'm not trying to be funny, I mean. I honestly want to know if there's anything else you want to tell me?"

"Why do you keep saying that?"

"Saying what?"

"That dumb thing about, 'anything else'?"

"I don't know," Anthony said. "I just figure there's got to be more."

Amy closed her eyes and heaved a deep breath. Now he's really going to hate me, she thought.

"He's white, okay?"

"He? He, who?"

"My baby's father."

Anthony's brow knitted, but he didn't turn away from her.

"Sooo, what does your mother say about that?"

"She's making me give the baby away."

"At least it's not the other way around."

"The other way around? I don't understand what you mean."

"I mean," Anthony said, looking straight into Amy's eyes, "if the father were Colored, and you were white, they'd eventually find him hung in a tree somewhere. My dad told me about that happening to a cousin of his."

Amy stared blankly out into the night. "What happened to the girl and their baby?"

"Don't know. My pops also said sometimes it's better not to ask."

Amy looked back at Anthony. For a long while neither said another word.

"I better go in," she finally said.

"Okay. Let me get the door for you."

Anthony got out of the car and came around to the passenger door. He opened it and took her hand as if he were her very own Prince Charming, but the prick of pain in her stomach reminded her that he couldn't ever be.

They walked to Amy's front door hand-in-hand.

Rowena startled them by opening the front door. She was in her bathrobe and a head rag, and pulled Amy inside without a word.

She slammed the door in Anthony's face so hard that it hurt his ears. And probably woke up half the neighborhood.

Anthony walked forlornly back to his car.

As he opened the door of his car to get in, he failed to pay attention to another car careening toward him. The car veered deathly close to his body.

"Better watch it, nigger," someone yelled at him through the car's partially rolled down driver's side front window. In nearly the same instant, someone in the rear seat of the car rolled down their window and hurled spit into his face.

The car's tires screeched and burned as the car sped away.

Anthony wiped the fluid from his face only to look up and see another white boy, who looked to be practically his same age and build, staring at him from across the street. They were even dressed much the same. Leather shoes, dark slacks, white shirt, dark jacket, apple cap.

The two of them glared across at each other, but neither made a move. Their duel would have to wait until another night.

The sun was rising, and a police car had turned onto the street, heading their way.

Charlene A. Porter

Chapter Fifteen

D r. Locke and his Imperial Kouncil unanimously endorsed Devin's plan. Although August 23rd was still a little more than three weeks away, the Kouncil members were bragging among themselves that this particular cross burning would be Colorado's most talked about event of 1925. *The Denver Post* and *Rocky Mountain News* headlines, they predicted, would read, "Largest KKK Rally in State's History."

Klaverns from the entire western territory, which included Wyoming, Nebraska, Utah, and Kansas, would convene on top of Ruby Hill, in South Denver.

The Kolorado KKK Ladies Auxiliary also wanted the occasion to be a success. It would help draw attention to their efforts to shut down bootleggers and speakeasies, and perhaps gain them hundreds-hopefully, thousands-of new members.

Their inital write-up, December 8th, 1924 on page C3 of the *Denver Post*, had been very helpful. Since then the women were the subject of the various feature articles.

The incorporators and directors of the organization are Meta L. Gremmels, Dr. Ester B. Hunt, and Laurena H. Setzer, all of Denver.

Objects of the organization are given as the procuring and enforcement of just and equitable laws, upholding the constitution of the United States and State of Colorado, teaching of respect for laws and law-enforcing authorities, furtherance of American principles, ideals and institutions, and relief work to alleviate suffering and distress.

Only white women of American birth over 18 years old are eligible for membership.

At Devin's insistence, Margaret had reluctantly accepted a leadership role in the Auxiliary. With both he and she wielding influence in the Klan, Devin reasoned, his overall power in the organization would be solidified.

This afternoon's Auxiliary luncheon was being held in the basement of one of Denver's most prominent Protestant churches. Other than the women in attendance wearing their Klan regalia, there was little to set them apart from a gathering of the Christian Women's Benevolent Society.

The festive air in the hall was due, in part, to the women's eager anticipation of the special presentation that had been promised. Many of them were trying to out guess each other about what the program would entail, but their only clues were that the church's basement stage, the very same stage where the church presented its annual production of the Passion play, and its yearly Christmas pageant, now featured a ten-foot painted backdrop of a burning cross, and a foot-pedal ax sharpener sitting downstage right.

Each table, down on the floor in front of the stage where the audience was seated, sat four, and was covered with a white linen tablecloth, and adorned in the center with a slender, cut glass vase with two yellow roses.

Extra tables were being set up to accommodate the overflow caused by the guests of guests, while the girls' auxiliary served those already seated Margaret's homemade angel cake on crystal dessert plates, and strawberry ice cream in matching crystal bowls, and poured the ladies glasses of the pastor's wife's famous sassafras iced tea into crystal goblets.

Backstage, Margaret was listening for just the right moment to make her entrance. She wanted the audience to be completely caught off-guard.

She waited until the women's chatter reached a peak, and then ordered the hall's lights turned off.

Just as she expected, with the sudden darkness came the clinking of forks and spoons being set down on plates, and a nervous murmuring throughout the audience.

Then, a spotlight beamed onto the ax sharpener...which brought a sudden hush.

The mood in the hall shifted sharply from gaiety to wonderment. A few of the women even felt a rush of panic before Margaret finally emerged from backstage left.

She was gowned in a floor-length red satin Klan robe and carried a long-handled ax.

She strode into the circle of light and held the ax high over her head, for all to see.

The finely sharpened blade of the ax glinted in the light.

The women o-o-o-ed and a-w-w-ed.

"Sisters," Margaret called out to them. "I say, sisters, the time...has come!"

She received only scattered applause.

As her eyes began to adjust to looking out into the darkened hall, she began to distinguish the various faces.

She turned toward a table of women who seemed eager to hear her message, then continued. "The enemy, the dark and evil scourge, lurks within. Within our neighborhoods, within families, indeed, within some of our very own cupboards. Yet and still, we must not surrender."

This time, the entire audience clapped, albeit timidly and politely. She went on, determined to win their minds, and hopefully, their hearts. "We can, we will, we must, fight back."

Someone, from the rear of the hall, stood and echoed Margaret's plea. "Yes! We can, we will, we must, fight back."

Margaret felt encouraged, and repeated the call to action. "We can, we will, we must, fight back. We can, we will, we must, fight back."

This time, a few others joined in.

As they chanted, she paced the length of the stage back and forth, all the while, holding the ax high for all to see. Again, she chanted, "We can, we will, we must, fight back. We can, we will, we must fight back. We can, we will—"

A woman at a table near the front of the stage stood and waving her linen napkin, joined in, "We must, fight back."

One-by-one, others stood too, each adding her voice to the slogan, "We can, we will, we must, fight back."

Before long, all of the audience was standing and joined in shouting, "We can, we will, we must, fight back."

Margaret lowered her arms, bringing the ax waist high, and continued to pace as the women continued to chant. After several minutes two of the oldest girls, from the girls auxiliary entered from each side of the stage, and bid the women to sit again.

Margaret waited for the audience members to regain their composure, then sat down herself, at the ax sharpener.

One woman leaped to her feet again and cried out, "Yes! Yes!" to Margaret as Margaret placed the blade of the ax against the sharpener's flint wheel.

At first, the sharpener's pedal resisted the pressure she applied with her feet, barely budging, but little by little the pedal did begin to move. Up a few inches, then down a few inches, thus, moving the belt positioned around the wheel of the sharpener, a few inches.

Then, Margaret applied all of her might to the pedal and it began to move rapidly and completely up and down.

She could feel the women's admiration for her growing.

All at once, she thrust the ax so firmly against the fast spinning flint wheel that sparks flew from the ax as it was sharpened.

Some of the women seated nearest the stage squealed in alarm, but Margaret only worked the wheel more.

It took several minutes, but the panicked women eventually saw they weren't in danger.

Everyone was fascinated to see what would happen next.

In measured succession, three more spotlights beamed down on across the stage.

One revealed a family kitchen.

One a saloon bar and stools.

The last a cemetery headstone.

All the while, Margaret continued sharpening the ax, and sparks continued to fly.

A woman in an apron entered from backstage right and started setting the table in the kitchen scene, while the lights over the other two sets and Margaret, dimmed.

Moments later, a boy, really a girl dressed as a boy, in an outfit to make him look about seven years old, holding a toy truck, and a girl, dressed to look about a year or so younger, and carrying a baby doll, ran into the scene and to the woman's side.

"Mama, mama," they almost sang, "Daddy's home."

A tall, blond, strong-jawed man in a suit, entered right behind them.

The astutest members of the audience giggled, realizing that the man was really a woman in the guise of a man.

"Good evening, dearest, the male character offered in an unlikely tenor voice, and kissed the mother on her cheek. "Something smells awfully delicious."

"Dinner will be ready any minute," she said, on her way to the stove. "It's your favorite. Beef stew."

"Great," the husband said, "I'll just have a shot of bourbon, and relax until then."

The man went to the cupboard, took down a crystal decanter and a small glass, then took them to the table and sat.

The children sat down on the floor, in front of him, and played with their toys.

He filled the glass and belted the drink back, then, immediately poured another glass full of the whiskey, and quickly downed it too. In a short while, the bottle was nearly empty. He started to pour another drink, but instead, drank straight from the bottle.

He hiccupped and spilled the rest of the whiskey down the front of himself.

After tilting the bottle to determine that it truly was empty, he got up, stepped clumsily over the children, and went to the cupboard for another bottle of whiskey...this one hidden in a sugar canister.

"Children," the mother said as she placed a bowl of stew at each of the four place settings, "supper."

The children and mother took their seats at the table, then waited as their father stumbled back to his chair.

He slammed the new bottle down on the dinner table, causing the children to jump in fright.

Mother, and the children, were obviously embarrassed for him. "Will you say grace, dear?" mother asked.

Father's head bobbed up and down, up and down again, then settled at an angle. "Whhhy surrre," he said, slurring.

The wife and children all clasped hands and bowed their heads, and the son and mother tried to reach for the father's hands, but to no avail.

Father's head was bobbing again as mother and the children waited for the prayer to begin.

Mother, and the children, peeked up at him just as his face plopped down in his bowl of stew, splattering each of the others in the face with juice.

He was out cold.

The spotlight over the family went dark, and before the audience could fully react, the spotlight over the saloon scene came up.

Downstage right, still in the dimmed light, Margaret reapplied the ax to the sharpener and created more sparks.

Two women, both outfitted in bustiers and bloomers, and wearing feather boas around their necks, entered the saloon scene.

One of the women, the grown up little girl from the first scene, went over to the victrola, cranked it up, and put on a scratchy jazz record, while the other woman went behind the bar and brought out a liquor bottle and two highball glasses.

The woman at the victrola put her hands on her hips and began gyrating to the music.

The other woman poured a drink and handed it to the woman dancing, and then poured herself a drink.

A man, another woman dressed as a man, entered the saloon, and took off his overcoat and hat and hung them on a brass tree.

"Evening, ladies. How's tricks?"

The dancing woman slinked her way over to him and pulled her feather boa across his chest.

"Just fine, ducky, now that you're here."

The woman at the bar pushed up her bustier, then held out her glass to him, and asked, "What about me?"

"What about you?" he said, took the drink, swilled it down, then held the glass out for a refill. His attention was on the dancer. He went over to her, grabbed her arm, turned her toward himself, and then forced her up a flight of stairs. The music blared, then went silent as the light over the scene dimmed.

For a moment, all that was visible were the sparks flying from the ax Margaret continued to sharpen.

Then, the third, and last spotlight went up, highlighting the headstone and cemetery.

Snow-soap powder-was falling.

The mother and father, now old, and the boy, now grown, from the first scene, all shabbily dressed and shaking from the cold, entered the scene huddled together.

The mother fell across the headstone and cried out, "Oh my child, my baby, by precious little girl. It was the demon rum that did this to her."

But then, she brought out a whiskey bottle from under her shawl and took a long swallow from it before handing it to her husband...who also took a gulp from it, and then handed it to the young man.

"Here's too ya', Sis," the young man said, holding the bottle up high before sprinkling a few drops from the bottle on the grave, then downing the rest of the alcohol himself.

Then, the light over that scene went dark, and the light over Margaret brightened.

Practically every woman in the audience had reached for her handkerchief, and was dabbing away tears. Sniffles and delicate sobs could be heard throughout the room.

When the middle spotlight went up again, the saloon scene had been cleared away, and in its place was a stack of large wooden barrels, three on the bottom, two in the middle, and one on top. Each barrel was clearly labeled whiskey.

Margaret rose from the sharpener, went to the spotlight, and stood next to the barrels.

The women in the audience sucked in their collective breaths as Margaret again raised the ax high over her head.

The actors from the scenes came from backstage and stood beside her. Altogether Margaret and the actors chanted, "We can, we will, we must, fight back."

Alone, Margaret asked of the audience, "Sisters, are you with us?"

At first the audience sat stunned, mute, but finally, someone replied strongly, "Yes! Yes, sister, we're with you...for we can, we will, we must, fight back."

Table after table, all the others in the audience stood as well, saying, over and over, "Yes, sister! We're with you, for we can, we will, we must, fight back. Yes, sister! We're with you, for we can, we will, we must, fight back."

Within minutes, all of the women were standing, some even on their chairs, clapping and stomping. "Yes, sister, we're with you, for we can, we will, we must, fight back."

Margaret held the ax still higher, then waited for the others on the stage with her to back safely out of the way.

Once they were a few good feet away, she swung the ax down into the front of one of the middle barrels.

A stream of whiskey-colored liquid spouted from the gash in the barrel.

Members of the audience began to urge her to do more damage to the barrel.

She raised the ax again and asked, yet again, "Sisters, are you with me?"

The women, Margaret's Klan sisters, replied in earnest, "We...must...fight. We...must...fight. We...must...fight."

Margaret brought the ax down into another of the barrels, but had to swing several more times before it too released a stream of the dark liquid.

The women, were behaving like boxing fans cheering a knockout. "Fight! Fight! Fight!" they demanded.

The liquid from the two broken barrels flowed down to the lip of the stage and over.

With Margaret leading the charge, The Kolorado KKK Ladies' Auxiliary had declared war against bootleg liquor and prostitution...and every woman in the room had enlisted.

Chapter Sixteen

Devin twisted the cap off of his flask and thrust the bootleg bourbon in front of Margaret's face. As had become Devin's evening ritual, he was having a nightcap and he wanted Margaret to join him.

She recoiled at the liquor's strong smell, but was afraid that if she pushed his hand away, he might feel insulted and become violent. "Please, Devin, stop. You know that I can't drink anything that might hurt the baby," she said, and tried to go on brushing her hair.

She was glad that she was sitting at her vanity table where she could look in the vanity's large oval mirror to see what he was doing.

He backed away from her and fell onto their bed. "Oh, that's right," he said, "I forgot, you're a, a...a whadya call it? One of them temperance leaders, now. Well, here's to you, missy," he said, and held up his flask in a mock toast, as he swigged another drink.

Margaret was trying her best to ignore her husband, but she had an uneasy feeling that he was on the verge of another one of his alcoholic rages. She began counting her brush strokes out loud in an effort to distract him.

"Thirty-seven, thirty-eight, thirty-nine, forty, forty-one…" The way he was staring at her gave her chills. She was terrified that now that she knew the truth about herself, he would discover it too.

"Damn it, Margaret," he said, raising up off the bed and coming back over to her, " no matter what else I think about you, I have to say you're one of the prettiest white women this side of Peak's Pike."

She started to correct him, to tell him that he meant, Pike's Peak, but caught herself just in time. He was too drunk to know what he was saying, which meant he was also drunk enough to want to hit her.

He walked back to where Margaret was sitting and stood behind her so that his thighs pressed into her back. He spoke to her looking at their images in the mirror. His body odor and breath reeked of his two-day binge.

"And, if I ever catch that nigger, Walter, looking at you again, I'll kill both of you. You hear me? Just because my fool mother promised him the job his father had, don't mean I won't take matters into my own hands. I think the boy actually forgets, sometimes, that you're a white woman."

Devin grabbed a handful of Margaret's hair and yanked her head back, forcing her to look up into his face.

She cried out in pain, but he only yanked her head again, and didn't let go.

"Sometimes, I think you forget, too," he said, and wrapped and wrapped her hair around his fist so that he had a tighter hold of her.

"Forget what?" What are you talking about, Devin?" Her eyes were watering from the pain.

"Don't smart mouth me, missy. You know damn well what I mean. I mean that if I didn't know better, sometimes I'd think you was a nigger lover, too... like that father of yours."

Devin pushed Margaret's head back up with his fist, and let go of her hair, but tossed a spurt of the flask's contents at the mirror, which splashed back into Margaret's eyes and face, and onto her nightgown.

The jolt to her head caused her to bite her lower lip, which opened a cut and also sent blood trickling down her chin and onto her nightgown.

Devin just turned his back on her and went over to the chaise longue and plopped down on it.

Margaret's scalp felt like it had almost been torn off, and her eyes stung from the liquor. Still, she had to think of the baby. She couldn't afford to react in a way that might provoke Devin even further.

He was walking back toward her, issuing some kind of command, but her mind would not make sense of it.

"No, Devin, please, no," she pleaded as he pulled her to her feet, then forced her out of her robe.

"Oh, yes, yes, Margaret. Besides, is that any way for a wife to talk to her husband?" he said, then tore her gown off of her body. After all, I enjoy looking at you. Your skin," he said running his hand across her shoulder, "is so white. So beautiful."

He began to circle her as he unbuttoned his vest, and then his shirt.

"But, Devin," she pleaded, "I'm eight and half months pregnant. The baby..."

Devin didn't answer. He just pushed her onto the bed.

In a last vivid thought, she felt grateful that neither Kyle, nor Walter, was home to hear her screams, and that Mother Browne was too sedated to be aware of anything.

*   *   *

When finally it was all over, Devin just rolled away from Margaret and dropped off to sleep.

She tried to cover herself with the sheet, but most of it was trapped under Devin's body.

She didn't dare risk waking him, yet, she didn't dare get up either. Instead, she curled into a fetal position, to wait, and just tried not to cry.

*   *   *

The sound of the front door slamming woke Margaret.

She looked over at the clock on her vanity table.

It was only a little past midnight.

"Hey," Margaret heard Kyle yell up the stairway, "anybody home?"

She could only pray that he didn't open up her and Devin's bedroom door in search of them before she could get up and put her gown and robe back on.

"Yes!" she called out to Kyle over his father's snoring. "Meet me in the kitchen, and I'll fix you a sandwich and a glass of milk.

"Great. Thanks," Kyle said.

Relieved, she heard his footsteps back down the stairs.

Only, instead of going to the kitchen, Kyle made a detour to the library.

After flinging open the doors he went straight to the desk and turned on the lamp.

The dim light cast an eerie glow onto the oil painting over the fireplace mantel, the portrait of his paternal great grandfather, the Colonel.

A faceless wire-form mannequin, standing in the far corner of the library, had on the very same Confederate uniform that his great-grandfather wore to pose for the painting.

Kyle went over to the mannequin.

"You won't mind if I borrow this, now will you, great granddaddy?" Kyle said, as he glanced up at the wizened old face of his ancestor, then took the faded gold sash and moth-eaten gray jacket off the mannequin, and put them on himself.

The dust on the jacket, and its loosened fibers from decades of nonuse, caused Kyle to choke.

"Whew," he wheezed as he waved the particles from in front of his face, then buttoned up the jacket. Other than the shoulders being too narrow, it was a perfect fit. He mimicked the heel clicking snap to attention of a real soldier, then saluted the painting.

"At your service, Colonel."

"What? I can't hear you," he said, to the picture, then reached up and lifted the portrait from its hook.

He studied the painting close up for a long minute, then heaved it into the fireplace.

It landed on the wood grate, and one of the grate's spikes tore a hole through the canvas.

Kyle looked down at the painting and spoke to it.

"Oh, you say there's no piss-drinkin' yanks to run into the river tonight? No belly-achin' turncoats to shoot at dawn? No lip-quiverin' niggras to tar and feather? Come on, great-grand-daddy, that ain't like you."

Kyle raised his foot and brought his boot down squarely on the old man's monocled eye, then, on the middle of one side of the frame, causing the frame to splinter and break, and the canvas to rip more.

"Come on, come on," Kyle shouted as he stomped his heel into the picture over and over again. "Come on, you stupid coward."

Kyle didn't see his stepmother standing in the library doorway.

Margaret had on Grandmother Browne's old chenille robe, but she was trembling as if it were late December, rather than the first week of August.

She stretched out her arms to him. "Oh, Kyle, what have you done?" She didn't mean the painting so much as she meant his appearance. He hadn't been home in almost a week, and he looked drawn and disheveled.

He looked blankly at Margaret without uttering a word. Instead, he went over to his father's desk and picked up the business ledger that listed every new Klan member and how much each man owed on dues.

Kyle opened the large red leather book and noted his father's meticulous bookkeeping.

The first column after the individual names was for the accounting of the six dollars of the ten-dollar annual dues, which went to Dr. Locke.

The second, third, fourth, fifth, sixth, seventh, eighth, and ninth columns noted the total payments on the four remaining dollars – which Devin accepted in fifthy cent installments to insure affordability even for poor white trash – went straight to Devin's pockets.

Margaret walked over to Kyle and tried to take the ledger from him, but he wouldn't release it.

"You know that you shouldn't be going through your father's things."

If Kyle heard her, he didn't let on. He simply pushed past her like she was any stranger on the street, and went around to the front of the desk, and opened one drawer after another, rifling through each one, for what she didn't know.

He's barely more than a boy just out of his knickers, Margaret thought, while watching him. And that face. That innocent, sweet face. Was I wrong to raise him as my own child?

But his mother died when he was a mere infant. He needed a mother. What else could I have done, but love him?

Did losing my own mother when I was so young leave me totally ignorant of a child's needs?

Did losing my own child to the world cause me to be insensitive to him, or overlook some need he had?

What in the world is he looking for?

Finally, Kyle took out a box of matches from the desk's bottom drawer.

He waved the box at her with a childish glee.

"You want to stop something, Pop?" Kyle ranted to an invisible adversary. "Then, stop this."

Margaret's efforts to grab the box from her stepson were futile. He was more man than boy suddenly, and his size and strength were too much for her.

He went to the fireplace again, but this time he was ripping page after page from the ledger.

Some of the pages he balled into his fist, then tossed on top of the discarded painting. Other pages he tore into strips, and let the strips flutter to the floor.

Somehow, Margaret, realized desperately, she had to stop him from this madness. What she needed was a weapon of some kind to scare him with.

She searched about the room for something to use.

The Colonel's saber was mounted on the wall, along with other Confederate swords, but a sword could easily be turned back on her.

The muskets and pistols on display on another wall seemed equally ominous.

Finally, she noticed the fire poker, and decided it would have to do.

She grabbed it, and held it high over her head.

"Kyle, stop this. I'm warning you. I won't let you destroy this family."

Kyle ignored his stepmother, not even glancing at her.

"How many times do I have to tell you, this doesn't concern you?" he said. "You're not my mother, and I don't want your help. All you need to do is to stay out of my way."

Margaret winced. He sounded just like his father.

He even used the same hate-filled tone of voice, and had the same scowl on his face.

This was all a very, very bad dream. Somehow she had to wake up.

Except, it wasn't a dream, and before she could stop Kyle he lit a match and threw it into the fireplace.

The ledger papers caught fire immediately and sputtered and crackled with flames.

The Colonel's portrait, thankfully, was still buried underneath the papers, but just as she reached with the poker to try to retrieve the painting, someone from behind pushed her violently to the side.

She fell against a chair, and crumpled to the ground. She looked up to see Devin with a hand raised to slap Kyle.

"Damn it, boy," Devin blurted, and whipped his hand through the air, aiming for Kyle's face.

But Kyle darted, and missed the attack, and just kept on tearing pages and throwing them into the fire.

Now, the Colonel was aflame, too.

"No!" Kyle said, "Damn you, and everything you stand for."

Margaret saw the vein in Devin's forehead bulge and throb. She also saw that his bathrobe pocket sagged from the weight of something odd shaped and heavy.

Please, she prayed silently, please, Kyle, turn around.

Her plea was useless, and the sound of yet another torn page made her stiffen like a frightened child.

Devin put his hand in his robe, then brought his hand back out in the open.

He was holding a pistol.

He fired the gun once, and hit the woodwork on the side of the mantel.

Kyle still didn't stop tearing the pages.

Devin walked closer to Kyle and put the pistol to his son's back. "Boy, if there's one thing I ain't never gonna tolerate, it's you sassin' me like some uppity niggra."

Kyle finally turned and looked at his father, but laughed.

"Why? Ain't that how that Colored whore of yours talks to you?"

Devin's face turned nearly as red as the fire.

He cocked the gun's hammer. "Damn you, boy!"

"Devin! No!" cried, Margaret.

Devin looked at her just as she whacked the poker across his arm.

He screamed in pain and the pistol fell from his hand onto the floor.

It was only seconds before he regained composure, but then he saw the welt on his arm.

He lunged at Margaret, and clasped his hands around her throat, trying to strangle her.

"You crazy bitch."

Margaret felt herself losing consciousness.

Then, she heard a "pop" sound, and smelled something like a whiff of smoke as Devin's hands first went slack, then, dropped away.

He was bleeding from a small hole in his shoulder.

He looked stunned, and pale.

She looked over at Kyle. He was still holding the pistol he had just fired.

"Oh dear, heaven," she gasped. "Quick, Kyle. Help me. We have to stop your father's bleeding, or, he'll die."

Chapter Seventeen

Walter had the night off. Again. Or rather, he had discreetly taken a second job as the Brownes had been unable to pay him for nearly five months.

Margaret was concerned that he would leave them all together; on the other hand, she was secretly grateful for his increasing absences. She could change Devin's bloody bandages, and wash and dry them, without Walter ever having much of a chance to learn that Devin had accidentally been shot.

She was likewise responsible for more and more of the cooking now. Broths for Devin, who was still too weak for anything else; stews or casseroles for Kyle, who, at seventeen, was still growing and always seemed to be hungry; mostly mashed vegetables, and some of the broth, stew, or casserole, and small salads, for Mother Browne; and, for herself, whatever was left.

She was frighteningly underweight to be so near the end of her pregnancy, yet she felt the others in the family took priority. She worried constantly about the baby's health, monitoring every little tweak, twinge and kick.

Fortunately, Walter had introduced her to the only woman Negro doctor in Denver, Dr. Justina Ford, and in exchange for Margaret doing her mending, she gave Margaret full and excellent medical care. Probably better even than Margaret would have received from Mother Browne's doctor…who also hadn't been paid in quite some time.

Kyle came into the kitchen, and sat right down at the table without the least hello.

Margaret ladled out a large bowl of steaming hot rabbit stew-the butcher had given her two rabbits in exchange for the charcoal drawing of his storefront-and set the bowl, and a spoon, on the table in front of Kyle.

"It's good to have you home early, son," Margaret said, and sat down across from him. "How was your day?"

"Look, for the umpteenth time, I'm not your son. More important," he said, shoving the bowl away, "what'n hell is this slop?"

Margaret forced back tears. Didn't he realize all she had to go through just to feed him? "Try it, Kyle," she managed, weakly, "it's pretty good, if I say so myself."

Kyle let out a contemptuous laugh. "You eat it then."

He stood so abruptly and violently that he caused the bowl of stew to spill over.

"Ugh!" Margaret cried as the hot stew poured into her lap, then soaked through her skirt and burned her thighs.

She looked to Kyle for help, but he was already on his way out of the kitchen and didn't bother to look back.

And the doorbell was ringing.

She called out to Kyle as she rushed to the sink to splash cold water on her burns. "Can you see who is at the door? I have to go upstairs and change clothes."

"Yeah, okay," he hollered as he was about to go up the stairs, but detoured back down to answer the door. "I still need something to eat, though."

She was wringing the cold water out of her skirt when Kyle ran back into the kitchen.

"Hey, it's Mr. MacDuff, and Spud. They want me to go somewhere with them," he reported, then dashed back out.

Margaret hurried after him, trying to compose herself on her way into the foyer. She caught Mr. MacDuff's look of surprise when he saw her. She refused to be embarrassed.

She dried her hands as discreetly as possible, and offered the right to MacDuff to shake. "Good afternoon, Mr. MacDuff. What is this Kyle is saying about your wanting him to go somewhere? I'm not sure his father will approve. Kyle's sort of on...on punishment."

He slapped the backs of Spud and Kyle rather than shake Margaret's hand. "I'm taking a few of the boys on a little ride through Five Points. Thought Kyle, here, might want to come along. Be a good education for him to see where the niggras live...in case, well, you know, just in case."

Margaret noticed the flicker of dismay in Kyle's eyes. She could also see in his eyes that he'd made up his mind to go. She had to think fast.

That's a wonderful idea, Mr. MacDuff. I'll go along. I want to learn what my son is learning.

"Stop," Kyle mumbled under his breath, "calling me your damn, 'son'."

Of course, Spud and Mr. MacDuff heard him.

Margaret stared at Kyle, dumbstruck that he would be so rude in front of outsiders.

Still, this was no time for her to show weakness. Kyle might not want her to act like his mother, but she was all he had. She wasn't about to give up on him without a fight, no matter what vile things he said, or did.

She looked quickly up the stairs, then back at MacDuff. She hoped Devin was awake and could hear her. She spoke as loud as possible without seeming suddenly odd.

"Devin. I'm going out for awhile. Kyle is going too. We'll be back shortly." She didn't wait for Devin to reply, and headed straight to the door. MacDuff was clearly stunned.

"Now, see here, Mrs. Browne, me and the boys are goin' on a little more than a hayride. If you'll pardon my saying so, I don't think it's such a good idea for someone in your condition," he said, nodding his head toward her advanced state of pregnancy, "to be along."

Margaret's hand was on the doorknob. She drew up tall and met MacDuff's eyes directly.

"Mr. MacDuff, as my husband's appointed representative while he is…is recovering from his, his…illness, it is my duty to know as much as possible about his territory and anything that involves it. So, don't worry about me. I am a very strong woman, totally capable of taking care of myself."

With that, she opened the front door and walked out ahead of MacDuff, Spud, and Kyle.

But MacDuff might have won the hand. She gasped when she saw five more young men in the back of Mr. MacDuff's pickup truck, all changing into Klan robes.

* * *

"If you don't mind, Mrs. Browne, we're on a schedule," MacDuff said, "could you hurry a bit, putting on that robe?"

MacDuff had handed her the long white Klan robe the minute they'd gotten in the truck, yet it was still folded on her lap.

Kyle was sitting in the bed of the truck, along with his new friends and Spud, but she could feel him glaring at her through the back window.

At last, she held up the garment, and pulled it on over her head. How ironic, she thought, that, except for the Klan emblem, it looked so much like a choir robe. She struggled to raise herself, and pulled the robe the rest of the way down, tied the sash, then donned the hood.

She glanced in the truck's side view mirror. Two more old trucks were pulling up behind MacDuff's truck, the bed of both trucks filled with more young men in robes.

MacDuff was more dangerous than Devin realized.

*   *   *

A rain storm had been threatening the entire day but the clouds had grown even darker and more ominous during the fifteen-minute ride from Capitol Hill to Five Points. It was only dusk as the two Fords turned onto Welton but the street lights were already on.

MacDuff, who was driving the lead truck, slowed the speed of the truck until he exactly matched the pace of a well-dressed Negro man walking up the street.

The man seemed not to notice the two trucks, or the trucks' hooded passengers, even as MacDuff blared his horn at him. He just kept on walking and whistling as carefree as when they'd first driven up beside him.

MacDuff scowled. "So this damn nigger wants to play high and mighty, huh? Well, I'll show him high and mighty."

MacDuff put his arm out the window and gave Spud a hand signal to stay close.

Margaret wanted to scream for the man to look out but she knew that she couldn't. If she did, MacDuff would accuse her of being a traitor and would probably make a report to Dr. Locke. That was the last thing she could afford to have happen. She had to force herself not to look away as Spud drove up on the sidewalk and nudged the back of the man with the Ford's bumper.

Yet, for some reason, the man still didn't turn around, even with both of the trucks' horns blaring at him.

Kyle leaned out the truck window and shouted at the man. "Maybe you oughta be a smart nigger, and move out of the way. That is, unless you wanta be a dead nigger."

Suddenly, the man did run. He went about half a block, then ducked into a locksmith shop's doorway.

Spud hit his brakes and screeched to a stop right on the sidewalk. MacDuff drove up beside Spud. Everyone in the two trucks, except Margaret, was howling with laughter.

"Bet that nigger won't ignore us the next time," MacDuff said to his backseat passengers.

"Ain't that the sure enough truth," Kyle said.

Margaret just sat quietly, praying that this would all be over soon.

As she looked out at the buildings they were parked in front of she was startled to realize that she recognized them.

Her body went cold.

MacDuff and Spud drove back into the street and started blaring their horns again.

This time, the trucks in front of them pulled to the curb and let the two Fords pass.

As they continued slowly down Welton, MacDuff asked, out loud, "Who's ready back there?"

The boy sitting next to Kyle hollered, "I am! I am! Let me do it."

MacDuff braked.

Spud had to swerve to avoid hitting him.

Margaret felt queasy all over again. They were parked in front of the same church in which she had taken refuge that awful night. The night that she had found out that—

No! She mustn't think of that night ever, *ever again*.

She tried to listen to MacDuff give the boy instructions, only his words seemed to blur as she watched a young Negro boy and Negro girl walk up the church's steps, then pull open the church's heavy wooden door and go inside the church.

A banner above the church door announced:

Annual Summer Revival
Saturday, August 16th
All Welcome!
Soul Food Dinner Immediately Following

Margaret felt panicked as she tried to remember the day's date. Finally, it came to her; it was Wednesday, the 13th. She had never felt so relieved.

The Klan Caravan to Golden was the Saturday after the church's revival.

She strained to hear the music and singing coming from inside the church, but her attention was distracted when the boy in the backseat suddenly got out of the truck.

He ran up the church steps, and like the boy and girl before him, went inside.

Unlike them, within moments, he ran back outside.

As soon as the boy jumped in the truck MacDuff sped away, with the other trucks following closely behind.

"Man, you should've seen them niggers' faces when I held up that pop bottle, then, threw it at the altar," the boy said, panting. "They was yellin' and screamin' like the place was really on fire. Too bad wasn't nothing more than root beer in that bottle."

MacDuff's guttural laugh caused chill bumps to rise along Margaret's arms and across the back of her neck.

She turned around to look at the church, but with the quickly widening distance between it and the trucks, as well as the onset of evening, all she could see was a faceless crowd running out of the church and gathering in the street to shout at the two Fords.

*   *   *

Rowena decided to drive around the lake one last time. If she didn't see Devin's car parked along there somewhere by now, he was one white man gonna get a piece a her mind.

She never understood why he insisted on them meeting in City Park, anyway. It was like playing with damn fire as far as she was concerned. Especially now that it was getting toward the tail end of summer, 'cause everybody and their grandmamma was out trying to catch themselves a breeze.

And, that was all she needed. The wrong people to see her with an ofay.

He should a been worryin', too, about the wrong people seeing him with a Colored woman.

To hell with it, she decided. He hadn't even showed up.

She turned onto the road to York Street and headed home.

Still, the thought nagged at her, something about Devin not being there didn't add up. He hadn't even been so much as late all the other times.

She decided to do like she always did. Follow her instinct.

After all, it wasn't like Grant Street was on the north side of town. Besides that, it was almost dark. No one would even see her drive by his house.

She remembered the night he'd shown the house to her.

They had parked practically in front of it and he had pointed out each window, then described each room, down to the knickknacks in it.

Not that she had wanted to know all that, but afterwards, for some reason, he was kinder to her. He said that in a lot of ways, she was the best thing that had ever happened to him. That, around her, he could be his real self.

She hadn't said anything back to him but she could have said the same thing about him just as easy.

He didn't even laugh when she told him she wished she could a gone to one a them colleges.

When she arrived at York Street, she turned left, or south, then kept going the couple or so blocks to Forteenth Street and turned right, west, onto it.

She was at Grant before she knew it, and turned left onto it, and continued to the twelve hundred block.

She decided to park at the far end of the block, just in case. If anybody looked out their window, and saw her, they'd likely think she was just a maid, coming or going.

Devin's house was in the middle of the block. It reminded her of the English castles she'd seen in the picture books at the library. Huge, made of big gray blocks of stone, and, about as home-like as a witch's den.

It was noticeably dark, especially among the other houses which all had various lights on. She had only one thought.

If no one was home…this was her chance to get inside and see the place for herself.

She walked around to the back of the house.

As she had expected, the service door wasn't locked.

She went in and found herself in the Browne's kitchen as easy as if she was entering with an engraved invitation. She could just see it; their creamy white stationery with the name, Mrs. Rowena Johnson, written on the envelope.

But not in this century.

The whole place was as dark as a cave. She had to wait for her eyes to adjust. Was that rabbit stew she smelled?

Finally, she began to be able to distinguish objects. The wood stove, the sink, the ice box. A doorway. She ventured onward, into the front of the house.

"Wow!" was all she could say at the sight of the foyer's chandelier. For a minute, she allowed herself to imagine that this was her home.

"But that tin man over in the corner is gonna be the first thing on the trash heap," she said, laughing.

She tiptoed across to the library doors, carefully opened one, and went in.

Directly in front of her was obviously Devin's desk, just like he'd described it. And, his Civil War collection.

She looked above the fireplace, for the portrait of Devin's grandfather, The Colonel, but all that was there was an empty space the shape of a large painting, lighter than the rest of the wall, as if a picture had been there but was now gone.

Still, she'd seen enough of The Colonel's type when she was growing up in Mississippi. Old white men sitting in their porch rocking chairs, wearing their faded Confederate uniforms, talking about the war, with anyone who would give them the time of day, as if the whole thing was still going on and Lincoln hadn't freed the slaves.

She knew the thought of a Negress wandering around, free as you please, in his inner sanctum, would have caused The Colonel to have a heart attack.

She stopped at the mannequin and ran her hand down the buttons of The Colonel's uniform. "I bet you's turnin' over in your grave now-ain't you?-you hateful old coot."

She left the library, respectfully closing the doors behind her, and stood again in the foyer, looking over at what, if she remembered right, was the parlor.

Nothing of interest in there, she decided. She'd seen grand pianos before...in most of the houses she'd cleaned to get the money to open her shop. Usually, they were just expensive decoration that needed a lot of dusting.

No, it was upstairs that she really wanted to see. The private part of the house.

She put a hand on the stairway banister, listened for signs of anyone, then, hearing nothing but more quiet, tiptoed up one... step...at...a...time.

Upon reaching the second floor landing, she found it was even darker, and scarier, than the first floor. Nevertheless, the room she was looking for was either on this floor, or the next one up. She decided to try the hallway to the left. As she waited for her eyes to adjust again, she thought about Devin.

She couldn't exactly call him her man, but she had invested the prime years of her life caring about him. What could it hurt for her to know this little bit more about him?

As soon as she could see better, she walked down the corridor, past the first two doors, to the third door. To what she believed was Devin's, and his wife's, bedroom.

The glass doorknob felt curiously cold,, but she went in anyway.

The sight of Devin, asleep on the chaise lounge with a blanket over him, nearly took her breath away.

She tiptoed near.

He was snoring like a freight train.

Just as she bent to touch and wake him, he moaned, and shifted to his opposite side, causing the blanket to pull off of his shoulder.

"Uh!" she gasped, quickly covering her mouth to hold in a scream. His chest and shoulder were bandaged with wide strips of cloth, and in the area near his shoulder, was a dark blotch.

She touched it lightly with her fingertips.

Blood!

Devin coughed and turned again.

She had to hurry and get out of here. Forget the rest of the house. Whatever had happened, she didn't want any part of it.

She backed cautiously away from the bed, to the open door, but once in the hallway, saw that a light had been turned on downstairs. She had to hide. Fast.

She decided one of the bedrooms across the hall would probably be safest, at least until she could figure out what to do next.

She darted across to one of the other doors and chanced opening it. It was to a large, white tiled bathroom.

A shaft of moonlight beamed in through the open window.

She looked around, frantically. Other than the claw-foot bathtub, generous porcelain sink, and toilet, all that was in the bathroom was a large white wicker hamper.

She was desperate to find a hiding place, but something about that hamper bothered her.

She gently·closed the bathroom door, then tiptoed across to the hamper, set the hamper's lid on the floor, and began sifting through and examining the hamper's contents.

All she found among the items dumped on the floor were several damp, used towels and washcloths, a woman's dress-practical; plain, front buttons, simple white collar and cuffs, no waist-a slip, brassiere, panties, and stockings, a woman's floor length, long-sleeved cotton nightgown, and some bloodied strips of cloth tied together.

Maybe her instincts were wrong this time. More important, she needed to be finding a way out of this damn house without getting caught. She kicked a pile of the items in disgust.

"Owww!" she caught herself in time to muffle the whisper.

She'd kicked something in the pile hard enough to hurt her toes. She felt around for it, then held it up for examination.

It was a man's white shirt, tied in a knot around something. Something that felt oddly like a gun.

She tugged at the knot until the shirt's sleeves came loose and an old pistol clamored to the floor.

She bent to retrieve the pistol, then straightened back up and smelled the pistol's barrel. There was no mistaking it. It had been fired recently. She also gave the shirt a good once over. It had a hole at the top of a sleeve that was surrounded by a large dark stain. She smelled it too. More blood.

"That crazy bitch tried to kill him," she said so loudly, there was a slight echo.

A second later, the bathroom door swung open and Rowena found herself flooded in light, with Margaret Browne staring straight at her.

"What in heaven's name are you doing in my house?" Margaret screamed.

"Oh, right, Miss High and Mighty," Rowena said, waving the pistol in Margaret's face. "Like that's what's really eating you, Miss White Lady. Well, when I take this piece down to the police station it's you what's gonna have to come up with the answers. Or…maybe…if you just get out of my way, and let me out of here, peaceably, I'll keep my Colored mouth shut."

"First of all," Margaret said, as Rowena tried to bully past her, "you've got this all wrong. And second, I'm not afraid of you. You go to the police and you'll get a rude awakening. Half of the police are Devin's friends and associates."

"Oh yeah," Rowena said, and belted Margaret in the face with the butt of the pistol to make her move, "well, I have friends and associates of my own."

Blood spurted from the left corner of Margaret's mouth. That side of her face throbbed with such pain, the only way she could remain upright was to lean against the wall.

Her head ached too, and she felt dizzy.

The vision from her one good eye was blurred, and there was two of everything, including Rowena and the pistol.

Rowena was taunting her and waving the pistol back and forth in front of her face.

"You white folks think you can get away with any and everything. Except this time, it ain't gonna be so easy, 'cause here's the evidence.

"No!" Margaret pleaded and lunged for the gun as Rowena escaped into the hall. "You don't know what you're talking about."

She stumbled down the hall after Rowena who was already at the landing.

Devin appeared at the bedroom doorway, and called to Rowena. "Stay out of this, Rowena, I'm warning you."

"You warning me! I done stood by you, and helped you, all these years, and you warning me? Both you ofays crazy."

Margaret had crawled down the hall to Rowena, then managed to stand and put a hand on Rowena's arm. "Please," Margaret said, "we don't want trouble. Leave us alone and we'll leave you--"

Rowena jerked her arm away from Margaret's grasp, causing Margaret to loose her balance.

Neither Rowena nor Devin could move fast enough to prevent Margaret from falling.

She tumbled and tumbled to the bottom of the steps, where she lay, groaning, on the floor.

"Oh, Lord, have mercy," Rowena cried and started to run to Margaret, but someone had grabbed and was squeezing her shoulder. It was Devin.

The foyer chandelier was on, providing enough light for them to clearly see Margaret's crumpled body.

"I think you better get out of here while you can," he said in a strangely calm voice.

Rowena nodded, almost imperceptibly, only rather than run, she slowly walked back down the stairs.

When she reached the last step, where Margaret lay nearly unconscious, she simply stepped over Margaret as if Margaret were merely an inconveniently discarded doll...then, hurried on to the front door.

Before opening the door, Rowena paused, and looked back for a last look at Devin.

While their eyes met, the door opened against Rowena's back and bumped her out of the way.

Devin's emotionless expression became one of pure hatred.

Rowena turned to find the reason.

"Walter!"

Walter didn't answer. It was clear all he cared about was Margaret, as he ran to her, kneeled beside her, and gently lifted her into his arms.

"Call Denver General," he yelled up at Devin. "Tell them to send an ambulance, right away." Blood had soaked Margaret's Klan robe. There was a deathly stillness in the air.

"My baby," Margaret suddenly wailed. "I'm losing my baby."

Chapter Eighteen

An old Indian legend has it that all the stolen hunting grounds will be reclaimed on a night blazing with fire.

Angus looked out of his bedroom window at the bolts of lightning crackling through the sky and hoped the spirits of the great chiefs hadn't chosen this night.

He made the sign of the cross, prayed for his sins to be forgiven, blew out his bedside candle, and went to sleep. Except for a once-in-awhile nightmare, he usually slept well.

His daughter, Margaret, teased that he still lived over the store because he liked being as close as possible to his money.

Contrary to what people thought, however, he wasn't so much miserly as prudent. Wisdom he'd learned in childhood.

Indeed, he had become a wealthy man by valuing every hard-earned cent, investing, rather than spending, his wages whenever possible.

Moreover, maintaining residence above the store insured that he opened promptly at eight AM, and that nights, he could stay as late as necessary, for paperwork and inventorying.

The real reason he had bought the building, though, and turned the top floor into his living quarters, was that it kept him from having to deal with prying neighbors. And when Margaret was growing up, he had only allowed her the two friends, the Jewish girl from the family with all of the money, and the Chinese girl, who lived around the corner in Hop Alley, because he knew that with both girls' parents being immigrants, they wouldn't want anyone nosing in their business either.

Other than that, he had done everything possible to discourage Margaret's curiosity about other cultures, and above all, he had brought her up white, and done all in his power to bury the truth.

He tossed, and turned, hoping that sleep would come soon.

*　　*　　*

"We must remember to tell Margaret about Ming's graduation dinner," Mr. Hwang said to his wife as he locked the laundry door behind their last customer of the day.

He beamed with pride whenever he spoke of his daughter's soon to be realized accomplishment.

"Yes, dear husband," Mrs. Hwang replied as she cleared the shop's countertop. "You are right, of course. I will go by Mr. O'Shea's store tomorrow and leave a note for Margaret. Perhaps, he will also accept our invitation to dinner."

"Let us not seek miracles, my flower," Mr. Hwang said, then walked down the hall to their back of the shop apartment. "If Angus O'Shea wishes to be a private man, then we, of all people, must respect that."

They entered the living room of their apartment and settled into the evening's routine.

Mr. Hwang at work on the family genealogy chart.

Mrs. Hwang preparing the evening meal of rice and fish.

Ming, who had finally settled on a young man to marry, would be home soon from her classes at Emily Griffith Opportunity School, where she was taking courses for her secretarial certificate.

The Hwangs had worked hard to make a success of their life in America, and wanted Ming to be able to do even better.

They could hardly wait to present her with the money they'd managed to save for her wedding.

"Look, husband. Here are two more dollars," Mrs. Hwang showed her husband before she added the money to the amount already in the secret drawer at the bottom of the dove cage.

"That lovely Mrs. Wright admired my hair comb again today, but when I offered it to her she would only take it if I let her pay for it. She gave me much more than that old thing was worth, but brought good fortune for all."

"Yes, my flower. Now please, let me work. Tonight I am writing in the names of our ancestors, my great-great-great grandmother and grandfather, who first told me of America, and whose first son helped build the railroads here. I do not wish to make any mistakes, so I must give it my complete concentration."

"I can help, father," Ming said, as she came into the apartment through the kitchen door that led out to the alley.

"Ah! You're late daughter," Mr. Hwang scolded. "I was about to worry."

"My beloved father, you worry too much," Ming said, and kissed her father on his forehead. "And mother, you rest tonight. Let me cook for once. I need the practice, don't I?"

"What a good daughter you are, Ming," Mrs. Hwang said, and handed Ming her apron. "Your father and I are so fortunate."

A strange sound, like breaking glass, shattered the quiet.

"What was that?" Mrs. Hwang said, nervously. "And that?"

The three of them looked at each other blankly.

"Ming, stay with your mother," Mr. Hwang said. "I shall go up front and see what has happened. I'm sure it is just a strong wind that blew the shop door open."

"But, Father," Ming protested, "the door is locked. Or, at least, I meant to lock it. Perhaps I forgot to turn the key. You and mother just sit down and remain calm. I will be right back."

But Mr. Hwang was already halfway down the hall when there was another sound of breaking glass, only this time, Ming and Mrs. Hwang knew which window had broken because they were standing right by it when the bottle that broke it came sailing through.

Within seconds, the kitchen smelled of gasoline, then burst into flames.

"Mother!" Ming cried, "We have to get out of here. Through the front." Ming put her arm around her mother's shoulder and led her mother down the hall, to the laundry.

They could barely see through the smoke that was already choking them as they entered the shop. Then, Ming saw the flames climbing one of the laundry's walls, and her father trying to put the fire out with the drape that divided the laundry and the apartment hallway.

There was a broken pop bottle on the floor and the burned remnants of a rag near it. The window shades were disintegrating, and the paper-wrapped bundles of freshly laundered shirts, neatly stacked on shelves behind the counter, were also on fire.

And the smoke had blackened and thickened. It was nearly impossible to see even as far as a foot ahead. "Father, we can't see you. Where are you?" Ming called out trying not to choke.

"Here, daughter," Mr. Hwang said as he stepped close and looped arms with his wife. "We must hurry before all falls down around us. Come. I have the key to the door."

Mr. Hwang tugged at his wife but she wouldn't move. She was screaming something, in Chinese, something about the bird cage. Finally, Ming understood. "No, Mother, let me go for it. You and Father wait outside."

Ming ran back down the smoke-shrouded hallway before either her father or mother could stop her.

Mrs. Hwang shrieked as her husband shielded her past the flames and forced her outside.

Many neighboring buildings were also on fire, but a citizens' brigade was doing the best it could to douse the fires with hand-passed buckets of water.

Anyone could see that it was too late to save the laundry. It had already become a roaring furnace.

The clanging bells of the arriving fire trucks were little comfort to Ming's father and mother as they kept vigil, hopelessly waiting for Ming to emerge from the flame-engulfed building.

"Hey, Captain," a fireman near them shouted," this one's a goner. But look, there's smoke coming from about where the dry goods store is, around the corner."

*　*　*

The Denver Post had reported the death toll from the night of fires at two, but the *Rocky Mountain News* said it was three, because a missing child was presumed dead.

"Let me take you there," Gwen said to Margaret. "You shouldn't go alone."

Margaret didn't answer. She had no more words, or even tears. Within one week, she had lost her baby, and her father.

Gwen tried again. "Of course, there's no rush. There isn't much left to see." She went over to a chair with a brown paper bag sitting on it, and took a carved wooden box out of the bag and set the box in Margaret's lap. "But a really nice fireman found this under your father's body and thought you might want it. He said it must have really been important to your father for him to protect it with his life. I cleaned as much of the soot off of it as I could."

Margaret didn't even look at it so Gwen sat down on the edge of the bed and opened the box for her. There were a handful of brass buttons scattered around, a lock of red baby hair, a ribbon-tied stack of letters addressed to Margaret's father from Ireland, and more.

"Oh, you're not going to believe this," Gwen said, "here's your first grade report card."

She noted the column of straight A's.

"Boy, you were a real Miss Smarty Pants, weren't you? And, how about this old pouch? I wonder what's in it."

Gwen opened the pouch and poured a small treasure of shiny yellow nuggets into her palm. "Uh! Margaret, look! Gold! Real gold!?

Margaret glanced at the nuggets, but all they looked like to her were plain ole rocks. Something else in the box, though, did catch her attention. A silver framed picture of a sailor and a young woman.

She took it from the box and examined the faces in the picture. "I think this is a photograph of my mother and father. She was beautiful, wasn't she? And, so blonde. I don't really remember that much about her."

"Yeah, she was a real looker all right," Gwen agreed. And your pop wasn't too bad himself."

At last, Margaret smiled. "I wonder what this is?" she said and reached for a well-worn envelope and opened it. It held a sheaf of receipts which she put aside and a birth certificate which she unfolded and read over and over.

"No! No, no, no. This can't be," she finally said in a near whimper, and held the certificate up for Gwen to see. It was for a baby girl named Amelia Grace O'Shea, born seventeen years ago. The very same day as her daughter.

She looked at Gwen for a long while. "My father knew all along where she was. And these receipts…" She picked up the receipts and studied them one by one. "They're all made out to Dwight. One for every year since her birth. But, how in the world, could Dwight have betrayed me like this? My father must have paid him off to take her."

For once, Gwen was speechless, too.

*   *   *

As she stood outside of Dwight's gate, Margaret felt grateful for the cover of night. The summer downpour had soaked her clothes, yet she had to see him.

Just being there brought back so many memories. In fact, at least the front of the house was still much the same as when she and Dwight had known each other as teenagers and it was his parents' house. Even the porch swing that his mother had ordered from Sears catalog was still there. It had hurt her to read that his parents had died in an automobile accident.

What had shocked her even more was to learn of Dwight's marriage so soon after her father had forced them to part.

With Gwen's help, however, she had eventually understood that it was probably better for Dwight to have a Colored wife.

Someone from his own background and community.

The ache of the past seventeen years, and of all that she had been denied, was reawakened. She fell to her knees and cried out. "Please, Dwight! Please tell me where our daughter is. Tell me where I can find her."

269

* * *

Trixie Hudson stared out her window and cursed under her breath. She'd always known this would happen one day. Why, she wondered for the thousandth time, hadn't Dwight's parents shipped his bastard child somewhere down south, instead of allowing her to be raised by some woman right here in Denver?

She walked back to their bed and jabbed Dwight in his side until he awoke. "That damn woman is outside;the mother of your child. If you don't get out there and shut her up, our son is going to find out everything. Thank God, his train doesn't get in until tomorrow."

Dwight sat up and tried to understand, for all he was worth, what his wife was ranting about now. Then it came to him. The woman she was talking about must be Margaret. Except, that didn't make sense. He hadn't seen Margaret for almost seventeen years, and she had no way of knowing that he knew anything about their daughter's whereabouts. Trixie must be drinking again.

"Trixie, I thought I told you to stay out of the liquor cabinet."

"Don't you wish that's what this was about. Well, just look out the window and see for yourself."

But he didn't have to. He heard the woman's cry and recognized her voice immediately. It was Margaret.

He grabbed his robe and ran past Trixie, out of their bedroom, barefoot. Out to Margaret. The love of his life.

She looked at him with the most accusing eyes as he approached her, but he kneeled beside her anyway and held her until her sobs quieted to whimpers. Almost the very same thing he'd done seventeen years ago, the last time they'd been allowed to see each other.

Also, like then, she rested her head against his chest.

He could feel her warm breath against his skin when she spoke. "Why? Why?" she asked in a voice so tortured, he could barely take it without breaking down too. He was grateful that she wasn't looking him in the face.

"I didn't have a choice," he said. "As it was, I had to plead with your father not to put her up for adoption. There was a family waiting somewhere back east. But, finally, he relented. He said that as long as I kept my promise not to see you again, our daughter could grow up in Denver, and that she would have everything she ever needed. And, if I did try to see you, she would be sent, immediately, to someplace I'd never be able to find her."

Margaret drew away from Dwight and looked into his eyes again.

He had never seen such anguish. "I did it for you, Margaret," he said. "I thought that if at least I knew where our daughter was, there was still hope for us to, someday, be a family."

"But, you got married, and had your own family."

"Yeah, that's true. But I didn't plan it. I'd known Trixie forever. Since we were children. When the fella she was pregnant by skipped out on her, I felt sorry for her, especially after what we'd gone through. I was just trying to do something right for once. Our son's name is Anthony. I've raised him just like he was my own."

"Can I see her? Our daughter. Please. I just need to see her." Margaret asked.

"What about your father?"

"My father is dead. His store burned to the ground last night. He wasn't able to get out in time. I found out about all of this when I looked through a box that he died holding in his hands. Her birth certificate was in the box, along with other sentimental keepsakes.

Dwight took a long time to answer, but finally did.

"All right, but then what? She's been raised by a good, hard working woman, who Amy believes is her mother."

"Amy? That's her name?"

"Short for Amelia, just like you told me you wanted it."

"Did you know that I wasn't even allowed to hold her one time? Not even to see her?" Margaret asked. "Can you imagine what that was like? At least, you've seen, and probably held her, when she was a baby. All I've had over these seventeen years are nightmares and prayers. I don't want to unravel her life. I just want her to know that I've always loved her and would never have given her up. Please, will you take me to see her? Now!"

Dwight took Margaret's face in his hands.

"Yes, of course, I will. Right this minute. I just have to go inside and get my shoes and car keys. Would you like to sit on the porch swing while you're waiting? I remember how you and Mama used to sit there, talking and shelling peas."

* * *

It was still very early, but the feel of it being a Sunday was unmistakable. Dwight parked the car two doors down from Rowena's and turned off the ignition. He wasn't used to not being in charge of what happened next.

Margaret already had her door open. "Is this where she lives?" she asked with one foot on the ground.

"No. Two doors down. I just thought it would be better for us to park back a ways until we figure out how we're going to do this."

Margaret didn't answer Dwight. She was out of the car and on her way to the door he had pointed out.

"Hello. Hello," she called out. "Is anyone home? I'm looking for my daughter. Please. Someone. Anyone. Just tell me if you know where she is."

Dwight hurried out of the car and rushed to Margaret's side. He knew there was no stopping her, but he also knew Rowena was going to be as mad as a wild cat.

She opened the door still wearing her Saturday night dress. When she saw Margaret, her eyes narrowed to slits.

"I'm warning you, white lady. Stay away from us? You don't know who you messin' with. Now get away from my door…and stay the hell away from my child."

Rowena started to shut the door, but she saw that Margaret was straining to see something, or someone, in the upstairs window. She ran outside and looked up too.

Amy was standing at the window staring down at Margaret just as hard as Margaret was staring up at her.

Rowena ran out of the house and began pummeling Margaret with her fists.

Margaret didn't budge.

Dwight had to wrestle with Rowena to pull her back.

"I don't mean you any harm," Margaret finally said, absently to Rowena, while not taking her eyes off Amy for even a second. "I just needed to see my daughter. She was taken from me right after she was born. The doctor and nurse didn't even allow me to hold her. Not even to look at her."

"Don't tell me your sob story, lady. I don't want to know about it. Amy is my daughter, and I'm warning you not to come anywhere near her – *ever* – again."

Margaret ignored Rowena and stared up at the window again. Amy was still there.

Margaret had never felt so certain of anything in her life. The young woman looking down at her was indeed her daughter.

Rowena fought harder against Dwight's hold and kicked his shin. "Ow, damn it. Margaret, get back in the car. I can't hold her much longer."

"All right, but I'm not going to give up. One day, I'm going to be able to tell her the truth," Margaret said.

"Sure, lady. Over my dead body," Rowena said, then wrenched loose from Dwight's grip and turned and kneed him where it really hurt.

Chapter Nineteen

Margaret kissed Mother Browne's forehead, then smoothed a lock of the woman's remarkably still mostly black hair back into place. She wanted to do something special for her mother-in-law but they had so little in common, Margaret feared making the wrong choice. For some reason, her thoughts kept coming back to the realization that it was Sunday.

Of course. Church.

Mother Browne loved her church, but she hadn't been able to attend a service since suffering the stroke.

Yes, that's it," Margaret decided as she straightened Mother Browne's blankets, "I'll ask Devin if we can all go to church next Sunday, like a real family, for once."

Margaret was so pleased with her idea that, briefly, she felt like a gleeful child. The emotional pain of losing her baby had nearly destroyed Margaret, but for Amy's sake she had to somehow go on. Everything, now, was about finding a little more strength each day.

"Papa," she said aloud to her deceased father, on her way

to the windows to tie back the curtains, "I know you're not going to like my setting foot in a Presbyterian Church but you're gone now. I have to start doing what I think is right.

She flung open the windows. The August sun brightened the room. It was just past seven AM, but already warm outside. On her way out of the room she looked over at her mother-in-law with genuine love. "Don't worry, Mother Browne, I know how much you hate the heat. I'll be back to pull the shades after you've gotten a little fresh air."

Mother Browne responded with her usual blank stare but Margaret refused to be daunted. She and Mother Browene needed each other, and she wasn't going to allow either of them to give up.

She closed Mother Browne's door as quietly as possible, then lingered momentarily in the hallway listening for sounds of Devin's and Kyle's whereabouts in the house.

She heard the quiet rustle of newspaper pages turning down in the parlor.

As usual, Devin was engrossed in the Sunday newspapers, but he had consistently made it clear that he preferred his solitude.

Kyle, on the other hand, was most likely still asleep, for it had been well after midnight when she had finally heard him come in.

She had at least a few hours to do as she wanted.

She hurried down the hallway to the back stairway, then went up the stairway and entered a small room used to store old steamer trunks.

Without anyone's knowing, Margaret had turned the room into a makeshift art studio. The little porthole-like window provided her light during the day, and on the occasional nights that she worked, she used candles to work by.

One of the trunks hid her pencils and sketch pads. She

opened it and took out her pencils and a book of drawings she had completed of Columbine flowers.

As the state flower, picture postcards of Columbines were popular with tourists and curio shops bought whatever she drew. On one page of the sketch pad, however, was the outline of the drawing that she would never sell. She flipped through the pages of the book until she came to it, then sat on the trunk and studied the drawing on the page for a long while.

This portrait of her daughter, of Amy, was going to be the best work that she had ever done. Now if only she could capture the crinkly texture of the hair. She thought of how surprised she had been that her daughter's skin had Dwight's same caramel coloring. Margaret put herbpencil to the paper and for the next half hour was absorbed in the joys of her effort.

She hadn't heard Devin's footsteps until it was too late. By then he had slammed open the door. The Colored woman, his mistress, was standing next to him.

"Maybe now you'll believe me," Rowena said to Devin as they stared down at the portrait of Amy.

Devin backhanded Rowena in the mouth.

"Aaggghhh!" she cried. "What was that for?"

Devin glared at her. "Just be glad if that's all I do. Now get out of this house."

Rowena-still holding her face where she had been hit-started to argue back then seemed to change her mind.

Devin grabbed her by the arm. "Don't ever come back here. Do you understand?"

Rowena nodded and wriggled her arm out of Devin's hold, then fled.

Margaret realized that she had just witnessed the parting of two people who loved each other.

Devin stepped closer to her and held out his hand for her sketch book.

"I, I don't understand," Margaret said, praying that she could somehow placate Devin.

"Like hell, you don't," Devin said and snatched the book out of Margaret's hands, "I'm married to a goddamn nigger lover, that's what to understand."

He whacked Margaret across the face with the book, and she barely let out a sound as she crumpled to the floor.

"You don't ever learn, do you?" he said, and yanked her up. Figures. That white trash father of yours didn't either."

"Please," Margaret begged, "I can explain."

"Just shut up," Devin said. "You've got a meeting to go to. And, you'd better come back with the right results."

"Oh, no, Devin. No. I can't be part of all that anymore. What you and the others are planning isn't right. No Colored people ever did anything to you."

Devin stopped just short of hitting her again.

"You know," he seethed, "you'd better be glad I need you right now," he said, then maneuvered Margaret around toward the door.

They were both shocked to discover Kyle standing there.

"God damn it, boy. What d'you want?" Devin said.

"Nothing, Pop," Kyle answered. "I just heard all the racket and thought I'd see what was going on. What's with the book?"

Devin shoved the sketch book into Kyle's chest. "Your stepmother, here, is a nigger lover, that's all. But don't worry, she's going to make amends. Ain't that right?" Devin asked Margaret as he steered her past Kyle.

Tears were streaming down Margaret's face. "Yes, Devin, that's right," she said.

* * *

The banquet room was well lit, but Margaret had arrived at the meeting after the mugs of complimentary ale had been downed. By then, most of the men's powers of perception had dulled appreciably. None of them seemed to notice Margaret's unusually heavy face powder.

Or, at the least, no one had dared comment on it.

She found it curious that some of the men were dressed in tuxedos, instead of their robes, like her and the rest of the men.

Dr. Locke pounded his gavel again. "Gentlemen…" he said, then noticed Margaret's barely raised hand. "Oh, yes, pardon me. And ladies. This Klancilium has been convened to discuss the Table Mountain march, which…" he nodded ceremoniously at Margaret, "Mrs. Browne's husband so brilliantly proposed."

"But, Doc," one of the advisory board members piped up, "Browne ain't even here. If we're really going to do this, don't we need someone who knows what they're doing?"

Margaret drew a deep breath and stood. "But, sir…that's exactly why I am here. To help you successfully plan and execute this day. Believe me, my husband wouldn't have sent me in his place if he didn't have complete confidence in my abilities. Now, may I suggest we start by deciding how much lumber we'll need? We'll certainly want enough to burn crosses-from sundown to midnight."

Even MacDuff had to agree.

"And the kerosene, I think, should be brought in from outlying counties as we absolutely don't want the *News* or the *Post* in on this, lest some ignorant do-gooder try to stop us."

The men had to agree again. This dame did know what she was doing. The Table Mountain march was going to be a topnotch extravaganza.

Over the next hour, most of the rest of the details about the march were pinned down, including the date. Saturday, August 23rd. Then the various committees were selected.

Any and all resistance to Margaret's involvement seemed to have dissipated.

Dr. Locke and four of the nine other board members got up to leave. "Boys..., and Mrs. Browne," Dr. Locke said, "a few of us have pressing business down the hall. I'm going to trust any other matters about the march to you."

"We'll do our best, Dr. Locke," Margaret replied with as much feigned conviction as possible.

"Oh, my dear, of that I am quite certain," the Grand Dragon said, and then led his entourage out of the room.

* * *

Amy awoke from the dream in a panic but she was even more startled to find herself in complete darkness.

She leaped out of her bed and ran to the room's closed door, afraid that she was locked in again.

"Mama, Mama, let me out," she screamed and twisted the doorknob. To her surprise, the door wasn't locked and opened easily.

The whole house was dark. She went out into the hall and called down the stairs to the first floor. "Mama?"

It was a long moment before she realized that she was in the house totally alone. Maybe the searing pain in her stomach would just go away.

She decided to go back to bed but her legs were almost too weak to carry her. She had to lower herself to the floor and crawl back, then could only manage to sit up against the side of the bed. The pain was worsening and she was sweating and short of breath. Even rocking back and forth didn't help. "Mama," she cried, "where are you? I think the baby is coming."

Just then she heard the front door open and the voices of a man and a woman. They were talking and laughing but they sounded drunk. Someone turned on the light at the base of the stairs.

Amy folded her arms against her stomach and called out. "Lulu? Is that you?"

There was no answer, just the sound of footsteps up the stairs. Amy cringed.

Lulu stopped at Amy's bedroom door and leaned in.

A short, balding white man in a tuxedo tiptoed past the door and continued on up to the third floor.

"Yeah, kid, it's me," Lulu said. "What are your doing on the floor?"

Amy ignored the question. "Where's my mother?" she said, feeling like she was about to pass out.

Lulu had the hiccups and could barely answer.

"Where she, uck, always is on Sunday, uck, nights, The Palace, uck, Hotel. Uck."

Lulu leaned back out in the hallway and looked up the stairs. "I'll be, uck, right there, Judgey. Just, uck, make your-self, uck, comfortable," she said. Then she leaned back into Amy's room and took a swig from the whiskey bottle she was holding. Her hiccups disappeared.

"You know, kid, your Mama's real smart. She sneaks us through them tunnels, then into the kitchen and upstairs by the back elevator. Makes a killin', I bet."

The judge bellowed down to Lulu. "Hey, doll-face, hurry. I gotta be home in less than an hour."

Lulu waved goodbye to Amy with the whiskey bottle. "Sorry, kid. Gotta, go."

Amy closed her eyes and waited to hear Lulu's door close. In another few minutes, she heard the springs of Lulu's bed.

Amy felt like the night was closing in around her. And the pain still had not subsided. She had to get to her mother.

She clutched the edge of the mattress and pulled herself up. The real struggle was getting dressed and downstairs to the first floor.

But then she realized that she had forgotten her purse, upstairs, in her room. For the first time in her life she was grateful for the beauty parlor. Especially for its cash register and telephone.

She opened the register and borrowed the money for a taxi, then made her call.

"Hurry," she pleaded to the taxi dispatcher, "it's an emergency."

* * *

She recognized the taxi driver from the train station. He also worked as a redcap. He was looking at her in his rearview mirror.

"Little sister, you gotta be crazy," he said. "Everybody knows they don't let Coloreds in Denver General. But I can take you to Dr. Ford. She's one of us, and don't never turn no one away."

Amy tried to make sense of the man's words but she was gulping for air and couldn't think.

"No! If I can't get to the hospital, then I've got to get to my mother. Take me…"-something was piercing her womb with what felt like a long, sharp knife-"…to the Palace…Hotel"

"To the what? Now, I know you're cra—"

"Please. I'm not crazy. I just need you to hurry. And I want the front entrance. Not the back."

The driver shook his head but said nothing more.

He had Amy at the Hotel's awning-covered main door in less than five minutes.

She tried to pay him but he refused her money.

"Next time, little sister," he said. "I just hope you know what you're doing."

She didn't. She just had no other choice. She *needed* her mother.

The bellman opened the taxi door and reached for her hand but drew it back, shocked, when he realized that she was a Negro.

She struggled out of the taxi without his help and rushed past him.

"Hey, lady," he shouted and ran into the lobby after Amy, "Coloreds aren't allowed on these premises. Where is it you think you're going?"

"To find my mother," Amy said as she entered the lobby.

Even in the haze of physical distress, she was dazzled by the opulence of the hotel's lobby, though not intimidated.

Her years at an exclusive boarding school, and all that came with it, prevented that.

She was halfway up the grand staircase before the guests in the lobby realized what was happening.

She reached the mezzanine and hurried to an elevator just as its doors were closing. No one in the party of revelers on the elevator seemed to notice her.

She rode with them to the top floor, and exited in their midst.

She chanced tagging after them until they were halfway down the corridor, then made a spur-of-the-moment decision to duck behind a potted palm.

The group never detected her absence as she disappeared around a corner. But now, how to find her mother?

She heard loud voices coming from rooms in opposite directions. It was worth a try to knock on both doors.

She went to the nearest door first, knocked, and surprisingly, was invited in.

It was as if she had opened the door to a nightmare, yet it was all too real. Six robed Klansmen were sitting around a poker table, arguing with each other.

She backed out so quickly she nearly tripped. They had barely gotten a glimpse of her.

She hurried down to the other room, but this time pressed her ear to the door for a better sense of things.

There was definitely a party behind this door.

Again, she knocked, but this time, no one answered.

She tried once more. The torment in her stomach had returned at double the intensity. There was no way these were ordinary labor pains. She needed help right now.

She tried the door, found it unlocked, and went in.

The air inside the room was hazy and smelled of cigars, bootleg liquor, and a clash of dime store toilet waters.

Colored women were sitting in the laps of white men and jazz was playing on a phonograph.

"Come here, gal," a grandfatherly looking man said to Amy as he grabbed her by the wrist.

"No!" Amy shouted. "Get your dirty hands off of me."

"Now see here, darlin', we've paid good money for you all's services. Why so unfriendly?" the man said.

Amy was trying to pry loose the man's hold on her when Rowena came between them.

"Captain, see that real chocolate girl over in the corner, the one waving at you?"

"Yeah," he said. "She is a mighty pretty filly."

"She's been wantin' to meet you the whole evening. Why don't you go over and strike up a conversation. She's kinda on the shy side. You know, new in town."

"Well, all right, Rowena, anything for you," the man said and let go of Amy.

"Thanks, Captain," Rowena said as the man walked away, "I's indebted to you again."

She kept her arm around Amy's waist, but waited until the Captain was nearly across the room before turning to her. "Baby, how'd you know where I was? Better still, why are you here?"

Amy tried to answer, only couldn't catch her breath.

"That's all right," Rowena said, "we's gonna jest get on outta here."

Rowena shielded Amy's eyes and directed her toward the door. They were safely out in the corridor within seconds.

"Come on, baby, this way. We's gotta go out the same way I came in, by the kitchen elevator."

Amy screamed and fell to her knees. "But I can't move. It hurts too much."

Neither one of them saw Margaret emerge from the room that she had been in. She saw them, however, and ran to help.

"Here, lean on me," she said as she bent down to Amy. "We'll get you down to the doctor."

Both Rowena and Amy looked up immediately except their expressions couldn't have been more unalike; pure hatred versus confused longing.

"Get away from this child," Rowena screamed, "She's mine. I told you, don't never come near us again. Amy is *my* daughter."

Doors along the corridor were opening, and guests peeking out to see what was going on.

Margaret's only choice was to leave, but now that she had been face to face with her daughter, she was more determined than ever to claim her.

She swore to it on her own life.

Chapter Twenty

The ill-mannered brew in Rowena's speakeasy– of honky-tonk jazz, boisterous talk, and raucous bursts of laughter-tinged with all varieties and strengths of tobacco smoke, the vague scent of marijuana, and the aroma of concocted whiskey–escaped into the basement air vent, traveled up through the house, and permeated Amy's bedroom.

If Amy had to hear strains of da da, da da, da da dadda da da, she was going to scream.

She hated Saturdays.

More specifically, she hated being subjected to her mother's incessant business ideas, especially this latest; opening the speakeasy for Saturday afternoon poker games.

The three dollar admission included one basket of Rowena's to-die-for crispy southern fried chicken, a generous side of her home-style coleslaw, and two-for-the-price-of-one drinks...until five o'clock p.m., maybe six.

Amy's labor pains, the previous night, had been a false alarm. Dr. Ford had prescribed complete rest, so Rowena had insisted that Amy remain in bed all day.

What all three women had forgotten to consider is that it was Saturday, which eventually meant Saturday night.

Amy hated Saturday nights at Rowena's. It meant the speakeasy would be going full tilt with honky-tonk jazz, boisterous talk, raucous burst of laughter, all varieties and strengths of tobacco smoke and concocted whiskey, and all manner of gambling, from dice to poker.

Most especially, if Amy had to hear more strains of...

da da, da da, da da dadda da

...she was going to scream.

Worse, Dr. Ford was coming tomorrow to talk to her, again, about giving up the baby for adoption.

Their first meeting, last week in Dr. Ford's office, which was in her home, stunned Amy. She remembered that her mouth had gone dry when she'd realized what Dr. Ford was saying to her. She recalled that morning for what had to be the hundredth time.

"You'd like them, child. They're a nice Colored couple, a preacher and his wife, from Virginia. Newly settled in Nebraska. They can give your baby everything ima-"

"You mean, my baby?"

"Yes, child, of course. What can you do for a baby at your age? You won't even have graduated from high school when he or she is born. How will you keep a roof over its head, and feed and clothe it, let alone yourself. Work in your mother's hair salon...or...the speakeasy. A baby is a lot of responsibility. Have you ever even washed the dinner dishes, or had to make up your own bed? A baby is a real human being. It has a great many needs. Every day. Every night. Every hour. Every minute. Every second. Whether you feel like it, or not."

Gratefully, someone pounding on Amy's bedroom door brought her awareness back to the present and snatched her from the brink of more crying.

But she wanted them to please go away. She'd already

turned down the plates sent up to her earlier. Starting with breakfast, then lunch, and less than an hour ago, dinner.

Amy sat up, faced the door, and shouted, "Haven't I said all day that I'm not hungry? All I want is out of this jail my mother has me in."

"Girl," came Lulu's voice from the opposite side of the door, equally adamant, "you one hard-headed number. Just like your stubborn mama. You sure gonna be sorry one day."

Amy glared at the door and threw her pillow.

It hit the edge of her vanity table missing the lamp on it by mere inches.

"You change your mind, just slip a note on out here under the door," Lulu said, again through the closed door. "I'm sure your mother'll be sending me back up here before too long to check on you."

Amy jumped off of the bed, ran to the door, and yanked on the knob.

"Luluuuuuu! Please! Tell my mother she's got to let me out of here. This is so unfair,"

She waited for Lulu to respond, but all that came back was silence. She fell against the door and let go her tears of frustration. She wanted out of here. Now.

Except for chaperoned trips to the bathroom, Amy had been locked in. She was nearly ready to do something desperate. But what?

She felt the baby kick. It wanted out too.

Without warning, she felt weak, and wobbly.

She took minced steps across the room to the window seat and collapsed onto the cushion.

Her breathing was suddenly heavy and labored. Trying to calm herself she peered out the window at the front yard. Her attention was drawn to activity across the street.

Was her eyesight playing tricks on her?

There were two boys, young men, really, about her age–one Colored, one white–going at each other with fists.

She closed her eyes, breathed deeply several times, then looked again...confident that this time she would see nothing except shadows cast by a late-in-the-day sun. Only, it wasn't her imagination.

Anthony, and Kyle, in plain view, were punching each other like boxers in a prize fight.

Anthony's knuckles raked Kyle's chin.

Seconds later, Kyle retaliated with a right jab at Anthony's nose.

Both times Amy winced and cringed.

She struggled to raise the window, leaned out, and yelled, "Stop it, you two. Just stop it."

Either they didn't hear Amy, or she was flat out being ignored, as the match continued unabated. She yelled louder.

"Are you both crazy? I said, stop fighting!"

As if choreographed, Anthony and Kyle's next attacks on each other halted midair, yet even with the distance and dim light, Amy could see they were still glaring at each other.

What in the world were they doing here? Fighting?

Simultaneously, as if she'd called both their names, they looked up at her.

All she could do was stare back at them, still not believing what she was seeing. The first Colored boy she'd ever liked, and the only white boy she'd ever loved...beating each other senseless.

Hadn't her mother made it utterly clear to both to never come around here again? Didn't they understand that her mother wasn't someone to be trifled with?

Maybe, months ago, it might have been her fantasy to have Anthony and Kyle duel over her, but she had grown up since then.

She was going to be a mother and all that was important to her now was protecting her child.

This was a nightmare.

Or, was it?

She waved for Anthony and Kyle to cross the street. To come near.

Both stared blankly at her, as if struggling with mutual bewilderment.

She waved at them again, more urgently.

*　　*　　*

"I think, she means both of us," Anthony said.

"Yeah. I think so too," Kyle said, warily.

Without so much as a rope, Amy had lassoed both of them like ponies in a rodeo. In tandem, they looked for on comin traffic.

Left. Then right.

They had to wait a minute for a clippity-clop horse pulling a vendor's fruit and vegetable cart, then the street was clear.

They bolted across, ran onto Rowena Johnson's forbidden front lawn, and stood beneath Amy's window, staring anxiously up at her.

Each young man's gaze declared an eagerness to please.

*　　*　　*

For a long moment, Amy studied Anthony and Kyle. How was it, she wondered, that she had never realized how similar they were to each other. In height and build. Even their facial features were more alike than different. Especially, their eyes. In fact, if it weren't for their different skin colors, in a first glance at a distance they might be mistaken for twin brothers.

The baby kicked again. If Anthony and Kyle were going to help her escape, they had to move quickly.

This time when she spoke, her voice was muted to just above a whisper. "My mother locked me in. She's going to make me put the baby up for adoption. This might be my only chance to get away."

Kyle's face contorted.

"What? What the hell are you—?"

Anthony quickly stepped in front of Kyle and interrupted him. "So what do you want us to do?

Amy pointed to the flowerbed.

"There's a little metal box buried behind that shrub. A spare key to the front door is in it. Find it, then hurry and come up and get me out of here."

This time Kyle nudged Anthony aside.

"Oh, yeah, right. We bust through your front door, then your mom unloads her 12-gauge in our guts. How 'bout we try to come up with something that gets us all out of here alive?"

Amy heard Kyle's question, but she couldn't answer right away. She was dizzy from more pain.

Finally, she caught her breath. "You're right," she said.

"That was a stupid idea. Maybe you'd both better just get out of here while there's still a chance. I don't want to think about what she'd do if she caught either one of you here, let alone the two of you together. Besides, she sends someone upstairs to check on me every hour, on the hour."

* * *

Anthony and Kyle gave each other sidelong glances, signaling an unspoken, if only temporary, truce.

Kyle spoke so that only Anthony could hear. "Tell her to throw down what she wants to take. I'll find the key."

Anthony nodded, "Uh, sure," but his attention was on a passing patrol car that slowed down, and then sped off.

When he turned back around and looked up at Amy, he was unprepared for what he saw. Her unmasked affection as she watched Kyle search for the key.

Anthony shook his head. "We'll, I'll be a--"

But before he could finish his thought Kyle was calling to him.

"Hey, I found it."

*   *   *

Anthony turned the key in the lock, opened the front door, and tiptoed into the house. Kyle followed close behind.

The din of music and voices downstairs captured their attention immediately.

"Wow!" Kyle said, peering curiously down the hallway that led to the basement stairway.

"Yeah," Anthony agreed. "Wow!"

But Kyle was already looking elsewhere and stepped a foot inside the beauty parlor. "Hey, this is some set-up," he whispered admiringly.

"True," Anthony whispered back. "Except, we've got trouble." He nodded at a couple, a professorish looking white man and one of the house girls, making out near the top of the stairs. "How we gonna get past them?"

Kyle looked up at the couple.

"Oh, shit!" he said, and ducked back into the shadows.

Anthony ducked back too. "What?" he asked in a hush.

"Dr. Locke's Kligripp," Kyle said.

"Dr. Who's what?"

"Dr. Locke's Kligripp. My Dad's boss's personal secretary."

"Maybe this isn't going to work so great, after all," Anthony said.

"Are you kidding?" Kyle said. "Amy's depending on us."

He thought a moment, then reached for the lone cap on a nearby coat and hat pole. Fortunately, the cap was several sizes too big for Kyle, and when he put it on, the bill fell down over his eyes.

"Okay, clever," Anthony said, and gave Kyle a thumbs up. "But just to be safe, stay crouched behind me."

The precautions proved unnecessary.

The moment the man heard the stairs squeak under the weight of Anthony and Kyle's footsteps he untangled from the woman, and within seconds, had scuttled down the stairs, past Anthony and Kyle, without a word or a glance.

Abandoned, the girl came down too, but she stopped to speak. To Anthony.

With her palm pressed against his shirt and chest, she inquired, "How 'bout you, handsome?"

Anthony blushed and gently removed her hand.

"I'd rather you went back home to your family," he said. "They can't possibly know this is what you're doing with your life. And you're still so young. And beautiful."

Her honey colored features were finely chiseled and her wide-set

brown eyes mesmerized with their hazel tint. She replied with only a skeptical laugh, but gave Anthony an innocent kiss on his cheek before continuing down the steps.

Kyle tugged at Anthony's sleeve. "Come on, we gotta hurry."

Anthony nodded. In seconds, they were at Amy's door.

Anthony started to knock but Kyle blocked his hand.

"Hey," Kyle said, "how do you know where--"

"Look," Anthony said, "it's you she wants. Let's just get through this and get the heck outta here."

Kyle's face tinted pink. He moved aside.

But before Anthony could rap on the door, Amy whispered loudly to them from her side. "Anthony? Kyle? Is that you?"

Kyle leaned close to the door.

"Amy. There's no key in the lock. Stand back. We have to break the door in."

Anthony glared at Kyle in disbelief, and mouthed, "Are you nuts?"

Kyle hunched and held out his palms. "You got any better ideas?"

"Okay, okay, maybe not. But you two are on your own once we're outside."

"Sure. No problem."

With that, Anthony and Kyle each angled their bodies so that both of them had a shoulder pressed into the heart of the door.

Anthony started the count.

"One," he said.

"Two," Kyle added.

"Three," they called in unison, then rammed the door.

It only buckled. They heaved into it again. And again.

At last, the wood splintered and Kyle kicked open a hole big enough for Amy to step through and reached in for her hand to help guide her out.

Anthony turned his back momentarily as Kyle and Amy embraced. They were still kissing when he looked back around. "Look," he admonished them in a weak attempt to hide his own feelings, "you two are gonna have to hold off on all that for awhile. If her mother catches us, it ain't gonna be pretty."

"You're right, man," Kyle said. "Let's go."

But before any of them moved a step, Amy put a hand on Anthony's shoulder. She wanted his full attention.

"Thank you," she said softly, and kissed him lightly.

"Sure," he sighed deeply. "I'm a real Boy Scout."

"In my book, too," Kyle said, his hand extended to shake Anthony's.

Their hands clasped, and in spite of all, the gesture was

warmly given as well as received.

"Hey," Anthony said as they started down the steps, "I've got my Dad's car, around the corner. Its got enough gas to get as far as Dearfield and back. My folks have a ranch out there. You can both stay overnight in the barn."

Kyle searched Amy's face for her response.

She nodded yes.

Kyle hugged her closer.

"That's real swell of you," he said to Anthony. "I owe you one, buddy. But you're right, we'd better get going."

*   *   *

Anthony turned the car east, onto York Street. The drive to Dearfield was going to take four or five hours. To play it safe, Amy was riding up front with him.

Her head rested against his shoulder as she slept.

Kyle was lying on the back floor covered with an old army blanket.

The honking horn of an oncoming car alerted Anthony to an out-of-control driver. He held his right arm across Amy to brace her, and used his left hand to maneuver the steering wheel back and forth as he worked to avoid a collision.

"What 'n the hell?" Kyle protested from his secret berth. "Try to kill me, why don't you."

"Sorry," Anthony replied nonchalantly, trying not to wake Amy. He didn't want to let on to either of his passengers that they had nearly been run off the road by a dairy truck driven by someone dressed in a Ku Klux Klan robe.

Amy roused and shifted away from Anthony.

Except for the mile or two another car trailed close to their bumper when they went through Limon, Colorado, the last twenty-some miles to Dearfield were without incident.

By the time they parked in front of the barn on his family's ranch, the prairie's evening sky was changing from swirls of deep magenta and antique gold to a vast stretch of navy blue.

Still, Anthony felt the need to remain vigilant. Too much had happened in recent times. Such as Negroes kidnapped–from their homes, or as they walked down a road–then beaten or tarred and feathered and dumped in the middle of town for all to see.

Bloody race riots incited by white mobs.

Decorated Colored G.I.s, real heroes, spit on.

And lynchings, hundreds of them, all across the nation.

His father had told him to ignore the cross burnings-in North Denver, on Ruby Hill, and in Golden, on Table Mountain-but the fire last month, downtown in Hop Alley, had had all the indications of being started by the Klan.

Five Points had had its share of threats, too.

Which meant Dearfield was on tenterhooks, too.

A lot of nearby farmers resented that Negroes had homesteads and incorporated the town, and made no bones about wanting to keep even the plains "for whites only."

Yep, ole Jim Crow was alive and well everywhere in the U.S.A. Anthony knew, like all Negroes did, out west, down south, or wherever, in this great democracy, a Colored man, woman, or child, best stay alert.

They had to get out of the car eventually, though.

He decided to let Kyle and Amy sleep while he went in and found a lantern and made some sort of bedding for them.

But when he opened his door, Amy moaned.

He leaned across the seat and felt her forehead.

She was running a fever and seemed to be shivering.

"Kyle!" he shouted, "Wake up! Something's wrong with Amy!"

Kyle bolted upright, threw off the blanket, and stood to look over at her.

Her face was ashen, and her skin beaded with perspiration.

Kyle was about to put the blanket on her when she cried out and balled up in pain.

"Oh my, god," he cried, "something is wrong. We've got to go back. She needs to be in a hospital."

All Anthony could do was look at Kyle. It wasn't the time to try to explain to him that Negroes weren't allowed in Denver's hospitals.

"Let's get back to town, first," said Anthony. "We'll find someone who knows what to do."

"But what if--"

"Look, just stay down," Anthony warned Kyle, as he floored the Cadillac's gas pedal.

Chapter Twenty One

Margaret gleaned what she could from the estate's resurrected side-yard strawberry patch, carefully placing the plump, juicy fruit into her basket.

All the while, with the morning sun kissing her bare arms, she thought of her father.

From her earliest memory, until she left home a married woman, he had insisted that she plant, weed, and harvest her own patch of land just as he tended the much larger family garden behind their small, brick house.

It was only now that she understood what he had really been doing; teaching her how to survive. No matter what. He would've been proud to know that this garden not only helped feed her own family, but gave her a modest income, as well.

A rivulet of perspiration ran from her forehead down to her cheek and intercepted a tear. She blotted her face dry with the hem of her apron.

It was nearly the middle of August and probably going to be the hottest day of the whole year. "Plantation weather," as her father used to call it.

Through the open kitchen door she could hear the phone ringing from inside the house. Momentarily, she forgot that Walter wasn't here to answer it. He hadn't been, for weeks.

Devin hadn't paid him in so long that Walter had finally had to take another job. With one of the families of the so-called Sacred 36, if the gossip she'd accidentally overheard at church was at all reliable.

The phone's ringing was insistent. She set her basket down and ran up the stepping-stone path to hurry inside. Mother Browne slept through most everything these days, but the discordant noise had probably already awakened Devin.

The thought of yet another of his ill-tempered beratings made Margaret cringe. If only Dr. Locke would give Devin permission to leave his sick bed. He didn't even have bandages on anymore.

Her hand was inches from the screen door when the phone suddenly stopped ringing.

She paused, statue-like, drew a breath and waited.

It was apparently worse than what she'd feared. Devin's blistering words to the caller, which could be clearly heard through his open bedroom window, indicated a problem far greater than an irksome banker demanding payment of a delinquent loan. It seemed to be something about MacDuff.

Each time Devin spit out the man's name it was embedded in a saloon epithet.

A brief silence was punctuated unexpectedly by the sound of breaking glass.

Margaret looked up to see the ripped out telephone flying through the air, and was just able to bolt clear of the shards raining from Devin's shattered bedroom window.

He came to the window cursing and shouting like a madman, leaned out, and yelled down to her.

"That bastard, MacDuff, went behind my back and convinced Locke to move the rally up a week. To tonight.

MacDuff thinks he's won, that he's going to move in on my territory. But Denver belongs to me. If he wanted to stake a claim here, his granddaddy should've shipped over and burned out the Indians like my grandfather did. I'll be double damned before MacDuff gets his limey paws on what's mine."

Devin's cough returned more violently than ever. He had to hold his side where he'd been shot. Margaret was almost as afraid for him as she was of him. "Devin, please," she called to him, "you're not well enough to…"

He was hunched over in pain but anger radiated off of him like heat from a blast furnace. "Margaret, shut the hell up," he croaked, "and don't dare try to tell me my business. Just get up here, and get your Klan robe on. Then, come and help me with mine. We're going to be the ones with Locke at the front of the damn Karavan.

Margaret's mind froze with horror. She'd given every reason she could think of at the Kouncil meetings to dissuade the leadership from carrying out another Karavan, but she'd been shouted down. Accused of being a typical woman.

To quote Dr. Locke, this Karavan was going to be, "the mother of all parades; a little something…the Jews, the Catholics, the spics, the kikes, the wops, the gooks, and especially, the niggers…would never forget."

It meant more burning crosses, more hate speeches, more vile threats…except this time not just through a working-class neighborhood, or on a local hillside, or even out in a prairie farm town. But from the plateau of Table Mountain.

Worse yet, the burning crosses would be visible to all of Denver. Even beyond.

And what if the men got liquored up, like they always did? Especially MacDuff and his bunch of, of…criminals.

God, help us, Margaret wanted to cry out. There was going to be trouble, soon, like this city had never seen.

* * *

By late afternoon, the broiling summer temperature had barely eased. The westward procession up Colfax Avenue of five or six hundred cars and trucks and even a few horse-drawn buckboards kept to five miles an hour so as not to overheat any engines...as well as to ensure being a real spectacle.

In spite of the speed, the participants were whooping and clowning like a big-top circus was in town.

Dr. Locke's chauffeured Buick was in the lead, followed by Devin and Margaret's Oldsmobile.

Devin had been unable to locate Kyle anywhere.

He wasn't even with MacDuff, who was driving an old farm truck, and was back, in the very rear, loaded down with planks of lumber. Kyle's friend, Spud, was at the wheel, and MacDuff was the passenger.

By the time the Karavan reached the foothills the convoy had doubled, if not tripled, and the way into Golden was lined with waving, shouting well-wishers.

There was still adequate daylight by the time the Karavan reached the mountaintop but little effort was given to orderly parking. The excitement of arriving, and getting the meeting underway, was too great for most. They simply abandoned their vehicles helter-skelter, and ran with their blankets and picnic baskets to the site: an expansive, grassy plateau over-looking not only Denver the Queen City, but also Colorado's great plains for as far as one could see.

Two or three stars barely had begun to twinkle visible through the early evening's coppery light, while somewhere far eastward, the ghosts of once great buffalo herds stampeded in the bowels of a seasonal thunderstorm.

Denver, only twenty-five miles away as the crows fly, had never appeared more peaceful.

Table Mountain, on the other hand, was all hustle and bustle as a detail of bare-chested men assembled and hammered together three fifteen foot crosses, and others, also from among the soon-to-be-robbed brethren, dug three deep holes—spaced apart in a straight line that extended the length of half a city block—in which to post the crosses.

Fresh volunteers raised the crosses, shoveled and packed dirt back in the pits to anchor the crosses, and hefted sandbags and stones around the bases of the crosses to stabilize them.

Three open barrels, full to the brim with kerosene, were put near each one of the crosses with each barrel accompanied by infinitely more barrels crammed with long, sturdy sticks, with all of the sticks knotted with rags at one end.

The Klavern's Nighthawk, the keeper of the fiery cross, reported that nearly two thousand men were in attendance but the circle of men around the field had swelled well beyond that number. Their mass of white robes and hoods cast a nightmarish pall against the darkening night.

The entourage of women and children, most also hooded and robed, were shunted to the side of the field closest to the cars.

One of the men began humming, then, across the way, a choir-worthy solo was offered of *"Mine eyes have seen the glory of the coming of the Lord."* Bit-by-bit, others joined in until soon there was a crescendo of all the men's voices.

Margaret watched from among the women, but Devin, identifiable by his robe's special insignia, had succeeded in claiming the position nearest Dr. Locke, who was even more noticeable because of his crimson Grand Dragon's robe.

Oddly, MacDuff seemed to be nowhere in sight.

As for the others, their identities were protected by their

sheets. Even the man who broke through the circle with a gasoline can, and doused the bases of the crosses with a clear liquid poured from the can, was anonymous.

A chant started by another of the men caught on and soon overruled the hymn. At first the words were indistinct. Then they sounded more like a deep growl. Finally, however, the incantation took on an ominous, if mystifying, clarity as more than two thousand voices recited...

Klakom, Kulkom. Koken, Klikom. Panther, Anther Hokum, Sibla. Bunko, Piffel. Siffel, Ribla

...over and over.

An hour later, the curse was still being invoked, but the sky had become forbiddingly black, with no moon or planets visible, and strangely few stars.

Dr. Locke accepted a box of kitchen matches from Devin, took out one of the matches, and struck it against the sulfur strip on the side of the box.

His pressure on the match was too heavy and the match broke, as did the next one, and the next one.

Devin conferred with him.

The box was handed back.

Within seconds, a lit match was thrown onto the base of the middle cross.

Licks of flame began to play among the sandbags, then suddenly burst into claws of bright orange as the wood caught fire. The unexpected heat forced Devin and Dr. Locke to cower back...toward the circle of Klan rank-and-file.

A great applause went up as the flames snaked onto the limbs of the cross, then shot the rest of the way up.

Devin went over to one of the barrels of sticks, chose the longest two, and returned with them to Dr. Locke.

He kept the shortest one for himself and gave the otherone to Dr. Locke.

He followed Dr. Locke's example and put the rag end of

his stick to the flame, then, they both turned back to face the circle and held high their blazing torches,

The crowd whooped, the circle began to move clockwise.

As it did, the men passed the barrels and chose their own sticks and likewise lighted them in the fiery cross.

Dr. Locke retreated to a cooler corner of the field and left Devin to light the two remaining crosses.

Somehow, more than two thousand torches were ignited in less than an hour. To Margaret, it looked like the residents of hell had taken over the earth. She couldn't take any more. The flames and heat were too much for her. She had to get away. But to where?

And how?

Her father's family came to mind. Maybe they would take her in, but...Oh, heaven! They lived in Five Points! And, so did her daughter. Why hadn't she thought of this before?

She still hadn't really recovered, physically, or, emotionally, from the miscarriage, and now, her surviving child might be in danger.

Her head swirled with fear and she wanted to wretch. Only, she couldn't afford to.

If anyone detected that something was bothering her, she'd be a suspect. One line of questioning would lead to another. Maybe even to the discovery that she was really a Negro. She didn't fear for herself, but for her daughter. She had to get back to Denver before the Klavern did.

She studied her surroundings.

A sickly, orange, reflection danced on the other women's faces. They all seemed mesmerized. The men were certainly entranced.

No one would miss her.

She looked over at the cars. If only she could drive.

Her only chance was to at least try...only, Devin's car was

blocked in by some of the other cars. She'd have to run down the road and hope there was a car on the outskirts she could manage to operate.

She edged to the rear of the clutch of women, then away from them, toward the cars.

When she felt safely hidden by the cover of night, she turned and ran through the maze of cars, down the hill.

She ran for at least ten minutes before getting anywhere near open road...only to stop at a car that had a pair of tangled, out-of-breath lovers in the back seat.

Next, she considered a paint-worn delivery truck, but it had a flat front tire.

At last, she found a Model-T, the same type of car that her father had last owned, and that was even facing the direction she needed to go.

Fortunately, it was easy to crank. She had closely observed the process many times. All she had to do after getting in, was remember her father's hand and foot movements when he drove.

She put her right foot on what she imagined was the gas pedal, and shifted into the gear she hoped would make the car go forward.

The car lurched three or four yards, and smashed, head-on, into the snout of a shiny, pastel yellow Packard.

Her mouth hit the Model-T's steering wheel and blood spurted across the sleeve of her robe, but after a dazed minute, she was otherwise all right.

She tried to get out of the car, but the door was jammed shut. She had to scoot across the seat, and exit from the passenger side.

She was too far down the hill now to be able to actually see the burning crosses, but the sky over the crest of the hill remained a glowing red.

She could hear laughter and chatter, though. Perhaps people were beginning to disperse. She had to hurry.

She prayed, and ran further down the hill.

Around a bend, parked as if an angel had left it for her, was another Model-T, only newer than the one she had just crashed.

Five minutes later, she was rumbling down the hill at over fifteen miles per hour, but eventually, navigating as straight as a trolley on a track. All she needed were the headlights on.

She fumbled around with the different console knobs and, at last, found the vital one. She hoped.

Great! Except, that the sudden beams of illumination revealed a deer bounding across the road, a mere fraction shy of missing her fender.

She screamed, yanked the steering wheel right, careened into a ditch, and nearly sheered a pine tree.

Miraculously, she maintained her composure and brought the car safely back onto the road.

Realizing a new measure of confidence, she accelerated.

As she neared Denver, she slowed momentarily and looked over her shoulder.

A long string of bobbing headlights was descending the road by which she had just escaped.

Even from the twenty-plus mile distance, she could see that the burning crosses were now bonfires.

Chapter Twenty Two

The road from Dearfield, by way of Limon, had been an open stretch the entire distance back to Denver. Anthony had used it to their advantage and mashed his foot to the Cadillac's gas pedal most of the way.

He eased up only when they proceeded onto East Colfax Avenue and once again encountered city traffic.

The last thing he, or especially Kyle and Amy, could afford, was to get pulled over by the cops. Not out of fear of getting a ticket–his father had an in at the local precinct for those type of matters–but because the majority of Denver's force consisted of not-so-secret KKK members.

Kyle, undoubtedly, was on their "most wanted" list for his treason against them.

It just naturally followed that anyone complicit in Kyle's betrayal was even deader meat.

Anthony stole a sidelong glimpse at Amy.

She was still writhing and moaning.

She had told him, on the way to Dearfield, during the half hour Kyle had dozed off, that she wasn't due to give birth for another month. But, either something was way out of whack with her health, or her baby wanted to be delivered ahead of schedule.

Anthony was hoping, or more like praying, that it was the later problem.

He checked his rearview mirror and sneaked a glance at Kyle who was hunched down in the back seat staring blankly out the window.

Kyle's expression was hard to read. He looked like he'd aged ten years in ten hours. One thing was evident, though.

White, black, or plaid, he really loved Amy.

A traffic light seemed to skip yellow and turn directly to red. Anthony smashed his foot to the brakes just in time.

His mind wandered while he waited for the green light.

Poor saps. They got about as much chance at happiness as Negroes got of gettin' a fair shake. Don't they know it ain't even legal for them to get married in most states? And just because one has brown skin, and the other white?

None of it made any sense.

Anthony shook his head in bewilderment.

An impatient driver behind him blared the horn.

Anthony's first instinct was to cuss the guy out, but he quickly reconsidered and simply drove on.

Amy moaned louder.

Kyle bolted upright and leaned over the front seat to caress Amy's shoulder. "Don't worry, beautiful," he said, unsuccessfully trying to mask the fear etched on his face. "We're gonna get help soon. You can hold on, can't you?"

Amy's response was unintelligible.

She cried out again.

Kyle grabbed Anthony's shoulder, and pleaded. "Man, hurry! Something is wrong. Maybe it's the baby."

Anthony didn't answer. He didn't know what to say.

All the way in from Dearfield he'd been racking his brain about where he could go to get Amy medical care, but he still hadn't figured out anything.

It was occurring to him that, in a lot of ways, Denver was a western version of the Deep South: Restricted housing covenants; no Negroes allowed in most department stores (except by the rear entrance); and their seating in the movie palaces confined to the balcony, the "crows' nest."

All that was missing were the "whites only" drinking fountains.

No wonder he couldn't think of any Colored people, besides himself, who might sympathize with Kyle and Amy.

He had always sought his father's advice on really tough matters, but going to him about this might cause a rift between the two of them, which, until now, Anthony had believed to be impossible.

Anthony was a junior, named for his father, Dwight Anthony Hudson, Senior.

His father was the most enterprising, visionary, industrious man Anthony had ever known.

His father also had one, all-consuming passion. He hated white people…for all they had done to Colored people.

Dwight had even almost become a Garveyite, but his father wasn't a joiner. He preferred handling things his own way.

If Anthony had admitted to him that he was trying to help a sheet wearing white boy and a pregnant Colored girl–elope, no less–he could hang up Dwight paying for him to attend Howard Law School.

A whispering thought gave Anthony pause.

Maybe his father was the solution after all. Not his father exactly. One of his tenants. Euphrates.

She was the closest Anthony had ever gotten to experiencing a grandmother, and she had once said to him, "Child, trouble slip under everybody's door now and then. And some of it just ain't possible to handle all alone. Don't ever let foolish pride hinder you askin' me, or some other body, for help."

On another occasion, Euphrates had commented that Anthony had some of the same qualities that she had admired in her brother, Angus, her twin. Intelligence. Resourcefulness. Courage.

It had made Anthony feel good about himself.

He also recalled the day he'd suddenly realized that she must have been through a lot in her lifetime. That maybe she'd even been forced to be a slave, like Mr. Joe, his parents' handyman, had been in South Carolina.

But whatever the details of Euphrates' life, they remained a secret. She was like a sphinx about her past, forever refusing to discuss it.

Except that once, when he'd helped her carry groceries home, and she had got to talking about how she and her brother had grown up on a Virginia plantation, and all the tricks she used to play on her brother, for fun.

She also started to say something about the Yankees, and the Civil War, but she had suddenly turned quiet and sad.

Anthony had tried to ask her then about the keloided welts along her forearms, which he had seen the time he was helping her weed her garden and her dress sleeves had been rolled up. But she scolded him in language he didn't know a Christian woman like her knew. Then, she sent him home after issuing a threat to tell his father if he ever dared be so rude again.

He learned a valuable lesson. Never pry.

Mostly, he was aware that Euphrates lived by one commandment: Treat others the same way that you want to be treated.

She *always* extended respect and compassion, and never passed judgment, on anyone.

Yeah, he concluded, she was the one person they could trust.

He floored the gas pedal again and bet himself that he could get from Colfax and York, to her house, in five minutes.

He won! But from the curb, the house appeared dark inside.

'You two stay here," he said to Kyle and Amy. "I'll be right back."

He went to Euphrates's door and knocked. Then knocked some more. He wished now that he had repaired the bell like he'd been promising to. He would definitely get to it tomorrow. But where could she be this time of night?

He heard the neighbor's screen door squeak open, then, bang closed. He looked over at the neighbor's porch.

A gray-haired, wiry-limbed, old black man was standing on the porch. The light shining through the man's living room window revealed that the man was in his skivvies.

"Say, boy," the man called over to Anthony, "what's your problem? You can't see they ain't home?"

"Pardon me, sir," Anthony said. "Didn't mean to disturb you. It's just that I've got an emergency on my hands and Euphrates is the only person I know who can help."

The man had come to the edge of his porch and was squinting at Anthony. "Say, ain't you Dwight Hudson's boy? Euphrates, and her people, ain't 'bout to get 'victed, is they? That'd be a low-down shame. They done painted, patched, and planted so much, that house and yard jest about the prettiest durn place on the whole block."

Anthony wondered how someone so old could be so long winded. He hurried to reply before the man started up again.

"Yes, sir, I am his son. And, no, sir, my father would never evict Euphrates and her family. I just need her help with something. It's kind of an emergency. If you could just tell me where…"

The man made a quick U-turn back to his door.

"They's probably at the revival. You know how Euphrates lo-o-o-ve the Lord. Even got me to go church once, In fact…"

Anthony, already on his way back to the car, didn't hear the man's last sentence.

Not until Anthony opened the car door did he realize that he hadn't gotten enough specifics.

He yelled back to the man. "Sir, what church did you say that was?"

After a moment, the man's screen door squeaked open again, his body silhouetted by the vestibule light. "Didn't. But try Mount Bethel, over on twenty-fifth and Marion."

Anthony waved at the man, and hollered, "Thanks!"

The man looked toward Anthony's car as it pulled away from the curb. He shouted, "Say, junior, you in some kind a trouble?"

But it was too late. All that the man heard back was the squeal of tires as Anthony's car rounded the corner.

* * *

Margaret kept looking in the rearview mirror but it was the gas gauge needle, hovering just above empty, that had her panicked now.

She could hardly believe that her first time driving, furthermore without one lesson, she had made it safely through Golden, then, all the way down West Colfax Avenue, back into Denver. Now all she had to do was find her way to Five Points.

To Amy.

But it had been a long and excruciating day.

Every sinew of her body felt tired and achy. Worse, she could barely keep her eyes open. She'd already allowed the car to drift, once or twice, to the wrong side of the road. Her greatest worry though, was staying ahead of the returning Karavan.

They couldn't be more than fifteen, or twenty, minutes behind her.

Fortunately, it was getting late. Most of the Karavan participants would want to go straight home, especially the women. MacDuff, and his hooligans, however, didn't consider cross burnings an adequate show of force. They had boasted that the night would officially end with a march through Five Points.

The thought of it made Margaret shudder.

She was even more worried about how Devin must have behaved after he discovered her absence from the mountain. He would surely punish her for humiliating him like that. His greatest concern, of course, would be assuring that no one–absolutely no one–ever found out that she was part Negro.

Aunt Euphrates had called her a "quadroon," and tried to explain a few other facts.

"Honey, far as white folks is concerned, whether you's half Colored, what they calls 'mulatto,' like myself, and my brother, your father…because one of our parents was Colored – African – our mama; and one white – this case, Irish – our pap; or, one-fourth, like you is; or, one-eighth, octoroons, like a whole lot a folks; or, only gots one drop, like too many peoples to count, you might's well be one hundred percent Colored 'cause they's gonna treat you like they don't know you jest as much God's child as they is.

"'Sides that, a goodly number of folks what calls themselves white, just lyin'. Some, for what they claim is practical reasons; some, cause they just sick 'n tired of bein' treated so poorly on account of what skin color they got born with.

"I mean, look at me and my brother. Same mama; same papa; same birthday; still, God seen fit to give us different tallness; different heart, mind, eyes; different skin colors, just like he do the flowers...but that don't make us no less brother and sister.

"All this nonsense got a whole lotta people jest goin' 'round telling what Mama used to call, 'boldfaced lies,' bless they's hearts.

Margaret decided that if she could just get across the Colfax viaduct, which would put her close to Union Station, she could somehow wind her way to the house where Amy lived.

She had only been there that once, when Dwight had taken her, but she'd made sure to note landmarks so that she could find it on her own when the opportunity arose.

A hellish light reflected in the car's side and rearview mirrors and blotted out that portion of the night sky over the burning mountain. The fires around the crosses must have been stoked and built up one more time.

She mashed her foot to the gas pedal.

In another minute, she drove across the viaduct bridge, its metal grids clattering loudly, then turned, north, onto Wazee. She was relieved to see the lighted Mizpah, Welcome Arch, which dressed the entrance to the train station.

The car sputtered again, but, thankfully, kept going.

Her heart was thumping so hard she was afraid of it exploding. The only other times she had felt like this was when she'd witnessed Devin's attempt to murder his mother.

Thinking back over that awful day gave her a nearly paralyzing realization. That if Devin had resorted to something that despicable, just to get money to pay his gambling debts, nothing would stop him from trying to kill her. Even if she was his wife. He didni't just hate her he detested her.

After all, he had only married her to use her. At first, for her father's money, then, ultimately, for her to support him in his scheme to work his way up the Klan hierarchy-which had been soundly accomplished with his promotion to Dr. Locke's second-in command.

Only, who could have known that her father had been passing for white all those years? It was merely logical that Devin would now have to get rid of her. Otherwise, Devin would be banished from the Klan. More likely, he'd suffer an even more dreadful fate.

Her mind kept filling with the images of the thousands of Klansmen marching around the three burning crosses. Their incantations had called for blood.

They would need to prowl Denver's streets, like animals out for the kill, until some hard-working Colored man-one who refused to say, "Yes, sir, Massa. No, sir, Massa," or, who had withstood the front lines of war and returned home, believing he'd at last be accorded dignity and equality, or who simply wanted to check books out of the public library-was hanging, broken and breathless, from the end of a suspended noose...like the more than two hundred other Colored men who had died in this way the last so many years.

The car wheezed, then chugged, to a dead stop.

Margaret forced herself to remain calm; to accept that no matter how exhausted or frightened she was, she was going to have to walk the rest of the way to Amy's.

She gave up the car and set foot in the same direction she had been driving. If she stayed out of the light of the street lamps she had a good chance of avoiding harm.

She forgot that she was wearing her Ku Klux Klan robe.

*   *   *

Anthony hadn't been to church in so many years, he felt embarrassed simply driving up to one. He parked a block away from Mount Bethel for Kyle and Amy's sake as well as his own.

A large, hand-painted, muslin banner was stretched across the front of the church. Its three lines read:

Mount Bethel Summer Revival
Saturday, August 16th, 8:00 pm
EVERYONE WELCOME!

Anthony walked up the church's concrete steps, opened one of the heavy wooden doors, went in, and was stunned to hear Pastor Carlisle, his childhood minister, in the pulpit.

Anthony decided instead to go around back and to enter through the fellowship hall.

The church mothers were bustling about in the hall, and to and from the kitchen, setting out cakes, pies, and punch bowls of lemonade, on two long, white linen-covered tables.

Anthony gave the women a respectful nod and headed directly for a wheel-around clothes rack filled with mostly empty hangers, the exception being the hangers holding two leftover choir robes.

He chose the longest robe, and put it on. The hem skimmed the top of his knees, and the ends of the sleeves reached just below his elbows.

One of the church mothers saw him and nudged her friend to look too.

Anthony sheepishly avoided their quizzical gazes and hurried down the hallway toward the sanctuary.

He stopped at the end of the hallway and listened. The pastor had the congregation's rapt attention.

Chancing a glance around the corner, Anthony scanned the sanctuary.

Euphrates was sitting with the choir, in the loft behind the altar, in the middle of the second row.

Anthony ducked behind the large potted palm just in front of him and waited for his chance to go over to her.

Finally, the sermon ended. The choir stood and the ushers went into the aisles to pass the collection plates.

If he dashed, he could make it to Euphrates' side without attracting undue attention to himself.

He mumbled apologies as he brushed past members of the choir.

They frowned and complained, nevertheless, he made his way to Euphrates, and squeezed into place beside her.

He got right to the point, whispering, "Mrs. Russell, I'm sorry to bother you, especially here, but we, I mean, my friends and…"

"Ssshh, child. Whatever it is, goin' to have to wait. My solo's coming up. But you help me with it and when we finished, we'll just keep on out the front door."

"But…"

Euphrates didn't hear Anthony's attempted objection. She had already gone down front and was looking back at him, waiting for him to join her.

The pianist had already started playing.

Anthony excused himself again, and made his way down to where she was standing.

The comments he heard this time were louder and more sarcastic.

He ignored them.

The song was, "Amazing Grace." Euphrates sang first.

Amazing grace! How sweet the sound, That saved a wretch like me! I once was lost, but now am found, Was blind, but now I see.

Then she looked at Anthony, indicating it was his turn.

Fortunately, he knew this hymn by heart. It was his favorite. He looked out over the congregation and was surprised to sense their support. He didn't want to disappoint them. He cleared his throat.

His singing voice, a rich baritone, was rusty and his first few words...*'Twas grace that taught my heart to fear...were hesitant.*

Then Holy Spirit touched him.

His next words resonated strength and feeling.

And grace my fears relieved; How precious did that grace appear The hour I first believed!

He and Euphrates alternated four more verses.

Euphrates: *Through many dangers, toils and snares...*

Anthony: *The Lord has promised good to me...*

Euphrates: *Yes, when this flesh and heart shall fail...*

Anthony: *The earth shall so on dissolve like snow...*

The last verse they sang as a duet.

When we've been there ten thousand years, Bright shining as the sun, we've no less days to sing God's praise Than when we'd first begun.

All the members of the congregation jumped to their feet, clapped, and shouted praises. The Right Reverend Carlisle raised up an, "Amen and Amen," and waved his Bible high in the air.

After a few moments of accepting acknowledgment, Euphrates and Anthony took their leave up the center aisle.

Just as they reached the front doors, Anthony extended his arm over Euphrates' shoulder and pushed one of the doors open, holding it until she was outside.

Again, he followed.

The congregation continued singing without them.

He hadn't realized, until this moment, as he took off the choir robe and left it on the stair railing–how oddly muggy and uncomfortable the night was.

Euphrates kept her choir robe on.

Neither Anthony, nor Euphrates, had taken a full breath of air before she pulled her humbled frame up to its full height and addressed Anthony, in her usual no nonsense manner.

"Child, you better have a mighty good reason for all this. Now, what in the world is going on?"

He explained everything to her, and then asked if she would come to his car to meet Kyle and Amy, and tell them where they could find a doctor for Amy.

Before Euphrates could answer, a fiery glow in the sky caught both their attention. They turned their faces to it.

The wicked glare reflected on Euphrates' mink-dark skin. She set her jaw.

"More of that Klan nonsense," she said, indicating the not-far-enough-away-burning crosses atop Golden's Table Mountain.

"Yeah," Anthony agreed. "Afraid so."

The air smelled scorched, and tasted…? Dead.

Euphrates continued staring up at the foothills. There was agitation in her voice as she spoke.

"Them children can stay in my attic," she said. "Once, they's settled, I'll goes to get Dr. Ford. She ain't never turned nobody away. Not even white folks what can't pay their bill. Meantime, we'll figure out how to get them children out a town. Safe."

Euphrates nodded, again, toward the burning crosses.

"Them Klan characters tryin' to run us Colored folks out a Denver. 'Cept we's got as much right–more, if you ask me, since we the ones mostly built the bridge they walked over to get this far–to be here. Nope! Be damned if we're going anywhere."

Anthony was pleased for Euphrates to have the last word. As if escorting a queen, he gently cupped his hand under her elbow and assisted her down the church steps, and up the sidewalk to where his car was parked.

Chapter Twenty Three

Margaret rounded a corner and went from walking along an empty, darkly-shadowed side street, to standing on a crowded, neon-emblazoned avenue.

She instantly recognized her location. The heart of Five Points. The same bustling village of restaurants, shops, offices, and clubs, she had first seen the day she learned that she was part Negro.

She was a stranger here, yet she no longer felt unwelcome as now she knew that these were her people too. She enjoyed the way so many of them lavishly greeted one another, as if they were reunited relatives.

She overheard unfamiliar words that she wished she could ask the meaning oflike copacetic and gAms, but she'd have to do that another day. Right now she had to get to Amy's. She was looking for the market that was a few doors from the cross street she needed.

People were staring at her, she realized, with their mouths agape as she walked by them.

She had hoped not to draw attention but suddenly she re-alized that she was still wearing her Klan robe.

She overheard a passerby exclaim, "Hey, Bub, check out the crazy ofay," and knew by the man's tone of voice that he meant it. That she must be crazy. He just didn't know, had no way of knowing, how wrong he was about the ofay part.

Her father's blood, the Negro part of her, meant that she was as Colored as if she was pure African.

More importantly, this was the clearest-minded she'd been in all of her thirty-four years.

She was walking so fast that faces were mostly a blur, except, once again, she couldn't help noticing the extra-ordinary array of the Negro peoples' skin colors. They seemed to range from lightest light to darkest dark, and every hue in between. Like Amy's, which was like coffee generously diluted with cream.

She envisioned a cup of coffee, particularly, like Mother Browne preferred...with so much cream added that the unaware might believe it to be a cup of milk. So, did that mean it was milk, or was it still coffee? Mother Browne called it coffee.

She crossed an intersection behind a quartet of apparent friends. Two men in tuxedos, and two women in long silk eve-ning gowns. One of the women kept turning to look at her.

"Honey," the woman said, "are you lost, or something? We can give you a ride if you need."

The woman's eyes conveyed sincerity. And concern.

Margaret was grateful for her kindness. "No, but thank you," she said. "I just have to get to my daughter. She only lives a few blocks from here,"

"Okay, if you're sure," the woman said, ignoring her com-panion's urging to, "Come the hell on."

The woman had dropped back and was walking beside Margaret.

"Yes, I'm sure," said Margaret. "In fact, here's the little grocery store I was looking for to remind me of which street to turn on. I take a right at the corner, go two blocks, and then left, then I'm there. I can't miss the house. It's the biggest house on the block."

Margaret started to thank the woman again but stopped short when the two men halted and cocked their heads as if listening for something.

Margaret heard it too. A faint, yet distinguishable sound. The still distant cacophony of a multitude of honking horns sent chills down her spine. Unmistakably, it was the Karavan…on its way to Five Points.

She couldn't determine how many miles away it was, but the two men and the two women became clearly distraught.

One of the men seized the kind woman by her arm, exhorting, "Let's be smart and get the hell out of here."

The woman nodded reluctantly, yet maintained another brief moment of eye contact with Margaret, while allowing herself to be moved onward.

Then the four elegantly dressed companions were gone.

An aloneness engulfed Margaret. She was so near to where her daughter lived, yet the Karavan was definitely on its way.

"Oh, no, Lord. I beg you…don't ask this of me," she cried aloud, but within an instant, realized, this wasn't the Lord's doing. It was ignorance's doing. And self-hate. Because anyone who loved truly loved themselves, didn't have the capacity to go around hating others. If she didn't resist evil, how could she expect anyone else to? Besides, she was the only one who could sound a warning.

The scale was so unmercifully unbalanced. One life, versus, an entire community.

Margaret blinked back her tears. She needed to act fast.

The problem was, if she went running up to people, one-by-one, they would only think what the earlier group probably thought. That she was simply out of her mind, and just ignore her. Frantic, she prayed for a solution.

A banner across the front of the church on the adjacent corner, caught her eye. The public was invited to a revival. Tonight.

"Dear God, p-l-e-a-s-e let them still be there."

She ran across the street, without watching for traffic, and was grazed by a motorist unable to stop in time.

She pitched forward and fell across the curb.

The driver of the car swore and shook his fist at Margaret, but didn't stop to help her.

Dazed, she stood back up on her own. She just needed a few seconds to regain her equilibrium.

She was dirtied, and bruised, but not bloodied.

She limped to the church steps and ignored the pain in her thigh as she climbed the steps. Perhaps a bone had been broken, but a minor injury wasn't going to stop her.

When she reached the church door, her stomach knotted. She denied that feeling too. This wasn't a time for uncertainty, and especially not for fear.

She pulled the door open by its wrought iron handle and hobbled through the narthex, into the church, and started up the center aisle.

Most of the congregation gasped and some even screamed.

She cried out to them, "You have to get out of here, now. The Klan is on its way, in a Karavan. They could arrive in half an hour, or, in minutes. Either way, if you want to avoid trouble, there's no time to delay."

She had reached the edge of the altar, and looked up into the pastor's eyes, pleading, "You've got to believe me.

There's no time for explanations. The warning must be sounded as quickly as possible."

The congregation was whispering comments back and forth. The initial shock–of a white woman dressed in a Ku Klux Klan robe running into their service–was giving way to instinct.

The women hugged the children close and the men pushed the women and children closer together.

The sense of alarm was palpable. Some people moved into the aisle as if to block Margaret in.

Pastor Carlisle raised his hands and demanded, "Everyone! Quiet! Hear her out. As you know, thousands of Klansmen met tonight, up on Table Mountain…and burned crosses. Perhaps this woman's conscience spoke to her and she truly is here as a Good Samaritan."

The congregation's respect for Reverend Carlisle's leadership was evident. There was suddenly complete silence. Margaret continued.

"Those men have been drinking bootleg whiskey since practically sunup. Most of them just to get the nerve to cause something bad to happen."

A woman shouted, "But, Pastor, what if she is just some crazy old…?"

"Sister," Pastor Carlisle, interrupted, sternly, "I don't think a good Christian woman, like yourself, wants to say anything she'll be ashamed of later. Furthermore, whoever this woman is, she was clear. There isn't time for debate."

No one could have been more stunned to see Margaret enter the church than Walter. An elder in the church, he was sitting in his assigned chair, next to the pastor's.

As he maneuvered past the individuals obstructing the aisle, on his way to Margaret, he loudly declared, "She's telling the truth. And, she's not white; she's Colored, just like the rest of us. If she says those murdering bast…, I mean, the Klan, is on its way. We'd want to be ready."

Walter reached Margaret and pulled her close.

As usual, she felt comforted by his presence and grateful for his support.

She looked into the face of the woman who had spoken on her suspicion of Margaret. The woman's expression softened.

Margaret appealed to the pastor, again. "Everyone needs to get off the streets. And to stay in their houses, there's no way to know what those men have planned, or what they're capable of. It'll be harder for them to succeed if we pull their bluff."

"All right," declared Pastor Carlisle, "all of you know what to do."

As if rehearsed a hundred times, the women and children exited the pews by the side aisles, then hurried down the rear hallway.

The men, including the pastor, filed quickly into the center aisle, then rushed out the front doors.

Walter remained with Margaret, holding her to him. She was sobbing.

He held her at arms length and looked into her face. "Is something else wrong?"

They were now alone in the church, but she couldn't breathe. "I, I…need to get to my daughter. That's why I was nearby. And I almost made it. Then, I heard the Karavan. I had no choice but to…"

Walter put his fingers to her lips. "What you've done was very brave, Margaret. And, there still might be a way for us to find your daughter. I think there's a connection between her and another incident that happened here just a short while ago."

"I don't understand. What do you mean?"

Walter seemed to be weighing what he wanted to say.

Margaret gave him a look that begged him to speak plainly.

"Dwight Hudson's son blew in here, in the middle of the service, looking for your Aunt Euphrates. The word is, he's been spending time with your daughter. Did you know that she is pregnant?"

Margaret was, all at once, alarmed and perplexed.

Alarmed to learn that Amy was pregnant. Perplexed that Walter knew about her Aunt. And Amy.

As if reading her mind, Walter added, "Look, Five Points, just like Harlem, the south side of Chicago, Central Avenue in Los Angeles, or any other Negro side of town in an American city, is a world within a world. Under such circumstances, not too much escapes the grapevine."

"The grapevine?" Margaret asked.

"The gossip mill," Walter answered, "the staple of all Colored beauty shops and barber shops. For instance, a fair number of folks around here had known for years that Angus, your father, was passing. That sort of thing is a popular topic, especially among old-timers. He also helped a lot of them get through tough times with loans, and so forth. The unspoken agreement was that they'd never go into his store, or call him out on the street. He seemed to visit Five Points, whenever he was, in a manner of speaking, homesick. Which, actually was quite often."

Margaret was incredulous at what else she was learning about her father. It was occurring to her that she might never have truly known him. However, her only concern now was Amy. "You said you might be able to help me find my daughter?"

Walter hesitated answering.

He was listening to the sound of the approaching chaos, outside.

Innumerable car horns were blaring and racial epithets being shouted.

Something glass shattered against the outside of the church door.

"It's them!" Margaret said, trembling.

"Then, we'd better get out of here."

"But what about Amy?"

Walter took hold of Margaret's hand. "It's just a hunch, nothing I know for sure. I think your aunt may be able to help. She left the service early, with Dwight's son."

Walter started to brush the smudge from Margaret's temple, only to see that it was caked blood from a bad scrape.

"Come on," he said, tenderly, "let's go out through the back. Through the fellowship hall."

* * *

Except for the Karavan madness a few blocks away, all was dark and quiet as Walter and Margaret waited in hope of Euphrates coming to the door. They had knocked and knocked, but no one had answered.

Perhaps the family had thought it wiser to stay elsewhere for the night.

A car turned onto the block then shut off its headlights and continued slowly down the street.

A young boy, not even as old as ten, leaned out of the car's passenger side, yelling, through a bullhorn, with the skill of a side-show huckster, "Come out, come out, niggers, wherever you are. You can't hide forever. The mighty White Knights of the Imperial Invisible Realm will find you, and you'll wish you'd run tail when you had the chance. Come out, come out, niggers..."

And so the refrain went as the car drove by.

Walter, again, pulled Margaret close.

Something–a rock, or a baseball, or a bottle–broke a window in the house next door, and the car sped away.

A dim, yellowish-orange light started to flicker in the living room of the house, then, noticeably brightened.

Licks of flame were suddenly climbing the curtains.

Margaret looked on, petrified. The mindless destruction of businesses and homes, and the deadly assaults of faultless and vulnerable individuals, were happening again.

Within moments, acrid smoke was billowing out of the broken window.

Walter looked anxiously at Margaret. "I've got to go for the fire department," he said. "The old man who lives in that house doesn't have a telephone. Will you be all right until I get back?"

"Of course, I will, Walter. Just, please, be careful."

"I promise," he said, and lightly kissed the tip of Margaret's nose.

Then they heard the screams, from the upstairs of Euphrates' house.

"That's Amy," Margaret cried, "I'm sure of it. It sounds like she might be in...in labor. We have to break down the door. Or, something. My child needs me!"

Walter examined the door, then gently pushed Margaret aside.

He kicked and kicked the door, but had to kick it still more before it finally splintered.

After that, he used his fist to open a hole in the door and reached through the hole to turn the lock.

The fire was eating through an outside wall of the neighbor's house and hot embers freckled the air.

Some landed on Walter's and Margaret's skin. Some in Margaret's hair, which Walter quickly brushed away.

She was trying not to grimace as she didn't want to reveal the pain shooting down her leg, or that an ember had burned her cheek.

"Walter," she said, "if Amy is in labor, she shouldn't be moved. It could jeopardize her and the baby. I'll stay with her until you come back from alerting the fire department and finding a doctor. And, don't worry, I'll find my way around inside the house. I've been here before."

"All right, Walter said. "I'll be back as soon as humanly possible. By the way, Margaret," he yelled back to her from the sidewalk, "you should know...I love you."

✳   ✳   ✳

Margaret decided it was best not to turn on any lamps. Instead, she extended her arms and hands to help her avoid the furniture, then worked her way across to the stairs.

As she struggled to overcome the excruciating pain throbbing the length of her leg, and to climb the stairs, she heard Amy cry out again.

She called up to her, "I'm coming, Precious."

A young man holding a lighted lantern appeared on the landing. "Euphrates hid them, Kyle and Amy, in the attic," he said, "But the baby is coming, and Euphrates hasn't come back with the doctor."

Chapter Twenty Four

I'm sorry about the awful way I treated you," Kyle said, earnestly. "I wish I'd known better."

Margaret was amazed, and gratified, to hear her stepson's change of heart. But it wasn't a change, really, for she had known all along that Kyle's true character was loving, and good. He had simply been a boy seeking his father's approval.

But never receiving such an accolade, he tried what any child might. To become a replica of his father in the hope that that approach would succeed in his winning at least a compliment now and then.

And so the cycle between Devin and his father, and probably between Mr. Browne and his father, had repeated between Devin and Kyle. With ever more dire consequences.

"I appreciate knowing that," Margaret said. "Particularly now. It gives us, this family, a chance to start with a clean slate. I'm mostly glad for my daughter's sake, though. I couldn't stand it if you treated her like your father treated me."

Kyle looked at Amy, shamefaced. She had closed her eyes during the last few minutes but he knew that she was listening to every word.

She gripped his hand and cried out. The contractions were starting again.

Anthony returned with the pan of water and the towels Margaret had sent him downstairs for. He smelled like smoke and was choking. He whispered to Margaret.

"I hope that baby comes soon. I don't think we have a lot of time. The house next door is in flames.

Amy weakly lifted her head from Kyle's lap. "What did you say?"

Both Kyle and Margaret subtly shook their heads to signal Anthony not to answer.

A waft of smoke seeped in around the edges of the attic's hatch door.

Anthony, Kyle, and Margaret glanced at each other with alarm.

"What's the matter?" asked Amy, and again received no reply.

Margaret tore a square of cloth from an old cotton dress she'd found in one of the trunks, and dabbed the perspiration from Amy's face. "Try not to worry about anything right now," Margaret said. "All we want you to concentrate on is bringing that baby into the world."

"He, or she, must have heard you," Amy said. "Because I think, o-o-o-o-h-h-h, the wait is over."

For the next ten minutes Anthony and Margaret worked as a team, while Kyle did all he could for Amy.

Their unified effort resulted in a miracle. The birth of a healthy baby boy. "Oh, Amy, you have a son. And he's so handsome," Margaret said, then placed the baby in the towel Anthony was holding open.

"But, he's got a little brother, or sister, coming right behind him."

"What?" Kyle said, looking at Amy who was pushing again. "You mean, twins?"

He had to wait a few minutes for his answer, but when Kyle got it, he was all smiles.

"Yep, twins, it is." Margaret said, at last, and then held up the second child. "Mommy and Daddy, meet your gorgeous little girl."

"I can't believe it," Amy cried, this time with happiness. "Kyle, we're the parents of twins."

"Yeah, and they're both beautiful, and I bet, brilliant, exactly like their mother," he said, proudly.

Anthony quickly handed the boy baby to Amy and Kyle, then held open a towel for Margaret to lay the baby girl in, but Anthony was having difficulty seeing. More smoke was escaping into the attic and causing his eyes to tear. "I'm telling you," he reminded Margaret as she wrapped Kyle and Amy's little girl, "we don't have anymore time. We've got to get out. Now."

Margaret nodded, clearly understanding, then handed Kyle and Amy their second baby.

For a brief moment the new family, Kyle, Amy, and the two babies, were the picture of bliss.

"We've decided to name them Jake, and Iris," Amy said. We talked it over in the car. We had chosen both a boy's name, and a girl's name since we didn't know which one we were having. Good thing, I guess."

Kyle was doting on the babies already and just grinned in agreement.

"Well then hello, Jake. Hello, Iris. And welcome," said Margaret, trying not to inhale more smoke. "And now, we have to take you on your first trip. We're going downstairs, then outside."

The instructions were really for Kyle and Amy. As Margaret expected, it took them a moment to break from staring and cooing at their children, but they too began to realize that the attic was filling with smoke.

"Here, man," Anthony said, "hand the babies to me. You and Margaret can help Amy."

Kyle quickly complied.

The babies looked like little dolls in Anthony's arms.

Now Amy was choking as well. "Anthony, ughh, ughh, please, you go, ughh, ughh, ughh, ahead. Get my babies out, ughh, ughh, of here."

She was very weak and had to put her full weight on Margaret and Kyle.

However, Margaret, herself, needed assistance. Her injured leg had swollen and the pain seemed to be branching out through her entire body. She managed not to let on though, and put an arm around Amy's waist to help steady her as Kyle lifted her to her feet.

Anthony was waiting for them with the hatch open.

A spit of fire was creeping along the quilt Amy had just gotten up from.

There was creaking overhead. Suddenly, a ceiling beam fell and nicked Anthony's shoulder.

"Oh, no, my babies!" Amy screamed.

But the babies, and Anthony, were fine.

The real problem was that beam now blocked the hatch door.

They were trapped, and smoke was pouring in through the floor boards.

Flames began to snake up the wall Kyle and Amy had camped against.

"Get back," Kyle shouted, and rushed over to shove the beam off the door, It was heavy, but finally budged.

He reopened the hatch and ran back to Amy.

Only, as he reached out to touch her, his foot dropped through a weak spot in the floor.

He tried to wrest his foot loose but when he did the hole expanded. The impact of his falling to his knees was more stress than the floor could withstand.

Kyle disappeared into the pit of fire below.

"K-y-y-y-l-l-e!" Amy shrieked. Only, it was too late.

Margaret turned Amy's head away from the gaping hole, and yelled over the sound of the crackling fire beneath them. "Anthony," she said. "Go! We'll be right behind you."

She hoped he'd heard her. She could barely see him through the voluminous smoke.

He yelled back, "Just watch where you step." Then, still cradling Jake and Iris in his arms, he carefully descended the attic stairs.

Margaret slapped out the lick of fire on Amy's skirt. "Come on, precious, we can do this," she said and steered Amy toward the hatch. They crossed the attic floor together, as tightly bound as two can be without mashing into one.

And they almost made it.

Until Amy's ankle twisted, and she too fell, hard, onto the weakened floor.

It couldn't take the pressure, and caved in around her.

Her legs dangled into the heat below as she fought to pull herself back up into the attic. She cried out to Margaret.

"Mama. Help me."

Margaret fell to her knees and grasped Amy's arms. "I'm right here, precious. Just hold on," Margaret cried back to her daughter, even as the weight of Amy's body was pulling them apart.

"I can't. I can't. I'm too…"

"Oh, yes you can. I can't lose you now. Amy, please, don't let go, please. I'm begging you," Margaret wailed, although her grip on Amy had already slipped from Amy's arms, to Amy's wrists.

Then, she had her only by the hands.

Then, only by her fingertips.

"Mama, Mama!" Margaret heard her daughter cry a last time… and then…was gone. Forever.

"Awwwwwggggghhhhh! Amy! No…no, no, no no! Oh, Amy! My precious, precious child."

Margaret's own life suddenly felt sucked out.

Fire was nipping at her skin, but she was numb to it.

She balled herself into her stomach, and rocked.

Everything ached. Her head. Her body. Her heart.

Especially her heart.

"Oh, my precious child. My baby. My baby," she repeated,over and over, oblivious to her own peril.

Someone was calling her. She didn't understand. What could they possibly want? Didn't they know that her daughter, her beautiful, precious daughter, had just…

"Awwwwwggggghhhhh!" she cried out again.

"Margaret," Walter called to her, reaching for her, "those grand babies of yours are going to need you. You're all they've got now," said Walter as he lifted her into his arms. "And I need you just as much."

"But…Amy?"

Walter didn't have the chance to reply.

Another ceiling beam crashed onto the exact place on the floor where Margaret had lain only a moment ago.

He carried her down the attic stairs then down the main stairway to what used to be the house's living room, but was now just a charred mess.

A fireman met them and led the way outside. Two minutes later, Aunt Euphrates' home was completely ablaze.

An hour later, a crowd of onlookers had gathered.

A total of four houses on the block had been destroyed, including one across the street.

Margaret was dazed, but, except for her leg, was doing remarkably well.

Dr. Ford had examined her and made Walter promise to bring her into the office-just blocks away, in her home parlor-first thing in the morning.

Margaret leaned against Walter's chest and gazed blankly at the various faces.

Euphrates, and her daughter, Lee Dora, brought the babies over to Margaret. She was much too weak to hold them, but it was a great relief to see that they were safe, and, unharmed.

Already, she loved them dearly.

She noticed Anthony at the front of the crowd, talking with his parents. She wondered if Dwight knew that his daughter had died tonight. His sudden change of expression-from detached curiosity to horrified shock-at something Anthony was telling him, told her that he did.

She wanted to feel sorry for him, this man who had been her first love, yet a deep-seeded feeling prevented her extending him any sympathy. After all, he had allowed her father to bribe him, and had helped her father put Amy up for adoption. Did he, at least now, feel any regret...or remorse?

However, it was two others she couldn't believe had the nerve to be there. MacDuff, and that boy, Spud. They were gawking and talking loudly, showing utterly no respect.

"Hey, boss," she heard the boy say to MacDuff, then something about a payday.

But MacDuff knocked the boy in the head, and yelled at him. "Learn when to shut up, will ya."

The people nearest them turned to look at them.

MacDuff revolted Margaret as much as ever. She decided then and there not to let his type win.

Walter nodded, and cupped his hand under Margaret's elbow as the coroner's assistants came out of the still smoking house with two stretchers, each bearing a white sheet-covered body.

Margaret realized what she herself was still wearing. The dress-up version of a white sheet.

Silently, she vowed to her daughter, and to her stepson, to strive toward that day that every white-sheet-wearing man, woman, and child, would disavow such garb, and all that it represented. Most especially, the destruction and pain that it caused, both to individuals and communities.

A man in the back of the crowd was arguing for his right to get through. Margaret recognized his voice immediately.

It was Devin.

"Walter," Margaret said, "Devin's here. I'd like to speak with him, alone, if you don't mind."

"Of course," Walter said. "I need to talk with the fire chief. I'll be just over there," he nodded in the direction of Fire Station Three's group of exhausted firefighters, all of whom were Negro, "if you need me."

As Walter walked away, Devin approached.

Devin began to say something vile to her, but was struck silent as the medical personnel carrying the stretchers neared.

He extended his arm, palm open and fingers up, signaling the men carrying Kyle to stop.

The men halted.

Devin started to lift a corner of the sheet covering Kyle, but Margaret delicately pushed Devin's hand away, then peered into Devin's eyes.

With her gaze, she guided Devin to look, instead, at the boots sticking out at the opposite end. "I'm so sorry, Devin," she said, while also nodding to the men carrying the two stretchers that they may go on.

Devin stared at Margaret, his face revealing the innocent boy she had once known, and loved.

Suddenly he let out a spiteful laugh. "Not as much as you're going to be," he responded to her pity. "You've humiliated me, Margaret, and you know, I don't take that sort of thing well."

"Don't threaten her, Devin," said Walter, startling Margaret, who didn't know that he had returned.

"It's all right, Walter. He doesn't scare me anymore."
She glanced around to find Lee Dora and Aunt Euphrates.

"Devin, look over there. Those two women are part of my family. The babies they're holding are my–and your–grandchildren. Jake, and Iris. Two precious, innocent babies, of our own flesh and blood. For their sakes, if not our own, let's find a way to live in peace with each other.

The past is the past. We have to bury it, with our children. But their children can live free of hate.

"You don't get it, do you, Margaret? The Brownes don't have mongrels. As far as I'm concerned, I didn't even have a son. As soon as possible, I won't have you as a wife."

Devin turned on his heels, and walked into the night.

Margaret watched him go.

How tragic, she realized, that even after all of this, he'd rather continue hating than love.

She saw a Colored woman grab Devin by the arm. The woman and he appeared to be arguing.

The woman slapped Devin.

He yanked loose of the woman's hold, and slapped her back.

Margaret suddenly recognized the woman. It was Rowena.

"Walter, I have to speak to someone," Margaret said. "I'll be back in a moment."

She hurried over to Rowena.

Rowena was crying, almost uncontrollably. Margaret embraced her.

"Let's get through this...together," Margaret said. "In honor of...of Amy.

"And of her family."

Epiloque

It was a splendid, Sunday May afternoon. All azure sky, snow-capped mountain peaks, and robin red breasts hopping through budding Daffodils.

Warmth and happiness abounding.

Walter had suggested to Margaret that they prepare a picnic basket and take the family to City Park for the evening band concert. The children could delight in the accompanying fountain display, which always garnered audiences' "ooos," and "awws," as the middle of the lake structure sprayed plumes of water illuminated by rainbow-colored lighting gels.

As soon as they had arrived and claimed a picnic table, Walter and Aunt Euphrates went to feed breadcrumbs to the ducks, while Anthony, home from Howard University for a brief visit with his parents, romped in the grass with Jake and Iris.

He had dubbed himself the children's uncle, and though they hadn't yet turned two years old, he spent as much time with them as his being in school in Washington, D.C. permitted.

Margaret was worried that Anthony still held himself responsible for Kyle and Amy's deaths. She prayed daily that he would someday realize that the truth was that he had saved the lives of two innocent babies.

She stretched out on the blanket and contentedly watched her new family. She couldn't help reflecting on how much her life had changed, and, how much she had to be grateful for.

Jake and Iris were becoming quite the little personalities. As well, both were completely – thankfully – healthy.

Iris, the more curious one, and always into everything, had Kyle's pale skin color and dark brunette hair.

Jake, the fearless one, and ever climbing up on, or, jumping off of, something, had Amy's cocoa complexion and blondish hair.

They reminded her of how her father, Angus, and his twin sister, Aunt Euphrates, reflected each of their parents' heritage.

If only she could know that Kyle and Amy would approve of how she and Walter were raising Jake and Iris. And, of where she was raising them: In East Denver; in Five Points. Within the Negro community.

No one there ever questioned Margaret, or Walter, about the children, or about her and Walter's marriage. Indeed, many of Margaret's new friends assumed that she was Colored, just like they were.

She had even begun to think of herself as Colored.

And Walter, well, he treated Jake and Iris as if they were his own; true to his pledge to her upon his proposal of marriage.

Margaret was just as appreciative of Aunt Euphrates.

In fact, she had forgotten that their lives hadn't always been so intertwined. Furthermore, Euphrates had made the ultimate sacrifice when her sister and family had moved to California shortly after the house had burned down.

They had urged Euphrates to go with them, but she had insisted that they get settled before she joined them.

Walter had guessed, correctly, that the real reason Aunt Euphrates had remained in Denver was to help Margaret raise Jake and Iris, and so, the day of his and Margaret's wedding, had asked Euphrates to come live with them.

Margaret already loved him, for abundant reasons, but all that he did for her family made him her hero.

She wanted to believe that her father, Angus, would have—sooner, or later—approved of Walter. Likewise, that Angus would have been very pleased that she was finally, and truly, happy.

A mother duck, and her five ducklings, waddled out of the lily pond, quacking excitedly, and guarding her brood closely as she led them across to the lake.

"I hope I'll do as good a job as you, mother duck," Margaret said to the feathered family as they ambled past.

While watching the feathered family continue onto the lake, Margaret also noticed that the Municipal Band was beginning to assemble on the floating platform and that other picnickers were setting up. Especially atop and across the slope of Museum Hill—which overlooked the lake.

There were also numerous promenaders, roller skaters, and bicyclists, including several unicyclists, enjoying the path around the lake.

Margaret was at peace. With her life. With herself.

She looked over at the children and laughed at their antics as they played, noisily and joyfully, with Anthony.

Walter caught her attention as he waved to her from the lake's shore. Beside him, Aunt Euphrates was still tossing food to the ducks.

Margaret stood, and waved back to him.

A letter fell out of her dress pocket onto the blanket.

She picked the letter up and went to sit under a nearby Cottonwood for a bit of privacy. It was Gwen's latest, and this time, the envelope was postmarked, Paris, France.

It was an entertaining report, about Gwen, and her new pals; a group of expatriate American writers and jazz musicians, many of them Negroes.

Gwen was most thrilled about having met Josephine Baker, a young Colored woman, also from the states, who performed in dance revues and was all the rage in Europe.

Gwen had heavily underlined that even royalty courted her.

Jake and Iris ran up to Margaret and fell into her lap, giggling.

She refolded the letter, returned it to the envelope, and put the envelope back in her pocket.

She felt great hope for the children's futures.

Mostly, Margaret wanted to believe that the time had passed that caused a person to feel the need to make a choice like the one her father had made; to lie...about his true identity.

Which meant that she, Walter, Aunt Euphrates, Anthony, and others, must instill pride in the children about the truth.

About themselves.

Margaret looked at each child's precious face, and stretched out her arms to them.

"Jake. Iris. Come give your Grandmother Margaret a big hug.

WOMAN LEGISLATOR SAYS KLAN IS TRYING TO CONTROL ASSEMBLY

Mrs. Martha E. Long of Denver Declares That Ku Klux Is Punishing Her Because She Voted Against Their Program on One Bill.

A statement by Mrs. Martha E. Long, one of Denver's representatives in the lower house of the legislature, charging the Ku Klux Klan with attempting to control legislation in the general assembly, is being widely circulated thru the state. The statement follows:

"Yes, it is true that I was a member of the klan and that my card of membership was taken because I did not vote for the nurses' bill. It is also true that they have been punishing me ever since. Let me say right here that I have no ill feeling. If that is their way of doing things it is all right and I'm not complaining.

"I joined the Women's Klu (sic) Klux Klan last summer. That is the official name for the organization. Women friends of mine asked me to join and I did. It is a wonderful organization so far as ideals taught in the ceremony is concerned. One of the prinicipal things I remember were the addresses of the members about patriotism and loyalty to the country. Especially do I remember an address that was delivered one night on Table mountain by Governor Morley. Mrs. Morley and the governor are both members and I have often heard him talk before the meetings of the klan and also before the klan caucuses of the Denver members of the legislature. Let me say (that) Governor Morley never in any of his talks abused anyone. He always based what he had to say on what I believe he thought was for the best interests of the state and the nation. Of course he, like all the other members was loyal to the klan and wanted to see it succeed.

"Following the election the klan members from Denver held many caucuses. I attended some of them but not all. When Governor Morley spoke before us at these meetings it was always(s) on what he believed would be best.

"After the session opened we were told that we had to follow the program. In fact, that was the order all the time. When the bill abolishing the state board of nurse examiners came up I realized that I could not support it. I indicated that much in one of my votes one day. That afternoon Mr. Atchison

347

handed me a note which read:

"Go straight down the line. No excuses taken.

(Signed) "ATCHISON."

"Mr. Atchison was at that time floor leader for the klan. I went to him and told him I could not vote for (the) program. I told him I would go to Governor Morley and get excused from voting for that bill. He told me Governor Morley had nothing to do with it; that I had to get my excuse from Dr. Locke; that he was handling the excuses of those who wanted to be excused. I told him I would not go to see Dr. Locke on the matter. The next day I voted against the bill. That afternoon Miss May Rankin Fox, secretary to Carl De Lochite, came to ask me for my klan membership card. I asked her why, and she said I had failed to follow instructions on the nureses' bill. I asked her who sent her, and she said the leaders of the klan. I told her it was at home, but I would bring it the next morning. I brought it as I had promised, and she came to my desk and I gave it to her. Since then all my bills have been killed. They told me they were going to kill them just to punish me as they punished Representative Payton of Pueblo. I only care for one of the bills. It was a bill that the school teachers of the state want. Under the present law, if a school teacher is on a pension and teaches just one day the pension stops. Such a condition is not right. No teacher should be penalized for teaching one day, even if they are on a pension. My bill corrected the defect in the law. Yet it was killed along with the rest.

"As I said, I am not in any way sore or put out. I am a Republican. I feel very much concerned about the future of our party. Our greatest fight next year is within our own ranks. We must clear the party of this control. The klan leaders are determined to control or wreck the party: There was nothing in the oath I took to bind me to any legislature course. That all came in the talks of the leaders at these meetings and at the klan caucuses. I refused to be bound. I got thrown out. Dr. Locke cannot be blamed. He wants power. If he can get it thru the Republican party by having its elected officials subservient to him I do not blame him."

Denver Post, February 26, 1927

Author's note:

PLEASE BEWARE...The Ku Klux Klan's motto is:
"Yesterday, today, and forever."

About the Author

Charlene A. Porter, a graduate of Howard University, began her professional life as a trade association writer and editor, and went on to become a tenured public high school English teacher, twice nominated by students to Who's Who of America's Teachers. She is also a professional scriptwriter. ***Boldfaced Lies*** is her debut novel and the first book in an on-going saga about an achievement-oriented African American family. Look for the first two sequels, ***Eeny, Meeny, Miney, Mo*** and ***If She Hollers*** in 2008. The first books in her children's series— ***The Hope Street Children; Cheryl's Clarinet*** and ***Tiger Woods, the Boy Who Loved Golf,*** both with illustrator James A. Davis— can be ordered from her web site. She lives in Denver, Colorado.

Visit the author's web site at:
www. CharlenePorter.com